CAST AWAY

or, The
Surprising Adventures
of Alexander Selkirk

FRANCESCA DE TORES

BLOOMSBURY CIRCUS

LONDON · OXFORD · NEW YORK · NEW DELHI · SYDNEY

CAST AWAY

BEING THE

TRUE

AND

SURPRISING

ADVENTURES

OF

ALEXANDER SELKIRK,

OF *NETHER LARGO*, SCOTLAND:

Who survived many Years,
all Alone on an un-inhabited Island far from
the Coast of SPANISH AMERICA;

Having been cast on Shore by his SHIPMATES,
Abandoned with only GOATS and CATS for company
in a Savage Landscape.

WITH

An account of his TRIALS at the hands of said Island.

Written by Himself.

LONDON

BLOOMSBURY CIRCUS
Bloomsbury Publishing Plc
50 Bedford Square, London, WC1B 3DP, UK
Bloomsbury Publishing Ireland Limited,
29 Earlsfort Terrace, Dublin 2, DO2 AY28, Ireland

BLOOMSBURY, BLOOMSBURY CIRCUS and the Circus logo
are trademarks of Bloomsbury Publishing Plc

First published in Great Britain 2026

A catalogue record for this book is available from the British Library

ISBN: HB: 978-1-5266-6139-5; TPB: 978-1-5266-6144-9;
EBOOK: 978-1-5266-6140-1

2 4 6 8 10 9 7 5 3 1

Typeset by Six Red Marbles India
Printed and bound in Great Britain by Clays Ltd, Elcograf S.p.A

To find out more about our authors and books visit www.bloomsbury.com
and sign up for our newsletters
For product-safety-related questions contact productsafety@bloomsbury.com

For my son, Max,
the best fellow.

I was myself the compass of that sea:

I was the world in which I walked, and what I saw
Or heard or felt came not but from myself;
And there I found myself more truly and more strange.

From 'Tea at the Palaz of Hoon', Wallace Stevens

Prologue

In the ordinary way of things, a man would find himself cast away by some catastrophe: a storm, or running aground, or being marooned by pirates. But I am cast upon this island only by the catastrophe of my own personality, which is a sobering thing, even for a man little used to being sober.

If a fellow keeps busy it is quite possible never to be confronted by oneself. Indeed, the sailor's life might be designed for this very purpose, each day parcelled into four-hour shifts, and each of them filled with labour or with sorely needed sleep. One might live to a great age without ever being forced to face the grim fact of your character – though few sailors live to a great age regardless.

But on this island, where I have no looking-glass at all, I am confronted squarely by the fact of myself, and having little else to contemplate, I cannot avoid examining the whole mess of it, and my manifold flaws. Viz., I am a man of choleric disposition, much inclined to rage. I am intemperate, and ashore am more like to be found drunk than sober. I have sinned in many ways, both large and small, and the worst of it is that I am no fool, so know myself for what I am, which is a wretch and a reprobate.

And here on the island, with none of those things that make a man – company; women; his occupation; a house, nor even a bed – who am I? Can a man crack the shell of himself like a crab, and cast off his scoundrel nature, to reveal the fleshy goodness within? I fear it is not so simple, though I would wish it so. Against what do I crack myself open? Against this island, its unyielding stone. Against time, which neither budges nor softens. Against my memories, sharper by far than the rocks.

And what if what is within me is not wholesome flesh and goodness but something else? Something rotten as the rest of me – intemperate, hasty, and curdled with sin?

A family may pack a troublesome son off to sea to be rid of him. But it is harder by far to be rid of yourself. There is no escaping oneself, although I could wish it, for my father has told me many times I am a scoundrel. I will allow that I have been a scoundrel, and a sinner too. Whether I have any good in me remains to be seen. Certainly my brothers would say I have none. There are a number of women in the region of Nether Largo and in ports around the world who would likewise agree. As for my father, he would give a hearty oration about my many flaws and weaknesses, which have ever been a favourite topic of his.

In truth my parents did not send me to sea to be rid of me – and though I warrant my father was glad to have me gone, he had for many years importuned me as to the unwiseness of going to sea. I did not listen, never having been inclined to listening of any kind, my inclinations being much more of the active sort, for brawling, drinking and leaving.

It is a hard thing, to know oneself for what one is. But the sea is a great one for starting over, and thus perhaps I shall.

PART ONE

I

When they leave me on the island, I do not scruple to beg. I chase the last boat into the bay, wading and shouting, 'Sir, sir, mercy, have mercy, you will not leave me here to die?' When Captain Stradling ignores me I shout to the other men aboard: 'Will you not show me mercy? Am I not your comrade and your friend?'

My sea chest is still on the shore, all my belongings within it – my treasured astrolabe, and all the other tools of my work – but I will leave it there if this is what it takes. I will flee this island however I may, for its rocks can grant me nothing but a slow and lonely death. Sobbing, snot warm on my face, I yell after them – and what shame for proud Alexander Selkirk, to beg in this craven way. But this is good, I think, as I stumble behind the boat – surely the shame is the point, for having shamed me thus, so utterly, it will cost Stradling nothing to admit me aboard. He has won this encounter, and I have lost, and none could think otherwise. He will appear magnanimous by sending the boat back for me – and what would it avail him to leave me to my death? That will serve only to rob him of his navigator, and to set the men against him for a brute. And when he lets me aboard I will kiss the wretched and worm-riddled hull of the *Cinque Ports*. I will lie on her decks and repent.

The sea is up to my chest. I trip on the stony ground and plunge altogether beneath the water, and though a good swimmer I am taken by surprise, and when I flounder to the surface I see two of the rowers laughing very heartily. And somehow the small indignity of this dunking, atop the great humiliation of my entire plight, is the thing that sets me raging, and I yell, 'Damn you all for villains, and a parcel of rogues and curs.'

I am in the deep water now, swimming. I try to grasp the boat's side and Stradling shouts, 'You fool, you'll overset it. Don't make me shoot you,' and indeed he has his pistol out. Surely he will not use it on me, his own ship's master – but perhaps I do not, after all, have such a fine grasp of what Captain Stradling may be capable of.

'Loggia,' I call, for my friend David Loggia is right there at the bow, neither rowing nor watching me. He keeps his eyes fixed down; when that is no longer enough he closes them, and whether it is to shield his own shame or mine I do not know.

I cannot keep pace with the boat, four men at the oars, yet still I swim, they shall see I mean to swim and to holler all the way. My voice tears itself ragged and hoarse, 'Save me, save me goddamn you has no man among you a heart?'

But they outstrip me fast, and I am forced to retreat a little, back to where I can stand, chest-deep in the water, the better to scream after them. 'Please,' I yell. 'Please. Don't leave me.' They reach the ship, and the men are taken up from the boat. There is a flurry of activity as the anchor is weighed. I do not turn my back, not even when my body gets to shaking, for it is October and the water fierce cold.

Hope is a wicked slippery thing. Even when the ship is out of sight and I am forced from the water by my shivering, still I watch. Surely that is the pennant of the ship; surely that is not just the crest of a wave but the *Cinque Ports*; surely those petrels must be there for a reason, hovering above the ship as it returns for me.

In the east rises the moon, a bowl of spoiled milk. The indifferent horizon owes me nothing. I am alone.

Dark is coming, and I have a mighty thirst, my throat parched from salt water and from screaming. Fresh water, at least, I have aplenty – for its reliable streams of water are one of the few reasons any ship would stop here, on this stony blemish in the ocean. Two good streams run down to this very bay, and water may be got with no greater hazard than the mud that our crew has churned on the banks of the stream during our month of camping here. I fill my mug and drink. *Water*, I think, and I give a short, sour laugh, sweeping my arm at the sea that surrounds me. *Oh yes, I do not want for water.*

I change into dry clothes from my sea chest, my fingers shaking so that I can scarce fasten the buttons on my shirt. I have no shelter – the tents where we all slept ashore have been struck and taken aboard. It is a mercy that it is not raining, for this last month here we have been plagued by rain, and even when it did not rain, a thick sea fog settled over the island in great drifts. I have my flint and steel, and without venturing too far from the shore am able to salvage enough fallen wood to start a small, smoky fire. I sit so close to the flames that the skin of my face grows tight and hot, like earthenware in a kiln. I eat nothing – partly from a desire to eke out my small supply of food, and partly because fear and anger have tied a knot in my guts.

My fire burns a small hole in the night. I wrap my blanket tight around me and try to sleep.

Although this island is bleak, in three things it is rich indeed; viz. goats; cats; and black rats. The wild goats and cats give me no trouble, but the rats are a torment.

My blanket affords me no protection, and they seek me out. When I slept here with the rest of my crew, all of us quartered together ashore, the rats were less bold. Tonight, without the great press and noise of so many men, they creep upon me in the dark. Something is forever moving in the corner of my vision. The worst of them is not even their sharp teeth, but their tails, obscenely hairless. Their black fur has a greasy sheen, as though they are always wet – as though they ought to leave a damp trail as a slug does. They come upon me rat-wise, nose first, sniffing and whiskering. Again and again I wake to find them upon me, right under the blanket, some testing my flesh with the fish hooks of their teeth. I kick out, but a man may only stay awake so long, and so I slip into a sort of delirium: sleep; nip; wake; kick; sleep; nip. When I sleep I dream of rats, their serpent tails and their splayed fingers; the ghastly wetness of their noses.

After sunrise, when I am yet half asleep, one daring fellow runs up the leg of my trousers. I don't know which of us is more alarmed for I leap up and dance a great horrified jig and beat him to death against my own leg, crush crush of little skull and sharp bone bits, and then when I have shook out the corpse, with much swearing, I bind the legs of my trousers with string so that no more may come in that way.

———

And what of this island, where I am forsaken? This outcrop of rock and forest, nearly 400 miles from land, and that land Chile, which is full of both savages and Spaniards.

I thought I knew this island already – I may be a bad man, but I am a good navigator, and I know my charts. This was the *Cinque Ports'* second time at the island, and we passed several weeks ashore – as we did the previous time, with the *St George* and her crew besides. Yet now that I am entirely alone, and doomed to remain so, the island takes on a different complexion altogether. I must learn this place anew.

I turn my back to the sea and gaze upon the heavy mass of the island, a sheer and savage jag of rock. Much of the coast is bound by cliffs, rising so fierce and unforgiving that there is but one decent harbour, in this bay on the north-eastern coast, where a ship may safely anchor in thirty-five-fathom water. A lesser bay, west of the island's northern tip, may serve for ships of a shallow draft, but offers less in the way of shelter, wood and water.

The island is perhaps twelve or fourteen leagues all around, but irregular in shape. It makes a haphazard triangle, pointing west, north, and south-east. Westward it stretches long and thin, nearly an isthmus, and that part of the island is favoured by the wild goats. Beyond that western extremity is another island, known variously as Isla Santa Clara or (as I have seen it on some French charts) Isle aux Chevres – however it is but a tiny outcrop, offering only what may already be got on the larger island: goats, rocks and silence.

If you were to glance at the island on a map, its size is such that you might fancy a man could walk around its edge in two days, if hard-pressed – or that crossing the island at its narrowest points would be the work of but a few hours. Any man who has been ashore here knows better, for it is a wicked hostile manner of place, a welter of sheer cliffs and dense forest. There are pleasant valleys to be found, but also treacherous precipices and entire bare plains of wind-scoured dirt or rocks.

Oh it is a very sharp island altogether. Sharp in how it slits open the sea; sharp in its peaks piercing the sky. Even the island's silhouette is most forbidding, setting against the air its rocky carapace, bedevilled with spurs and spikes. The violence of stone.

It is not long after dawn, and now comes the daily clatter of goat hoofs on rock, as the goats come down from the island's high places and begin their unhurried grazing – a goat's hunger must be a fearsome thing, for they are forever at the task of eating. The Spaniards many years past set some goats on the island, for the benefit of ships that land here. The goats have quite overrun the place, but they promise better than the rats, for at least the goats shall feed me.

On this grey dawn the great profusion of goats seems to me a grim token of the island's remoteness – for if ships were in the habit of stopping here often, the goats should not have reached such a tremendous number, nor be so bold and unwary, some even coming close enough that I could toss a stone and strike them. But as the sun emerges a little, I consider that the goats should be a comfort to me – not only as a source of food, but because it suggests that they have no predators here. I confess that I have not been altogether easy in my mind for thoughts of fearsome beasts – lions, or tigers, or other monsters of the jungle – but surely there can be none, or the goats would not be so abundant. By the same token, I am reassured that no savages frequent this place – which my knowledge of the island's remoteness had already inclined me to believe – but the goats are further assurance, for surely even savages would not neglect such a rich source of food.

The cats, too, I suspect have been left here by some sailors, and have since run wild. They are alike to an ordinary cat in size, though their fur is shaggier, and they have about them a greater fierceness, mighty wary of men. A tabby stalks the beach above me now; idly, I toss a pebble. It lands short of her, but she turns and hisses, her bared fangs a very clear reminder of lions and such beasts. While perhaps these cats could not kill you as a lion could, I believe most ardently that they would try.

———

I resolve to take a kind of census of my possessions, spreading them out before me on the shore. It is a meagre collection, and offers me little comfort.

Of food, I have some small quantity of cabbage leaves and a joint of goat meat, which remain from our last meal as a crew. I have also three ship's biscuits, and the miserly supplies that Stradling deigned to leave me: a small sack of flour and a cask of flip.

My clothing (in addition to the shoes, shirt and trousers I am wearing), consists of two shirts; one warm undershirt; one jacket; one pair of trousers, much worn; two pairs of stockings. Also in my possession are several yards of linen cloth. I have my blanket, but for once it is a disadvantage to have been an officer, for instead of having a hammock like the common sailors, which I could have brought ashore, I was furnished with a bed, which has sailed away with the *Cinque Ports*. A musket, though this will not serve me for long, having not more than a pound of powder and but a small quantity of bullets. I have also some practical pieces (viz. my mug; a flint; my knife and marlinspike; a kettle, which is not so large as I would now wish). Of money I have nine shillings and eight pence in coins, carefully husbanded during the voyage, and entirely worthless to me now. My pipe, and my small pouch of tobacco; the further pouch of tobacco that Stradling left for me in his grand show of generosity.

Also a small quantity of cord, which was not left out of kindness but by error, in the haste of the men striking the tents, leaving this rope where it had fallen at the base of a tree. You may readily believe I was delighted to find it, as few things are as useful to a man in my situation as good rope. 'If only to hang myself with,' I say aloud. A nearby goat looks at me, exceedingly doleful, and returns to his chewing.

Scattered elsewhere along the shore are other such pieces of detritus, abandoned as junk. Two broken barrels, a small quantity of sailcloth, rather torn. Just yesterday, I too would have considered these things no great prize – now, though, I fold the sailcloth as delicately as though it were a reverend's vestments, and drag the barrels away from the waterline, already wondering to what use I may put their wood, or their broken iron hoops.

It is a source of boundless distress that I do not own a telescope, hungry as I am for the horizon, and dreaming of rescue. Instead, I have only my mathematical instruments. These I had previously reckoned amongst my greatest treasures, most particularly my astrolabe. Now, far from being a comfort, they seem to taunt me. My most diligent navigational readings would confirm only what I already know: that I am stuck here, and like to remain so. My divider, my scale, my nocturnal and my traverse board can be of no use to me – indeed they are as worthless to me here as my small quantity of coins, and I would trade any of them for a pound of powder, or of tobacco. The books I consulted in my work – a mathematical treatise and an astronomical almanack – are likewise useless now, unless I use their pages to kindle a fire. I resolve that before I die here, alone, I shall carve some kind of plaque that will read: *Here died the unfortunate Alexander Selkirk, navigator, who knew precisely where he was but not how to leave.*

If I were not a ship's master, and familiar with the charts, I might hope to escape this island. I might scurry about and construct myself some kind of craft and hope to make landfall. The curse or the blessing of my particular circumstance is that I know too much. I have perused the charts many times. To the east, it is more than 380 miles to the coast of Chile. To the west, a mere 100 miles would take me to

Mas Afuera, the westernmost island of these Juan Fernández isles – an island the twin of this one, but even more removed. Beyond that, open ocean for thousands of miles. There is no escape that would not end in drowning, particularly in the brutal seas of this part of the world.

The last item in this grim accounting of my few possessions is my Bible. My father gave it to me as a young man, and given the nature of my youth, and its many sins and misdemeanours, I confess the Bible felt more like a censure than a gift. Nevertheless I have never quite brought myself to sell it – not through any piousness, but rather through a filial fondness, and a wish that he might come to think better of me. Today this is a melancholy reflection, for I shall not live to see him again.

These thoughts of my desolation, and the very great likelihood of my death on this forsaken place, lead me to open the cask of flip that Stradling gave me. Before I drink, I raise a toast to him: 'To Captain Thomas Stradling, who took pains to seem benevolent even when abandoning me to near-certain death.' I commence drinking, and looking about me at the desolate island, its mountains propping up the sky, I see no reason to stop. I have many pressing tasks, but none seems more pressing than the contents of the cask. I drink not for pleasure but for oblivion; oblivion, my faithful companion, does not disappoint me. Rain comes; I drag my sea chest to the nearest stand of trees, and drape the length of sailcloth over the chest to make a hasty and primitive tent, where I may hunch out of the rain. I gnaw at the joint of goat meat and watch the bay for the return of the *Cinque Ports*. I drink, and drink again – how else is a man to bear such a blank horizon? The sun slips like a coin into the sea. When the rats come to find me, I yell mightily at them; it does not discourage them, but it gives me some pleasure to hurl at them all the calumnies I can summon, and to laugh heartily at my own wit.

Not being a temperate man, nor one accustomed to restraint, I spend three days in a state of violent drunkenness. I talk to myself, as I stumble through the hours. There is at least a certain freedom in this – for at sea, in the inordinate press of bodies that fills any ship, a man may not so much as fart without a noisy chorus of ribaldry and complaints. Here, on the island, I mutter and shout; when the mood takes me, I even sing. There is nobody to hear nor care, though when I sing a particularly obscene song, one old, white goat looks at me with what I fancy is disapproval. I throw a pebble at him, and miss, and he takes off inland.

I watch him dart uphill. A hill on the island is nothing so gentle and rounded as the word might conjure. No – the island's hills are blades, sharp and narrow, fit to cut the sky to shreds. The hills of Largo, that my brothers and I used to roll down as children, are nothing like these shards of rock, jagged walls thrown up against the horizon. Largo Law, the mountain that used to seem such a towering great height above our village of Nether Largo, seems now a mild and tame thing, its top flattened the way a woman's breast settles when she lies on her back. And this sets me thinking of women and the prospect that I shall never again see a woman, and I confess that as the dark thickens, I slump against my sea chest on the shore and alternate between frigging myself and weeping.

By the third day I have eaten two of the ship's biscuits, and all of the goat meat. My fire has long burned out, for I have been in no state to feed it. Only ten yards from where I sprawl, the old goat is staring at me again. He is white all over, with huge curved horns and a splendid beard. I lean back on my elbows and call out to him: 'Why do you hang about here, old man? Do you not know that I may eat you too? Why do you drag your long ears about, and stare so? And what manner of beard do you call that, so bushy and long?'

The goat, unconcerned by my shouting, lifts his tail and shits, dropping little pellets round as so much musket shot.

I lean back against my sea chest. And in this bleary state, awash with drink, the years are dislodged and slosh about in my mind, I am beset by thoughts of my childhood, and all that led me to this accursed place.

My mother is soft, too soft. She feeds me love as a mother bird feeds its chicks: great wet gobbets forced down the throat. She feeds me love like pap, and I want none of it.

Thus I must be wicked, and if I am not born wicked I am at least determined to become so, so that I may join my brothers and they will cease their mocking of me, Mam's pet, her special wee dote. And a better school of wickedness I can scarce imagine than our cottage in Nether Largo, with my herd of older brothers, quick with their sharp tongues and quicker with their fists. Thus I grow up throwing rocks at shutters and yanking the tails of cats, and saying to the village lasses such things as would make my sweet mother blush if ever she heard them, and indeed she does hear from time to time and weeps and chides but even then cannot bring herself to box my ears but gets my father to do it. I wish Mam would hit me herself – not because she lacks my father's strong fists, but because then I could be rid of her cloying grip on me, and could take my rightful place amongst my big brothers, that fierce tribe.

For myself, I can never see why a woman with six sons living should wish for more – least of all when the sons were as wild as my brothers. But my mam did – she wished for more, and there were two born before me that died, and those dead babies set a fearful wanting in her so that when I came along she wanted too much altogether, and made of me her special pet. I am the seventh living son and Mam takes it as a benison, and says I shall always carry luck with me. Furthermore I was born in my caul and had to be cut from it, which is reckoned a blessing against drowning. Thus Mam always tells me I am doubly charmed. 'Blessed, not once but twice, and no harm can come to you,' she says. When she presses me against her she is soft as risen dough, and smells as good. It is not always easy to despise her, but having made up my mind, I am nothing if not stubborn.

I am four years younger than my youngest brother. For that gap I blame the two dead babes that came in between. I cannot forgive them, for those four years made a mighty gulf between me and my six big brothers. They are their own gang; I am forever an after-thought, left with Mam, or trailing behind my brothers, calling out to them to wait.

The village of Nether Largo sits hard on the shore, so that a drunken fisherman may easily stumble into the water, and several indeed have done so. Raised here, where the sea-spray smears the windows and rots the window frames, a lad's thoughts turn easily to going to sea. I am barely five when I fall into the harbour (my brother Andrew was standing close behind me, and I could swear I felt a shove between my shoulder blades). Yet somehow I stay afloat until my father wades in to pluck me from the water – and to Mam my survival is certain proof that I shall always be spared. She is not fool enough to believe me a saint, for I am neck-deep in mischief most days, but she does sincerely believe me blessed, and most especially that I can never be drowned and should therefore go to sea.

My father is hard where my mother is soft. His work has hardened him – a cobbler and a tanner, his very skin is stiffened, his palms coarse and tough. This I learn to my cost, for I receive many beatings at Da's hand, and deserve nearly all of them.

When I am older and begin to speak seriously of going to sea, my mother smiles and kisses me and says, 'And so you shall, and make your fortune, too,' at which Da grows angry.

'Don't encourage the lad. He nearly drowned in the harbour – what do you think will become of him at sea?'

Mam only smiles, always mild, saying, 'But he did not drown, and what's more never shall; will you not show a little faith?'

But no Selcraig has been a sailor – and though a mere cobbler, Da sees himself superior to the fishermen and sailors hereabouts. And he is fierce set on me helping him in his trade, though why that should fall to me I do not see, for have I not six brothers who could do so, and John already working with Da at the business, and William too? Altogether I have a great hankering for the freedom of the sea. The local herring fisheries are not enough for me, for I am young and full of tales of daring and discovery. Thus when Mam harps on how she believes I shall make a fine sailor, it suits me to believe her, for I readily wish myself far away from Nether Largo.

My brothers, too, give me a good reason to wish myself gone, most particularly Andrew. Mam does not see how she condemns me to mockery and torment by making a great deal of my blessedness – for a gang of boys likes nothing so well as to tease, and who better to tease than Mam's little pet, her blessed one, her charmed lad?

As for Andrew, he is a most canny rascal and since our early child-hood has tormented me with a variety of pranks large and small, viz. I can never put on a pair of shoes without finding several sharp stones therein. Also a prodigious quantity of pins in my pockets, and the tying of my stockings into knots pulled very tight, and other like pettifogging things. Such japes may hardly be accounted serious, but when for years on end you have not even been able to dress your-self without torments you may ask yourself how grave you would consider these insults.

Andrew is of no mean intelligence, so he is at pains to show me fondness when our parents are about. He saves his taunts and jests for when we are alone, knowing how to provoke me precisely to the point of anger, until Da and my older brothers lament my temper, and even my mother wonders aloud how all this vexation could come about when Andrew is such a sweet-tempered boy.

'He is merely spirited,' she tells me. 'If you would just yield a little. You are so stubborn. If Andrew must have his little jokes, do not take them to heart so.'

Our older brothers are inclined either to ignore us both, or to side with Andrew, for he was their comrade many years ere I was born. And when my brothers make sport of me, my mother draws me close, saying, 'Pay them no heed, Pet – for we have each other. And we make a good team, do we not?' She squeezes me, and from the crush of her embrace I look over her shoulder and out of the window, to my brothers playing together outside.

And the more my mam calls me *Pet*, the worse it is, for my broth-ers take to calling me the same, in cloying tones, and what's more encouraging all the lads at school to do so, until every lad in Largo is calling me *Pet*, except for Angus Cameron who is too small and weedy to mock anyone. And my shame is not allowed to be forgot-ten until more than a year hence, when I coin a new name for Angus Cameron himself, which catches on throughout the school, concerning as it does Angus's simpleton sister and a rhyme both memorable and obscene.

Thus my brothers school me very well, and my dearest wish is to either kill them or become them.

Thus you may begin to see how a man such as Alexander Selkirk was shaped, and shaped in such a way that my course was set early for disaster, and this island the greatest disaster of them all. How I found my way to this particular calamity, however, I am too drunk to contemplate – or perhaps not drunk enough.

It is the third day. The last of the flip has been poured down my throat, and no small quantity of it brought up again the same way, in vomiting. I tip the cask above me to be sure it is truly empty, and with much swearing I drop it on its side and give it a hefty kick to roll it down towards the shore. Then, realising that I can ill afford to lose any such thing, I stagger to the water's edge to retrieve it, cursing, and with my head pulsing most alarmingly with each step. All that night I shake and retch, and my sad fire does not keep the rats at bay, but serves only to illuminate their glistening tails as they creep closer.

Yet by next morning things begin to take on a less dire complexion. Although my hands still tremble, now that the flip is gone, and my headache subsided, I find my spirits considerably improved. Indeed it is a kind of relief, for having no drink whatsoever has absolved me of any need to exercise restraint, or to reproach myself when restraint fails. Just as I was at my best aboard a ship, with the purser in charge of rationing our daily tot of drink, I find that there is no sterner purser than this island. The drink being gone, it is gone, and there is no beseeching the island for more. It is time instead to set about the business of surviving.

3

A better camp than the beach must be my first concern. I alight on a place but a little removed from the shore. The ground is flat, if rather damp, and covered with a pale grass, with pimento trees all about. Of water I have a plentiful supply, for a good stream runs hard by my small clearing, and thence down to the bay. Most importantly, my camp offers a clear view of the sea, so that I shall not miss any ship that passes the bay, which I can reach in less than half an hour. In this spot I rig a hasty tent with one of the pieces of sailcloth, determining to use the smaller part to make a hammock.

As for food, the sea hereabouts being very rich in all manner of fish, I think at first to provide for myself in this manner. Even without a net or line, a man may easily gather a good supply of crawfish, which grow prodigious large in these parts. When we were anchored here, we all ate heartily of this good meat. However, without the provisions of the *Cinque Ports* I am sadly lacking in salt, and discover that any quantity of this fish, unsalted, occasions a mighty loose-ness of the bowels, so that I spend half a day shitting and am much reduced to tremors and weakness.

Thereafter I turn my attentions to other foods. My great succour is the cabbage tree, which gives large quantities of cabbage leaves, indifferent sweet but plentiful. The leaves are so big that some of their threads cannot be chewed, so that I am often left working away at a fibrous mass, like a ball of string, as a cow works at its cud. These I fish from my mouth and set aside, like little nests. Sometimes I see the old goat with the long beard taking up these leavings and eating them, a goat being tremendous hardy in eating all manner of things.

But a man, not being a goat, cannot be satisfied on cabbage leaves alone, which leave me hungry no matter the huge quantities that I eat. I must seek meat.

When we anchored here in February, before our final and disastrous visit, the shore was packed thick with seals. Now there are none, it no longer being the season. These fat, finned creatures were entirely harmless, troublesome only for the great yelping and grunting that they make, and for their vast numbers, at times so many of them ashore that we had to holler and stamp to clear a path to the water. They were much prized for their fur which is exceeding soft, some silver and some the rich colour of well-oiled wood. They were so plump about the middle that they rolled helpless onto their sides, as though they contained altogether too much seal for their skin. During our time ashore we used sometimes to eat them, but only to spare other victuals, for seal meat is coarse-grained, dark and only tolerably good, tasting very strongly of fish and of liver.

In the absence now of seals, my meat must come from the goats, so abundant here. They are surprising tame, and some I may approach quite close, though when they do dart away they are both quick and nimble. The long-bearded old goat, the same one who watched me at my shitting, is forever hanging about my camp, often but a short distance from me. Sometimes he scratches his back against a tree, giving a long and gruff series of hees and haws, like someone working a set of rusty bellows. But most of the time he simply watches me. The way he stares puts in me in mind of those in our crew who fancied themselves naturalists and men of science, such as Dampier's mate Funnel, who was forever writing notes and making sketches of the creatures and the savages that we encountered on our voyage. This old goat examines me with the same fixed curiosity.

I take to speaking to him, as I busy myself about my camp: 'And do you see how the Christian man occupies his days? Is it as you expected, sir?' As for eating him, he looks a bony old fellow, and there are hereabouts many others with an appearance altogether more succulent.

I guard my shot and powder jealously for I have but a pound of powder and less of shot, and once gone neither can be replenished. But I am weak with hunger and this perpetual shitting, and resolve to shoot a goat. This I do with little trouble, lying in wait

17

awhile in the woods above my camp until a good-sized fellow strays near enough to kill with one neat shot – and I have always been accounted a decent shot. But though I hit him squarely, he then confounds me by staggering to one of the many crevasses amongst the rocks, and either falling or darting down it. Swearing heartily I rush to the edge. I cannot see him below – but it matters little, for whether he is dead or has merely escaped, I shall have no meat, and my powder and shot are wasted, my precious store depleted – and for nothing.

I am more cautious the second time, choosing a place further inland, without any such crevasse within reach. Perhaps my aim, too, is better, for this goat obliges me by dying on the spot, very tidy. Before I move the carcass I take my knife and I dig about inside the shattered chest to retrieve the shot, a messy and arduous process, only to find the ball much deformed, likely where it struck bone. Even were I able to retrieve a ball still in good shape, I will nonetheless run out of powder. So I account this time wasted, and although the goat meat, broiled in my little kettle, is tolerably good, I must at some point master a means of catching and killing the goats without my musket, so that I may preserve my shot and powder. I'm reasonably confident that this island harbours no fearsome beasts, but a man alone in such extremity feels better with a weapon in his hands. And even if there are no giant serpents nor tigers to pounce upon me, the Spaniards or the French are more fearsome still, for at least beasts do not take slaves, but grant you the mercy of a prompt death.

That night I eat more goat meat than is wise, so impatient that I do not even wait for it to cool. Crouched in my humble tent, I lick my burned fingers. It is my fifth night on the island. Already I am become used to the treachery of time – each day is too short for me to complete my tasks; each night, beset by rats, refuses to end.

Given that a man is not like to starve in this place, you may wonder at my certainty that I will not leave this island alive. You might think that, having led a life full of misadventure, and survived thus far, I should feel myself blessed and be sanguine of my rescue. Yet the opposite is true: having seen what I have seen, I know for sure that even a seventh-born son cannot be so fortunate. Such luck as I was born with I have surely exhausted.

———

My camp is a meagre one – but rescue is more urgent than comfort. Should any ship pass, I shall need a signal fire, and to this end I drag a good stock of wood on the beach, laid out ready like a pyre. The climate being rather damp than otherwise, I secrete a further stock of kindling where it may stay dry – tucked in a cave by the shore. The small tin box containing my flint and steel I have taken to carrying with me always, in a pouch by my belt, the way some papists wear a saint's medallion about their neck. I pray to no saints but to my flint, and have hopes that it shall yet be my salvation.

Yet what I know of the island's history offers me little encouragement. When the *Cinque Ports* stopped here in February, we were forced to leave eight men behind when we gave chase to a French merchant ship. Not able to return until September, we found only two survivors. The others had been taken unawares by the French, who had hunted them out with dogs, and shot or seized those they found.

There is one other story of abandonment in this place: an Indian slave, left here by buccaneers. Dampier himself rescued him, ten years or more ago. This Indian fellow went by the name of Will. He had survived – being an Indian and a savage he had, most likely, an affinity for the wilds, and less need of company and discourse. Even so, it was three years before the fellow was rescued. Three years – in which time a man might find divers ways to die on this sorry island – by beasts, or starvation, or illness, or hunted and killed by Spaniards or the French.

I will allow that there are likewise plenty of ways for a sailor to die – I have proof enough of that in my own calamitous career. But at least if you die aboard a ship, a note is made in the ship's log, which will record your name, and then, *departed this life*, or something similar, and there would be a sea burial with the captain presiding, and all the solemnity that the sea endows. And if you are swept overboard in a storm, and cannot be granted the dignity of a sea burial, at least your death would be known, and your shipmates could later raise a toast to you, and your name recorded in the log nevertheless.

Here, though, if I die, I am lost to all knowing. The rats will have my flesh and the wind will scour my unburied bones, and no record will ever hold my name nor tell the story of my passing. It would be a dying more complete than any other.

I am known for a man bluff and choleric, and not given to cowardice. I am a sailor and no stranger to storms, nor to battles. Yet here, on this ruinous shore, I will allow that I am afraid.

4

While my thoughts are much preoccupied by mortality, the rats are my most pressing daily concern. A rat will not kill a man but I begin to think they shall be the end of me nonetheless, for they torment me so grievously that I cannot sleep nor even rest easy. I begin to feel feverish with exhaustion, my body tremoring and quick to sweat. I jump at every movement in the dark and fancy every shadow a rat. Coming back at night from a piss, I spy a rat by the opening of my makeshift tent and kick it across the clearing, only to discover, after much swearing and clutching of my foot, that it is my tin mug.

I decide that I must beseech the cats for their help – it is common to see a cat stroll past my camp with a fat black rat held fast in its mouth. My father, a cobbler who cured his own hides, was wont to keep a cat or two about his workshop, to keep off any vermin. I think that I might contrive a similar arrangement with the cats hereabouts, and that if I can persuade a few of their number to make my camp their home, they will keep the rats at bay.

Yet how to win the cats to my service? They are not so bold as the goats – indeed, they keep a good distance from my camp, and if I come across one elsewhere, they are quick to dart away, with a mighty hiss.

Taking many good morsels of goat meat, I lay a trail from the woods all the way to my humble bed. Yet rather than cats I find only a tremendous increase in the rats, who are prodigious pleased by my gifts, and come that night in greater numbers than ever.

I am learning that a cat will do nothing that does not please it, for a cat is a very indifferent thing – particularly a cat that is not hungry. Thus I resolve to take a different approach, for I fancy it will be easier to win the affection of a young cat, not yet so fierce as the grown beasts who prowl these hills. And so for some weeks I am alert for a litter of kittens. One dawn I see a cat carrying a kitten in its mouth; by tremendous good luck the cat is cornered against a cliff and cannot flee when I pounce, and its burden makes it slower so I am able to grasp the cat and seize the kitten, at the cost of a nasty scratch to my arm – only to find it is no kitten at all but a rat, still alive, which, far from showing gratitude for its rescue, bites me deeply before twisting free of my grip and darting into the scrub.

But four days hence I am more fortunate. I have been watching for some time a cat with a white chest who was used to frequent a stretch of the shore, and is either fat or pregnant. I do not see her for a week or more, and then when I do again glimpse her she is much reduced in size and without that ungainly waddle. By much careful stalking of her, I am at last able to come upon her hiding place, which is a burrow half concealed beneath a fallen log. I do not disturb the kittens, which are mere parcels of fur, still blind, and anyway could not survive without their mother's milk. But I watch the place carefully, and when many weeks have passed and the kittens have started to venture from the burrow, I wait until their mother has left to hunt, in the early evening, and I snatch up one of the kittens – a girl, who can furnish me with more cats in the future. The one I choose is grey all over, except for a fetching white patch on her chin.

I have no milk, for while killing a wild goat is one thing, catching one alive is quite another. I shoot a goat and set aside a saucer of blood, and I take the soft hot liver and chop it very fine, and feed the kitten off the tip of my finger, a little at a time, which it takes most eagerly. It is but tiny yet fierce determined to live, eating lustily with a tongue that, although small, would make a good rasp.

I have never had, nor thought to have, a pet. Da's cats served a purpose and no more – and they learned quick to keep a distance from my brothers, who would tease them with throwing of stones and yanking of tails. As for tenderness, my father's only contact with the cats was to toss them the occasional scrap, and to drown their kittens. 'Else the place shall be overrun,' he used to say, holding those small slick bundles beneath the water. Each season his cats whelped more kittens, reliable as chickweed.

I cannot win the affections of this kitten merely with food, as the rats of this island provide an easy feast for any cat. I busy myself instead with many blandishments and caresses. To keep her close, and also to help her grow accustomed to me, I fashion a kind of pouch from goatskin, with the fur turned inwards. This I wear about my neck, the kitten nestled within. I go about thus for several weeks, and the kitten likes it very well, purring mightily. She has a habit of standing on her hind legs in the pouch so that she may press her little head beneath my chin. In my clearing she entertains me often with her antics, for she will chase her own tail, and if I take a twig with a leaf at the end and wave it along the dirt, she will stalk it most intently, and pounce.

After three weeks of this I begin allowing her to roam, and am heartened to find she never strays far from my little camp. I give her a name − Pickle, after one of the lads on the *Cinque Ports*, for the cat's white chin puts me in mind of his white beard. When I call her name she comes running as smart as a little dog, and whether it is for affection or for the good supply of liver, the result is the same. I confess that she is not a prodigious hunter, and perhaps it is my fault, for being too free with the liver and other scraps of goat − but it seems that the mere scent of cat about my tent has a discouraging effect on the rats, who have become less bold. And although I still suffer sorely from my lack of human company, a man feels less miserable with a warm creature perched on his lap.

Do not mistake me − even amongst the diverting antics of my kitten, my first thought is always of rescue. My camp offers a fine prospect of the bay, where any ship intending to come ashore will anchor. Yet this is not enough for me, for I am plagued by notions of ships passing with no intent to stop, who may not pass by this side of the island. Thus I make it my business to seek out a lookout, and some hours' walk from my camp I find a most satisfactory one, a sort of saddle slung between two peaks. From here, the thin stretch of land to the west is split by a central ridge of mountains, fearsome sharp, as though the island is some great and starving monster that has lain down, this ridge its bony spine. Beyond it, the smaller island of Santa

Clara. To my east, the milder slopes that lead back down to my own bay. And beyond everything, and in all directions, the sea.

I cup my hands about my mouth and give a mighty halloo. I had thought to feel bold and powerful – to make the island ring with my cry. But my yell, be it ever so loud, is made small by the boundless space around it. My voice drops into the rock crevasses and is swallowed by the forests, and is lost long before it ever reaches the sea.

———

I make the journey to my lookout several times a week. Already the climb has become easier, for in these weeks and months I have worn a path through the forests of the island's lower reaches, though I must still go carefully on the steep rocks, where a single slip would mean death. Once up here, I stay an hour or more, searching the horizon.

Stare long enough at the sea and you may imagine any thing. When the westerlies blow savage and the white crests of waves ride the horizon, I imagine white sails. On grey days such as today, when heavy clouds sit right on the water, I can see a towering man-of-war come for me, solemn and stately. Oh, a fellow as desperate as I can imagine the whole English fleet, and on the flagship all the whores of Southwark on deck, tits out, coming just for me.

Then I rub my credulous eyes, or the wind shifts, and all is gone, and only the waves remain.

How can it be so long – so very long? Three months – summer has the island gripped in its clammy fist. Surely a ship must soon come, as my own ship came, not once but twice, and the French ships that we chased and battled. Now: nothing. Each day here is a hoax played on me by time. The miserly horizon refuses to grant me a sail.

The island is so small, and the sea so endless, that it seems a miracle that it has ever been discovered at all. Juan Fernández himself, who gave these islands their name, came upon the islands when he was essaying a new method of sailing south. Sailors have long known that the northward currents that beset the west coast of Peru and Chile make for slow sailing, so that ships heading south from Peru can take as long as a year to reach Chile. Fernández discovered that a ship may make better speed by first heading west, far out to sea, and hence southward, avoiding the curse of the coastal currents. Ever since, this knowledge has been a boon to sailors in these parts – but is a curse to me now, for I know all too well that a ship may come all this way and yet not stop here at all. Ships may pass these islands without a thought, and with no intent of stopping. Most ships in these seas are Spanish, and I must pray indeed that the Spaniards do not come ashore, for I would have to flee them or be enslaved or killed. But I am plagued by the thought that a rare English ship could pass within sight but never drop anchor. Such a notion would drive a man to despair, if I allowed it.

I kick a rock from the lookout; it shatters as it hurtles against the rocks below. I glare at the vast disloyal sea, which carries men the world over, yet traps me here.

Determined as I am to spare my powder, which has already dwindled most alarmingly, I make a study of the best way to hunt the goats without using my musket. This proves less difficult than I had feared, for as the weeks pass I find that goats are surprisingly regular in their habits. From much stalking of the goats, as well as from my foraging about the island for other food, I have learned that they use particular paths, almost as men use a road. Once I know these paths – which the passage of goat-hoofs has marked very clear – I can find places well suited to ambuscade, where I may spring out and catch the creatures unawares. With a little skill it is no great thing to wrestle a goat to the ground – and there is not much call for chasing down the goats, as I had first supposed.

As to the killing: it is quickest to slit their throats, but I wish to spare my knife, which I treasure above all things, and don't wish to blunt unduly. At first I think a rock to the head will serve – but I swear a goat has a harder skull than any other animal, for it takes a tremendous bash to knock it out, and on several occasions it takes me many blows before the animal drops, and it is bucking the whole while. I learn to my cost the hardness of a goat's skull, for when I fumble at knocking out a good-sized buck, and lose my grip about his neck, he butts me in my ribs, knocking the air clean out of me. I count myself lucky not to have been caught on his horns, which could easily kill a man, but the injury is nonetheless enough to have me moving gingerly for a week or more. Henceforth I return to using my knife, though it is a messier business, and the poor blade grows sadly dull.

My work does not end with the hunting – as soon as a goat is killed, I must swiftly set about dressing the meat, for the rats and insects wait for nothing. There is a spot a short way from my camp which serves as my butchery, so that I may keep the stench of blood and offal (and the rats and flies that are drawn to them) away from my living quarters. There is a stout bough at a good height where I have fixed a little of my precious rope, and with this I hoist the carcass by its hind legs, the better to drain the blood and strip the hide. The blood I catch in a bowl for Pickle who, whether by nose or by study of my regular habits, is always here, weaving in and out of my legs, by the time I string up the goat.

I cut free the flesh around the hind hoofs – here cursing my blunted knife – and then slit downwards, and around the genitals, and use the tip of my knife to loosen the flesh. Then, to tear the hide free, I grasp it very firm, and yank downwards, like a man trying to rip off a woman's skirt. It takes a tremendous pull to tear the hide free – and where the skin does not come away clean, I must once more get out my knife and loosen the flesh, before pulling again and again, until the hide hangs down over the head of the upside-down goat. To cut the hide away from the front legs, I must again resort to my knife.

Now the meat is exposed, startling red, and cobwebbed all over with stringy white fat. Next, the long belly slit, which I do most carefully, having learned by wretched experience that if my blade digs too deep I split the guts, and they spill all over the good, clean flesh. So I slice cautiously to open up the carcass, until I may pull out the innards, still steaming, which loop and slop wetly onto the rough-hewn wooden dish, which I set below for this purpose. The great mass of guts, the slick tubes and the swollen sheen of it all, remind me of nothing so much as a polypus, a sea creature I once saw dredged from the deep, a wet tangle of eight twisted legs.

I keep the hefty slab of liver, and the kidneys, those two glossy beans, for these when broiled make a most tender meat. The heart, too, I keep, for my cat relishes a slice of raw heart above all other morsels that I give her.

The offal and the feet and head I toss into a pit, and scatter fresh dirt over them in a futile attempt to keep the flies at bay. The pit cost me two days of labour to dig, having no proper shovel, only a sharpened stick and my hands. Yet even after these few months it is nearly full, and smelling prodigious foul, and I resolve to begin taking the innards to the cliff and throwing them over, to feed the sea.

The butchery itself takes hours – and then there is the cooking to be done. Without salt, it is no simple thing to preserve meat – for the most ravenous of men cannot eat a whole goat in a day. After various experiments with smoking the meat, I find the simplest way is the best: a long, sharp bough, pierced through the arse and chest of the carcass, its hind and forelegs bound together at each end. This I suspend above the fire, between two wooden tripods. By feeding the fire steady and not letting it run too hot, the meat smokes tolerably well, though it is a task of at least five hours, during the whole of which I cannot neglect the fire, and must turn the carcass too.

Smoking keeps the meat unspoiled for longer than otherwise – but no meat here can outlast the rats. Wherever I store it they nose it out, and the allure of the meat is even greater than their fear of my cat. When I store some meat in the small cask that once held my drink, the rats gnaw clean through the wood, and the meat that remains is ragged from their teeth. I mend the cask as best I can, fasten it to a rope and, tossing the rope over a bough, hoist the cask near twenty feet from the ground. The rats' infallible noses lead them to it nonetheless, and they run up and down the rope, effortless as sailors on rigging. I even try burying the cask, but nothing avails: the rats will not be deterred, and all I have to show for my efforts is a ruined cask, and a company of plump and cheerful rats.

Thus I learn that it is barely worth my time to labour over smoking the meat, when I am only preserving it for the benefit of the rats. Instead I settle into a pattern, killing and butchering a goat every ten days or so, and feasting on it for several days thereafter, with goat meat at each meal – and plenty, too, for Pickle, who grows stout. In this manner I usually manage to eat nearly all the meat before it begins to spoil, and by the time the carcass is consumed I am sick of it, and heartily constipated furthermore. And thus for a week or more I get by on cabbage leaves and berries and the odd fish or crawfish, until the craving for meat takes hold of me once more, and I take up my knife.

I choose younger goats to hunt these days, for it is a waste to kill a larger one, and furthermore will cost me more effort, particularly in the case of bucks with well-grown horns. I fancy the young meat is more tender, too, though in truth I would gladly never taste any goat meat again. A sailor is not precious about his food, nor does he expect any great variety, for salt meat and ship's biscuit and dried peas can make up his shipboard diet for months on end. Yet here, the endless goat meat and cabbage leaves, unsalted, has made me a man who eats because he must live, rather than for any pleasure. And I, who have always had a lusty appetite, so that even my doting mother complained that I would bring us all to ruination by my hearty eating, must now sometimes force myself to eat, and then only because I know I must fuel the labours of the next day, and the next.

5

And where is God in all of this? No citizen of Nether Largo can be free of the kirk and its cold and dreary Sundays – and yet I confess that I have never been accounted a godly man. From a lad I was inclined to daydreaming during the Reverend William Moncrieff's sermons, and later found myself hauled up more than once before the kirk sessions, for outrages against propriety, much to the shame and anger of my family. Thus I had not thought to find much by the way of consolation in the Bible that I have with me here. Indeed, I have oftentimes heartily wished that I had been stranded with some other book, most particularly of the manner popular amongst sailors, with illustrations not fit for a reverend's eyes, and tales and poems of the ribald sort. The carpenter of the *Cinque Ports* had a volume entitled *The School of Venus, or, The Ladies Delight*, which was much passed about below decks, and I used to borrow that volume many more times than I turned to my neglected Bible.

Now, however, the Bible at least offers more in the way of story than my astronomical and navigational almanacks, which are concerned only with calculations and with the mechanics of my trade. And with little else to amuse me, particularly in the long dark evenings, I spend many hours reading. This is not easy – nothing on this cursed island shall ever be easy – for I must read by the light of a taper, a stick dipped in oil that I have rendered from goat fat. By this stinking and uncertain light, I am forced to peer mighty close to make out the words. Nevertheless over these many months I have quite exhausted all the stories within the Bible, excluding those sections which are a mere listing of names, stating who begat whom. These chapters, despite containing a very great deal of *begetting*, provide none of the delights of *The School of Venus* and other such entertainments that a man stranded alone might wish for. Thus I admit I merely skim over these sections in search of more diverting fare. This I find largely in the Song of Solomon, and it is not piousness that leads me to return to these passages many times, but rather the woman wishing that her beloved *shall lie all night between my breasts*. Through diligent study I also discover that the Book of Ezekiel has some amusement of that sort to offer, hid amongst the strangeness of the prophet's visions.

But even a man of lustful appetites cannot read the Bible only in search of the occasional breast, and I find within its pages diversions of a less bawdy sort. Tales that I used to find dull, when recited in Largo kirk in the high and droning voice of the Reverend William Moncrieff, I now find more gripping. Being of a nautical bent I am particularly taken by Noah and the details of his ark, and I note bitterly that God is most precise in warning Noah to prepare the ship with pitch, *within and without*, and I could wish that Captain Dampier had been as prudent in preparing his fleet for our ill-fated expedition. I am struck also by the tale of Jonah and his big fish, which I take for a whale or shark. And while the story of Jesus itself has suffered from being rehearsed so many Sundays in the kirk, I do find myself strangely moved by the detail of Peter, and his denial of Christ after his death. Peter is warned by Christ that he shall betray him three times before the cock crows, and yet he does so nonetheless. He is a man wading straight towards his own disaster – a story I know all too well.

I stumble all too often upon passages in the Bible that put me in mind of my own predicament. When I read that *it is not good that the man should be alone,* or of the man *whose house I have made the wilderness, and the barren land his dwellings*, I almost wince.

Yet other passages serve as a balm. When the Book of Psalms assures me that *the sun knoweth his going down,* I take it as a kind of benison or incantation. I say it to myself, over and over, as I go about my works, so that if a man were to alight on this island and come across me here, hunched over a goat hide and muttering those words repeatedly, he would think me mad indeed. *The sun knoweth his going down*, I say again. For I must cling to this: that while all is cast into chaos and disorder, there is yet a kind of order in the world itself, and this at least has not forsaken me.

────────

My stockings are worn almost to shreds, and my shoes have long since fallen apart, so that even a cobbler's son such as I can no longer patch them. I go barefoot now, which is less strange to a sailor than it would be to many. From long usage, and the island's sharp rocks, my feet have hardened, so that even when thorns pierce them they do not pain me; at night, I pull them from my soles without wincing. When I am saved, I think, I shall not be fit for shoes. I shall have to learn again how to be a man in company.

Shoes I can well manage without, but I am sadly lacking in cordage, which I need for so many things, from holding up my trousers to securing my tent against the endless wind. Thus whenever I am abroad I am always looking out for material that can be twisted or braided into decent rope. At the very top of some of the palms, right where the trunk erupts into huge leaves, the tree sometimes yields a wiry nest of fibres. This stuff is well worth the hazardous climb, and makes sturdy rope. The palm fronds, too, have within them thick threads, as do some of the stands of tall, spiky grasses that grow hereabouts. These fibres, though, can only be got by retting. I soak the grasses in water for a few days to soften the weaker parts of the plant, so that the strongest fibres can be stripped out. Thus, with much labour, and with a fresh crop of blisters and callouses on my fingers, I am able to produce a decent supply of rope for my various needs. Here on this island, I who have nothing must be everything: I must be roper and chandler and tanner and carpenter all at once. Watch my busy fingers; see how they conjure rope from this island's scraps. In the long evenings, hunched before the fire, the tail of rope grows longer and longer, spinning and twisting out from my hands like a story.

────────

Thanks to my cat, the rats no longer torment me in my hammock at night, but they still creep about the margins of my camp and make free with my belongings. My kettle is overturned and my goat meat eaten; a goat hide patching the roof of my tent has a hole gnawed in it, and the rain soaks my hammock; the spit I use to cook meat above my fire collapses when the rats chew the rope that bound one of the tripods.

You might think: *Oh, he need only tidy his possessions away to keep them from the rats.* You do not understand: there is no *away.* No firm closing door, no tight-fitting lid, no wall through which the rats will not chew. There is no place out of this island and its creeping damage, its rot. Not for my possessions, nor even for myself, chilled and damp and forever chased by wind.

I begin gathering logs for a raft, the same way a man in a tavern may finger the hilt of the knife in his pocket when an argument threatens to become a brawl. When he does not want to use his blade — when he fears what will happen if he does — but likes to know it is there all the same.

I understand all too well that escaping the island is impossible. Even great ships of war fear these southern seas, in which the island is a mere speck. A man ignorant of geography might dare to dream of escape; a navigator such as I knows any attempt would mean death.

Nevertheless, whenever I come across a likely tree or bough, I set to work to cut it to size. Having neither axe nor saw, I use a crude axe-head fashioned from a shard of stone, split in such a way as to leave a sharpened edge. This I drive into the wood by striking with another stone. It is a primitive and painstaking method, and makes for coarse results — but with patience I am able to trim a log to size, then drag it to the bay and add it to the pile.

You might think palm logs would suit my purpose, being both plentiful and uniform in shape, neatly round and without protruding boughs. But after I have blunted an entire stone axe-head bringing down a palm trunk, I discover that its wood is not wood at all, but a kind of mass of fibres, tightly packed. Freshly felled, the palm trunks are wet and spongy in the centre and will not float; when left to dry out, they are weak, disintegrating into long shreds, good only for twisting into cordage. Thus it is the pimento trees that provide most of my logs, though they do not come neatly shaped as the palm trunks, and cost me many hours of chopping and hauling.

At the bay, the log pile is growing – it puts me in mind of the Tower of Babel.

'And just as like to succeed,' I say aloud, 'for counted in miles, I'll warrant heaven is closer than the mainland of Chile.'

I begin to learn the peculiarities of the island. In addition to the useful pimento tree, the place is much overgrown with a plant that I (being no botanist) have christened the parasol tree, on account of its leaves, which tower high above me, and form a sort of upside-down parasol. These leaves, huge as a lady's skirt spread out wide, will fill with water when it rains, a little reservoir in the sky, so that a high wind will sometimes dump this water upon me when passing, unwary, below. These leaves grow on a thick stem, not unlike rhubarb, but on a monstrous scale. The stem is entirely covered in spines nearly the size of thorns, so that when once I stumble and grab at one to steady me, my palm is cruelly pierced, and for several days I can scarce use my hand, and wish very fervently that I had instead taken the fall. When in season, this tree produces a huge clustering flower rather obscene in shape, and beaded all over with orange berries, like the member of a man with the pox. When I tried eating these berries, they gave me the gleets – and as the berries were also sour, I was not tempted to try again.

The island is also home to hummingbirds – a name I take to refer to the whirring noise made by the ceaseless motion of their wings, rather than to their song, which has little of the hum about it, being more of a chirp or trill. These birds are smaller even than a wren – why, there are beetles hereabouts larger than they. Each time I see a hummingbird I am startled by delight, having forgot how tiny and how magnificent they are.

There are two varieties: one a scalding bright bronze with black-tipped wings, the top of their head the shiniest vivid green, as though gilded. The other is white or grey, with that same unlikely green running all the way down the back, glimmering like the scales of a fish.

Their wings beat so very fast that they seem to have a dozen pairs, or none at all, for the wings blur and become quite invisible. They dart not only forwards but backwards too, their bodies perfectly still while their sharp beaks jab and their wings do their busy work. A hummingbird follows its own precise geometry. What darters, what sky-needles, what strange and shimmering machines of air.

I have made it a particular study to look out for them, though they are so small and swift that I count it a piece of luck if I see one during the day. If I go quietly, I can occasionally come across them feeding in the gaudy orange flowers of the cabbage tree. The birds are so tiny that when they delve amongst the long, slack petals, the flower swallows them entirely.

They are elusive during the day, but at night I see more of the hummingbirds than I should like, for they cannot resist my fire and, as a moth will throw himself at a lantern, these birds dart into the flames, so that many mornings there is a little offering of charred bodies amongst the ashes. I should perhaps not mind if they furnished me with any meat, but being so tiny, they are fit only for the rats and cats. I would shoo the birds away from the fire, were they not so quick and so fixed on their own destruction. It is perhaps an unfortunate consequence of their tiny size that their understanding is correspondingly small, for they seem not to learn, and even after many months here my fire has lost none of its deadly appeal to them.

When, at my life's end, my many sins are laid at my account I shall consider it no small thing that I have been the cause of so many tiny deaths, simply through being here and by having need of a fire.

And I begin to see that the hummingbirds and their lust for flame is very typical of this island. What fierce malediction was laid upon this place, that it should squander its beauty so?

I hunger for salt.

In my Bible I read of Lot and his unfortunate wife, who turns to a pillar of salt when she makes the mistake of looking back. When my brothers and I were set to study the Bible, these chapters caused us much hilarity and whispering, concerning the sins of Sodom and Gomorrah, and also Lot's daughters who trick him into bedding them. Now, though, I linger instead over the pillar of salt. I long for salt, more even than a good axe or a feather bed. You do not know blandness until you have eaten of unsalted meat, and unsalted fish, for many months, unchanged. I try boiling the fish or cabbage leaves in seawater, which helps a little, but my kettle is too small even for a good size crawfish, and cannot help me when I have a whole goat carcass to cook before it spoils. Chewing my unseasoned goat meat, I read about Lot and his wife, and I think that even had I a woman here, I would gladly see her changed into a pillar of salt, and not mourn.

February brings a tremendous boon, in the form of the discovery of turnips. When the *Cinque Ports* was at anchor here back in February of last year, the men found and harvested many, not far from shore. Being unable to find any since, in that place or elsewhere, I believed them lost or failed, or thought the greed of our crew had left none behind. But the old goat is on this occasion my deliverer, for one day I see him foraging very cheerfully and vigorously at a certain patch of ground a little way off my path to the lookout, and when I push through the shrubs to investigate, I find he is grazing on the fresh green tops of new turnips. I do not even wait to fetch my rough-hewn trowel; no, I squat and scrabble with my fingers, loosening the dirt so that I may pull a turnip from the ground: a fat, yellow bulb, with its straggly beard of roots.

To a man in my situation, with the fibrous strands of cabbage leaf forever stuck between his teeth, and bowels perpetually blocked up by bland goat meat, you may imagine how wondrous even an ordinary turnip may seem. For days I eat almost nothing else, and am prodigious grateful for the perpetual greed of goats. The small turnips I eat raw; the larger ones are bitter and must be cooked. The stalks and leaves, too, can be eaten, though I must beat the goats to them, for they also find them a delicacy.

The wild cats keep their distance, but for one. Reassured, perhaps, by the presence of Pickle in my camp, a wild tabby cat spends a great many hours at the edges of my clearing, cleaning herself and sleeping, as though her life has no concerns but her own leisure. When I go to my butchery tree to bleed a goat carcass, and set down a bowl of blood for Pickle, the tabby comes up mighty bold and takes the blood while it is still hot, a little steam coming off it. If Pickle tries to approach the bowl, the tabby will hiss, a mighty loud sound like a bolt of canvas being ripped. She drinks her fill before she suffers Pickle to come near.

Afterwards, when the wild cat's white nose and whiskers are red with blood, she spends many minutes cleaning herself, by tongue and by paw. She has a white face and bib, and a very white belly, and one startling white plume at the tip of her tail. The rest of her is all over stripes, palest grey to black. Down her back is a dark stripe, as though all her licking has smudged her tabby colours into one thick streak. I would reach out and stroke it, but I value my hands. Her disposition is not affectionate, nor gentle.

Pickle has grown sweet and biddable, trotting to me when I click my tongue, and sleeping nested close by me in my hammock. And yet it is this tabby that fascinates me, and each time she deigns to come to my camp, I watch her intently. It is perhaps in man's nature that the amiable and willing creature will preoccupy him less than the aloof and reluctant one, and so I admit that I pay this wild cat greater attention than my own sweet Pickle.

The wild cat begins to come closer, and even at times to sit near me, which I account a triumph. She sleeps for much of the day – she has a tremendous facility for indolence. She curls herself in a ball to sleep – and no circle carefully drawn with compasses has ever been as perfectly circular as a sleeping cat. When she wakes, she stetches and gives a huge long yawn, gaping wide the wet red nest of her mouth. But while she seems docile enough, I nonetheless take each yawn as a reminder, for cats do nothing carelessly, and the yawns display to perfection her sharp teeth, each one a hook for flesh.

In June the sea lions return, each of them hauling their immense, unwieldy shroud of loose flesh.

When the *Cinque Ports* last landed here, before I was abandoned, the shore was crowded with these beasts, sprawling about a musket's shot from the water. A sea lion is a seal conjured in a nightmare, and on a fantastical scale. A man who has not seen these creatures can never comprehend the size of them. Three men laid head to toe would scarce match the length of the largest; the weight of a single one would rival that of a ship's pinnace, for each of these beasts is a landslide of flesh, a catastrophe of sound and of stench. I am a sailor, no stranger to either sharks or whales – and while the largest sharks may match these beasts in length, they have not their uncompromising bulk. They are considered a prize, and our crew slaughtered several, for there is a huge quantity of oil to be got from them. But I felt it a mercy that, before the *Cinque Ports* left me here, the last of the sea lions had taken its cumbersome flesh back to sea.

Now they are back. It must be their season for breeding, and they mass upon the rocks. The largest, which I take for males, have a great snout, bulbous and prodigiously wrinkled, a sort of foreskin of the face. When they throw their heads back to give their fearsome grunts and calls, I fancy this snout is used in the manner of a horn or trumpet, for the sound they produce is vaster even than their bulk would suggest. Like that, heads back and mouths agape, they look fit to devour the sky. Their grunts and calls are fearsome resonant – each sea lion is its own chorus.

When they settle on the shore they change the whole topography of the island – a map-maker would have to make a different map in this season, for they come in such numbers that they become the shore, and the whole coast heaves with their slow breath and their awful throaty cries. To reach the water in that part of the bay, a man would have to walk on their backs like stepping stones – but you would need to be tremendous nimble not to lose a foot in doing so. They are mighty fierce if roused and can turn their necks and snap with huge sharp teeth. Our crew used to hunt them with pikes, eight men together, bleeding the beasts a little at a time. Sometimes, when the men tired of their sport, they would dispatch the sea lion by a pistol emptied down its roaring throat. For myself, having no need of more oil than can be rendered from goat fat, I am wise enough to leave the sea lions alone.

Sometimes two male sea lions fight. They rear up, then clash against one another, raking their enemy with their teeth, which are savage sharp. Oftentimes the blood runs down so that both beasts are dripping red.

A civilised man might watch their brawling and be frighted, or disgusted. I watch them fight; it is not disgust I feel — it is recognition. I see the ugliness of their rage, and I think, *Yes, yes.*

6

I decide to kill a seal. They had left the island at the time of my abandonment, but have since returned for their season of breeding – and still the young seals sprawl on the beach, growing temptingly fat. I am weary of goat meat, and whereas the goats are nimble, the seals lay about like so many sandbags, and only if startled by a close approach do they swing into a lumbering motion, hauling themselves ungainly towards the water.

The task of hunting seals has never before fallen to me, but I have seen it done by our men – and in truth it is not fit for the name *hunting*, for it suffices simply to stroll up to them and strike a good blow to the nose with a stout club. Today it is the work of but half an hour to fashion myself a crude wooden club, thicker at one end than the other. Yet when I approach, I find that the seals have great beseeching dark eyes that look upon me very trusting. This colossal parcel of flesh is mine for the taking, for these beasts have not yet learned to fear men – yet I do not find it easy. I am not squeamish – no cobbler's son could be so, for in the home where I grew up there was always a hide to be scraped of its fat, and another soaking in the leeching pit. But it takes three blows to kill the seal, while its fellows yelp and grunt and drag themselves away. The seal looks at me all the while with its big stunned eyes, and its long whiskers shaking, and its tail thrashing this way and that until it has gouged in the sand a little trench, which begins to fill with blood. At last my final blow stoves in its face altogether which is both a relief and a horror.

After all that, and the messy work of butchery, the meat is as poor as I remembered it – indeed, it is worse for now I must do without salt, and my stomach protests as it was wont to do with the unsalted fish, and for the rest of the day I do huge oily shits that stink of seal. The white, bearded goat has wandered close enough to watch me, a condescending look about his face. A man with the gleets does not need to be pitied by a ragged old goat, and so I shout at him, 'Begone you son of a bitch, you cur,' and hurl a rock at him, though my shaking hand sends it wide, and as he scampers off I yell, 'I'll eat you next, you bastard.'

At least the seal gives me a wealth of oil to render for tapers. Were the meat itself more tolerable I don't doubt I should have overcome my reluctance at the ungentlemanly way of killing – I have done much in my life that is ungentlemanly, after all. But these hours of shitting have left me feeling like a husk of a man, and I resolve to hunt seals only when I must, for their oil. I will not deny that it has something to do with those great round eyes, the softness of them. I was not wont to be troubled by such things; if I have become more troubled by such softness, it is perhaps that I have become unused to it, when all about me this island is so very sharp and hard.

The last few shreds of my tobacco I have eked out by mixing with fern fronds, dried slow in a kettle on the coals of my fire. I also experiment with some seaweed, dried and chopped fine. And I have high hopes when I discover a moss that grows on the island's western reaches, for when dried it has the look of tobacco. However, none of these things gives me anything but a nasty cough, chest-deep. I still take out my pipe in the evening, after dinner, for there is a certain comfort just in its familiar weight in my hand, and its polished stem between my teeth. But even that habit eventually drops away; the more the rats chew at the pipe, the less I wish to do so, and in time the pipe becomes nothing more than a sort of ornament, resting on an upturned log, where a spider makes a home in the pipe's empty bowl.

Summer's last days offer me an unexpected gift. It is a sweltering afternoon, the rocks so hot that even my leathered feet burn if I do not walk quick. I find a spot where a shallow rock pool has dried in the sun, leaving only its outline: a crust of white salt. Squatting, I lick my finger and press it to the salt, then bring it to my tongue. The sharp tang is a shock after so many months, and I grimace at the same time as I whoop with delight. Salt – how I have longed for it. And if salt gathered this way also tastes strongly of fish, I cannot afford to be particular.

Henceforth on hot days I look out always for these salt ghosts of rock pools. When I find them, I scrape the salt gently with the side of a leaf, careful to avoid digging out grit along with the salt, and place it into a goatskin pouch that I have fashioned for this purpose.

There are not so many rock pools, nor so many hot days, and thus I can never gather salt in the quantities required to preserve meat. Knowing the determination of the rats, this does not trouble me, especially given the ready supply of goats. It is boon enough to have a little salt from time to time. To see me squatting, painstakingly scraping each grain into my little pouch, you would think me a miner who has discovered a seam of gold.

Such consolations as the island offers, I gladly seize – but my thoughts are ever of rescue. Whatever I am doing, I stop regularly to search the long horizon; I have climbed so many times to my lookout that my path is well-trod. I may have learned to survive here, but still I curse the island, my gaoler. I do not neglect to add to my pile of logs, nor to contemplate how best to make these into a raft. Do not mistake my small gains – the salt; the turnips – for contentment. How could a man be content, so alone that the ceaseless winds that buffet the island begin sometimes to sound like howling voices? I am very far from being reconciled to this place, and being abandoned here is the crowning calamity of a life built of calamities.

As to how I came to be abandoned here – to remember that only casts wood on the fire of my fury, and so I am resolved not to do so.

———

I pride myself that I have become an excellent hunter of goats. Having few diversions on the island, I sometimes take a notion to hunt even when I do not want for meat. I occupy myself with running down the goat, but when I have seized it, and have it by the neck, still kicking and bucking, and the veins jutting proud of its throat, I take my knife and cut a small notch in the right ear. I fancy it a sort of project: to see if I may one day catch them all. And when I see the goat skitter away, a trail of blood spreading below the ear, I feel magnanimous indeed, as though I have bestowed upon the animal the gift of life.

The old goat with the lordly face and magnificent beard continues to haunt my camp. When he sniffs at something, he has a particular manner of lifting his upper lip, so that it curls quite over his nose, exposing his lower teeth and presenting a most comical air. As for upper teeth, he has none whatsoever at the front of his mouth, though when he opens his jaws wide to yawn or to bleat, I can see he has some at the back. Before he settles down in any spot, he paws at the ground for some minutes, exceedingly fussy and precise, as if he is preparing a feather bed and not a patch of grass amongst the scrub.

I stare often at his eyes, for the eye of a goat is a queer thing, having not a round pupil like most creatures, nor even a vertical slit as cats do, but instead a thick horizontal slit, its corners squared as few things are in nature. A line within a circle – the eye containing its own horizon. A goat's eye being so very different from all others, it gives the whole creature a foreign and even ungodly aspect, and while I am used to the old white goat, I begin to understand better why goats have so often been linked to devils and demons and such.

This particular goat has a prodigious appetite, and I have witnessed him eat divers things, viz. a pair of my stockings, washed and hung to dry; a dead hummingbird from the ashes of the fire, scorched black; several pages of one of my navigational almanacks, until I chased him, looking much affronted, from my camp; the bones of a fish carcass, which I had picked quite clean; a great quantity of turnips that I had set aside for my own supply.

Whether he gains any benefit by these meals or whether it is merely a sort of mischief, I do not know – only that when I came upon him with the last scrap of my stockings hanging from the corner of his mouth, he fixed me most deliberately in the eye as he chewed, and I could swear there was a roguish tilt to his face as if to say: *How do you like your fine stockings now, Mister Selkirk?*

Though he must have watched me many times while I butcher his brethren, he seems mighty sure that I will not kill him, and indeed he is right, for he has the protection of his grand age and his bony features. But although he looks most unappetising, I nonetheless decide that he shall not escape my knife, and determine to count him among my conquests, for if nothing else it shall show him who is master here, and put an end to his mischief.

So tame does he appear that I think I shall simply be able to seize him at the camp. However he is more wily than I guessed, and leaps clear of me, and I will allow that he gives me some good sport, and shows a surprising turn of speed, particularly upon the rocky slopes where I must tread with care. When I have seized him at last, and notched his ear, he gives a loud donkey-bray of outrage, and if he is chastened he gives no sign of it. The very next day he is back at my camp, chewing contentedly on the rope that holds up the northern corner of my tent. Where once I kept my time by the sandglass and the ship's bell, on this island I could measure out my days by the rhythm of the old goat's constant chewing.

The wild tabby cat is often watching me from the edge of my clearing. I call her Sleek, for her fur is less shaggy than that of many of the island's cats, and when she sets about washing herself with her diligent tongue, her coat grows wet and slick as an otter's. And while she will not tolerate being touched, she comes each day, and when I am butchering she demands her bowl of blood as though it is her due. Sometimes she brings a rat, which she deposits carelessly at the tent door. I am not yet reduced to eating rats, but I am glad to see their number depleted. This is our exchange: I give her blood, she brings me rats. Such is this island's currency.

Just as a ship's hull fouls and decays fast in these seas, on this island my clothes rot away mighty swift. Between the sun and the damp and the great deal of scrambling through rocks and shrubs, and the sharp teeth of the rats, which gnaw at any soft thing, my shirts soon fall apart. All sailors are handy with a needle, for the mending of sails is an endless task aboard a ship. But I have no needle – only a nail, which I must use to pierce the cloth, and then with much pinching and poking, to force the thread through. As for thread, to make it I must spend half a day delicately unravelling what remains of my worsted stockings. And after all this labour, when I set about mending my ripped shirt, I find that the cloth itself is perished, and no matter how carefully I stitch, the fabric simply falls apart, like meat boiled too long.

My warm undershirt and my jacket are of a stouter material, but even these have been much chewed by the rats, and are in a sorry state. My trousers are likewise worn almost to shreds, and have lately developed a tear across the arse that would make me sorely unfit for company, if I had any.

The linen in my sea chest is still serviceable and furnishes enough for two new shirts – although even after much labour with my nail and thread, they are barely worth the name of shirt, being more like tunics, having neither buttons nor proper sleeves. Nevertheless they will serve to shield me from the sun in summer, and to offer a little warmth in winter. As for trousers, these must be of goat hide. The hides being somewhat stiff, I must make the trousers exceedingly loose, even more so than the ordinary sailor style, so that they do not limit my nimbleness. Of these hides, at least, I have no shortage, goats making up such a very great part of my diet.

With an eye to the coming winter, I resolve also to make myself a warm jerkin. The goats I hunt for meat are but small – for my jerkin I have need of a larger hide. And although this island has stripped me of what vanity I had, I allow myself to deliberate over the colour, watching a herd a while to pick out a goat. When so much of my daily toil is a matter of survival, it's a welcome change to have before me a choice of so little consequence: do I choose the white fellow, speckled with grey? The imposing black buck with his shaggy fur, or the piebald goat in his brown and white motley? In the end I choose a stately buck, rich chestnut all over. It takes me two days to catch him, for he is wily and quick, but I do not account it wasted time.

When his throat is slit, I give Sleek her bowl of blood, and only when she has had her fill does she permit Pickle to lick the bowl clean. The butchery and the cooking take the rest of the day, and well into the night, and the next day I begin the curing of his splendid hide.

This task always puts me in mind of my father. As a child, and a wayward one at that, I wished myself a gentleman's son, and not the son of a humble tanner and cobbler. But here I have cause to be grateful for Da's craft, and I wonder what he would think of me now, to see me squatting over a fresh hide, and diligent in my tanning work as I never was in his workshop.

I wash the hide, taking pains to go downstream, so that the water which runs by my own clearing is left unspoiled by blood.

My meagre supply of salt is not enough to cure hides, and so I combine the curing stage with the soaking, by softening the hide in seawater. No tanner nor currier would countenance this – but the island gives me no choice. Above the high-tide line at the shore, I shift the rocks from a space, and in the sand below I dig a hole deep enough that the seawater seeps within. Here I bury my hide beneath heavy stones, in case the rats should brave the water.

The next day I retrieve the hide, spread it over a wide log, and set to scraping. In my first attempts, months ago, I tried using a broken barrel hoop as a scraper, but it tore the hide. Later I shaped a scraper from a goat's thigh bone, by digging a long groove in it and leaving a ridge on either side, which I ground against a stone. This, being more yielding than the metal hoop, serves very well, the fat coming off neatly as I drag the tool downwards with both hands, the knob at each end of the bone making a sort of handle.

Even with this much-improved tool, it is messy work. I think of my father who taught me to cure and tan a hide, and the many ways in which I failed him. Here on the island I have no kirk in which to repent my sins, which are many – but as I work at the hide of the chestnut buck, I wonder whether this greasy labour could be accounted a form of penance.

I do not bother to remove the fur – for although it gives me a savage appearance, it adds both to the warmth and the robustness of the hides. This spares me the soaking of the hide in ash and lime, to loosen the hair, as well as the labour of scraping it off. And if skipping this stage of the curing means the hides are not quite so well preserved, I can but say that I have become less precious regarding smell, and that anyway the smell of a well-grown buck goat is so strong that imperfect curing can scarce make it worse.

I have none of the oak trees that my father used to chip into his tanning liquor – indeed, I have not even a proper axe, for the making of wood chips. But I have found an alternative that serves well enough, for not long after my abandonment a gale uprooted one of the giant parasol trees, revealing a bulbous spread of roots. The smaller clusters of these may easily be grated by scraping at them with the broken hoop, and these shreds when boiled slowly in fresh water yield a good dark tanning liquor, though with my small kettle I must brew batch after batch. I think often what a tremendous increase to my ease and happiness would be brought about by such a simple thing as a large metal pot or cauldron. Before I came here I had not spared a thought for such an item my entire life – but now it is the object of my most fervent imaginings. I dream of how much I could cook at once, and how much I could store safely within. And if I were granted such a thing, a fine big pot with a tight-fitting lid to keep the rats at bay, I should think myself a rich man.

For leeching the hides, I have gouged a wide, shallow trough into a huge fallen trunk, and coated it thickly with fat so that no liquid shall seep from it. Into this I pour, batch by batch, my tanning liquor, now the rich brown of good beer, and lay the hide, which must wait there at least three weeks, and I take pains to turn and stir it every few days, and to add ever stronger batches of my liquor.

A final rinse, downstream, and then the hide must be wrung out. For this I use the same bough that I use for cooking, which stands on two tripods. I lay the wet hide over this, looped over itself, then roll it loosely inwards from both ends, as my father taught me, so that it hangs over the bough in a ring. Into this ring I place a stick which, when turned around and around, contorts the hide into a tightly twisted rope, so that the water pours from it. I repeat this several times, turning the hide each time, until when finally I unravel the hide it is barely damp. Next it must be stretched, or it shall dry small and stiff. For a stretching frame I use two trees that stand a little more than an arms' span apart, and with my precious rope threaded through holes at the hide's edge, I stretch the hide side to side. The top of the hide I stretch with ropes fastened to boughs above, and the bottom by using wooden pegs to fix the rope in the ground. By the end, the rope forms a kind of web between the trees, the hide at its centre, as though some monstrous spider has caught and flayed an entire goat.

Once the hide is completely dried, I lay it flat and, using an oval stone with a rounded edge, work seal oil into the hairless underside, stretching and scraping with the stone as I go. For the hides intended merely to line the roof of my tent, a quick application of fat is sufficient, and will help keep out rain. But for hides such as this splendid large chestnut, that I plan to wear, or to use on my bed, I spend a considerable time rubbing in the oil, so that the hide softens to the touch, and takes on a rich lustre. It transforms beneath my hands, becoming wondrous soft and pliant.

The chestnut hide is a thing of beauty indeed, and I stitch it into a jerkin that would make a chief of savages proud. I wear it for the first time, running my hands down the lustrous fur. It is some comfort to know that I am arrayed for the coming winter.

The old goat looks at me gravely and gives a kind of nod. Is it me he recognises, or the fur of an old companion? And if the *Cinque Ports'* crew, or my family, were to see me now, clad as I am, and with my beard and hair long and unruly, would they recognise me?

7

Midwinter, the mountains buried in cloud and the wind in great gusts, south-southeast. By my reckoning it is now July of 1705. I have come to feel quite complacent about my survival – I have been nine months on this island and though I often fear for my sanity, I have ceased to fear attack by either beasts or savages. I have lived through one summer and the start of one winter, and have grown accustomed to the island's temperate climate – for in summer it remains mild, and winter has so far not been too harsh, though it rains prodigiously. And while I have grown heartily tired of goat meat and cabbage leaves, and am even beginning to weary of turnips, I no longer fear that I shall starve.

My tame cat, little Pickle, is sweetly behaved with me, but cats have no more notion of propriety nor chastity than sailors, for she is barely eight months old when she produces a litter of her own: tiny mewling bundles of grey, white and ginger. I do not drown the kittens, as my father used to, for I aim to populate my camp entirely with well-disposed cats. And while nothing can rid my camp of rats, my scheme works neatly to keep them from troubling me at night – and if there is a certain sharp tang of cat piss about the edges of my clearing, I soon become accustomed to it, and consider it a price well worth the paying, for delivering me from the torment of the rats.

Do not mistake me and think that I am at ease here. I wade daily through a kind of despair so vast that I cannot make out its horizon, nor fathom any way to navigate it. In my primitive tent I have few comforts, and while the cats keep the rats from my hammock, there is no keeping at bay the insects, which plague me day and night. Any pleasure I might have is tarnished always by my wretchedness and misery; I am furious when I eat, and desolate even when I frig myself, and in every way I know for certain that this island has ruined me. And yet I live, and I do not know whether I account it a comfort that I shall not soon die.

It is cold, but a bright clear day, and I decide to swim, for I have not washed for several weeks. I say to the old goat who hangs about the camp, 'It would not do for rescuers to come ashore, and refuse to take me on account of my unwholesome stench.' I leave my clothes on a rock at the shore, which is no longer crowded with seals. Last season's pups have grown so large that they begin to essay the waters themselves, their mothers returning less and less often to suckle them.

The water is fierce cold but bracing, and I give little whoops and gasps of shock with each new step, and most particularly when the water reaches my balls. It is a still day – I should not have chanced it otherwise, for even in the bay a strong wind can raise vicious waves – and when I turn my back to the sea and face the island, I can grudgingly acknowledge that it has a certain stark beauty to it. The things that make it foreign and unwelcoming – its sheer rock faces; the mountains, cruelly jagged – make it spectacular from the waterline.

A seal surfaces not twenty yards from me. This I am quite used to, for at times the water fair roils with the creatures. I pull further from the beach; many sailors cannot swim, but most lads of Nether Largo are fine swimmers. And it gives me some satisfaction to draw away from the island. Sometimes I fancy swimming onwards and never stopping, letting the island grow small behind me, and swimming towards my own death, rather than dying of old age alone on that forsaken shore.

Another seal breaks the water, much closer – but this is bigger, too big for a seal, and for an instant I think perhaps it is just kelp, for there are great thickets of kelp all about here, a slick and tangled forest that shifts with the tide. But this thing is too fast for kelp, and does not move with the sea, which is glassy and calm. I turn, treading water, and although I am fervently wishing to see a sea lion, I already know that it is not, for this beast is pale grey, nearly white, and its fin is a blade that slices the water. A seal at leisure will circle and roll about, very playful – but the shark moves with a terrible purpose, nothing wasted.

He is right at the surface, so close that I could almost reach and touch him. I can see everything: the neat angle of the gills, a row of slashes such as a razor would make. His tiny eyes, all blackness, revealing nothing. He moves tremendous slow now, but I do not mistake him, for to see him is to know that the whole of him is a machine for speed, the angles of his tall fin perfectly calculated, and the lazy switching of his tail which drives him with so little sign of effort. His mouth is open – perhaps that fearsome armoury of teeth does not even permit him to close it all the way. And as he passes me, I get a true sense of his size – twice my length, he is as thick as a forty-two-pound cannon, and looks about as solid.

I have drawn my feet up tight to my chest, my arms floundering to keep me afloat. He is circling me, for with his eyes set deep in the side of that great slab of face, he must turn to examine me. Having passed me, he turns once more, to come again, and I hear my own breath – little rough gasps – and know that there is no point in screaming. This time he passes so close that his broad flank would have brushed my arm, had I not snatched it away.

Before he can turn again I flail for the shore, trusting that if he is to charge me, his huge length will take a few moments to come about. But I know this hope to be vain, even as I thrash through the water. My only chance is that seal I saw just before the shark came upon me, and I most fervently pray that a shark finds a plump seal more tempting than a man. Yet a seal is swifter by far than I, and though I do not cease my swimming, I know full well that my fate is entirely in the black eyes of that shark.

I swim, not daring to look back, and expect with each stroke to feel his teeth in my flesh. I am so far from shore that the nearest land is not the sloping pebbled beach where I waded in but a mass of rocks at the bay's eastern side, and this is what I make for, eyes clenched as though that could keep a shark's teeth at bay. I swim and I swim until the only thought I have room for is *breathe, breathe, breathe.*

I heave myself onto the rock, careless of my flesh so that I am much scraped and cut, hands and feet and knees, but I am alive – my heaving breath, my storming heart, my heavy heavy body streaming water.

I squat on the rocks and let the shaking come. Had the shark resolved to eat me, I do not doubt I would be dead – I am not fool enough to fancy that I can outswim a shark, least of all one of so great a size. Most likely it had already dined on fat seal pups. Perhaps it looked upon me and considered me an ill meal, as I look upon the old goat who hangs about my camp.

You might think I would be gleeful at such an escape. Yet all the rest of the day my hands shake, and will not be stilled. I have learned this: that I may have grown accustomed to life here, but I am never safe. The island has reminded me that it has teeth.

This incident with the shark has two immediate effects. The first is that I go no longer out into the depths of the bay, and when I must bathe, or wash my clothes, I stay in the shallows, which I consider not cowardice but merely prudence.

The second is that I am cast very much into my thoughts, and in particular to thoughts of my past. A sailor's life is never vouchsafed, but there is something about a shark's teeth that makes the question of mortality pressing indeed, even to a man not ordinarily inclined to philosophy. Thus I find myself preoccupied with the nature of my past, and of my conduct.

When I survey the choices that have brought me to this island, my conclusions are not heartening. I have not lived a virtuous life. My life thus far has in the main been unruly, and I have allowed my rage to be the master of me.

I should like to be a better man. But this island has stripped me back until I feel barely a man at all. Where, on this God-forsaken spur of land, may a man find his better self?

And while the actual circumstances of my being stranded here remain too ugly and too painful for me to dwell on, I find my thoughts turn more and more to what came before: my childhood, and all the things that took me to sea.

8

I spend my childhood beset by my brothers' taunting on one side and by Mam's tenderness on the other – and all the time dreaming of the sea. This unhappy state of affairs continues until I am fifteen years of age. We are traipsing through a mizzle to the kirk on a Sunday, to suffer the Reverend William Moncrieff's sermons.

'And I swear they grow longer in winter,' says Andrew, out of earshot of Mam and Da.

Ahead of us, Moncrieff waits at the kirk door. He is a tall, thin strap of a man, as though God has taken an ordinary fellow and stretched him. I will say of Moncrieff that at least he is no hypocrite, for he appears to live as he preaches, exceeding strict and proper. He shares his house with his sister, and they are always together. She is built along the same lean lines as he – or perhaps it is their frugal living that has shaped them so. Today they stand with their hands clasped before them at their waists. They smile and bob and turn together to greet the parishioners, the two of them looking like two hanged men swinging in the wind.

'If they kept a dog it would starve, for Moncrieff would begrudge it even the bones,' George says.

'Surely,' says Andrew. 'And having made a meal of the bones for himself, Moncrieff would have his sister make a broth of what's left, to last them both till the next Sunday.'

'And they would make the dog pray, too,' I say, 'and attend kirk twice a day.'

But Da has come up behind us and overheard me, and cuffs me smartly on the ear for mocking the good minister, and Andrew snickers and says nothing, and George looks away, and my older brother John and his wife walk faster to separate themselves from the disgraceful scene. Mam catches up to me and strokes my cheek where Da struck me, which kindness only adds to my mortification.

Fortunately I am at an age to have discovered a most welcome diversion from my family, in the form of Effie Breck, a lass only a little younger than me. The Brecks sit two pews ahead of us, and I confess that my attention in the kirk has lately strayed very much from Moncrieff's sermons to Effie, and the curve of her neck, and to imagining the other curves that might be beneath her winter shawl.

Today, for the first time, Effie looks back. While Moncrieff holds forth about the virtues of industry and prayer, she turns to face our pew, fixes me in the eye, and smiles. If anything would make a fifteen-year-old lad yearn for Sunday kirk it would be the smiles of Effie Breck.

In the weeks that follow I grow to know Effie better, for the two of us contrive to meet, and it becomes the whole joy of my life, so that every day is measured only by when I might see her next. I think of nothing but her neat body, her belly and her behind so sweetly round as though the whole of her were made by turning, like a wooden spindle. She is rather bold in her speaking, always quick to tease. And because my mother is so soft, I am drawn to this forcefulness in Effie: the decisive quickness in her hands, and the way the dimple in her cheek puckers just before she laughs – and she laughs loud and easy. And her laughter and her smiles are such an enticing promise that even when I am away from Effie, I cannot be roused to anger even by Andrew, who shares my bed (which he counts amongst his many grievances against me) and is very expert in scraping me with his toenails, and also in the delivery of foul farts. But in these weeks so full of newness and the thrill of Effie turning her brown eyes onto me, I only ignore him and will not be drawn into our usual scuffles.

'She is a hoyden, that one, and shall come to no good,' my brother John says, as we walk home from kirk, after a service during which Effie again turned and grinned at me a great deal. 'Her parents ought to have taken her in hand.'

'For what sin?' I ask. 'For smiling?'

'For her malapert ways,' he says, which seems to mean the same thing. Having lately married, and not seeming to have gained any joy by it, John is keen to ensure no others shall enjoy greater happiness than he.

'I've a mind to take her in hand myself,' Andrew says, and runs his tongue along his wet teeth. 'In both hands, what's more,' he says, and mimes grabbing her breasts.

And although I have lately been complaisant, this is not be to borne, and I give him a shove, and he shoves back, and the two of us take to the ground with our wrestling, and as always Andrew goes too far, finds a soft place and jabs it with his sharp elbow, or sinks his nails into the skin of my neck, and John shouts at us, 'You two ruffians bring shame on our father's name.'

Effie and I contrive to meet often – we benefit from the unruly nature of her household, her family not being the kind to carefully chaperone their daughters. Her father is a notorious drinker, very free with his fists, and her mother counts it a blessing when the children are away from the house, where they cannot set him off. Even so, as we walk the shore together we keep a demure distance for Largo is a tremendous hive of gossips.

There is a handbill pasted to the seawall. Effie sounds it out slowly – the girls of the village not having had the schooling that we lads receive at the kirk school.

'*Run away on the 15th Instant from Mister Thos Cullan, Apothecary, a Negroe Slave named Adam, a well-set youth of nineteen.*'

My own schooling has been largely a sequence of beatings, on account of my conduct rather than my understanding, which is reckoned good enough. Indeed, in matters of geography and mathematics I excel, though the teacher, Mister Leslie, would be loath to admit this, due to a certain amount of scrapping in the schoolyard, and one incident involving a pail of water set atop a door.

Despite this unhappy relationship with Mister Leslie, I enjoy school, and reading most particularly, though I'm at pains to keep this from my brothers, not wishing to give them yet another reason to make sport of me. Our house has no books but the Bible, yet my oldest brother John has three, his wife's family being well-to-do. I read these whenever I can contrive to smuggle them away without any of my brothers noticing. One of the books is merely an almanack and offers nothing in the way of story or adventure; *Paradise Lost* I like better, for it is much concerned with disobedience and temptation, which to a lad of my age seem to make up the larger part of life. But the third in particular takes my fancy, *The Comic Romance of Monsieur Scarron*, a book that I quickly come to suspect neither my brother nor his wife have ever read, for as I discover to my great satisfaction, it is full of scenes of violence, fornication and absurdity. Thus it becomes my favourite, and I read it again and again, until it is no longer worth the effort of smuggling it from my brother's house to read in secret, because I can recall the whole of it.

This furtive reading has served me well, and I am happy to help Effie when she stumbles over *apothecary*. To her, a year younger than me, and with parents indifferent keen on learning, I seem a sort of oracle in matters of reading. This is very gratifying, particularly for a lad who has in his own house always found himself the subject of much ridicule.

'It's an odd thing, don't you think,' I ask Effie, 'that having become lettered, one can never again become unlettered.'

'What do you mean?'

'I mean, try as we might, we could never see this handbill and not know what's written there – even if we wished not to.'

'And would you wish yourself foolish?'

'No,' I say hastily. 'Only it seems strange – such a great change. As though when they teach us to read, they put fresh eyes in each of us.'

'That's it. Eyes – that's how you could do it. If you went blind, or put out your eyes, you would be back to not knowing.' She is ever a practical girl.

'Ah,' I say, grasping for her hand, and let the gossips be damned. 'But then I could no longer see you, and I would count that a far greater loss.'

She slaps my hand away, laughing. 'Your grand notions drop away mighty fast when you see a chance to flirt.'

Effie is not always so reticent in the matter of touching. When we can contrive to be alone together, tucked in the lee of a stone wall at the foot of Largo Law, or in the fishermen's shed by the shore, she is generous with her body. In the shed we sit on a bed made of herring nets, put away for winter and still reeking of fish.

She is very willing, hoisting her shift over her own head when I fumble with the laces at her neck. We lie down together, quite naked, and I kiss her slowly and then more quickly, and not all the herring stink in that dark shed can diminish my happiness.

She looks at me, her face grave. 'You know this is a sin.'

'We would not be the first to sin this way.' I run my finger along the side of her neck, which I have so many times admired from my pew in the kirk.

'No,' she says. 'But still it's no small thing.'

'Does it feel sinful?' I ask, and I move my hand lower, to her cunny, her hair springy and damp.

'Yes,' she says, but she presses back against my touch, and I begin to understand that this feeling of sinfulness is part of her pleasure. Perhaps it is part of mine too – certainly we each find our pleasure that day, and when we are spent, we find it once more.

I am no theologian, but you shall not convince me there are not other kinds of sacraments than those countenanced by the kirk. That what Effie and I do in the fishermen's shed is not itself a sacrament. And though the Bible says we sin against God when we do such things, I believe sincerely that I have never felt closer to God than in that shed, and that if I were free to meet Effie each day and receive a sacrament such as this, I would be devout indeed.

9

Saturday is Da's night for drinking. He has taken himself to my brother John's house, where the two of them will drink and talk, and I know that my failings will make a large part of their conversation, and that John's shrewish wife Margaret will eagerly join in, for it is a topic the three of them never tire of. Da will not stumble home until late. He is not generally an intemperate man – he drinks only on Saturdays, and Andrew often laughs about it, saying, 'Da is a good man of the kirk even when he drinks, for he does so very orderly, by schedule.'

This Saturday, when Da is long gone and all the household asleep, Andrew wakes me with a tremendous kick, and reaches below our bed to pull up a pail. He holds it out to me, and motions for me to smell it, which I do with some misgivings, having fallen foul of his tricks too many times. But Andrew is grinning and now so am I, for the pail is half filled with claret that he has stolen from Da's cask.

'A good deal better than a chamber pot, eh?' he whispers.

We dress in silence. With Andrew's finger pressed to his lips he ushers me to the window, past the beds where David, Simon and Peter are sleeping. With much hushed swearing, and Andrew's hissed imprecations not to spill the claret, we clamber outside, and I follow him up the log pile stacked against the back wall, which we use as a kind of stair, so that we may sit on the roof together, as we used to do when we were mere lads.

The stars are bold tonight, and beyond the seawall the ocean breathes its slow, wet breaths.

'Da will miss the wine,' I say. Our father is no fool – there will be a reckoning.

'Aye,' says Andrew. 'But not yet. Not tonight, he won't.'

I have always been a great one for doing what I will, and putting the consequences out of mind. And although I am wont to be wary of Andrew, I cannot but be glad that tonight he has chosen me, of all our brothers, for this escapade. Thanks to Effie, I am magnanimous with happiness, so I set aside my usual resentments and suspicions and take the wine from Andrew, and I drink deep, laughing when the claret drips down my chin, for the pail makes a clumsy vessel.

Soon enough we are reeling, good reeling. I have not been drunk before, and I discover that when I am drunk I am not myself at all, and I like that very well. Tomorrow normal life will descend like the fog that rolls off the sea, and we will have to traipse to the kirk, and soon enough my father shall discover what we have done. But tonight we can forget ourselves entirely and that is enough. We have stepped even outside our usual enmities – for now that we are thick with drink, even Andrew, bane of my days, is a jovial enough fellow. Indeed, his jokes have never been so funny, and nor have my own – and what a splendid sharing of jokes this is, the two of us on the roof with the stars punched out of the sky as though father has taken to the night with his leather awl.

And Andrew proves himself generous too, for he plies me with the drink, and takes his turn at the pail not half so often as I. 'Go on,' he says, passing it to me once more. 'For do you not deserve it, the scoldings I've given you over the years?'

I think, *Yes, yes I do deserve it.* Do I not deserve this one thing for myself, who has lived my whole life in my brothers' cast-off clothes and their mockery? I drink deep.

We watch my father stumble home, hands pressed to our mouths to stop our laughter as he trips at the gate. We do not sleep at all. At dawn Andrew takes himself off to wash his face, 'For I have not the stomach that you have, brother, an old man such as I am.' We laugh, for he is but a few years my senior – but it is true that I feel strong and young. He has left me the bottom of the pail to drain, and I do drain it, and feel stronger still. Is this how it feels to be a man? Effie has made a man of me, and Andrew has recognised it, and now he and I shall be friends and I shall be tormented no more.

Soon enough the household awakens. Father being concerned with his own sore head has no attention to spare us, even when I climb down from the roof with a great deal more noise than I should have liked, to find that Andrew has not only washed but even shaved and changed his shirt.

'Look at the state of me,' I hiss at him, looking down at my own clothes, much worn and dirtied by the climbing onto the roof.

But he just slaps my back and says, 'You fret over nothing – you look well enough.'

I feel well – I have never felt so well – never so quick-witted nor so handsome, and the walk to kirk passes mighty swift, and I near dance my way to our pew. My God the light in that place, and all the women in their Sunday best. There is a glow throughout the kirk which has not so much to do with the deep-set windows but more to do with me, the things I can now see that had before been hidden from me. It is enough to make a man become pious, this light. What a fool I have been to dread coming here today, when in fact it is precisely the place for me, yes – for where else would so many be gathered, so much beauty in each face? I could stare a long time at each one, and when I spot Effie I cannot help but call out and wave very fervent, and she giggles but others around look stern. I recall that this is a solemn place, despite its beauty, and so I enter into my solemnity: I nod my head gravely and slow to a stately march, until Mam nudges me from behind and Father says, 'Christ lad, what ails you?' and I say, 'Nothing at all, truly nothing,' in a voice I thought hushed, but which comes out fearful loud, bouncing around the kirk as though it has nought to do with me at all. And it is met with a chorus of hushing and whispering, and this strikes me as extremely funny so I join in, hushing back with broad exaggerated movements, my finger to my lips, 'Hush, hush now, won't you all just hush.' Moncrieff is coming down the aisle towards me; Da has me by the shoulders, saying, 'Jesus, by the smell coming off you you're half pickled.'

Moncrieff says, 'We'll not be taking the Lord's name in vain in his own house now, Selcraig.'

'No indeed,' I say, 'that would not do at all,' and then am sick right at his feet, very quick and very acid.

Thus I go to sea on a tide of my own disgrace. My father is still set dead against it – yet nor would he countenance my being hauled before the kirk session, Largo's sombre court, which Moncrieff says I must do the very next day, to answer for my indecent carriage in the kirk. I myself feel the mortification deeply, most particularly of having so shamed myself in front of Effie, whom I cannot bear to face.

Having created two ways to disappoint my father, I choose the one that pleases me best, which has ever been my way, and walk that same night to Leven, to beg my passage on a ship bound for Leith.

IO

This island has taught me to hate the sky, for there is too much of it. From my lookout, there is too much by far – and what is not sky is sea, or mountain, and there is nothing at all on the scale of a man, so that I feel untethered, and terribly small. No man likes to be humbled – and me less than most, having grown up as I did with a host of brothers at pains to humble me.

I turn all about, scanning slowly. By my reckoning it is mid-August, and more than ten months since I was abandoned here. Long enough for a woman to carry a child – yet what has happened on the island? Nothing but the seals returning; summer bleaching the grasses in the lowlands; the soft descent of winter. The winds on the island do not cease; even in my dreams, a scouring wind blows loud across the water. Awake, the wind is so deafening that I sometimes press my hands over my ears to try to vouchsafe a moment's peace.

But even after so very long, hope dies hard. It dies hardest of all in sailors, for we have seen ships emerge from storms that seemed to swallow the very sky. All of being a sailor is an unlikely enterprise – a kind of miracle, not so far removed from walking on water, after all. Only a fool or a sailor would still make the long journey up here to my lookout – perhaps I am both.

Today, though, when I stare to the south-east, there is something: a smudge, merely, but enough to set my heart clattering against my ribs. I close one eye, shake my head, open it again. It is still there. Holding my breath, I narrow my eyes and see it: the white of a sail.

I holler and leap, though the ship is but a faraway blur. I cannot make out the pennant – and if it is Spanish or French I shall have plenty of time to hide, but I know in my gleeful heart that it is not, for no ill can come on this day, made golden by good fortune. I cannot resist leaping and waving my arms above my head, though I know it cannot avail me from this great distance. Nevertheless I yell until my voice cracks, harsh and shrill, and continue even then, hurling my cries into the wind.

That same ceaseless wind has scattered some of the timber that I laid ready many months ago, for my signal fire. I squat to shield my flint from the gusts of wind as I strike, and strike again, and I am swearing heartily. The kindling is damp and will not take the spark; with shaking hands I cut the end of the rope that is my belt and use that instead to kindle the flame. Ordinarily I would begrudge this, for every inch of rope is precious to me – but now surely all such concerns are behind me. Now that I am rescued, I need think no more of such things, for there shall be whisky and ease and plenty, and no more goat meat nor cabbage leaves neither. Giddy, hoarse, I stand before the flames and weep – it is over, it is over.

And now the fire has truly kindled I add green leaves to make more smoke, and damp ones too, and even in the gusting wind the smoke rises tall and true, and I bless it, I bless the good thick smoke. I burn my hand and I bless the burn, I bless the wind for drawing the ship closer, and I can make it out clearly now, a frigate, her sails fat with wind. She looks a fair ship, in good trim and swift. Her lines are not those of a Spanish ship, nor the light and fast build of the French fleet, designed for the Mediterranean. No, this is stouter, a solid English ship, built hardy for the cruel Atlantic and beyond. And whatever enmities we Scots have with the English, I care nothing for them now, for there is no mighty Scots navy to come to my aid. An English ship is my best and only chance; an English ship means rescue, and nothing else signifies.

Yes – and the wind snaps the pennant taut and indeed it is the red ensign, it is an English ship, and as soon as she turns for the bay I shall be found, and she shall bear me home.

She does not turn. She stands off a great distance to the east, as if the island were not here at all. Certainly it does not figure in her plans, for she makes her stately way across the horizon and for three or more hours I watch her go, feeding my fire to a furious blaze even long after it is clear that she will not stop.

And now I curse the very fairness of that ship – for such a ship, well provisioned and polished to a gleam, has no need to anchor here. I should wish instead for a beaten-up old hulk, for it will only be desperation that drives a ship to this island. I cannot doubt that she saw my signal; perhaps her crew thought it the fire of a Spanish encampment, or of savages. Perhaps they have pressing orders and cannot stop. As the fire dies, I churn such possibilities in my mind. But in the end the reason matters not – for she is gone.

This missed encounter occasions a fresh melancholy. It is nothing like my sharp despairing fury when first I was abandoned here. It does not stir me to tears, nor rage. It stirs me to nothing – it is the opposite of stirring, for I am becalmed, barely able to rouse myself from my hammock of a morning. I would lie abed all day and never rise were it not for Pickle and her young, who are most insistent in demanding their food, and in taking liberties, viz. much nibbling of my toes and ears; howling exceeding loud; and scampering over my hammock as a game, regardless of the comfort of my person. Thus I am bestirred to rise and to hunt, if only to feed the cats, for my own appetite is sorely lacking.

I do not wish for food, but I long for drink, and I curse myself most heartily for drinking all my flip in that panicked frenzy of my first days here. I have left myself with no means of oblivion. This island permits nothing in the way of forgetting – it is here and it does not change, and I am ever the same, and stuck. The days mount around me like seals on the beach, dragging themselves so slow, so heavy.

I think often of my mother, and of her insistence that I was blessed, the seventh son, born in my caul – no harm could come to me. Perhaps she was right – for I survived an ignominious career at sea, and I am here, while the *Cinque Ports* was in such a wretched state when it left me that I doubt not it has sailed to its doom. Even this island has not killed me yet. It is true that my life seems mighty reluctant to quit me. But whether it is a mercy or a curse I cannot tell – for what manner of life am I now left with, alone here, and half mad?

I have taken a fancy that this island is in fact some kind of Hell, and that I have died – that the *Cinque Ports* sank after all, and I with it, and that all that has passed since then has been some kind of dream or vision. I look down at my body and wonder whether a man may not know he is dead.

It is hunger that jolts me from the apathy in which I have been bogged since the ship passed by. And since I am not dead, after all, and my appetite returning, I resolve to get myself a supply of goat milk.

I have no difficulty these days with catching goats, knowing their daily trails and where I may lie in wait to leap upon them. I do not much fancy the task of carrying a live goat all the way from the goat paths to my camp, for even the she-goats have a good set of horns on them, and are heavy what's more. I decide instead to snatch up one of the kids, for I trust that if I carry him back to my camp, the mother will follow.

In the rocky heights I seize a kid, brown and white, and small enough to tuck under one arm, though he flails. But to my dismay the mother scatters with the rest of the herd, and I am worried that goats are little troubled by motherly instincts. If I am not to have milk, at least I shall have fresh meat, and so I take out my knife, the kid bleating mighty noisy in my grip. I have scarce got my knife to his throat when I hear the scattering of hooves on rocks; the mother goat has come back and is watching warily from an outcrop just above us. She dances in uneasy circles, and cries piteously to her little one, who cries back. With this fearful racket we make our way down to my camp, the she-goat following close behind me.

I tether the kid to a tree, and the mother circles my clearing, skittering away whenever I move, but drawing near again when I am motionless. I watch her; certainly she should not begrudge me some milk, for her teats are engorged, her udder so swollen that it hangs between her hind legs, so that she must walk sailor-fashion, with bowed legs, the whole udder juddering as she moves.

For an hour or more I let her be. When at last she feels bold enough to creep closer, I am able to toss a loop of rope about her neck. Her horns would usually serve her well, but here they are her downfall, for when she bucks and tries to shake off my noose, it snags where her horns splay wide, and she cannot get free.

Even thus, it takes no little effort to secure and tether her to a tree beside her kid – and thence it takes an hour more, and many handfuls of cabbage leaves, fed to her piecemeal, to calm her enough that I may attempt to milk her.

I have never milked an animal before and am surprised to find it difficult – and made all the more so because the goat will not be still. My tentative pulling at the teats yields nothing, but I am loath to squeeze harder, the she-goat already being mighty restive. Yet having seen how mercilessly her kid butts and drags at her teats, I suppose a goat cannot be too precious about such things, and so I squeeze much more firmly. When at last I do get a good spurt of milk, it comes out not neatly into the bowl I have set below, but in all directions, including onto my feet. It takes some practice to direct the stream to the bowl, and even then, the sides of the bowl being sloping and shallow, and the stream now forceful, half of the milk blasts over the far side of the bowl and is lost. Furthermore the kid, whom I had not thought to tether out of the way, is jealous and butts and interferes, and I must fend him off with one hand while working her teats with the other. In this haphazard manner it takes me at least half an hour to fill my bowl.

The milk, when at last I drink it, has a flavour strongly redolent of goat. That does not stop me drinking all of it, and enjoying it heartily. Henceforth I keep both mother and kid tethered close to my clearing, and even when the kid begins to wean the mother stays in milk, which is a most welcome addition to my diet. Keeping the two of them secure is no easy thing – goats being such great ones for clambering about, they are forever getting their tethers tangled, or wrapped about the trunk to which they are tied. And although I move them regularly so that they may graze on fresh leaves and grass, you would think they had nothing to eat but rope, for both mother and kid chew at their tethers something terrible, and I must endlessly check and mend the ropes. But though I often curse them for infamous rascals, and begrudge the hours of twisting and splicing rope, I am nevertheless glad to have the milk. And while my diet would not please an epicure, it is a wholesome one, and I fancy myself in better health now than when I was at sea.

My knife is much blunted from being turned to rough work and to sawing. Even when I sharpen it carefully against a stone, its edge is sadly dulled. Today I am at work on a bowl when my knife tip lodges in a knot in the wood and snaps cleanly off.

In my old life, such a mishap would have been a thing of no great account – an irritation merely, and a small expense. I would need to buy a new knife from one of my crewmates, or ashore at our next port – and in the meantime there would be plenty of knives to borrow. Here, it is a calamity, and already I am thinking of all the things for which the tip in particular is useful (viz. prying open the shells of crawfish; slipping between the hide and the flesh when skinning a goat carcass; extracting thorns and splinters from my feet). Thus, even with the old goat looking on, I weep with anger and swear a good deal. I must grovel amongst the grass in search of the tip, sifting the dirt with my fingers. When at last I find it, I whoop mightily, and slip it into the tin box where I keep my flint. I store it away like a treasure, already thinking of how I may still put it to use.

Such is the very scrabbling sort of life that I lead now. When I am saved, it shall be different, and I shall never again take for granted such a miracle as a good sharp blade. *When I am saved* – this is my constant refrain, the chorus of my longing.

Since the sea lions have come ashore, the seals keep themselves to the bay's eastern edge. They keep a respectful distance from the sea lions – a wise precaution, for I have twice witnessed the sea lions preying upon young seals. To a seal, is a sea lion a god, vengeful and remote?

In need of oil for my tapers, I take my club and pick my way through the seals. At once they set up their bellowing and squealing. The nearest one, a slick silver fellow, lurches away, twisting his ungainly body around, the better to see me. In his rolling eyes is naked terror. He flails away, dragging himself on his fins – and I could have chased and caught him for a seal on land is never fast. Yet his gaze has gone through me like a harpoon, and I fall to my knees, my club dropping to the wet rocks, and my hand pressed over my mouth as if to keep my horror in.

The seal's terror should not shock me like this. In these many months I have come here often enough with my club and done my killing. It is beyond time for even these foolish creatures to learn the good lesson of fear. But the seal's horror has pinioned me. In this island without looking glasses, the seal's eye showed me myself, fearsome and savage. Is this what I have become?

The seal has reached the water's edge; he rears up to cast one last aggrieved look back at me. 'You wish me gone?' I shout after him. 'Do you think I don't wish it too?'

He slips into the water. He has the luxury of leaving the island. I do not.

I stand. The seal fled from me, for he saw me as a dread brute. If the island has made me thus, then I shall be thus. I take up my club again. The seals still on the shore are stirring and barking. Well should they fear me. I stride towards them. If this island is indeed accursed, as I have so often complained, I see now that it is I, myself. I am the curse.

II

I carry the seal carcass, heavy with death, back up to my butchery. As I walk, I recall the passage in the Song of Solomon that I was reading only last night: 'Set me as a seal upon thine heart, as a seal upon thine arm.' I say it aloud, calling to the old, bearded goat, who has followed me here: 'See? See? *Set me as a seal upon thine heart, as a seal upon thine arm.*' I press the carcass against my chest and let its tail flop over my arm with a wet slap. 'See? See, Master Goat? *A seal upon thine heart, upon thine arm,*' and this little piece of wordplay strikes me as the funniest thing I have heard in such a long time – for what have I heard these many months but my own voice, and the cries of beasts, and the wind and the sea which never cease? I set to laughing, and I am much stained by the blood of the carcass, and I cannot stop my laughter, until I must set down my burden and laugh until I sob, hunched over the little seal, and the goat looking on all the while.

———

This evening, when I settle down to read, the Bible falls open to the story of Noah. 'And that is most fitting, is it not?' I say to the old goat, and sweep my arm at the horizon. 'For Noah and I are both of us beset by water.'

Yet Noah was not so very similar to me, after all, for he started out tremendous virtuous: *These are the generations of Noah: Noah was a just man and perfect in his generations, and Noah walked with God.*

And so I lift a stick of charcoal from amongst the coals of my fire, and take it to the page. After all, in these many long months of reading, I have exhausted the Bible's stories. Why should I not make for myself some new stories, out of the old? I start to strip away at Noah's story. I am remaking it, and making it my own.

Noah was perfect in his

violence.

come

flood of waters destroy
the

covenant

of flesh

Come

clean beast take to thee
the

living

flood

I am left with something approaching a psalm, or perhaps a poem. And if it has a strange, staggering lilt to it, then that suits me well enough, for I am become slow and, perhaps, a little mad in my speech, having so little need for words.

What would Largo's Reverend William Moncrieff say, were he to see me take to the Bible with my charcoal? Is this blasphemy that I undertake with my black-smudged fingers? Is this a defacement of the Holy Book? Moncrieff would not be quick to understand, I think, for I was ever a sinner in his eyes. Yet it gives me some satisfaction, this strange work of words. *Come, flood of waters. Come, clean beast.*

When that ship passed by and did not stop, something in me snapped, a broken mast. I have tolerated my stagnation here, in the belief that rescue is possible. But since the ship failed to stop, I can think of nothing but escaping the island. Whether I have lost my mind, or found my courage, I am not sure.

I take myself down to the bay, and survey there the tall pile of logs that I have been gathering these many months. The old white goat follows me, watching with his head to one side.

'Master Goat,' I say to him. 'It is time for me to be going.'

Now that I have determined to go, it seems a wonder that I have not done this earlier. Yes, there is the sea to be reckoned with, the awful vastness of it – but I have endured the terrible expanse of time on the island, and no sea can be more deadly than that.

I am a navigator by trade – I have seen the charts and maps. I know that the distance to the mainland is so great, and the seas so vicious, that no man could hope to make the crossing in an open raft. I know that even if some miracle brings me to the coast of Chile, I am more like than not to fall into the hands of either Spaniards or savages. A sane man would not hazard such a thing. Listen well: I have long since pushed off the shores of reason; there is a fever in me now to be rid of this island, and it can only be answered by doing.

I examine carefully the logs I have set aside. The tall heap of lumber looks fit for nothing yet but a bonfire. I have work to do – for if nobody is coming to rescue me, I must rescue myself.

For weeks, I labour at my raft.

Once cut to size, and with any boughs removed, the logs must be stripped of bark, which is a veritable sponge for water, and speeds the rotting of wood. Here the broken barrel hoop comes into its own and makes a fine scraper. Then, before I fasten the logs together, I rub each one liberally with seal fat, as a further defence against waterlogging.

Half of my tent must be dismantled, to make a sail. I also strip my camp of every piece of cordage, unravelling it from the frame where I stretch my hides, and even from the tripods that support the spit where I smoke my goat meat. Each scrap of rope must be turned to the work of binding my raft together, for I am neither ship-wright nor carpenter, and even the simplest mortice and tenon joint requires better tools than I have.

Much of the assembly must be done in the shallows, for once the logs are bound together, the whole of it weighs more than any man could carry – if I build it on the shore, it will remain there. In the water, knee-deep, I labour for many days, and with much swearing and grunting, to build the raft that shall carry me away.

It can only charitably be called a raft, for it is nothing so neat as the word might suggest. A rough square, perhaps ten feet each side. A base of logs bound together as tight as I can manage; atop these, six larger logs for beams, laid crosswise for strength, with a gap between each one. And set atop these the final layer, which I hesitate to call the deck, gapped and uneven as it is. I have impaled her through the middle with a primitive keel, a broad plank wedged through gaps in the deck. At the top of this plank I've gouged two holes through which I hammer two long pegs, athwartships, to hold it into place. It judders and shifts, but should help to keep the raft steady in strong winds.

The mast is barely taller than me – anything more shall risk over-setting the raft entirely – and anyway, I have precious little sailcloth. She is lateen-rigged: a triangular sail, affixed on a long, light yard set at an angle across the top of my mast. This shall allow me to tack against the wind, though how much I can hope to manoeuvre so unwieldy a vessel I cannot say. As to steering, I have only a plank, carved to a handle at one end, which is to be paddle and rudder both. At the top of my meagre mast hangs a white pennant – the sleeve of a torn shirt, worn to rags – so that if I meet with a ship, I am declared a supplicant, in need of mercy.

The mainland being at such a vast distance, I tell myself that I need not even reach it – only draw a little closer, to where I might encounter a ship. From Spaniards and their slaves I avert my mind; and while the French may be our enemy the same as the Spanish, they have a less fearsome reputation, and are more like to ransom a prisoner than enslave them. A man must take his chance – what other choice is left to me but to die here or run mad?

I leave my raft moored in the shallows of the bay, tied fast to one of the huge rocks. The next day she is still afloat; when I check on the second day, I find three seals have clambered aboard and are resting there. This I take for as good a test of weight as I could wish, seals being so very fat. I chase them off, with much waving of my arms and shouting, and by jumping on the other side of the raft to set it rocking. When the seals, protesting noisily, slip quickly into the water, the raft jerks wildly and I am nearly flung into the water to join them.

My provisioning is dictated by the miserly size of the raft. I will not take my musket – if I find an English ship, I shall not need it, and if I meet with Spaniards, a single musket will not avail me. My raft is so small that I am more like to lose my musket overboard than to use it. The precious room that a musket might take shall instead be given over to water – my cask, two goatskin bladders, and my biggest wooden bowl, to catch any rain that falls. I shall bring my kettle, too, so that I can light a signal fire if needed, without making a funeral pyre of my raft. I pack a small quantity of kindling and a few sticks, rolled in a greased goatskin to keep them dry. To the handle of my kettle I affix a length of rope, for I figure that the kettle may also form a small sea-anchor to help steady my raft should I meet with heavy seas.

My most precious belongings – my knife; my flint; a fishing line of the finest cord that I could make, with a wooden hook – are fastened to my belt, so that they cannot drop between the gaps in my raft, nor be lost even if the raft is overturned. As for my mathematical instruments, I take only my compass, for I can take no reliable readings with my astrolabe on an unsteady raft. And while the distance I must cover is nigh impossible in such a craft, the navigation at least is simple, for I need only go east, which the meanest sailor can determine without aid of any instruments. East, and if I can but make the distance, the precise direction matters little, for all the great stretch of Chile is waiting to catch me.

For food, I have the fishing line, as well as a sack stuffed with cabbage leaves and cooked turnips. I slaughter both my she-goat and her kid, now a fair way to being fully grown. It costs me no pangs to kill them, for keeping them tethered, and rescuing them from tangles of their own making, has been tireless labour since first I caught them, and at times scarce worth the benefit of the milk. With difficulty, having dismantled the structure that suspended my spit above the fire, I smoke enough meat to last a goodly while.

For days, as I wait for the wind to turn, I carry the goatskin sack of smoked meat with me, to keep the rats from it. At night, I sleep with the sack beneath my head like a pillow, and Pickle and her offspring sniff it most eager, and nose themselves close about to my head to sleep. And as these are my last nights here, after all, I let myself imagine it is affection that draws them so very close, and not the pungent smell of goat meat.

Four days the wind remains stubbornly from the south; on the evening of the fifth, the air warms, and when I look up, the pennants of each palm are trailing eastward. I wet my finger and raise it: yes, the wind is westerly, and strong enough to whip my hair into my eyes. I will catch the next outgoing tide, at dawn.

Before nightfall I make a final trip to my lookout. The wind holds westerly, and the skies are clear. I could not hope for better. In my gullet rises a feeling that may be hope, or terror, or both.

That night my camp looks ragged indeed, my tent half disassembled and the place stripped of all that I shall take. Those treasures that I cannot bring (my musket, wrapped in an oiled goat hide; my sea chest, containing my astrolabe, Bible and my little store of powder) I have hidden as well as I may in a shallow cave not far from my camp, in case I should ever return, though God knows I hope not to.

I will not bring Pickle with me — for even a man as selfish as I could not justify that. Not only because she would be terrified to be set upon a tiny raft, or because I shall struggle to feed and water myself, let alone her. No: it is because the truth of this journey is that I do not expect to survive it. But if this escape feels hopeless, it is no more hopeless than waiting for a ship that will not come. At dawn, before I leave my camp, I stroke Pickle patiently, holding her to my chest, where I used to carry her in the pouch when she was a kitten.

Sleek, the wild tabby, looks on from the clearing's edge, and does not move. The old white goat likewise stares as I gather the last of my possessions.

'You are not usually here so very early,' I say to the goat. 'Are you come to make a procession, to see me off?'

He continues chewing, very solemn.

'I suppose this camp is yours now,' I say to him and the tabby. 'I wish you well of it.'

12

Wading to the raft, I think of the caul I was born in, that my mother always swore was a promise that I could not be drowned. I have usually paid my mother little heed, but now I hope fervently that she was right, for the raft looks fearsome small, and it rocks alarmingly when I come aboard.

At first my progress under paddle is slow – but once I pass the head of the bay and my sail catches the wind, I move at a fair pace. To move at all is a joy – to be carried by the wind, and not to trudge as I have done this past year, following those same weary paths to my lookout and back.

From my bay to the island's eastern tip is but a league or so. Before noon, under a fair wind, I sail beyond it. I would put my pace at less than one knot, but nevertheless the island, which has been my entire world, is receding. No liquor has ever been as intoxicating as this: the sheer giddy joy of breaking away from that place. Why did I wait so long? Why did the island seem so insurmountable, when in just this short time I have got free of it? At last I am the master of my fate. I built this raft myself; I am away.

Down here at sea level I cannot see above a few miles. In the late afternoon the island drops out of view altogether, I give a mighty whoop. Oh, to have my horizon not hemmed in by those same hills, those same bays! To have a rat nowhere near my person! For almost a year I have known it would be madness to attempt escape. If this is madness, let me have it. Let me have my fill.

The night is very much less comfortable than the day. In the great open sea, even this mild wind sets up a swell, the raft rocking and creaking, wood and rope straining. If I sit up, I am at risk of tipping off; when I lie down, the uneven logs jab at me, and the raft sits so low in the water that I am sorely splashed. I grasp the mast for purchase, but must grope around my possessions, which are fastened at the mast's base.

I may be uncomfortable, but I am still moving eastward. Nothing is asked of me in the way of sailing, for the westerly holds up, and my little sail does its work. Nothing is asked of me but to endure – and am I not Alexander Selkirk, who has already endured more than most men encounter in a lifetime? I catch a few moments of sleep; waking in blackness, I frantically grope at my possessions, to assure myself that they are still there: water bladder; sacks; kettle. I am parsimonious with my water, allowing myself but a single sip at a time. My eyes adjust to the dark; the quarter moon winks at me knowingly, and all the heavy black tent of sky drapes down to the horizon.

Before dawn, something changes: there are stars missing to the north, a swathe of unrelieved darkness. The sunrise confirms it: clouds are massing there, churning and heavy. I tell myself that at least I shall have some fresh water, and I allow myself four sips from my cask, along with a strip of goat meat. I do not permit myself to be afraid. I am master of this vessel, however small and ungainly she may be.

How quickly the sea reminds me who is truly master. The wind swings about, a fierce nor-easter, driving before it giant ridges of swell. Any notion I had of being able to sail against the wind is proved a nonsense, for my sail is too small and the waves too great. I am being dragged back, and all my painstaking progress shall be lost, those precious miles undone. In the distance, black columns of rain, and the occasional flash of lightning. The thunder, when it comes, is scarce louder than the furious roar of the water, whipped by wind. I drop my sail – in truth, even if I could make headway by tacking against this wind, I would not dare draw closer to the storm. Nothing matters now but to stay afloat, a task that grows harder with each wave, steeper and steeper until I must straddle the mast, legs and arms wrapped around both bundled gear and mast, clutching to stop myself from sliding from the deck.

I have let out the kettle behind me as a sea anchor, the rope hitched tight to a central log, to stop the raft from turning broadside to the waves. But even for such a small vessel, the bucket is too small; it slows the raft but a little, and still I am tossed haphazardly. Thick rain is upon me now, and from within the troughs of waves it is harder and harder to take my bearings. West – still I am swept west, faster than ever I sailed yesterday. How did I ever imagine I could cross nearly 400 miles? What lunacy, what hubris. What a longing for death must have been breeding inside me like worms in a hull.

All day I cling; all day I despair of living. Long hours, the sun quite lost behind waves and a sky so thick with rain and spray that it is a wonder I can breathe at all. My hands are too cold to feel. My paddle is swept overboard; I watch it go, and cannot even try to grab it, or I shall follow it down.

It is late afternoon when a shape emerges to the south-west: an island, long, dark and low. No – my island, rendered briefly unfamiliar, its peaks buried altogether beneath the storm that has reached it before I could.

And while I am mighty grateful to be delivered back to the island, that deliverance may also be my doom. In the open sea the waves were huge, but rolled in unbroken banks; closer to land they break, sharpening to steep peaks and tipping over in a fearsome churn of water. Nearer to shore lies the greatest danger – there, between the rocks and the breaking waves, in the very teeth of the sea's maw, is where I am being swept.

I can now snatch only glimpses of land – the storm has darkened the afternoon to a grey blur; my furled sail has been torn loose and slaps and snaps in the wind. I fend it off with one hand, clinging to the mast with the other. I am drawing close now – I can make out the cliffs. Cliffs much sheerer than those near my own bay – this is the island's north-western side. If I am swept much further I shall be carried past the island altogether, and past any hope of surviving, for beyond is nothing but the merciless expanse of sea, thousands of miles in which to die.

The waves are giant walls and trenches now. My mast is loosened – it is down, and it knocks me with it, clear of the raft. I am beneath the water and tangled in the grasping wet sheet of the sail. It makes a caul like the one I was born in, but this caul shall drown me, for I cannot get free of it. My arms are pinned tight to my sides; I thrash, but to no avail. I have no air left, my lungs nothing but an empty sack, soon to be filled with water. I bring my knees to my chest and then kick out, hard, against the canvas that binds me. Two more kicks, and I twist free. I shoot upwards, but come up under the raft, knocking my head hard. Half-stunned, I stare up through the cage of logs at the sky beyond. The pain in my lungs is fierce – a terrible thirst for air. Before I can get out from under the raft, a wave hurls me sideways. I am slammed again against the raft, but now it is lifted high and tumbled over and away from me. With a final desperate flailing I reach the surface and gasp a breath, and then another.

The next wave hoists me up; I can see land. I am being dragged into a bay, the shore but a few hundred yards away. But it is no shore – no gentle beach, such as my own bay boasts. This is a cliff, jagged and high, the waves smashing at its base. And I must swim away from land, against every instinct, for there is no safe place here where I may come ashore. If I let myself be carried in by the waves I shall be dashed on the rocks and soundly killed, and be ground to a paste by the cliffs what's more. I try to swim out, against both tide and waves, and when the largest waves rear up before me I dive beneath them, so that I am not picked up and dragged back. But the waves come so huge and fast that I have scarce surfaced from one when the next drops upon me, and all my effort is spent upon seizing a breath, rather than covering any distance. I swim but I get nowhere; my body, tested beyond endurance, is weakening now. The waves and the onrushing tide are hauling me towards land. It is as though I am trying to tow the island, the whole grotesque bulk of it fastened to me and pulling me back.

A seal glides through the waves not far from me. He skims across the wave face as though this is a mere game to him; a twist of his sleek body and he dives beneath. His ease enrages me – why should these lesser creatures slip so smoothly through the water while a man struggles and thrashes? And this fury fuels me a little longer and drives me on, stroke after dogged stroke, until I've rounded the point and the next bay is in sight. Cliffs – more cliffs – but a wave raises me high and before I am slammed down again I can make out a point where the cliffs relent – yes, a rocky slope a little way east, where the island's walls have given way to the sea and crumbled. Nothing so hospitable as a beach, but it is not sheer cliffs, and with my body failing I have not the luxury of holding out for better. I drag myself a little further from the point, then I let the waves take me in, though there is a great deal of going under in the process, and I swallow such a quantity of salt water that it is a marvel I can swim at all.

Closer to the shore there is a reef of rocks, which I discover only by kicking one of them, and if my foot were not so cold I fancy it would hurt more. I push away, and the waves shove me back against the rocks. I am too weak to push off again, so I let myself be dragged across the rocks, tearing up the flesh on my legs once more. There must be plenty of blood – in the ordinary way of things, I would fear attracting sharks, but in this vicious maw of rocks and sea, a shark could kill me no better than the storm is already doing.

The waves are higher than the rocks, and I am beyond them now, though I'll warrant I have paid handsomely in shreds of flesh for my passage. Yet I am alive still – and the waves are pummelling me swiftly towards land.

The shore has none of the pebbles or sand of my own bay – instead there is a jumble of sharp and broken rubble where a cliff has subsided. Onto those rocks I am thrown, and I cling on, and each time a wave draws out I have a moment's reprieve to drag myself a few feet higher. I lose my grip once and am pulled back out a few feet, but the water is shallow enough here that I can throw my arms around a boulder and hang on while the sea does its best to heave me out again.

When at last I am beyond the water's reach, I collapse, vomiting up a warm sluice of salt water. My heavy goat hide trousers have been swept away, and my shirt too; I cannot regret it, for they would only have dragged me down. Naked except for my belt, I lie with my bare arse in the air, my face pressed against the rocks.

If this is the sea's mercy, it is a terrible one. I have been spared – and I am condemned once more to this island.

———

I cannot make it back to my camp tonight – it is all that I can do, before the dark comes, to clamber further up the jagged and shattered rocks, and find a ledge a short distance above the sea. It is nothing so grand as a cave – merely a spot where one rock overhangs another, granting a little respite from the rain.

The cold water has stopped my gouged legs from bleeding too heavily, but there is blood nonetheless, and the insects swarm to my wounds. It is a warm night, but I am much plagued by chills. The sea has left me almost nothing, but it has spared the pouch which is fastened to my belt. I pour the salt water from it, and carefully take out my treasures. The glass of my compass is smashed, but my knife is still intact, as is the tin box (much dented) with my flint and steel. I have nothing to burn for warmth – even if I braved the steep rocks in the darkness, I shall find no dry wood in this storm. I tuck my chin to my chest and wrap my arms tight around me. Between my thirst and hunger, and the swarms of insects, I could swear I shall never sleep.

I am wrong: I wake with the dawn, much bruised and cold, but still alive. I watch a fly suckling at one of my leg wounds, and I have not the strength to wave him away. How he sups; how thirsty he must be. This awakens my own thirst – I shake off the fly and stagger to my feet. The wind is still high but the worst of the storm has passed, and the rain with it. I clamber up and find my way to a wooded plateau. There is no stream here, but a shallow puddle will suffice for a man as desperate as I. Lying down to drink, I slurp as a dog slurps, drinking until my stomach hurts, the muddy water sweet on my salt-parched tongue. With much searching and scrounging for dry wood, I make a small fire. I sit so close to it that I wonder if my flesh shall be smoked like the goat meat that I cook. Can a man be seasoned, like goat flesh? Yesterday I was well and truly brined, today I am smoked. A laugh breaks from me, but I swallow it quickly, for I sound mad, even to myself.

My hunger must be answered next – I stumble west, to the next bay; the tide is out, and in the shallow rock pools I am able to snatch three good-sized crabs, which I skewer roughly on my tip-less knife, and tear the meat from them with little regard for their thrashing, nor for the sharp shell, which cuts my gums.

Before I can permit myself to return to my camp, I have one last task. All day, I stagger along the north-western coast in search of my raft. It is not mere blind hope, for the swell still rolls from the nor-east. I was not so very far offshore when I was cast into the water, and the island being stretched out so long, east to west, it is a fair net to catch a wreck in.

Mid-afternoon I am rewarded by the sight of it, quite upturned, and tossed upon the rocks in a bay just a little west of where I came ashore.

All the belongings I had fastened to the raft are gone, as is the mast, and the sailcloth with it. My cask, my water bladders, my carefully gathered supply of food. But the sea grants me one unlikely gift: when I pull at a trailing rope, one end still hitched firm to the raft, there is resistance. I haul the rope in, and up comes my kettle like a fat, rusted fish. It is much battered and dented, but when I raise it, it holds water still.

It takes me but a few hours to disassemble what took me so many painstaking weeks to build. I take every scrap of cordage that I can salvage; the rest of the raft, now in pieces, I leave where it lies. It is scattered on the rocks as though some huge beast of the sea has run aground and only its bones remain.

It is the work of many days to reconstruct my camp. My milking goat and her kid are gone, slaughtered to little purpose, for their flesh is feeding fishes now. Half of my tent has been sunk, and what remains I must extend with goat hides, patched together. The bladders and bowl lost to the waves must be replaced. I work hard, and in silence. The wounds on my legs scab, then crack and bleed. I fancy that the old goat and the tabby cat look at me with scorn.

Pickle, at least, is pleased to see me. 'Here I am,' I say to her. Her warm head fits precisely into my palm. 'And I shall not be trying that again.' I think of the moment when I was tangled in the sail, beneath the raft. How the sailcloth became at once my caul and my shroud. Being a sailor, I have no objection to a sea burial, but I had thought to be dead first.

Had I managed to sail further – had I sailed for a week or more, before being blown back – I might be tempted to try again. But the sea has given me a most decisive answer. The catastrophe of the storm was so absolute, and so quick, that to try again would be nothing more than suicide.

My survival is a miracle – perhaps I ought to be grateful. Yet as I look up at the island's stark peaks, I am tired of miracles.

I

will

not   escape

the

mercy

of

salt.

Two weeks after my return, still limping from my wounded legs,
I find the skull of a buck goat. It is wedged in a crevice between

two rocks, with its horns entire. The island has scoured it perfectly clean – the bone bright white and the horns black, with ridges like the lines on a shell or a fossil. The horns spread near as wide as a man's shoulders, curving right about and ending in a sharp point. I have seen few specimens as splendid – even the old goat who makes himself a nuisance about my camp has not a pair of horns as fine as these.

I carry the skull back and set it in the fork of a tree at the clearing's edge. It stares over my tent with its black, empty eyes. Sometimes, when the old goat is absent, I speak instead to the skull.

'How do you like to see me eat your brethren?' I ask it, as I chew on a joint of goat meat. 'Do you condemn me? Or do you hunger too?'

The skull is a bowl of silence.

The sea lions are leaving. It is the end of September, and their pups are bigger now, and bold enough to try the water. Each night a great tide of sea lions takes to the sea, and each dawn fewer and fewer return.

I have always known that they would go – when the *Cinque Ports* was harboured here, we witnessed their leaving. They are creatures of their own seasons, and it is their season for going. Yet when they left last time, I had my fellow sailors still around me. I had not yet been left here, nor had I passed such a long time alone. And though I have much bemoaned the noise and inconvenience of these beasts – to say nothing of their stink – I find it very hard to bear their leaving. I gain no comfort from the thought that they will surely come again, next June – for to witness their return, I too must still be here.

I stand on the shore and watch them make their toilsome way to the water. I want to cry after them: *Don't go, don't go.* A broken man, beseeching these monstrous beasts to stay a while longer with me, and not to leave me on this island. Do not leave me here with myself.

13

I am lost to any sense of scale. There are days that I spend watching ants, and the intricate tracings of lichen, and I feel myself vast beyond all possibility. I look down at my own limbs and wonder how such a monument in flesh can even move, giant as I am? Other days, when the sky goes on forever, I feel myself minuscule – so tiny that I despair absolutely of ever being found, for no ship could ever spot me amidst all this space.

'Goat,' I say to the old white goat. 'Have you not wearied of all this sky?'

———

The leather thongs fastening the pouch to my belt having perished, the box containing my flint and steel drops and smashes onto sharp rock – of course it does, for what is this island but one sharp rock, after all? Amidst much loud swearing I fumble the box open to find my flint shattered into three, two of the pieces so small as to be useless, and the other much diminished.

When I am finished with my cursing, which takes no little time, I resolve that I must learn to make a fire by other means, so that I may preserve what remains of my flint for a sighting of a ship, when speed shall be most urgent. I have for some while been meaning to try a method that I once saw demonstrated by Captain Dampier himself, during my last expedition. He and the other officers of the *St George* had come aboard the *Cinque Ports* to dine, and conversation fell to the practices of the various savages that he had come across – and whatever my feelings about Dampier as a captain and indeed as a navigator, I will allow that he has seen more of the world than most men ever will, and has been a keen observer of those men and beasts that he has encountered. He tried to demonstrate how some of them make a fire with neither flint nor steel, by digging a groove in a stick and setting another stick into it. Dampier then twisted this upright stick swiftly between his palms so that it rubbed against the groove, whereupon he claimed that a quantity of wood shavings could be induced to begin smoking and, with much careful tending and judicious blowing, can be brought to a flame. That night Dampier did not progress beyond producing the smallest trail of smoke, before he let the stick fall and sat back, saying, 'Well you understand the principle, though savages have time to spare that we have not,' and called once more for the port.

For myself, I have never been a patient man – but I cannot say that I do not have time, and so I determine to try it for myself. The pimento wood must be entirely dry, which is not always easy, in an island that tends rather to dampness. For the kindling, amongst the rocks on the island's western side there grows a thick moss that, when dried, kindles faster than any wood shaving. The first time I succeed in lighting the moss with this rubbing method, I holler greatly, startling Sleek, the wild tabby cat, who has been watching me.

Even with these refinements, and much practice, lighting a fire thusly is not a swift process, and my hands grow new callouses. As I squat and rub the stick, my mind turns to a line I have lately read in Genesis: *Behold the fire and the wood*. It has a pretty rhythm to it, which I find answers very well in keeping my rhythm when rubbing the stick – and so I take to saying it aloud, over and over, as I work at coaxing the smoke from the sticks. And I am no heathen nor magician nor a fool neither, yet soon enough it has become a habit, such that I would not attempt to make a fire in this manner without saying my little refrain aloud, as though it is the incantation itself and not the rubbing that conjures the flames.

———

I have found myself returning many times to the Bible with my charcoal, until page after page is blackened, and even the covers become much smudged with black fingerprints. These new stories or poems are a most welcome diversion on the lengthening October evenings, when the sun is slow to quit the sky.

Today I open the Bible once more to Genesis, at the very beginning of the book:

In the beginning God created the heaven and the earth.

When I am done with my charcoal, what I am left with is altogether different:

Perhaps this is heresy, after all. Certainly it is different altogether from reading the Bible. Instead of reading, this feels more akin to whittling at a piece of wood – for I am removing word after word until what remains seems to be the truth.

I shall not starve, but the island kills me in a thousand mundane ways. In the utter tedium of gathering cabbage leaves, and of picking from between my teeth their fibrous strings. The fire going out, and the roof of my tent leaking – and all of this could be solved with ease through merely a good length of sailcloth, or a new flint – but not having these, I must continue always to repeat the same tiresome tasks. It takes me weeks of labour to cure a hide to patch my tent, and then the rats gnaw at it – and in these damp climes and with my imperfect curing, the hide shall rot soon enough anyway, and it all begins anew. I am impaled on the curve of time, as sharp and inevitable as the horn of a goat. It all comes around again.

Such small things can be the ruin of a man. I have never lived a life of ease – neither as a youth, beset by brothers and sermons and chores, nor as a sailor, a profession hardly known for its luxuries – yet there is something uniquely crushing about the thousand little ways in which the island thwarts me. It puts me in mind of the passage in Revelations, about what shall befall those who worship the beast: *And the smoke of their torment ascendeth up for ever and ever: and they have no rest day nor night.* I may not suffer the agonies of fire and sulfur, but sometimes, when I am stung in my hammock by insects, or pick rat droppings from the remains of my carefully stored meat, I think that the fire and sulfur might indeed be preferable.

I had thought the great question of my time here would be how to survive. That has been answered well enough, and I do not fear starvation, nor wild beasts. No. The great question I must answer here is: *who is a man, when all the things that make up his life are stripped away?* No. Not just any man, but *who is Alexander Selkirk,* without his troublesome family nor his shipboard duties nor even a tot of rum? Who remains?

What are the parts that make up a man? Your occupation – of which I have none, for how can I be a sailor when I cannot sail? Your family – and I was ever a disgrace to mine, who must by this time surely have given me up for dead. Your wife or lover – but here there are no women at all, and I run half mad with desire. Your attire – surely few men have ever been as strangely dressed as I, goat-clad and ragged, and my face half lost within my thick beard. Your conversation – and what have I of this, except for my own mutter-ings, which would condemn me as mad if any man were to hear me, for I have taken to a sort of recounting of my own actions to myself: *A fine hitch, that one, let us see – yes, yes, it holds well enough – the fucker, the fucker* (for the bough to which I am trying to fasten the side of my sagging tent has snapped) – *well that is more toil for Selkirk, toil toil and what for, fucking nothing, nevertheless we go again...* and so it goes on.

I did not know that other men are a mirror. When you live amongst people, you are always seen. I did not know what a deal of work is done by that witnessing: how a man is shaped by those expectations, and responses, so that he may measure himself against those who surround him.

Alone, all of that falls away. What remains? If I jest, who will laugh? If I sin, who will condemn me? If I am virtuous, who will praise me? Not the old goat, nor the tabby cat with her scornful gaze.

So what remains, when everything that once made me a man has been stripped away? The island, always. The dreadful patience of the sea. And Alexander Selkirk, whoever that may be – just a body on a small rock in an ocean very large indeed.

I succumb to a fever. For three days the sickness wrings sweat from me, and then the sweat chills my skin so that I shiver and sweat at once.

I throw up; when there is no food left to vomit my body does not stop, and I bring up bitter green bile, and then nothing at all, my body wracked with spasms that produce nothing. It is the same in my nethers: I shit hot liquid, and when I have shat myself dry, still my stomach cramps and protests.

Pickle and her offspring keep away from me. Perhaps they are angry, for I have not fed them – or perhaps there is some animal knowledge that warns them I am unwholesome. It may be the heat of me, which I swear would almost scorch them. For days and nights they do not come near me – my fever has drawn a ring about me in the dirt and no creature dares cross it.

'Pickle,' I call. 'Pickle.' Then I fall into laughing at how crazed I must appear: sweating and shouting *Pickle* at the dark.

The only cat that comes is Sleek. She walks to the door of my tent and sits there, very upright, staring at me unabashedly.

On the third day, in the glare of afternoon sun, I limp to the clearing's edge to shit, and whilst I am shitting I am taken by another bout of vomiting.

The old goat is there, chewing as he watches me.

'How do you enjoy the show?' I ask, my voice hoarse.

He looks solemn. I might almost fancy that he pities me.

I must grab a pimento trunk to haul myself upright. Steadied, I wrench the goat skull from its perch in the tree. I hold it by its wide black horns, sweeping back from the brow like some devilish cleft crown. It is a fierce relic, and the tremendous weight of it feels fitting.

I place it atop my own head and hold it there, turning to face the old goat. I take a shaky step closer to him. He draws back, hind legs skittering on stone.

My shadow is cast on the ground before me, fearsome large: a great horned beast. I like it. The seals were right to fear me, for I am become God. I test the words aloud: 'I am become God.' Yes – God of goats and cats. God of stone and sea. A fierce and wild god. *Come, flood of waters. Come, clean beast.*

PART TWO

14

I wake face down on the floor of my tent. The goat is at the tent door, his head low as he peers within, so that his long ears brush the ground.

'Good morning, sir,' says the goat. 'I trust I find you in better health.'

I scramble to my knees, unleashing a torrent of cursing and knocking over a jug of water.

'If you must curse,' says the goat, 'you will oblige me by doing so more quietly – for a goat's ears are much more acute than a man's.'

You need to understand that I have seen many strange things. I have seen a man dying of scurvy whose teeth grew so loose that when he coughed they flew across the deck and scattered on the floor like so many dice. I have seen a man so crazed with fever that he took a notion that he could fly and climbed over the gunwale to fall to his death, smiling all the while. I have seen a rat whelp a litter of pups and then eat them one at a time, while the living ones yet suckled.

Another thing that you must understand is that the goat's voice permits no doubt. He speaks perfectly clear, and with great authority. There is nothing goatish about his voice, and it has no bleating tone. He speaks with such gravity that one cannot do otherwise than take him seriously. His voice, and indeed his haughty way of holding his head, make it very plain that to doubt him would be an insult to his dignity.

His eyes being so much to each side of his skull, he can only watch me goatwise, by turning his head to the side, the better to fix me with one of those strange eyes. Close behind him is the wild tabby cat. If she notices that aught out of the usual is occurring, she gives no sign of it, for she is busy washing herself.

Is this my fever, playing tricks on my mind? A form of delirium, like that of the man who jumped to his death from the gunwale? No goat could master speech. I have only ever known one other creature to speak – a parrot, kept as a pet by a fellow named Curnow, aboard the *Caledonia*. The parrot was of a great age, and Curnow had taught it a number of words, which he used to yell, sudden and loud: *Can of flip* and *Sails Ahoy!* Curnow thought it good sport to teach it to imitate the bosun, which the bird did very well, so that at any point it might shriek, *Out or down! Out or down*! and exhausted sailors would stumble from their hammocks and hasten to dress, before swearing at Curnow or hurling blankets at his bird.

But who, on this remote and God-forsaken place, could teach a goat to speak? Is it I? I, who have taken to speaking to them, or to myself as I wander through my days, always muttering: *And wouldn't that be a fine thing, a chair, my God, a good sturdy chair, yet we shall make do with this old log, eh, goat? Eh?*

But the goat's words are not mimicry – this is no parrot repeating what he has been taught. There is no way to reason what is happening here. No way whatsoever to force this to make sense: a goat who speaks.

All that I can do is listen.

'You are well, sir? You have been grievous ill.' He speaks like the Reverend William Moncrieff in Largo kirk – as though he is behind a pulpit, rather than peering into a tent, ears dragging in the dust.

I sit up, and brush at the dirt that is crusted to my face.

'Goat,' I say. 'You are a goat.'

'Indeed, good master.'

I suspect him of sarcasm. 'And as a man, am I not indeed your master?'

'Last night you stepped in your own piss,' he says.

I regret that it is true – for in my weakness I did stumble in the dark when pissing against a tree, and step in my own hot stream.

'As you said - I have been sorely unwell, and not myself.'

'And we see you frigging yourself daily.'

This is not from the goat at all, but rather from the cat behind him – Sleek. She has ceased her bathing and is staring at me, one paw still raised. Her voice is smooth and deep, though unmistakably female.

'A man must have his pleasures,' I say.

She resumes her bathing. 'Must he have them quite so often, and quite so noisily?'

You might think that the advent of a second speaking beast would send me into paroxysms of fear, or disbelief. In fact the opposite is true: the one follows the other, so that all of a sudden both seem more ordinary. A speaking goat alone is a marvel; when a cat speaks also, suddenly it seems as though it were the most ordinary thing in the world to converse with beasts.

'Goat,' I say. 'Do you have a name?'

'Certainly,' he says. 'My name is the Reverend Vicarious Cronch.'

You must understand one further thing: if I doubt what is happening, I deny myself the prospect of company. You may call me credulous, but if I refuse this goat and his voice, I lose his conversation and condemn myself to silence. If even the meanest creature spoke to me – a clam; a slug; a rat – I would welcome his voice, rapt with attention. I would press my ear to the slug, keeping my breath gentle so as not to discommode him, and I would say: *Yes, yes, I am listening.*

I clear my throat. 'An unusual name.'

'It was the name my mother gave me.'

'And your father?'

'I had not the pleasure of knowing my father.'

I speak quickly, though he shows no sign of being embarrassed by this admission.

'And you are a minister? How do you go about taking holy orders here? There is no college here, no presbytery.'

'Goats have no need of such petty ceremonies. My name is Reverend, and that is sufficient.' He cocks his head, setting his ears swinging. 'It speaks of a certain dignity or piousness about my person – and I flatter myself that I have lived up to the name.'

'And Vicarious? It's not a name I've heard before.'

'I could not tell you its origins. As for Cronch, it is a family name on my mother's side.'

'I did not know that goats were in the habit of taking names.'

The cat speaks again. 'There is much you do not know.'

My mouth is dry, and I need to piss. These days of sickness have left me gravely weakened, and I can only stand slowly. When I have stumbled from the tent to the far side of the clearing, I hesitate. These animals have watched me for the better part of a year, and yet now they have spoken, I am newly bashful.

'Must you stare at me always?' I turn my back as I piss against a tree.

'You are ashamed, all of a sudden?'

'I am not ashamed. But no man wishes to be made a spectacle.'

'If you were better at being a man,' says the cat, 'you would not mistake yourself for a god.'

I dart a glance back at my camp. The horned skull lies on its side in the dirt, where I dropped it last night.

The cat has turned away and is stretching.

The goat chews on a pimento leaf. 'It seems to me that most troubles come from being what you are not. Me? I excel at being a goat, and thus have few troubles – excepting worms, of course, which are the curse of every goat.'

'They are the curse of sailors, too,' I say, 'though in a different way.'

'They do not make your arsehole itch?'

'They eat our boats. The *Cinque Ports* most especially.'

'A serious matter.' He nods sympathetically.

'Cat,' I say. 'You, cat. Have you a name?'

'I am neither man nor goat. What purpose would a name serve?'

'You must be known by something, amongst your kin.'

'I have no name that you could speak, nor understand.'

'Then what shall I call you?'

'Call me what you like. It matters not at all – a cat never comes unless it wishes.'

'Pickle comes when I call,' I say.

'She comes because she wishes – because you have fattened her on goat liver.'

'If you will not tell me your name, then I shall continue to call you Sleek, for it suits you well enough.'

She makes no reply.

This talk of Pickle reminds me that I have much neglected her during my illness. I call for her now, my sweet and faithful pet, and she emerges, most prompt, from the woodpile where she has made a nest.

I chuck her beneath the chin, as she likes best, and wait very expectant for her, too, to talk – yet she says nothing.

'Will you not speak to me, sweet?'

She looks at me very obliging, and allows me to rub the soft fabric of her ears between my finger and thumb, but still she does not speak.

'Come, little one,' I say. 'You must have plenty to say to me, my old friend.'

'She is not your friend,' says Sleek, 'but a pet. It is quite a different thing.'

Pickle, who is now grown plump with still more offspring, remains steadfastly silent.

I turn to Sleek. 'If a cat is to speak to me, why should it be you, and not my own Pickle?'

'A cat that consents to be a pet is no longer a cat.'

And I will confess that while I am inordinately fond of Pickle, she has never struck me as a cat of great intelligence, being particularly given to chasing her own tail. Perhaps it is not surprising that she, of all cats, has not achieved the power of speech.

I press my palm to my forehead and chest to test whether I am still feverish; my skin is clammy, but it does not burn as it once did. I am relieved to be emerging from a sickness that I feared would kill me, and yet I am sorely afraid that when the last traces of fever are gone, the goat and the cat shall again fall silent. I shall be left once more alone, my tongue good for nothing but working shreds of cabbage leaf from between my teeth.

But the cat and goat, having begun talking, do not stop. Indeed, I sometimes wish that they would, for the cat has a pert tongue. I am busy with the work of setting my camp to rights, which is no easy task after such a long illness, and with my limbs still shaky. With my makeshift shovel I dig the vomit and filth from the floor of my tent and carry it to the clearing's edge, where I toss it into my latrine pit.

'You are weak,' Sleek says.

'I thank you for your keen eye.' The illness has left me snappish with fatigue and hunger.

'Where is my bowl of blood?'

'You shall have it when I have slaughtered a goat. I am not yet well enough to hunt.'

'I have brought you luscious rats – and still you do nothing for me.' It is true that she delivered a rat to me but an hour ago – its limp and greasy body dropped at my tent door – but I am not yet reduced to eating rats.

'Did you master speech just to rail at me?'

'A luscious rat,' she says again. 'I even left you the eyes. Yet when you have killed a goat, you give me scraps. You keep for yourself the good fat liver, or waste it on your pet.'

'You would have me worship you, then? Build you a little altar, and lay offerings?'

'I would have the liver. The heart too.'

'A goat heart is not such a treasure.'

'Good,' she says. 'Then you will not begrudge it.'

'Leave off with your begging,' I say. 'I have work to do, and all of it alone.' In my days of illness, my small store of cabbage leaves has been entirely devoured by the rats, and I must gather more. While I was sick I let my fire dwindle and go out, and not having the strength to light it afresh, I eat the cabbage leaves raw.

The goat sighs. 'The work of staying alive is a burden for you, I will allow, a man not being as hardy as a goat. Genesis itself says it: *It is not good that the man should be alone; I will make him an help meet for him.*'

'I had not thought to meet a goat so well versed in the Bible.' Indeed, I had not thought to be conversing with a goat at all – but this day has begun strange, and grown only stranger. Yet the goat speaks in such a very grave and earnest manner, as if it is the most ordinary thing in the world for a man to converse with a goat and a cat.

'You give me little credit,' he says. 'Did I not tell you that I am a minister?'

'Well then, the Reverend Vicarious Cronch – if Genesis says a man should not be left alone, where is my help meet? Can you tell me how it is just that I should be abandoned here, with no help meet at all? To be left here to survive, and not vouchsafed even so much as a servant or a slave to help me?'

'A slave?' the goat asks. 'And by what authority would you rule him?'

'He would be my slave,' I say, 'and labour for me.'

'Ah,' he says. 'If there are but two men on an island, which is the slave? By what authority?'

'By the law's authority,' I say, impatient now.

At this Sleek snorts heartily.

The goat asks, 'And have you found the island amenable to your laws, thus far?'

The cat speaks over him. 'What are your laws here, where there are laws of claw, of rockfall or storm? Do you mean the law of shark teeth, or the law of goat hoof?'

'Fine,' I shout. 'By the authority of my gun.'

She sticks one of her hind legs in the air, as though it had nothing to do with the rest of her body, and she takes to licking her arsehole. I had thought we sailors were brazen, but a cat is worse, having no notion of modesty, and a great deal of flexibility. When she pauses, still not looking at me, she says, 'And what manner of man would this slave be, strong enough to take on all your labours, yet not strong enough to wrest from you your gun?'

'I should be curious to meet this slave,' says the goat. 'A veritable phenomenon, such a man must be.'

'Enough,' I say. 'Enough from the both of you.'

The cat ignores me. 'Are you so very sure that you would not find yourself the slave? Or find your throat slit in the night?'

She saunters away.

———

Towards the end of this long, strange day, the goat announces that it is time for him to be off.

'Shall you return?' I say, and then am ashamed at the need in my voice.

He turns back from the clearing's western edge. 'Have I not come here each day? I confess that you have become something of an object of curiosity to me.'

99

'But shall you talk again, when you come?'

'I am sure of it.'

'And the cat?'

He shakes his head. 'It would be an unwise fellow who speaks on behalf of a cat. She will do what she will – cats were ever thus.'

He takes his leave of me with a rather stately bow.

I go early to my bed, still giddy with both the remnants of my fever, and the peculiar turn the day has taken. Have I taken leave of my senses? Can a goat and a cat truly speak? And if so, how much can I trust of what they say? I can boast myself much travelled, and I thought I had a fair grasp of the many varieties of strangeness that the world contains. I see now that I have understood nothing. This island, which I thought I knew so well, can surprise me still. What does it mean, what omen or portent, when animals speak? All I know, very certain, is that I am no longer alone.

I take out my Bible and return to the story of Noah. With much careful rubbing and wiping I do away with the charcoal that had blacked out most of the words – and then, from the same passage, I make the story anew:

the earth was filled with

stories

I

have seen

the face of

the

beasts, and every thing

opened.

I am learning how the same story may be told in many different ways.

I read it aloud to myself, much satisfied. *And everything opened.*
Yes – it has been that manner of day.

15

The cat wakes me at dawn.

'Blood,' she says. 'Hot blood.'

'Can you not wait? I say, and throw my arm over my face.

'Blood.'

'Let him rest,' says the goat, forcing his head into the gap between the tent wall and the ground. 'He is not yet well.'

But the truth is that I am much recovered – and the sudden and unlooked for gift of conversing has filled me with a renewed energy. I had feared that the dawn would bring a return to silence, as I regained my senses after my illness – yet the goat and the cat show no sign of stopping speaking and, furthermore, speak as though it is entirely unremarkable, and merely the continuation of a conversation that we have already been having for some months.

Even had I the strength, I should hesitate to hunt goats under the gaze of the Reverend Vicarious Cronch. Before he spoke to me, I used to jest about it, waving my plate towards him and saying, 'How do you like to see me eat your kin, Master Goat?' But that has changed now, and I would fain not lose his company, which I need more than goat flesh. So today I make my unsteady way to the bay where, with little difficulty, I catch two large crawfish. I must set about lighting my fire, using the rubbing stick method. It is tiresome work when I am still weak from my long fever. The cat shall not have her bowl of blood today, but when I have eaten my fill I toss her some crawfish meat – and though she looks affronted, at least she eats it, and allows Pickle to have what remains.

Afterwards, the crawfish meat has the usual effect on my belly, occasioning a great deal of shitting. I had thought myself alone at this business, but the goat speaks suddenly from my left.

'You would do better with goat flesh, for you cannot be shitting so when you are still convalescent.'

I stumble forwards, swearing. Even without being startled, it is hard to converse with dignity in such a situation. When I have steadied myself, I roar, 'Is a man to have not a moment's peace, or am I to be tormented?'

His ears snag on the branches as he withdraws his face from the bushes, and for a moment I am afraid that I have frighted him away for good – but when I return to the camp a few minutes later, he is there, close by the cat. His solemn face gives no sign of mockery at what he has witnessed.

'I apologise for startling you earlier,' he says. 'But you will not survive without proper meat.'

I clear my throat. 'I had not thought to see you encourage me to hunt your kin.'

He chews, his jaw churning from side to side. He is forever chewing at something. 'It gives me no pleasure to see goats killed. Indeed, but a few weeks ago you ate one of my friends.'

I am hard-pressed for how to respond to this. After a few moments, I ask, 'Were you very fond of him? What manner of goat was he?'

'He had a superb grey beard. He was nimble on the sheer rocks. He was a prodigious eater of turnip tops. He was everything a good goat should be.'

'How, then, can you bring yourself to be here with me? How can you forgive me?'

'He was a goat, and he did goat things. You are a man—'

The cat interrupts him. 'And what men do is kill.'

I think this a mighty blunt assessment of men's inclinations, but before I can say so, the goat continues. 'As for killing him, it is in your nature, and I would be foolish to judge you for it.'

'And you do not fear me?'

'I do not.' He cocks his head. 'You already had your sport, when you chased me and cut my ear. I do not believe that you will eat me.'

It is a bold thing to say, when he stands within arm's reach. Even in my weakened state, I could have my knife to his throat in an instant – and for all that he is a scrawny old buck, after my long illness he would be a veritable feast. Yet he stays near to me, looking at me frankly with one bulging eye, his heard turned sideways.

'You may be sure I will not,' I say. 'You are a most singular goat. And I confess that I've been sorely in need of company.'

'I am obliged that you enjoy my company, sir. It is a novelty, too, for me to speak with you.'

'You speak very prettily, for a goat.'

'How did you think a goat should speak?'

'Not at all, as you well know. But certainly not in such a way. And very different to the cat.'

For the cat, who has now meandered from the clearing, speaks in a strange and savage manner. *Blood. Hot blood.*

'Ah,' says the goat. 'You must remember that we goats are famously adaptable. We can thrive in all manner of terrain. We can scale cliffs. We can eat nearly anything.'

'This I know to my cost.' I am thinking again of my stockings, and my cabbage leaves.

'There is little a goat cannot do,' he continues proudly.

'And cats?'

He looks around, to check that Sleek has indeed left the camp. 'A cat is a different thing altogether,' he says in a lowered voice. 'With cats it is not a case of cannot, but will not.'

The next day I hunt once again, using a little of my precious supply of powder, for I am yet too weak to chase the goats down as I have been used to. I shoot a fat goat on the path a short way above my camp, and butcher it on the stump that I use for that purpose. Into the rough-hewn wooden bowl I drain the blood for the cats. Sleek comes first, not even acknowledging Pickle and her kittens, and drinks her fill. As for the goat, he watches the whole thing.

I say, 'It surprises me a little, sir, that you can watch this.'

'If a thing is to be done, then it ought to be witnessed.' He looks solemn, but not angry. 'You will eat him, and you will live, and the cats shall have his blood, and they will live too. You shall find that few creatures on this island are sentimental.'

'Do you not mourn?'

He shakes his head, and his beard sways.

'When he lived, that was the truth of him. Now he is dead, that also is the truth of him. I do not mourn what is true.'

'These other goats – do you speak with them?'

'Certainly I do.'

'But I have never heard you. Nor will any other creature here speak with me.' To my shame, that same morning I even tried speaking with a seal, who looked at me dumbly and wallowed away, yelping.

'It is a different kind of speaking,' the goat says. 'We speak with the angle of ears, and the scent of arse, and the scraps of thorn and grass that cling to the long hair of our underbellies.'

'Milk scent,' says the cat, looking up from her bowl. 'Whisker twitch, and the language of tails.'

'That is not speaking. It is no language at all.'

'It is a language you cannot hope to understand,' she says, exceeding sharp.

I turn back to the goat. 'But you can tell me what the other goats say? What they are thinking, and what they have seen?'

The cat gives a warning hiss.

'I cannot,' says the Reverend Vicarious Cronch. 'It is not for you.'

'Yet you speak to me.'

'We do so out of kindness,' says the goat. 'But you must understand this: not everything on this island is for you.'

Out of kindness. It is an uncomfortable thing, to be pitied by a goat – and thus I speak more angrily than I had thought to, when I say, 'This island – always this island. You speak of it like a deity, when it is but a God-forsaken rock, and I wish I had never seen it.'

The cat turns to face me. 'You wanted it. You asked for it.'

'What are you talking about?'

'She is speaking of how you came to be here,' the goat says, 'and of the choices that you made.'

'You can know nothing of it. As for choice, what choice did I have?'

'You have been here a long time, and still you have not understood the story of how you came here.'

That is a story I have no wish to recall, and thus I say nothing.

In the strange days that follow, I unleash upon both the goat and cat a great torrent of questions. I ask them about William, the Indian slave abandoned here so many years before, whose rescue Dampier used to speak of. And I ask about the men of our own crew who were left here, and how most of them came to perish. Most particularly, I pester the animals with questions about the Spaniards and the French, and how often they come to the island, and whether any savages have ever reached here – but the goat and the cat do not wish to speak of the past.

'That is done with,' says the cat impatiently.

I beseech the goat. 'You, my trusty companion – you will tell me how the Indian passed his time here, and if you saw him?'

'You are much concerned with the past,' says the goat. 'But I can tell you nothing, for it is past.'

He is chewing – he is often chewing, for the business of eating seems to take up his entire day. Goats do not chew as men do – instead his jaw grinds round and round, a kind of millstone, tremendous slow.

'You might at least tell me whether you saw him? Or how often the Spaniards are wont to come here?'

'It is past,' says Sleek, as though that were an answer.

What is past and what is to come seem not to figure for them as such things do to men. To a beast, life is terribly immediate: the goat chews on his leaves, and is pained by the worms in his arse; the cat sleeps with the concentration that a man would apply to his labours, and wakes hungry for blood. To animals such as these, it is always now.

'Is it not enough that I have been abandoned to die on this God-forsaken island? Yet you will not even give me the small comfort of telling me what you know.'

'You might find yourself happier, were you to be more like us,' says the goat.

'Happier, perhaps – but less of a man. It ill befits a man to behave like a goat.'

He looks at me and blinks slowly. 'And is it such a very great virtue, to be a man?'

———

It takes weeks for me to recover my strength. I am grievously afraid of what shall happen should I fall ill again. Having no means of preserving food, nor of creating a stockpile that can withstand the rats, any illness that prevents me from hunting could leave me sorely at risk. I must keep some goats at my camp – but the method of tethering that I used with my she-goat and her kid cost me many yards of rope, and much time disentangling the witless pair. Thus I resolve to build a pen, and to capture a herd of young goats, as well as another milk-goat, so that I shall always have a ready supply of food and milk.

Building the pen is the work of some weeks, for to make an enclosure of any size requires a huge length of fencing. I mourn the simple tools that I lack. An axe – a simple axe! At my father's house, where it was my daily task to split wood for the fire, I would never give a thought to the miracle of an axe. Here on the island, such a thing would transform my days. With an axe I could construct a solid fence; without one, I decide to try my hand at a wattle fence, such as I have seen made with willow or hazel at home. To make the posts, I use my crude stone axe-head, and in this cumbersome manner I fashion a great heap of posts of pimento wood – yet when I begin to stake them, I find I have not made a quarter of those that I shall need. And the staking itself is no easy task, for the ground is rocky and they must be driven deep. A mallet – how I long for a mallet, a stout-handled one that swings true. As it is, a large, rounded stone is the best I can muster, and when I strike it at the top of each post, a fierce juddering jolts my shoulders and arm, until I feel I am being pounded as much as the stakes.

I plant them at intervals of about a foot, a task so tiresome that each hour my designs for the size of the pen grow more modest, until what I eventually have marked out with posts is small indeed. Even so it takes more weeks of labour to weave between the posts the palm fronds I have gathered, in the absence of willow.

At last it is done, and no mason has ever looked with greater pride upon some splendid monument than I look upon my goat pen.

It is a whole day's hard labour to catch five goats and bring them, one by one, to the enclosure. I choose young goats, though not sucklings. In the pen, at first they make free with the cabbage leaves that I have piled within, in my attempt to win them over to their new lodgings. These swiftly being eaten, they immediately set about eating the fence. With their teeth and their nimble lips they begin to gnaw and to pull, and within a few minutes they have worked loose some of the palm fronds that make the fence, and are swiftly eating them. Others use their brethren as a kind of ladder or stool, jumping onto their backs and thence over the fence, while I am frantically trying to shore up the sorely diminished fence on the other side of the pen. Two more set their heads to the ground and with much butting, pawing, and digging of their budding horns, lever up the post so that a whole section of the fence sways and sags. These last goats drop to their knees and slip beneath it.

I swear heartily and give chase, but tripping over one of the fallen posts I land jarringly on my front, near the feet of the Reverend Vicarious Cronch.

'We goats are very adept at all manner of climbing and jumping.' He looks rather smug.

'You are tremendous wily animals.'

'We were thus, before you built the pen.' He chews. 'If you are angry, it should be with yourself, and not with the goats for being goats.'

'You speak more prettily than the cat, but you are forever criticising me.'

'Is it criticism, to speak the truth? I deal in what is. We goats are skilled at escape. You must build differently, or find another solution.'

I speak no more to him that evening.

The next day I tell him what I have resolved to do: the pen alone is not enough, thus I must lame the captive goats so that they shall be less able to escape and, if they do succeed, to stray.

'And how do you like that solution, sir? Will that not cause your brethren more pain than a fence?'

'A fence is a great affront to a wild goat,' says he. 'No more and no less than a blade. If the goats are to suffer, you may as well get your meat, so that it is not in vain.'

After several days of painstaking repairs to the pen, I choose just two goats to catch, younger this time, in the hope that these little ones shall grow tame, as my cats have, so that I need not forever be shoring up the pen against their escape. While I ready to lame them

I leave them tethered by the neck, though already their indefatigable goat teeth are setting to work at my precious rope.

I seize the smallest fellow, squatting over him as he bucks and squirms, the stout cask of his ribs pressed between my chest and my knees, his hind legs flailing under my elbow. His head strikes the underside of my jaw, and I am mighty glad he has no horns to speak of, only little nubs, quite rounded. When my grip does not loosen, his arse unleashes a small barrage of shiny warm pellets, which scatter over my knees and feet. I must have become coarsened, I think, for such a thing hardly troubles me these days – indeed, goat shit offends me not at all, smelling as it does largely of grass.

I have my knife out, but before I cut him, I crane my head around to his head, and in a low voice ask him, 'Do you have aught to say?'

He only continues to buck blindly.

I spoke low, but the Reverend Vicarious Cronch's ears miss nothing. 'Should it make a difference, if he spoke back?' he asks.

I shrug over the kid's squirming body. 'Perhaps. I do not know.'

'You would be reluctant to put them to the knife?'

'Stop your badgering.' I once more ready my knife. What is it that angers me: the accusation of tenderness, or the accusation that I lack it? My life has not been of the kind to foster softness. A soft man would not have survived the life that I have led.

I try to be swift as I make a deep slice at the back of each hind leg. The sinew itself is shocking strong, and when cut, gives a loud snap like a loaded line on a ship, which if sliced can whip across the deck fit to take a man's head off.

The young goat is much alarmed and instead of bucking falls still, as though dead, although there is but little blood. It is shaking, and I am clutching it so tight that its shaking becomes my own. I set it down, and it stumbles and falls, its legs not working as they should. It drags itself away from me on its knees. It is a sorry business, for I wished both to lame and tame him, two things so very much at odds that I see no way to succeed in both.

I seize the other goat and begin again. Why do I hesitate, the knife held an inch from the quaking leg? I have ever been a man too quick to violence – but that is violence of a hasty kind, when anger rises in me and will not be stopped, until the answer to every question is a fist. This is a different manner of violence, being so precise and deliberate. I have butchered many a goat, but none so very small, and the cries this little one makes are most piteous. I find myself speaking aloud to him, a messy flow of words: 'I am sorry little fellow, it shall heal very well, I would not do it if I did not need, and all will be well soon and you shall forget this passing pain.'

'None of those fine words shall make any difference,' says the cat.

'I'm just trying to soothe him,' I say. 'Isn't that a kindness?'

'A kindness to yourself, perhaps,' says Cronch. 'Yes, his leg shall heal soon enough – but only so you may the more easily catch him later, and eat him at your leisure.'

'If you are a blade,' says the cat, 'be a blade. At least a blade doesn't lie.'

'Can the two of you never hold your tongues? Is my life not hard enough, without you forever watching and judging me?'

The cat rolls over, very leisurely. 'What made you think we were here to ease your life?'

Over the next week, I catch and lame five more young goats, and one she-goat with a suckling kid, so that now I have quite a little flock in the pen, skittish and limping, yet already tottering to greet me when I bring them feed, for they have cleared the last remnants of grass growing within the pen. With their nimbleness much reduced, the reinforced pen seems sufficient to keep them contained. And they have little reason now to escape, for being at pains to tame them, I am forever carting armfuls of fresh leaves and grass to them.

The new she-goat is no more willing to be milked than the last was, and the first time I milk her it takes an hour, and involves a great deal of kicking on her part, and swearing on mine. When at last my bowl is filled and I straighten, triumphant, the goat steps sideways and her hoof knocks the bowl and tips the whole of it into the dirt.

Of such petty frustrations is my life on the island comprised. It is but a small thing – a waste of an hour's work; a waste of good milk. Such a small thing – and yet the effect of being thwarted in so many small ways, day after day, of each task being harder than it should be, builds upon me like grime, until even a small frustration is enough to make me despair.

'It shall be easier next time,' says the Reverend Vicarious Cronch, gently.

'Keep your counsel – I did not ask for it.'

'You need a good stout pail,' says he.

'I know that,' I yell. 'But to make such a thing will take me a week, and all of it painful because I have not even the right tools to carve it.' The thought of using my makeshift axe to trim a log, and of gouging out the wood with my blunt knife, is enough to make me weep.

'If you want milk,' says the cat, 'take it direct.'

'What do you mean?'

'Suckle. Hot milk, and teat.'

'Jesus Christ.' There is something obscene at the very notion of taking in my mouth a swollen teat, the loud pink flesh blotched with brown spots, and on its upper parts, the white fur. Pendulous, each teat is closer in appearance to a cock than a breast.

'You do not want the milk?'

'I am not an animal.'

'You want the milk,' says the cat. 'So take it.'

'I will not suckle like a beast.' I take up the empty bowl, dirt clinging to the traces of milk, and hurl it at the cat. It does not hit her, but comes close enough, and she jumps, her back arched as if a string has been tied about her middle and yanked suddenly upwards. She lands with a hiss, and is gone.

Cronch cocks his head, one ear dangling. 'It is interesting to me, as a natural philosopher, to see the limits of what a man will and will not countenance.'

'I am not your subject,' I shout. 'Look elsewhere for your studies and reflections.'

Yet I will confess I am mighty thirsty for milk, after my long labour, and I do not wish to wait a week or more until I have fashioned some crude pail. I grasp a teat and, squatting, lean forward. I do not take it in my mouth – I have yet some dignity, I tell myself – but I turn the teat towards myself and squeeze, aiming the stream at my mouth. As before, the stream is unruly and I am much sprayed about the face, but manage nevertheless a good mouthful, and then several more.

'Does it make a difference,' asks the Reverend Vicarious Cronch, 'those few inches between your mouth and the teat?'

'A very great difference,' I insist, and turn away. He does not know how fearsome narrow the space between man and beast has become, and how I must uphold it – or what am I, and what shall I become?

In the week or more that it takes me to carve a deep pail, I continue to get milk each day by spurting it direct into my mouth. If ever I am rescued, I decide that this is a secret that shall remain between me and the island.

That cat, witnessing what I do, does not crow, as I feared she might, but merely gives a little nod. When I am sated, she steps closer and says, 'Warm milk mouth.'

Perhaps I am beginning to understand her better, for when she stretches her mouth wide, I direct the teat at her and spurt the milk straight in.

16

Any man who had endured such a very long time here would find his mind turning to drink. I have long become used to the absence of tobacco, but my yearning for drink is more barbed, and I cannot be rid of it. As to the stupor and sickness of my first days here, when I devoured the cask of flip, I begin to think that the sickness surely cannot have been as bad as I remembered – and a little stupor would be welcome indeed. To be sober is a terrible thing, when a man must reckon with days such as mine. Since it has proved impossible to escape this island by means of a raft, I resolve to escape it by means of drink.

I have no grains of any sort for brewing – let alone hops, nor grapes. But there is a palm tree here that yields great clusters of berries about the size of a cherry, bright red, with a large stone. These grow high, just below the palm's branches. I have tried them before, climbing with the aid of a rope to gather them, but they proved to have but a miserly layer of flesh about the stone. When raw, they are fibrous and unpleasant; cooked slow, they have a taste not unlike hawthorn berries. As they are neither convenient nor filling, I have not bothered with them except as an occasional novelty, to vary the monotony of my diet.

Now it occurs to me that I may set them to a better purpose, and try to make of them a sort of berry wine or liquor. It is already high summer, and the berries that I can gather are shrivelled, loose sacks of skin that leak red juice onto my hands when I pluck them. Those already fallen to the ground have been well chewed by rats, and those still on the tree have fared little better, for rats are expert climbers. Being less expert than they, and the berries growing high, it is the work of half a day to fill my kettle with the berries, which are already well on the way to being rotted.

Having no sugar, I can only brew them with time, and hope that they shall ferment as grapes do. And having nothing so complex as a still, nor the knowledge of how to construct one, I cannot hope to make liquor that is as strong as I could wish, nor as pure. I add water and crush the berries with my wooden spoon. The blackened skins peel away and stick to the spoon; I pick them off like scabs and toss them back into the mash.

Then I must be patient. I set the mixture aside in a bowl with a rough wooden lid, held in place by a heavy stone, and leave it alone for three weeks. By the first week it is giving off a sharp and cloying smell; by the second week, there are bubbles forming; by the third week, the entire surface is covered with a layer of green mould, like a baize cloth laid on a table.

Several times, as I scrape away the mould, I come close to abandoning the whole experiment. But my desire to be drunk again is greater even than my disgust – and you must recall that I have not the same notions of disgust as I once did, given all that I have survived in my career at sea, and since. Thus, clenching my nostrils, I persevere. I strain the liquid through a piece of cloth, and what remains is a syrupy black liquor, mighty foul-smelling. I fill a mug; raising it to my lips, I cannot help but gag at the stench of it. Yet sailors are no strangers to foul smells, and I tell myself that its very foulness is a good sign, a sign that I have managed to brew something potent after all. I hazard a sip.

'How is it?' asks the goat, who has watched the whole process with a disapproving air.

I cough. 'Like it has been brewed in a man's arse.'

He leans closer, to take a sniff; his nostrils flare and his ears shudder. 'Sir,' he says, 'surely this cannot be wise.'

'If I were wise,' I say, 'I would not be here.'

'Perhaps not,' he says. 'Though you still have not told me the whole of it.'

If I had been hesitant to drink again, the goat's raising the question of how I came to be on this island makes me need more than ever the forgetfulness of drink. I steel myself, exhale, and take another gulp, and another. I keep waiting for the sour taste to pass, but it seems only to grow stronger; my tongue is burning and my eyes water.

The goat shakes his head. 'You go to great lengths to avoid the subject of your coming here.'

I ignore him, throwing back my head to drain my mug. Then, my nostrils still stinging with the acrid stink, I pour another.

I asked for oblivion, and I have got it. Two hours, perhaps three, of good, reeling drunkenness. The old Selkirk would have been ashamed to be drunk after just a few mugs; this evening, I am just grateful that I do not need to drink more of my foul brew. I lie on my back outside my tent. The stars are moving faster than usual – terribly fast, so that each star tows behind it a bright trail of light like a comet, to trace its wheeling passage across the sky. It is a warm night; I say something to the goat, but at some time in my dazed stupor both he and Sleek have left my camp.

I am alone, but I am far enough sunk now into drunkenness that my memories have been drowned or washed away. I am made clean. This is a new man, who can watch the stars racing and who cannot even recall the flaws and errors that brought him here. I am a new Alexander Selkirk – it is altogether better this way. Why has it taken me so long to get to brewing? Why have I allowed my past to follow me around, when all along it could be shaken off by nothing more than a kettleful of berries?

I sit up, for I have a very strong wish to be singing. I sing 'Ward the Pirate', and then work my way through all the other sea-songs I can recall, Scots and English both. Indeed, tonight I discover in myself a tremendous talent for singing. The old Alexander Selkirk had but an indifferent voice; this one, though, sings loud and fine. The fire has almost gone out, but I do not bestir myself to feed it – it would not do to deprive the night of my singing. And if Pickle's offspring scatter from the camp when I reach the high notes, I do not take it personal, for I know myself to be a man greatly gifted in voice, and I shall not stop.

I sing 'Ward the Pirate' a second time, and am building up a tremendous volume for the rousing verse:

Go tell the King of England,
Go tell him thus from me,
If he reigns king of all the land
I will reign king on the sea.

Yet in the final words my voice swerves to a howl, for a pain has pierced my guts, a pain so sharp that, in my bleary state, I lift my shirt, for I must prove with my own eyes that I am not, in fact, being stabbed. It is a skewering kind of pain, and having started it does not cease. Hurt surges through me and my whole body convulses, and I vomit. Again and again this happens – the pain cracks my body like a whip. I cry out – but who will answer me? Sleek and the goat are gone; Pickle is startled by my yells and skitters from the camp in such haste that she knocks over my mug. There is nobody who can help me, and I am certain that I shall die.

There is a rock not far from where I lie; I try to calculate whether I can crawl there to bash my head against it to knock myself out and stop the pain. But that would mean moving my body, and my body has nothing whatsoever to do with my will, for now it obeys only the orders of pain. Lying on my side, I vomit again, and cannot even move my face clear of my own sick. Where is my song, so rich and full? Where has my fine voice gone?

I wake at dawn, with another fit of vomiting. Pickle has returned; she is at the edge of my vision, ignoring me to bat at a rat that lies before her. She tests it with her paw. She swipes it and swipes it, but it refuses to provide her with any sport, for it is already dead. Its little face is stained black with my wine. Nearby, two more rats likewise lie dead. One of them is lying in a starkly unnatural way, its chest and head facing down, its hind legs pointing upwards. It is twisted in the middle as if its convulsions have wrung it out.

When I can stand, I stumble to the bowl that contains what remains of the liquor.

'Do not drink that,' says the goat, appearing at the clearing's edge. 'How foolish do you think I am?'

He does not need to answer, given the evidence of my foolishness writ already very large all over the clearing, and particularly on my face, crusted with dirt and vomit as it is.

'All that effort,' I say, my voice cracking and hoarse. 'And my liquor was good for nothing but poisoning rats.' I dare not even put it to that use, in case my cats should taste it and be killed too. I lift the bowl, and the last dregs of the brew I pour away into the ground, kicking dirt over it for good measure.

For three days the pain comes every few hours. It makes a marionette of me, jerking me up and over, and making me retch and writhe. Worse, for a week or more the vision in my left eye is spattered with flecks of darkness, like a tarnished looking-glass.

I have never been a temperate man, but I do not attempt to make liquor again. The lessons that pain teaches, a man remembers well.

———

During my convalescence, the goat has watched me with the air of one who is gravely disappointed.

'Must you be always judging me?' I snap, when I see him studying me as I shuffle back from relieving myself.

'I have said nothing.'

'You don't need to,' I say. 'You with your parson-face — that is enough. You cannot blame a man for wanting a drink.'

'Is not the clear-running stream enough for you?'

'You know what I mean. Liquor.'

'Ah,' he says. 'I am still learning the many forms that a man's desire takes, and the many ways in which he may be dissatisfied.'

At this I am offended. 'No sailor can be called unduly nice in his habits,' I say. 'I'm no stranger to privation, or lean rations. It is a natural thing, that's all, to yearn for drink.'

'Natural,' says the cat, her mouth stretching wide, as if trying out the word for the first time.

'You find many things with which to be dissatisfied,' the goat says. 'Yet your dissatisfaction does not extend to your living quarters.'

'What do you mean?'

'I did not think you an idle man,' he says.

'No indeed,' I say, bridling – for you may well imagine the dili-
gence required just to scrape out my meagre existence here, the dull
daily labour of gathering cabbage leaves and digging turnips and
hunting my meat, and butchering and dressing it too.

'And yet you do nothing to improve this hovel.' He jerks his chin
at my makeshift tent. 'You have spent more effort on the goats' pen
than on your own shelter.'

I survey the tent where I have lived for more than a year. Even
now that I've cleaned up the mess of my sickness, my camp is a
sorry sight. My tent was pitched in haste when first I made my
camp, and in the time since then, rather than improving it I have
merely shored it up against ruin, and in a haphazard manner. Half
the roof was lost along with my ill-fated raft. What remains drapes
slackly over a long bough. The sailcloth, much patched with hides,
is pegged with rope, leaving a gap of two feet or more from its
lower edge to the ground. In this gap I have piled logs and branches,
to function both as a woodheap and a wall, though in this last
winter, when I burned nearly all my supply of wood, it became a
sadly sparse wall.

Below, my hammock hangs unevenly, from the tree trunk at its
head to a post at the feet. And all around it is clutter and disorder:
a goat bone that my cats have been chewing; a hide, waiting to be
cured, and smelling none too good. A heavy log laid on its side
is what passes for a seat. Beside it, piled on the ground, are my
carved pots and bowls, a trail of ants revealing how far from clean
they are.

'And what is wrong with it, sir?' I say. 'Is it not fit for a goat?'

'That is not the question,' says he. 'Is it fit for a man?'

It is not that I lack the skills to improve this dwelling. A sailor
needs must be a practical fellow, able to turn his hand to most things,
from carpentry to sewing – and after such a long time on the island
I now account myself a decent jack of all trades. No. I dare not
make this place more homely, for to do so is to admit that it is my
home. To pen the goats was a necessity, should I fall sick again and
need meat. But any concession that I make to my comfort is also to
concede that this is my life now, and that rescue may not come, or at
the very least will not come soon.

'It would cost you little labour to make yourself a great deal more comfortable,' he says.

It is true that while I cannot summon a ship to my rescue, it is in my power to make my situation on the island less wretched. Yet I do not acknowledge as much to the goat, for I can stomach no more of his condescension.

Over the days and weeks to come, however, I set about improving my shelter. My old tent, draped over an overhanging bough, had its position dictated by that tree. In the year or more since, I have often had cause to regret it, for the doorway faces south, which allows me no view of the water, and less shelter from the prevailing winds. Furthermore, in heavy rain, water seeps down the bough and into my tent, dripping noisily, soaking my hammock and turning the ground to mud.

I determine that my new home shall be a proper hut, standing free of the trees. Indeed, given the heavy winds that scour the island, I shall sleep all the sounder for not being directly beneath a tree, and not having to fear with each gale that I shall be crushed where I lie. I choose a place across the clearing from my bedraggled tent, a site where the door can face north and afford me a view through the trees to the bay. I am careful to heed the lessons that I took from building the goat's pen. I stake out a perimeter with good, stout stakes, and weave between then a wall of palm fronds. The Reverend Vicarious Cronch stays close by, and we chat as I work, and if sometimes he chews on a frond of my wall, I consider it a fair price for the diversion that his conversation provides.

I build the wall to a good height, so that I shall not need to be forever hunched over, as I was in my old tent. Thus when it is complete I have a kind of pen, without a roof, and with a gap for a door. This woven wall is both pleasant and sturdy, so that when I stand inside and survey it, the whole effect is of being within a tree, or perhaps within the nest of a bird. I am heartily pleased with it, but not trusting entirely to its sturdiness, and bearing in mind the island's tremendous winds, I make it my business whenever I walk abroad to gather loose rocks of the right size. These I carry back to my shelter and set about the outside of the wall, for greater strength, this stone wall mounting gradually higher and higher.

As to the rats, I make no effort whatsoever to keep them out, for it is futile – and because Pickle and her offspring, recently increased in numbers by a new brood, make an excellent job of keeping them away. I am grown prodigious fond of Pickle, though her latest clutch of kittens is all black, and thus I think her very wanton, for the father cannot be the same as the last litter.

For the roof, I lay out beams of pimento boughs, onto which I spread goat hides, for I have plenty of these. Atop this, I place the white grass that grows hereabouts, for when dried and fastened with strips of hide into tightly packed bundles, it could almost pass for a kind of thatch. Without a ladder it is no easy task to secure the hides and grass to the roof, and I accomplish this by reaching from below, balancing on a huge stump, which I drag inside with much swearing and grunting. And this work is not made easier by having Sleek underfoot, for she has taken to weaving between my legs.

'Friend,' says the goat, as I struggle to affix another hide to the roof's beams. 'You work as though you are constructing your own gallows.' He has taken to addressing me thus: *Friend*, he says, as though a man may be such a thing to a goat.

But he is right that I have worked with an ill humour.

'To make myself at home here is to give up,' I say. 'To allow that rescue is unlikely, and that there is no escaping this place.' I have never been one to give up, stubbornness being one of my besetting flaws.

'And is that not the truth?' the cat says.

I look out of the hut's doorway towards the water – the awful scar of the horizon. 'To be stuck here – it is a dismal thought.'

'But no less the truth for that,' Sleek says. She drops these words before me like a dead rat deposited at my feet.

Stuck – I am stuck here, however much I might wish it otherwise, and living in squalor shall not change the fact. I think of the goat's tremendous fussiness before he settles down on the ground, pawing at the earth and turning about several times. Yes – if even a goat can cater to his comfort, then a man can do the same.

Thus I persevere with my new hut through the clammy final weeks of 1705 and into the new year. Completed, the hut is a strange and makeshift dwelling – but when it rains I am dry, so what care I for appearances? In addition I have made a number of small improvements for my convenience, and confess myself well pleased with my own ingenuity. About the outside I have dug a drain, to funnel the water to the clearing's edge, so that in heavy rains the ground of my hut shall not become a swamp. Atop the doorway I have set a strong bough and hung from it two heavy curtains of goat hide, with a peg mounted at each side, behind which the curtains may be hooked in fine weather. In cold or rain, the two panels of hide can be closed, overlapping almost entirely, and hang so long that I may set a pair of rocks atop the hides on the ground, to hold the door firmly shut.

Even with both curtains held open, the Reverend Vicarious Cronch will not venture inside – he merely sticks his mournful face through the door and peers around.

'I never thought a goat would be so excessively polite,' I say, on my first evening in the new hut. 'Come in, so I can close the door.' With the goat hide door open, the insects flock to the light of my taper.

'Certainly not,' he says.

'You cannot fear me?'

'Of course not, sir.' His eyes roll as he surveys the ceiling, and his short, upright tail switches jumpily from side to side. 'But even in good company, a goat does not care to be enclosed, above all and around.'

'You would never make a sailor,' I say, 'for below deck is sometimes more like a coffin than anything else.'

'Few goats make good sailors,' he says solemnly.

Although the goat will not be persuaded to come in, to my great surprise Sleek slips inside the very first evening, stalks once about the hut as if inspecting it, and leaps onto the hammock, a thing she never once deigned to do in my old tent.

When she is still there in the morning, warm at my feet, I ask her: 'Were you not most scathing about Pickle, for letting me make of her a pet?' Indeed, Sleek has remained steadfastly aloof to Pickle and her offspring; when Pickle draws close to her, Sleek will turn her back, as though Pickle were not even there.

'I am no pet.'

Rising, I cross the tent and open the door. The goat is already grazing just outside.

'You slept on my bed,' I say to her. 'You take the blood I give you.'

'I take your offerings.'

The goat chortles. 'She has you there, sir. By that same token, a god is a pet.'

'I did not think to hear a reverend jest thus,' I say.

'We goats are a surprising folk.'

'Anyway,' I turn back to the cat, 'you also bring me offerings. What about the dead rats you bring me?'

'It pleases me to hunt them.'

'But why give them to me?' I sit again on the hammock, close to her.

'Blood for blood. It is a payment.' She rolls over, stretching her front leg so that it rests on my arm. 'I owe nothing.' Her paw on my forearm is soft, but as she stretches further, the claws protrude, like so many blades. They rest thus a moment, barely touching my skin, before she draws back her leg.

I consider myself warned.

I know better than to raise again the question of pets and masters with the cat, even though she has taken to creeping into my hammock most nights, after midnight, and sleeping there late of a morning. The Reverend Vicarious Cronch, however, is very happy to discuss the subject – he has a tremendous appetite for discussions of every kind, most particularly those tending towards the philosophical.

'You consider yourselves our master,' he says. 'Yet does not Ecclesiastes say: *a man hath no preeminence above a beast*?'

'Your knowledge of the Bible is better even than mine, and few men can have been forced to study it as closely as I.'

'Did I not tell you I am called Reverend?'

'Even so,' I say. 'Your knowledge of the Bible is prodigious.'

'Ah,' he says. 'I once ate an entire Bible. It was left unattended in the camp of some sailors who came ashore.'

I see that he is not jesting. 'Is that not sacrilegious? For a minister, no less?'

'Indeed not. What a goat values most greatly, he eats. Why should the Bible be any different?'

'Which ship's company was it?'

'It was many years ago.'

I raise an eyebrow. 'You say you cannot recall the ship,' I say, 'yet you recite your scriptures very smartly.'

'Thank you,' he says. 'But we digress — for still you have not told me what you make of Ecclesiastes. *No preeminence above a beast*, it says, perfectly clear.'

'You may bring me your Ecclesiastes, but what of Genesis?' I rifle through the charcoal-smudged pages for the passage. 'Here. God himself says: *Let us make man in our image, after our likeness: and let them have dominion over the fish of the sea, and over the fowl of the air, and over the cattle, and over all the earth, and over every creeping thing that creepeth upon the earth.*'

'*Every creeping thing that creepeth upon the earth?* And can you claim such a dominion, when you were telling me only yesterday how sorely you are plagued by insects?'

Here I must concede a point, for even though the cats keep the rats at bay, the insects still swarm about me at night. 'Not dominion, perhaps, but that does not mean I am not their superior—'

'You stray there into a different debate entirely, touching on the interpretation of *dominion*…'

And he can continue thus for many hours at a time. A younger Alexander Selkirk would have had little patience for such philosophising — or for Bible talk of any kind. But a younger Alexander Selkirk had not the luxury or the burden of so much time.

I have cause the very next day to recall the Bible's phrase, *every creeping thing that creepeth upon the earth*, for at dawn I am wakened by a dreadful scraping within my own head. An ant or some other tiny insect has crawled into my ear. It does not cease its moving, and whatever manner of creature it is, I know that it must have a great many legs for I feel all of them scuttling in there. I have never suffered from seasickness but this must be something similar: a giddy, reeling sickness, and all of me out of balance, so that when I leap from my hammock I stumble and stagger about the hut. I jab my smallest finger into my ear, to no avail. I tip my head to the side and thump at the opposite ear, hoping to dislodge the creature; when that does not work, I take my mug and tip water down my ear in hopes of flooding the insect out. This only increases its thrashing, and I cannot help yelping.

The Reverend Vicarious Cronch comes upon me just as I am kneeling outside my tent and setting about probing my ear with a twig, to try to crush the insect.

'Stop,' he says. 'You will do yourself violence – or deafen yourself. Be calm, for the ant will die soon enough.'

'I cannot bear to feel it moving in there.'

'Patience,' he says. 'An ant's life is not so very long, but you shall be deaf forever.' He shakes his head. 'A goat would never be so careless with his ears.'

One hand still pressed to my ear, I take several slow breaths to calm myself. I look at his ears – it is true that a goat's ears are wondrous things. They can turn about to trace a noise, even while the head remains still. And even on a goat such as Cronch, whose fur in the main is as wiry as the bristles of a scullery brush, the short hair covering his ears is marvellous soft. His ears express a tremendous variety of feelings – if he is curious, they tighten up like unripe tulips; if he is vexed, they draw backwards as though he is facing a strong wind. And though he has never complained of it, I feel more than ever how I wronged him by marking his ear with my knife, when I resolved to hunt him and make him one of my conquests.

I pass two days of misery while the ant fails to find its way out of my ear. The tiniest creature becomes prodigious large when it is within your head, and even a silent creature such as an ant becomes loud indeed. I am trying to work on my latest project – a low wall, enclosing my fire on three sides, to shield it from the worst of the southerly winds and rain. But the ant's jerking startles me each time, and often I fumble and set the rocks clattering out of place.

When I wake on the third day and find the thrashing and scraping in my ear has ceased, I could weep with relief. I lie in my hammock and relish the silence. Pickle has tucked herself right into my belly, where it is warmest, and Sleek lies on my feet.

'It is gone,' I say to Sleek. 'The ant.'

She stretches and strolls to the head of my hammock, where she sniffs, most deliberate, at my ear.

'Not gone,' she says.

'It has,' I say. 'It must have found its way out.'

'Dead,' she says. 'And it has made your ear its grave.'

'How can you be so sure?'

'A cat's nose is always sure.' She jumps lightly to the ground.

I shake my head, as though that will dislodge the dead ant at last. It is mighty discomfiting to think of it still in there. But even Sleek's unhelpful words cannot quell my jovial mood, and when I step from the hut and find the goat awaiting me, I say, 'Sir, I have in mind to make amends to you, for a wrong I did you some months ago.'

He turns his head, the better to watch me, and in my magnanimous mood, I think what a very fine beard he has: longer by far than mine.

'Am I to gather that you are no longer troubled by the ant in your ear?'

'Dead,' says the cat. She begins her morning vomiting, a protracted and noisy process that results in a narrow stream of frothy spit and a nugget of chewed grass. I have often scolded her for this unseemly habit, but today I ignore her, focusing instead on the Reverend Vicarious Cronch.

'I owe you an apology, sir – for the slitting of your ear.'

He is watching me gravely as he chews. 'There are thorns on this island that have done worse damage than your little knife.'

'I am glad it did not pain you.'

'It bled,' says the cat, sudden and loud. 'What amends can you make for that?'

The goat acknowledges her with a nod. 'Certainly it pained me,' he says. 'But a goat who has been hunted, and felt a man's knife held close to his neck, will count himself lucky to emerge with merely a nicked ear.'

'So you do not mind?'

His beard swishes from side to side with each chew. 'I did not say that. I am saying this: a notched ear does not diminish me. As to whether it diminishes you, you shall be the judge of that.'

'It is but a sport.' My voice is a little louder than I intended. When a man has lowered himself to apologise to a goat, he does not expect to be met with censure.

'Ah, yes. And where a man has sport, someone must bleed – is that not so?'

'I must pass the time somehow.'

'You are much concerned with time,' the cat says, stretching.

How should I not be? Time – the terrible gift of this island.

'A man must always be doing,' says the goat, 'as though time will not pass if you do not wedge your knife into it and heave it forward like some mechanism. Time will pass regardless, if you let it – you do not need to take up your knife, nor make your mark.'

'Enough with your preaching,' I snap. I have given him my apology, and still he lectures me. Whatever I looked for in a companion, it was not this. 'I did not think goats were so very apt to philosophise.'

'I am a very particular goat.'

'And I have said I am sorry for the slitting of your ear. As for the other goats: it is a project – a task to occupy me. I am a working man – not some idle gentleman, accustomed to having no occupation.'

'You wish to catch them all? Is each goat on this island to bear your mark?'

'Indeed. And they shall, by the end.'

'The end?' echoes the cat.

The Reverend Vicarious Cronch looks at me. 'Of what shall it be the end, Mister Selkirk? And what then?'

17

For several days after this uncomfortable discussion, I hunt neither for meat nor for sport, having devised a different project to occupy my time. I have finished the wall that shields my fire, and being so mightily satisfied with my new hut, I resolve to build a second one. I shall have the first hut for my living quarters, and another as a kind of workshop, to give me shelter while I set about my various tasks, such as preparing food and hides. And after my recent experience with the ant in my ear, it is my hope that if I keep the smelly work of cooking and tanning to a second shelter, the insects shall be less attracted to my sleeping hut.

I set about building the second hut on the southern edge of my clearing. The construction ought to be faster this time, for I have attended well to my previous mistakes – and yet I am also become more ambitious, seeking to make this hut both larger and more comfortable. I make two windows, and into the southern wall I build a number of shelves. They are not particularly sturdy, as is quickly proved when one of Pickle's kittens jumps onto one, bringing down the whole shelf, complete with a stack of wooden bowls. But they allow me to keep my few possessions in a more orderly fashion, and even to put about the place a few choice trinkets that I have gathered over my time here. A half-shell, big enough to serve as a saucer but which I keep largely because of the very fetching silver sheen of its inside, the whole of it polished like a pearl. A piece of old broken glass spat out by the sea, and now the precise colour of smoke. A hollow reed, which I have a fancy to fashion into a whistle or flute.

'Have you an ear for music?' asks the goat, seeing me whittling at the reed.

'Hardly,' I say, wincing to think of my heedless drunken singing when I'd attempted to brew liquor. 'I have a poor voice – but still better than the screaming of a goat, I'll warrant.' For goats, when distressed, have an ungodly shriek, like a drunkard falling and landing on a bagpipe. When they are amorous, too, they grunt most alarmingly.

'Ah,' says the goat. 'I understand that the music of goats would not be to everyone's taste.'

At this I laugh very loud, and the goat, that stouthearted fellow, is not offended.

I gesture at Sleek, who is sleeping in a patch of sunlight. 'The one thing to be said for the music of goats is that it's better than that of the cats, and their night-time shrieking.' In the dark, the island's cats sometimes caterwaul in such a way that I know that they must be either fucking or fighting – though they do both of these things so fiercely that from the sound alone it is impossible to tell which you are hearing.

Not being satisfied merely with building my new shelters, I set about furnishing them. For more than a year I have contented myself with a stump for a seat. I set out now to carve a proper chair. It is not a chair that any carpenter would recognise, for in truth it is just a larger stump, wide enough that I can hollow out a seat and still leave a back, and armrests furthermore. When I lower myself into it for the first time, I find myself weeping. What is it about a simple chair – a clumsy one, at that – that can reduce me to such sobs? It is not even particularly comfortable, its unsanded wood snagging the skin of my wrists where they rest upon it. Rather it is the feeling the chair summons – a sensation my body had forgot, and now recognises. If I close my eyes, I might almost be at my parents' table once more, or (better) at a dockside inn, a mug of good ale in my hand on the armrest. Thus my ugly chair I account more precious than any throne, for when I sit in it, I am once more a man. And it inspires me to build a table, having thus far merely hunched over my sea chest to eat or read.

To make a table is no small undertaking, for it needs planks, and here I feel most sorely the lack of a saw. The closest that I can arrive at is to hack out coarse planks with my makeshift axe, and then to scrape at the surface with the same broken barrel hoop that I use for shaving tree roots into my tanning liquor. What a boon those two broken barrels have been, and what a different life I should have led on this island had they not been carelessly left here. I wonder if the papists, with their many strange saints, have a saint of broken barrels, and other discarded things. I would worship such a saint gladly.

The table that I arrive at is an ungainly thing, its top so uneven that I must place my mug with care to be sure it will not tip. Yet it is such a tremendous improvement on my previous table that I feel a veritable gentleman as I dine at it, able to eat without hunching over, and then to lean back in my chair and take my ease.

Such are the meagre riches I find here. There is a small beach to the north all pebbled with stones, and when I walk there the stones set up a wondrous great clanking underfoot and I might almost imagine I am walking on a tremendous hoard of coins. 'Oh yes,' I say to myself, 'I am a rich man.' I look down at my ragged clothes. 'Rich indeed, my fine Mister Selkirk, esquire,' and I laugh like a man quite given over to madness.

———

While the cat and the goat are strange companions, they are companions nevertheless, and after such a long time in my own company, you may imagine with what delight I speak to them. The cat's conversation is savage and halting, but the goat takes enormous pleasure in discoursing at length, and thus we pass many hours, as I labour.

It should not be a surprise, given his name, that the goat takes a particular interest in theology. Before the island, this subject held no interest for me, but having now become, by sheer necessity, something of a scholar of the Bible, I am able to keep up when his conversation takes a theological turn.

'And far be it from me to criticise the Bible,' he says to me as I chop a felled tree, 'but I will say only that goats are sadly lacking in it, and that I should like to see them figure more in many of the stories.'

'Forgive me,' I say, 'but would the stories be improved by the addition of goats?'

'A goat improves most things,' he says gravely.

'As I recall, Leviticus is full of goats. What about the scapegoat, sent off into the wilderness with the burden of men's sins?'

'Ah,' he says, looking at me very knowingly. 'You feel a certain affinity with the scapegoat, do you not? Is that why it came so quickly to mind?'

'I know what it is to be abandoned in the wilderness.'

'*Abandoned*? I do not recall that the story says any such thing.'

I set down my stone axe blade, fetch the Bible from its shelf, and hasten to find the passage. 'Here: *And Aaron shall lay both his hands upon the head of the live goat, and confess over him all the iniquities of the children of Israel, and all their transgressions in all their sins, putting them upon the head of the goat, and shall send him away by the hand of a fit man into the wilderness: And the goat shall bear upon him all their iniquities unto a land not inhabited: and he shall let go the goat in the wilderness.*'

The Reverend Vicarious Cronch flares his nostrils. 'See? There is nothing whatsoever about abandonment. The goat is released.'

'Released, perhaps – but into the wilderness. What is that if not a punishment? If not a death sentence?'

'Hardly.'

'A goat would say so. To a man, it is quite a different thing.'

'If you are a scapegoat, Mister Selkirk, whose sins do you bear?'

'Stradling,' I say. 'My fool of a captain. Dampier, too. I have ever been made to suffer for the stupidity and bad decisions of others.'

'You are very quick to see yourself in the stories, when it suits you.' He chews, his ears swinging side to side like a pendulum. 'At any rate, the scapegoat is not my favourite goat in the Bible.'

'You have another?'

'I am quite taken with the passage in Proverbs: *There be three things which go well, yea, four are comely in going: A lion which is strongest among beasts, and turneth not away for any; A greyhound; an he goat also; and a king, against whom there is no rising up.* Is that not a fine thing?' he says. '*Comely in going – an he goat.*' And he takes a little promenade, the length of my clearing and back again, as if to prove once more the great dignity of goats.

His strutting annoys me. 'Does not Matthew state that the son of heaven shall divide all men, *as a shepherd divideth his sheep from the goats*?' It takes me some little time to find the passage. 'Listen – this is what he says to all those he likens to goats: *Depart from me, ye cursed, into everlasting fire, prepared for the devil and his angels.*' And I laugh, and nudge him in his side, where the hair of his belly is wispy and long. 'How do you like that?'

He gives a short snort. 'A man who cannot recognise an allegory has no business reading the Bible at all.' He shakes his head mournfully. 'This pernicious association with wickedness has long grieved me. I blame our horns – it is a grave misfortune to goats, that our handsome and useful horns happen to match men's image of a devil.' He has a tendency to loquacity, I have noticed – every sentence might be a sermon.

'You must allow that a goat's eyes are strange, too.'

'They are perfectly suited for seeing – whatever wicked complexion men have put on them, which has nothing to do with us.'

'But you will admit that goats most often figure in the Bible as some kind of sacrifice?'

He ignores the question. 'And what becomes of him, the scapegoat? Where does he go, laden as he is with all the sins of men?'

'The Bible never says – for in truth it's not about him. It's about the men, and freeing themselves from sin.'

'Aye,' he says. 'Every story of men is about men.' And then he laughs, which he does not do often, being of a rather magisterial bent. And if you had ever heard a goat laugh, you would count it a blessing that it does not happen often, for it is prodigious loud, a great eruption of hawing, like a donkey very much startled.

I think of the scapegoat that afternoon, when I climb to my lookout. Did he also yearn to be returned from his exile? How did he shoulder his burden of sins, and was it heavy upon him? I know that weight, the dread heft of it – for a man does not end up on this island without his own cargo of sins.

I search the vacant sea. I scream, and scream again, at the ships that do not appear. Alone in the wilderness, did the scapegoat, too, rage against the waste of his life, the hours and days all squandered upon aloneness?

In late summer the pimento trees begin to drop their berries. Last year I tasted them, but quickly stopped, for they are both tart and of an unpleasant texture, and being so very small, can scarce make a meal. This year, however, remembering that some men call the pimento tree the *allspice* tree, I resolve to see if it may indeed be made to yield some kind of spice. I take a notion to dry some of the berries and crush them to a powder. Gathering a quantity of berries, I spread them on a rock in the sun. My first attempt is wasted – after several hot, dry days I go to fetch the berries and find them gone, taken by goats or rats, and I curse all goats, all rats, and the island for good measure. Next time I choose a flat, high rock, more remote and a long way from any tempting foliage, and when I retrieve them four days later the berries are still there, shrivelled and hard. These I grind carefully with a stone, and use the resulting powder to season a joint of goat.

A miracle – a small miracle of the mouth! I will allow that any variation from the usual blandness would be welcome, but this is a wonder, for the spice gives the whole joint a new flavour entirely, at once peppery and nutty. An alchemist turning lead to gold could not be more delighted than I, and I close my eyes and savour each bite.

'You have the air of a man well pleased with yourself,' says the goat.

I proffer him my plate. 'You are most welcome to taste it – but I think you would not care to eat the flesh of your brethren.'

'You are correct,' he says, somewhat censoriously, drawing back his head from the meat.

'And what about you?' I ask, through a new mouthful. 'Do you never tire of eating the same bland things?'

He shakes his head briskly, setting his ears swinging. 'I do not find them bland. A leaf tastes of leaf, a turnip tastes of turnip – and thus am I satisfied. It is a quality particular to men, to always wish things to be other than what they are.'

'You are in luck,' I say, 'for today I am in too good a humour to be irritated even by your sermonising.'

Over the weeks to come, I find that crushing the leaves of the pimento tree has a similar seasoning effect, though less potent. And I make a great effort to gather and dry as many berries as I can while they are in season, so that I may have a store of them to see me through the winter months, when the sun's rays are too feeble to dry up the rock pools and no salt is to be had.

The more I read, the more I note that the Bible is full of stories of repentance. Saul repents his sins; the prodigal son does the same; even King David has sinned and must repent. In Psalms he begs for forgiveness, saying, 'Deliver me from bloodguiltiness.' I turn that word over in my mind: *bloodguiltiness*. What a fitting word it is – what heft it has, and weight. Not just guilt, which Moncrieff's sermons in the kirk were ever harping on about. But *bloodguiltiness*. It is a graver thing, the word soaked in blood until it takes on the sharp, tannin stench of it.

'But these fellows in the Bible,' I say to the goat. 'They repent their vices so neatly. They get a sign – a light from the sky; the voice of God – and they are forever changed.'

'Their suffering is not necessarily ended,' he says. 'David repents his theft of another man's wife – but still his misbegotten son dies.'

'Yes,' I concede. 'But he remains virtuous nonetheless.' They step out of their vices as easy as slipping off a jacket. I have not found my own vices so obliging – they are more barnacle-like. Oh those limpet sins are not so easy to prise away.

I return to Psalm 51, in which King David repents and begs forgiveness. When I am done with it, it is more black than white.

Hide thy ████████████████████████
████████ clean heart ████████████████████████ within me.
████ Cast me not away ████████████████████████
██
████████ I teach ████████████████
████████████ bloodguiltiness, ████████████ my
tongue shall sing ████ of ████████████████████
████████████████████████████████████
████████████ sacrifice; ████████████████ burnt
████████
████████████████████████████████ heart, ████████
██
████████████████████████████████████
offering and ████████████ offering████

'You are writing?' asks the goat. Poking his head in the door, he finds me bent over my Bible, my fingers blackened by charcoal.

I shake my head.

'What, then?' When he peers into my hut thus, the two flaps of the curtain frame his face, like a nun's wimple.

I hesitate to tell him the truth of my work at the Bible – what if he thinks it a form of sacrilege? He is in some ways strict when it comes to blasphemy, and in other ways surprisingly lax, viz. the eating of Bibles &c. My charcoal on the Bible page is a bold thing, after all – the Reverend William Moncrieff would disapprove heartily, and I am far from certain that the goat will be more sympathetic.

'Not writing,' I say. 'The opposite, really – a subtraction. From the words on the page I cross out those that I don't need.'

'Need for what?' asks the cat, from her place on my hammock. Pickle is relegated to the foot of the hammock these days, for Sleek has claimed the head for her own.

'Need, because they seem to capture something of the day – or of my life. Because I recognise them. Because they seem true, I suppose.'

I read him today's fragment, as he works his jaw.

'And in this one, where you say *offering and offering*. What are you offering?'

'Does it matter? For it amounts to nothing – that is the whole point of the poem.'

He nods. 'And would you consider these poems themselves a form of offering? A form of prayer?'

Before I can answer, the cat speaks, licking her lips. 'Bloodguiltiness.'

I look down at my hands. I suspect the cat of knowing too much – of knowing why I am so concerned with the question of repentance. Sometimes, when she stares so very bold at me, I could swear she sees through my silence to the many shames of my past.

Sleek saunters into the clearing, when I am hard at work on lighting a fire.

'Between your cock and your fire stick,' she says, 'you are forever rubbing at something.'

I ignore her. I am already in an ill humour, for it is through my own carelessness that the fire was allowed to go out. The cat's sharp tongue does not help matters.

Would I call her my friend? Unlike the goat, she is abrupt and demanding. She is contrary, too. I was delighted the first time she deigned to jump up to my lap, but when she sits there she is wont to stretch her front paws out to knead my leg, and with every press there is a baring of claws, each one a tiny scimitar such as the barbary corsairs carry. When I call her by her name, she never comes; when I am occupied with some task, she takes it upon herself to weave between my legs, or to stretch out across the flattened hide I am working on. Even now, as I hunch over my work, she strolls backwards and forwards before me, stepping over my fire stick, and parading her little puckered arsehole in my face, no matter how many times I shoo her.

I should hesitate to describe Sleek as tame – and certainly I would never be fool enough to call her that within her hearing, for an outraged cat is a dangerous thing. Yet she comes to me daily, and when I cease scratching her behind her ears she will butt her head against my hand until I start again. Sometimes she will even do as she does now, and lie on her back to unfurl the great white flag of her belly and indicate that I should stroke her there. This I have learned is an enterprise fraught with risk, for she enjoys these scratches mightily until a time of her choosing, when she will briskly set to savaging me with both teeth and claws, and has several times drawn blood. She does this now, catching me sharply on the knuckle.

'Why do you do this?' I ask, sucking clean the scratch. 'You demand to be stroked thus, and then you turn on me so sudden.'

'Cats are not known for constancy,' she says, unperturbed.

The goat nods sagely. 'A lady cat in particular is mighty changeable.'

'You are cruel,' I say to Sleek. 'And not only to me. What about the lizards that you torment?' Often, I've watched her taunt the little lizards that she catches, taking off their legs and tossing them about, or batting them with her paws. I begin to fancy she catches them only for sport, for she is growing plump on the blood and meat that I give her.

'I like the taste,' she says.

'You don't even eat them.'

She raises her chin and looks me straight in the eyes. 'I like the taste of their fear.'

'There you have it,' I say. 'You are cruel. You torture those creatures. You do not even eat them.'

'You wish me to kill the rats, though I have food enough without eating them. Is that cruel? Or is it cruel only when it does not serve you?'

'You take pleasure in the torment, though. You make of it a game.'

'And do you not take your knife and slit the ears of goats, for sport?'

Before I can respond, she stalks from the clearing.

Yet tonight, as with most nights, she slips under the curtain of my tent door, seeks out the spot between my chin and my chest and curls there very neat, and purrs, a tremendous rumbling noise that I like above all things: her faithless body betraying her.

'You are a riddle,' I tell her in the morning.

'No riddle,' she says. 'I am myself.'

'No,' I insist. 'You are a riddle indeed, for you are always changing.'

'You will not solve me,' she says. She arches her back and looks at me. 'If you wish for a riddle, I will give you one.' She jumps down from the hammock and takes a few steps towards the door. From behind, the curve of her tail, swayed to one side, and the spot of her arsehole just below it, are the very image of a mark of interrogation. Her whole body a question.

'Riddle me this,' she says, 'since you are so wise.'

I wait.

'Mister Selkirk. What is a church for one man alone? And who speaks but is never heard?'

The hide curtain sways as she walks through it, and is gone. I do not see her again until that evening, when she reappears, a dead rat in her mouth. She drops it at my feet. Its open mouth leaks blood onto the dirt floor of my hut.

'Can you not leave that outside?'

'Fresh blood,' she says.

I snatch up the rat by its tail, the hot dead weight of it, and stride outside to hurl it towards the trees. Today I will not argue with her, for I am impatient to show off my reply to her riddle.

Back inside, I squat before her. 'You had me there, for quite some time. All morning I turned it over in my mind – *a church for one man alone*. I was thinking: *pulpit; chancel; vestry*. Then I thought I had it, for in the old language *kill* can mean either a church or a monk's cell. But then I realised I was trying too hard, for it is right there: *Sel* – alone, sole. And *kirk*, of course.'

I sit back, hands on my knees. 'Yet even then I am not certain that I know the whole of it, for I cannot see how it fits with the second part – *who speaks but is not heard*? But as to the first part, I am sure I have solved it: *Selkirk*.'

She begins to lick her feet.

'Well?' I say. 'I have it, do I not? Will you not tell me? And what about the second part?'

'I promised you a riddle,' she says. 'As to answers, I made no promises.'

18

'Still you have not told me the story of how a man such as you finds himself here,' says the goat. He has a mighty curiosity, and is full of questions. He is as hungry for answers as he is for everything else.

'I thought you and the cat cared nothing for the past. Is it not the two of you who refuse to tell me anything of the other castaways this island has seen?'

'I cannot speak for the cat. As for myself, it is true that I am not concerned with the past. Yet a past that is unaccounted for is not the past at all. There has not yet been a reckoning.'

'And what makes you so certain that my past is not accounted for?'

'You are here,' the cat says. She is curled with her back to me and her eyes closed, and I had thought she was sleeping.

'She is right,' the goat says. 'You are here, after all. This is not the kind of misfortune that befalls a man with a well-ordered life.'

I cannot dispute this – the goat and the cat have been the closest witnesses to the catastrophe that is my life, and therefore can have no illusions about its nature.

'It is a long story,' I say. 'And an unwieldy one. To tell it in its entirety would take a great deal of time.'

'Time?' says Sleek. 'Mister Selkirk. You have nothing but time.'

———

My past is not a story I wish to tell. But do not underestimate what a gratifying thing it is to have a listener as attentive as the Reverend

Vicarious Cronch. His huge mobile ears betray his keen interest, sweeping forward when I recount a tense moment, or drooping with melancholy when my tale grows sad. He leans in as I speak, and takes great huffing breaths, his boxy ribs flaring. His entire body is a mechanism for listening.

As for the cat: if she is interested, she gives no sign. Yet I note that she stays near as I talk, and though her eyes are often closed, the telltale twitching of her whiskers makes me suspect she is listening nonetheless.

Over the days that follow I tell them of my childhood, and my plague of brothers, my doting mother and my censorious father. And I tell them of Effie, whom I had left behind without so much as a farewell.

———

Having fled from Nether Largo and the shame and chaos of my conduct in the kirk, none is more surprised than I to find that I make a good sailor. I am but fifteen, which makes me older than many lads learning the trade – but securing a position as a ship's boy aboard a merchant ship, I learn quickly. Having lived a rather disorderly life, I now find that I thrive in the strict routines of a ship and its work. And when a lad has any inclination towards intemperance, he could do no better than to go to sea, where the grog is rationed very regular, so that he is neither denied his daily tot, nor given any chance of drinking to excess. Ashore, I spend my new wages in taverns, and there I make up for the months of moderation that the sea imposes.

I have always been ready to argue, but even the most headstrong and contrary lad learns fast that there is no arguing with the sea. Thus I get on with my work, and do it well. And the better I do, the more certain I am that my father's refusal to let me go to sea is proved wrong. Far from repenting my defiant conduct, I am much encouraged, and when I am between voyages and in a tavern, I sometimes raise a toast to my father, and drink deep and bitter.

I am accounted neither a good nor a sober man, but after several years at sea, I begin to be accounted a good navigator. This I credit not only to my natural inclination to geography and numbers, but largely to a man by the name of Cooley, ship's master on a privateering frigate that I join in Bristol. Cooley has a mate and second mate under him, and when one of them leaves on the deck a pamphlet, I open it. It is an astronomical treatise, *On the Uses of the Astrolabe in Navigation*. I squat right there and open it, and am much absorbed, when a shadow falls across the page, and I look up to see Cooley. He is a man of stern countenance, and his thick grey whiskers look even more impressive from below.

I stand at once. 'Abercrombie left it here, sir. I was going to take it back to him, I swear.' Thievery is not tolerated aboard, where trust between men is what keeps the ship afloat.

'You have been reading it for some time, Mister Selcraig.'

'I was curious, sir. I swear I meant to return it.'

'And what do you make of it?'

'I think all sailors could benefit by making a study of it.'

'Then the captain would have a mutiny on his hands,' said Cooley. 'For half the men aboard cannot read, and the other half would find it dull work.'

'They would find it even more dull to be run aground, for want of understanding of navigation,' I say, hastily adding, 'Sir.'

'And you, Selcraig – you have an interest in navigation?'

'I like numbers, sir.'

'And should you like to try an astrolabe?'

This is how it begins – and Cooley is a good teacher, unhurried and steady. For my first few weeks under his tutelage I am waiting for him to realise the truth of what I am: a hapless lad, lurching from one disaster to the next, and condemned by both the kirk session and his own family for a fool and a bad fellow. Yet while Cooley is not a man for praise, he seems satisfied with my work. He sets me tasks, and I accomplish them, and he nods briskly and sets me another. In this manner we get along very well, and I make good progress.

Cooley puts me in the way of books, lending me volume after volume. These are not books of the bawdy sort usually passed about below deck, but real books of navigation, science and philosophy. I read them all, and understand most. My crewmates begin to jest that my way of speaking is become prosy and formal. The ship's carpenter tries to make sport of me for aping a gentleman. I beat him soundly, but in truth I am not displeased. I think of my brothers and wish they could see what I am become: an educated man, rising in his profession.

Under Cooley's careful attention I am able to make another version of myself, entirely new. This Alexander Selcraig is not a hothead, nor a drunk. This Alexander Selcraig is somewhat studious, and has an aptitude for navigation. He is a man who does not need to be told a thing twice – for I discover in myself a prodigious memory, so that having read an almanack once, I need not consult it as often as others might, the larger part of it committed to my memory. And if I am still stubborn, stubbornness is not such a bad trait in a navigator, who must be certain of fixed points.

Things continue thus until one night when we approach Cape Wrath, and Cooley says, 'You may plot our course around the cape, Mister Selcraig. I am for my bed.'

'Sir,' I say at once, 'I am bound to sink us.'

'I shouldn't think so,' he says. It is not precisely praise – certainly not the effusions that used to pour from my mother – yet he says it without hesitation, and it keeps me warm all that long cold night, as the north wind cuts across the forecastle and we round the cape.

When the second mate takes a fever and dies, I have his post, and when his belongings are auctioned on deck, I buy his pamphlets and almanack too. And in this way I become a fair navigator. It is rare to rise to second mate at barely eighteen – but the captain will not countermand Cooley's recommendation. I am reckoned by the men rather serious when on duty – but a ship's master and his mates have a serious role. The captain may determine our destination, but it is we who determine our course – and if we err, every man aboard could be lost.

I exchange no letters with my family, the circumstances of my going away being both hurried and shameful. I confess that I think of them rarely, and of Nether Largo not at all. I am young, and I have all of the sea to occupy me.

———

'And did you not miss Effie?' asks the goat. I begin to suspect him of being a sentimental fellow.

'I did,' I say, and it is the truth. 'But I must tell you that a mass of men, crammed together on a ship, does not incline to faithful talk, nor faithful thoughts.' There is much loose talk below decks, in the way of such things.

There may be no women aboard, but they are not put out of mind, for sailors talk ceaselessly of women. We swap stories of our conquests, and if few of the stories are true, it matters little. Above all, we sailors speak of cunny. All the particular things that make up an actual woman fade then, when you are far enough from port, and the men's stories summon one imaginary woman, all cunny and tits, until she is nothing but a warm wet hole, and perhaps that is the ideal of all sailors, or even of all men. This leads to naught but disappointment for, ashore, we find that the whores have grating voices, or faces much marked by pox scars – and thus can never live up to the great comforting wetness of the woman we used to conjure with our shipboard talk.

This disappointment does not stop us, when ashore, from making free with the portside whores, and with any other women who will have us. Nether Largo was a mighty small place, and the kirk loomed large within it – what a delight to discover that the world is so full of other places, bustling and huge, and that a man may go many months without giving a thought to the kirk, or even to God. The first time I go to bed with another woman, I am unsure and think very much of Effie – the soft folds of her armpits; her little bare toes like a row of naked hatchlings. But I am deep in drink, having just spent nine weeks aboard, and I find myself well able to forget Effie once my own pleasure takes hold of me, tremendous urgent. After that, it becomes a habit – we take women at each port as though they are a reward due to us for our months at sea. Oh they are willing enough and we pay them well, or if they are not whores we pay them all the same with the purchase of drinks and a fine arsenal of flattery. And while my shipmates still sometimes tease me for speaking too fine, or fancying myself a gentleman, I will say that my loquacity does me no harm at all with women. And when my life is all drudgery and dry ship's biscuit, I come to shore aching for softness, and take it wherever I can. Thus after a while I think little at all of Effie, and I have got myself a hearty reputation as a beard-splitter. When the men say, 'If you have a sweetheart at home, you sly dog, you will bring her home a pretty parcel of pox as a gift from all your whores,' I find I can laugh along with them.

I say, 'My mam always told me I was blessed as the seventh son – perhaps my true blessing is that I haven't caught the pox yet, for all my efforts,' and we drink, and drink again.

By 1698 I have been three years a sailor. Both Cooley and I are between ships, ashore in a Leith turned grim and ragged. The long war has provided work for the navy and for privateers, but the rest of the country has grown bony – and year after year of unseasonal cold and failed harvests have stripped what little remained. When country folk starve they flock to the city, but there is nothing for them in Edinburgh or Leith, except that they may die in company with others, I suppose. Greyfriars Kirkyard is become a kind of encampment for families fleeing the countryside. Around Leith harbour, the poor are grown poorer, and the thin are dead. When a beggar dies his corner is quickly claimed by another, sometimes so quickly that the body of the late incumbent is still to be seen, stripped even of their meagre clothes, for when people have nothing else, even rags become treasures.

'It is worse in the north,' says Cooley. 'My brother in Fraserburgh wrote that people are eating nettles and grass, and rancid meat.'

At this time there are a great many bills posted in the taverns and coffee-houses and on walls all about town, announcing the grand ambitions of a new expedition. Just as the English have profited by their East India Company, now we Scots shall have our own: *The Company of Scotland Trading to Africa and the Indies.* Cooley takes the post of ship's master on one of the fleet, and joining him seems too good an opportunity to miss, promising not only a post as his second mate, but also prodigious riches at the colony that shall be established. And I, having squandered my old life at Nether Largo, am particularly eager at this promise of a life entirely new. Of course nothing can be told of where the expedition shall settle, for fear that the Spanish or the English will rush to beat us there – and thus the scheme is spoken of always in terms of distant promise and future glory. Just as at sea we used to summon a fantastical and ideal woman, now we summon this imagined colony for ourselves: a verdant and pleasant land, there for the taking. And it is galling indeed to hear tales of how the savages in such places lead an easy life, while in Scotland we cannot get free of the famine.

The English withdrew their support, sorely threatened by what the project will mean for their own trade. This forced the Scottish people to raise the funds themselves, through a subscription – such is the national fervour for this scheme, even now that famine stalks the streets like a hangman. And while I cannot pretend to be abreast of international affairs, and of the many slights borne by my people from the English, I have enough older brothers to feel very ardently what it is to be always put upon, always imposed upon and neglected. So, if it is time for we Scots to forge our own empire, I for one am eager to be a part of it.

Cooley and I are to sail on the *Caledonia*, under Captain Drummond. She is one of a fleet of five, the others being the *Dolphin*, the *Endeavour*, the *St Andrew* and the *Unicorn*. Before our fleet can leave Leith, several stowaways must be chased from the ships – I find one myself, a young fellow curled beneath a boat on the *Caledonia*'s deck, and so keen is he to stay aboard that it takes three of us to drag him out, and he holds fast to the gunwale, talking all the time about how willing he is to serve. We have to pry his fingers loose.

When the fleet sails at last, crowds gather at the shore to see us off, the women waving kerchiefs. All our way along the Fife coast the crowds come; from our ship we can make them out, and see their waving, but the wide water has stolen their voices.

What I mean to say by all of this is that we sail not as individuals nor merely as privateers, but as the hope of a desperate nation. I stand on the deck of the *Caledonia* as we set our course north, and I taste on the salt wind something I have not tasted before: pride. I am a man who knows his business, and whose business is the nation's. Like all men, I have wanted to make my mark on the world. Now, for the first time, I am set fair to do so.

The goat sighs. 'You men are very devils for wanting. You will sail the whole globe for it.'

'Is that not boldness?' I demand. 'Enterprise, and courage?'

'More, more,' says the cat. 'More and always more. A man's hunger is a terrible thing. Too big for his skin.'

19

Despite our grand aims, the start of our journey is inauspicious. We are still not permitted to know our ultimate destination, for fear of intrigues or sabotage. For now, we must make our way up the coast before we can turn south, and thence to Madeira – but angry gales spring up almost at once.

'They should have launched from the Clyde,' I say to Cooley. Even his habitual calm manner is strained, for the gale is a cruel one and we are much tossed about on the giant slabs of waves. The *Caledonia* is a goodly ship, but this sea has become an anvil and a hammer both, and we are pounded between them.

'A shameful thing it shall be, for all of Scotland, if we sink before we've even reached Orkney,' says Cooley.

'Not to mention the small matter of our deaths,' I say, but Cooley does not reply, being much preoccupied with his chart, and anyway not being a man disposed to sentiment.

But we do not sink, nor lose any of our fleet, and pass at last between Orkney and the Zetland, and bear south. Our supplies, it seems, have been badly stowed, and so we are quickly put on short rations. When we stop at Madeira we are so hungry that we gorge on unripe fruit, which makes us ill, until two men at a time must share the heads in a great chorus of shitting, and the rest of us shuffling in line as we wait our turn. A number of the officers sell their coats, their hats, their shoe buckles, to buy meat – I among them.

Captain Drummond upbraids me when I come back aboard with neither coat nor hat. 'What sort of a figure shall you cut, in our brave new colony, looking thus?'

I can only tell him, 'I shall not live to see any colony if I do not eat, sir.'

Which is to give you some impression of the general disorder and mutinous feeling that has already taken hold amongst us.

At last Captain Drummond is able to announce our destination: the Isthmus of Darien, joining the north and south of the Americas. William Paterson, who fancies himself the author of this entire scheme, comes aboard from the *Unicorn* to address us, and standing on the poop deck speaks stirringly of what awaits us. This stretch of land, he says, shall give us 'the doors of the seas and the keys of the universe'. The isthmus is the key to unlock all trade on the Pacific and the Atlantic, for who would not wish to avoid the long and treacherous journey around Cape Horn, if their cargo could instead be ferried across the narrow peninsula?

We make landfall by the second of November, our fleet having lost only seventy on the voyage, which may seem a great many, but to sailors is accounted a reasonable amount, particularly given how large a company we are, and that many aboard were settlers rather than seasoned sailors, and ill-suited to the travails of shipboard life.

Our settlement is at a place distant about ten leagues from the Gulf of Darien. North-west of us, along the isthmus, are the Spanish settlements, and it makes for uneasy sleep, to know our enemy is so close. But if they have not yet had the wisdom to seize this particular place, we shall not make the same mistake, and still Paterson speaks winningly of the gold that lies in the earth, waiting to give itself up to our picks; the merchants who shall come to us, supplicant, when we have control of the isthmus and have established the crossing. Our settlement is named New Caledonia, and the town we shall build on the bay's eastern side is to be New Edinburgh. Cooley takes out his charts and we inscribe the names there, and for a lad from Nether Largo it is something indeed to be a part of such a thing. We are naming the world; we are making the world anew.

And what manner of place is this New Caledonia? The whole of it seems to be either mountain or marsh, the air both hot and dank, and the forest so dense that it feels outright hostile, a veritable affront to movement. Seeing it on a map, it had been easy to wonder why the Spaniards themselves had not bothered to settle at this particular place; seeing it in person, we have our answer.

You might think it would be peaceful and quiet here, being so far removed from civilisation. But the noise of the jungle is tremendous, most particularly at night. The frogs do not so much croak as bellow; the flies and mosquitoes set up a prodigious noise, like the warming up of a great stringed orchestra. Even the rain is loud, falling as it does on the wide wet leaves and the mud, so that in the midst of the heaviest downpours you could well imagine it is not rain at all but the beating of war drums, the savages raising an army against us.

It rains, and does not cease from raining. At least we sailors have berths aboard the ships. The settlers, who must fare as well as they can ashore, are the first to sicken. The rain seeps into the hasty tents and the makeshift shelters, and the damp is everywhere. One of the settlers removes his boot to show me how his foot, from being always wet, has begun to rot, like spoiled leather. The climate is altogether unwholesome, leading to a contagious distemper that carries off many of those who survived the voyage.

We rapidly begin to see how ill-equipped we are for this endeavour. Set to work unloading our stores, we pry open a crate to find it packed tight with wigs. Young Buchan, a Glasgow lad whose waggery has survived even our grim voyage, puts one of the wigs atop his head, and takes a turn up and down the narrow walkway between the crates.

'Am I not a very fine gentleman?' he says. And we laugh, for no fine gentleman ever wore such sunken cheeks, nor such ragged clothes.

'All this finery,' I say, 'and nothing whatsoever in the way of fishing gear, which we're sorely in need of.'

I stare for a long time at that crate of wigs, startling white, to be worn in elegant drawing rooms that have not been built, or for promenading on roads that are for now just ruts of mud where we have dragged the logs for huts. These wigs are artefacts from a different world entirely – certainly they have nothing to do with us, nor with this place.

We have no more stirring speeches from Paterson, for his wife dies shortly after our arrival, and his child too, and henceforth he is diminished, moving like a man whose bones have been broken and badly set. Yet I can summon no particular sympathy for him, because dying has become a commonplace thing, and rations now are so tight that though few will admit it, the sick oblige us by their deaths, for it means fewer mouths to feed.

Despite these privations, some of the men remain cheery, the younger ones most of all – and they long to see action against the Spanish.

'I wish that we might have a visit from them,' says Buchan, 'for once we defeat them, we shall have a claim on their gold mines.' I myself am but eighteen years old, but I think you must be young indeed to look around this place, at the wasting men and the sloppily built shacks, and see a conquering army, sweeping all before it. Our food supply is woefully short; our supply of liquor was quickly exhausted, and the water that we must drink instead is unwholesome and hastens the flux and pox that spread through the whole of our company.

The Spaniards do not come – they need not, for this place is defeating us without their help. As for the natives, they are not hostile, but nor are they much interested in us – nor with the trinkets with which we were supposed to win them over. They are no great friends of the Spanish, who have taken some as slaves, and mistreated others – but far from inclining the Indians to be our allies, this has only given them a general suspicion of white men, and none of our leaders' entreaties can rid them of it. I suppose we ought to be glad not to have encountered violent attacks from the savages – but there is something particularly galling about how they look at us: a look of indifference, or of pity.

The Indians of these parts are of short stature, but strong, with skin very copper and hair very black. The men sport a gold plate through the gristle of the nose. It is said that they once went about naked, but these days they are clad. There is much muttering amongst the men, for we had been told stories of bare-breasted native beauties, and instead we have these women, short and stout, and dressed (if a little oddly) in the Spanish style, sometimes even with a veil over the face.

Paterson had packed a huge quantity of combs and the like with which he planned to make fortuitous trades with the Indians, much to our advantage. But the Indians show no desire for such trinkets. In fact, many of the Indians are so much bedecked in gold that they make our wooden combs look sad indeed. The natives assure us that they know several gold mines; the plates they wear in their noses are enough to persuade us of the truth of it. It is commonplace to see a group of Indians sporting a hundred ounces of gold between them. The Spaniards have several mines on the southern side of the peninsula, which they work with the benefit of many hundreds of negro slaves. But such wealth as this land affords, it will not yield to us – and we are left scraping in the mud merely to survive.

In late January, the natives do us one great service, for they bring us warning that the Spaniards are at last mustering an attack and have taken possession of a native village to our south. Montgomerie is to lead a force of a hundred soldiers, guided by some of the Indians; Captain Drummond announces that we sailors, too, are to see part of the action, for he is instructed to follow Montgomerie 'with sixty fit men'.

'Good luck to him, finding sixty of us who could be accounted fit,' says Buchan – for already hunger and illness have done their work on us. Nevertheless Drummond manages to gather his men, and I number amongst them, and Cooley too. I am glad – for a man cannot fight against his hunger nor against the creeping jungle, but he may at least take up his musket and fight the Spaniards.

Montgomerie's company left at dusk; we are several hours behind them. Moving through the jungle by day is next to impossible; by night it is a special hell, for each time something drags across my face I do not know whether it is a python or a mere vine; each time something sharp jabs at my side, it could be the bough of a tree or the barrel of a Spaniard's musket. My own weapon, slung over my back, contrives to tangle in the vines, and catches on trunks as I pass between them, jerking me backwards. We are slow, and though Drummond hisses that we must be silent, our progress seems tremendous loud, for we cannot help but stumble and crash, and there is a good deal of whispered cursing.

We reach the Indian village but instead of the enemy there are forty of Montgomerie's men, left by him to hold the village, which they found already abandoned. This gives us heart; the Spaniards, Montgomerie's men tell us, have retreated to a grove but a few miles off, and Drummond is confident that we can catch up with them. We have walked all night; it must be morning, but the jungle begrudges the dawn, allowing us only thin hints of light. Nevertheless we have no trouble finding the grove, for suddenly comes the sound of drums, so loud that it shakes water from the ferns above me. Unslinging our weapons, we rush to the noise, no longer attempting stealth, for the drums have shattered all notions of quiet.

The trees stop, and a plantain grove opens out before us. The drums have halted, so as we enter the grove, we enter silence. Stepping into the open, I am glad to have Cooley close beside me. From the south, the drums start up again.

'It's Montgomerie, sounding the advance,' calls Drummond, and waves us forward, across the grove and back into the jungle's clasp. 'We shall be upon them any minute.'

We had expected hundreds of Spaniards; now, even in the half-light and through the clutching trees, we can see that there are but few – perhaps thirty at most, and instead of a battle it appears to be a rout. The Spaniards are fleeing, though where our men have caught them there is fighting, sudden and ugly. And what use is my gun now? All the world is trees with only gaps and glimpses in between – you could not see a man to shoot him until you were upon him, or he on you.

A Spaniard, running from the mass of Montgomerie's men, stumbles around a tree and barrels straight into Cooley. They fall together, knocking me with them. The man is swearing in Spanish and trying to regain his feet, but Cooley has him around the neck and drags him down. They are wrestling as I used to wrestle with my brothers – viciously. I raise my gun, but I dare not shoot at the Spaniard with Cooley grappling so close, the two of them kneeling and locked together. The Spaniard has his hands around Cooley's neck, squeezing so hard that his fingers disappear into the flesh, and Cooley gives a throttled gasp.

With the butt of my musket I jab downwards, striking the Spaniard on the back of the head. His skull breaks with a clean crack, the sound of a slate falling from a roof onto stone. I think he will drop dead but he staggers backwards, silent now, one hand against a tree to steady himself, the other to his head. He opens his mouth; I keep waiting for him to die but still he stands there. Cooley is on his feet, taking great gasping breaths and looking about him for his gun, which he dropped in the scuffle. The Spaniard's gun is slung on his shoulder but he does not reach for it; his face is slack and when he lifts his hand from the back of his head it is wetly red.

'Just die, you bastard,' I beg, for if he does not die then I shall be obliged to shoot him, and it is different, now that he simply stands there – a different thing altogether from killing a man who is doing his utmost to fight back. We have been told to take no prisoners – God knows we can afford to feed none. Cooley has found his gun; he begins to raise it, though his breath is still coming in long, noisy shudders, the whites of his eyes startling red. I cannot be thought a coward by Cooley, and nor am I one, so I shoot.

At such a distance I could not miss – the Spaniard is hit clear in the chest. I had thought that a musket ball pierces flesh; I did not understand that it pulverises flesh and bone into a kind of jellied mass. He falls forward, his body folding strangely, for the wound has put a new joint in him, in his chest, so that he bends where no man should bend. His blood is in my eyes; when I wipe my hand across my face it comes away covered not just in blood, but something grittier – blood ground up with bone.

In these hungry months of waiting we have all spoken very bold of our enmity with the Spaniards. Whatever I expected to feel, having killed one, it is not this. I cannot look at Cooley – I do not wish to see on his face what he thinks of me. When I came here to Darien I thought it would make a man of me. What manner of man it would make me, I have not until now considered.

It seems that we have benefited for once from the harshness and impassibility of this place, for the great number of the Spaniards were turned back by the terrain, so that the force we came upon is only their rearguard. Such fighting as there was may only be called a skirmish. By the time dawn is fully upon us the last of the Spaniards have fled. We have two dead, Swinton and Jaffrey, and almost a dozen wounded. The dead Spaniards we do not bury – the jungle shall swallow them soon enough.

Upon our return to the colony, the starving and the sick greet us conquerors – for this is what they need. Thus, amidst the mud and the gappy log huts, our ugly skirmish becomes a triumph. As for Cooley and I, we do not speak of what happened there.

This triumph, if it can be called so, heartens the men for a day or two, but is soon driven from their minds by hunger. We have fled a famine at home, and yet like pestilence it has followed us here. It is a kind of drunkenness, to be so famished. Everything sharpened, and my head light and giddy. Things slow down: I can stare for a long while at a drop of water on a branch; at an ant, his diligent procession along a leaf. There is a terrible brightness to the midday light.

The famine does not relent. If there were soft and kind-hearted men amongst us, they have not survived, and so what remains is a grim and flinted force, sharpened very keen on the whetstone of hunger. Those who survive are those willing to do what survival demands of us. We are experts in snatching at rations, and in steering clear of the diseased, however piteous their cries.

Each man is allowed two pounds of flour a week – and two pounds by the Company's weighing is one pound only. 'And a good quarter of that is maggots,' I say to Cooley, as we chew our meagre meal. We take our chewing mighty seriously these days, and can eke out the merest scrap of food for half an hour. If we are given dried peas, it is a handful between five men, and when we boil them, a scum of maggots and worms rises to the water's surface. We used to skim this off before eating. Now we do not, for a spoonful of worms will fill the belly better than nothing – though we do at least avoid each other's eyes when we eat them, for we have our shame, if nothing else.

Any man too sick to work that day gets no allowance at all, for the Company is set on the building of palisades and the mounting of the guns in their embrasures. The fort grows, and the men diminish. All are starving, but there is yet some hope, for we expect any day the arrival of supplies from Jamaica. Two sloops have been commissioned to trade there and return with food – and though we know they are bound to bring flour and salt beef and small beer, and some medicines if we are fortunate, a favourite game amongst the men is to imagine what manner of delights these ships might bring.

'Peas – fresh, not dried,' I say.

'Apples,' says young Buchan, and I can almost feel the snap of a crisp new apple between my teeth.

'Oranges,' say I, though I have never tried one, 'and currants, candied.'

'Claret,' says Cooley, who is not usually a drinking man.

Oh we make a tremendous manifest of our longings, in those waiting days, until in our imaginings those two sloops become galleons, laden to the gunwales with all manner of food and strong liquor.

But the ships will come too late for Cooley, who falls gravely ill – taken badly by the fevers that pass like malicious rumours around the settlement. The surgeon has no medicine to give; he bleeds Cooley, but afterwards Cooley seems weaker still. Being no longer young, and much reduced by hunger, he has not the strength to fight. He shakes mightily, the whole of his flesh merely a butcher's sack of bones, rattling.

'You shall be well soon,' I tell him. 'The surgeon will see to it.'

'I shouldn't think so,' he says.

He asks me for no further comfort, and nor do I offer him any. You must understand that the hunger has robbed us even of our words – we have so little, so little. Thus I do not find within myself any soft words for him, nor take his hand as he lies dying. Nor do I thank him for all he has done for me, training me to be a navigator when neither I nor anyone else saw any promise in me.

When I check on him the next morning, he is dead. I try to close his eyes but it is too late, for the stiffness has set in. He shall be buried with his eyes wide, to stare forever at the inside of his shroud.

In all my wretched life, three people have thought well of me. My mother did so in the tender way of mothers, and I did little to deserve it, being always a rascal and much inclined to fighting, and being ashamed of her fondness. Effie, too, was prodigiously fond of me – and when I think of the many women I have bedded since I left Nether Largo, I know how little I deserved her regard. But if Cooley thought well of me, he was not blinded by mere affection – indeed, he was not wont to show any. His good opinion I earned by my work: he considered me a good seaman and I gave him no reason to think otherwise. Now he takes that opinion to his grave.

Back home, the Reverend William Moncrieff and the kirk found me wanting – but none has ever judged me more harshly than I judge myself on the day we bury Cooley in the swamp of Darien, and he is not afforded even a grave of his own for we have too many dead and not enough time.

20

We had figured the Spaniards for our principal enemies, but soon enough it seems that the English will instead play that role. By May of 1699 a periagua sent in search of news and food returns with word of a proclamation by the English, forbidding any English subjects from trade with us. Our periagua's crew came upon a Jamaican sloop who gave them a copy of the proclamation itself, and Paterson nails it up on the door of his hut, 'that you may know our enemy, and see for yourselves that our endeavour here has them scrambling'. I fear that instead it will only destroy what remains of the morale of the company — for this document might as well be a warrant for all of our lives, so surely does it condemn us to death:

> *In His Majesty's name and by command, strictly to command His Majesty's subjects, whatsoever, that they do not presume, on any pretence whatsoever, to hold any correspondence with the said Scots, nor to give them any assistance of arms, ammunition, provisions, or any other necessaries whatsoever, either by themselves any other for them, or by any of their vessels, or the English nation, as they will answer the contempt of His Majesty's command, at their utmost peril.*

For our food, we have been relying entirely on trade from Jamaica and thereabouts — this now is closed to us. The sloops we have been awaiting, laden with food, shall not come. I picture them sailing over some far horizon and out of sight.

Paterson does his best to exhort us to courage. But since the death of his wife and child, his manner cannot match the zeal of his words.

He does his best, and tries to fire our resolve – but hungry men are wet kindling, and slow to catch aflame.

'The English would not be so riled, were they not certain of the great wealth this settlement shall win us,' Paterson says.

'Sure,' I mutter to Buchan. 'Can you not see already the great wealth we've won by our formidable empire?'

Buchan stifles a laugh as we look around: the starving crowd, blank faced; the haphazard fortifications, with none strong enough to man them; the graves, so marshy that they take our dead with a hungry squelch. I think often of the young stowaway that we found aboard the *Caledonia* before we sailed from Leith. I remember how we had to drag him off, and how he begged to be allowed to join us. What a mercy we did him, that day.

Sometimes the natives take pity on us and bring us some food – but we are in such numbers, and in such sore need, that it can but little avail us.

'They could do more,' I mutter to Buchan, 'for God knows they look stout enough.'

'And how much would we do for them,' he says, 'if they'd sailed up the Clyde and declared Glasgow to be New Darien?'

I have little patience for such soft-hearted speculations – and if we had not claimed this place, the Spaniards would have done so, and indeed may yet do so, for in our starved state, we could offer but a poor resistance.

Far from holding the promised key to all trade, we languish here as a kind of afterthought. We seem to have been forgotten even by the directors of our own company, for there is no word from Scotland, let alone the supply ships that we were promised would follow us. Depending as we were upon those, and upon trade, and being so much occupied with building and fortifications, we have barely done any planting. I look over our few small plots of yams, Indian corn and Jamaica peas. The soil is rich and looks to be fertile, but we have sown almost nothing. No – that is not true, for we have filled the earth with our dead.

We are not even authorised to make any raids on the Spanish camps, nor on their ships, beholden strictly as we are to orders from the Company – but the Company gives every sign of having abandoned us. Do they imagine that we thrive here? Do they picture us dining comfortably in well-built houses, and wearing the wigs that now moulder in their crate? The Indians bring rumours that the Spanish at Carthagena are massing against us; these days even the youngest and brashest lads no longer speak so bold about wishing for the Spaniards to come so that we may trounce them. We are already beaten – our own bodies speak of our defeat.

For wood to build our New Edinburgh we cleared several acres of forest. Already the forest is claiming back the cleared land, for everything grows prodigious fast in these parts, forever wet, forever hot. In the face of such implacable forest, this colony of ours begins to feel insubstantial – we make no impression on this place, can get no purchase. I take a notion that if I were to look at the charts on which Cooley and I proudly inscribed *New Caledonia* and *New Edinburgh*, I would find that our writing has disappeared. For the first time I wonder what name this place might have had before ever we came here.

I learn to admire my incorruptible hunger. It wants what it wants, and it is always true. A tooth loosens in my mouth and when at last it comes free, I keep it there, sucking it and dreaming of food. A young settler takes leave of his senses and gorges on stones; he dies smiling through a mouth full of broken teeth, and saying that at least his belly is full.

———————————

In this lamentable condition, it is at last announced that we shall abandon the colony. It is not yet eight months since we first landed here – but time has warped and mildewed in the mud of this place, and I could swear it has been years.

Six men are judged too sick to undertake the hazardous voyage; whether it is a mercy or a betrayal to leave them here, I do not know. I sail in mid-June, aboard the *Caledonia*, in convoy with the *Endeavour*. The *Unicorn* and the *St Andrew* being obliged to anchor outside of Golden Island, we are separated from them at the start, and do not see them again in all the voyage. As for the *Dolphin*, she was run aground and seized by the Spanish months back.

The sickness plagues us sorely on the journey. I remain well – what bastard strength is in me that I do not sicken when so many around me sweat and vomit and shit themselves? What manner of man am I, that even my death does not want me?

'It's sheer stubbornness,' says Buchan. 'You are too stubborn to die.'

I have not the energy to laugh. We are sewing the hammock about a settler, lately dead. He is so thin that his knees and elbows are great beads strung on the twine of his limbs.

Buchan nods down at the body. 'He makes it eighty, since we left Darien.'

'I stopped counting.' Indeed, I stopped counting long ago – for a number, however high, is a neat thing, and can have nothing to do with all these dead. A number cannot capture how we drop them overboard before they can stiffen; how they slop about inside their shrouds, their bowels loosened and mouths slack.

The *Endeavour* is in such a wretched state that she can barely keep pace with our *Caledonia*. By the time we reach the Caribbean in early July the *Endeavour*'s mainmast is sprung and her hull nothing but a net of leaks. She signals for help and we are able to rescue all aboard her. But *rescue* seems the wrong word, for none here can think themselves saved. The *Caledonia* itself in a bad trim, the sick and dying all about us, and the vengeful ocean yet to cross.

We were bound for Boston, but are forced by contrary winds, the illness of our crew, and the scantiness of our provisions, to put in instead at Sandy Hook and to seek aid in New York. When we limp into harbour in early August 1699, we have given many more men to the sea. Ten days afterwards, the *Unicorn* arrives, much battered; they tell us they sent 150 overboard on the journey. Even now our travails are not done, for we are stranded some time in New York, Captain Drummond not having the money to purchase the supplies we need, nor to hire the additional men we need to hazard the journey home.

One day there is a tremendous bellowing and shouting from Captain Drummond's cabin. The rumour spreads quick around the ship: the captain has a friend in the city, a fellow Scot, who has received a letter from the Company, and brought it to show the captain. As to its contents, the yelling and the sound of breaking glass give us some indication.

When we are all summoned to the deck, it is clear the captain has been drinking. Were he sober he might be more discreet, but he is all rum and fury, and fierce insistent on reading the letter aloud, 'so that all you men may see how the Company values our travails, that have cost us so many lives'.

And whereas we have received information from London of a very improbable story that those of the said Colony have wholly deserted their settlement there, and gone where nobody can give any account of them, we can give no manner of credit to the said story, all circumstances relating to it appearing so very inconsistent and fabulous that we can believe no set of men in the world of any reasonable measures of discretion and resolution, and much less those in whose fidelity and courage we have placed such an entire confidence, could be guilty of so much groundless cowardice, folly and treachery. Yet in case it should happen that through any unforeseen and unexpected accident you hear confirmation of the Colony being removed from their said settlement (which we cannot suffer ourselves to believe upon any account), then I earnestly beseech you, as a patriot, to use all means possible to advise the Council-General or Court of Directors of our Company as soon as may be.

And thereafter more of that sort. The men make the noises that the captain wants from us – he needs our anger now, just as a minister needs the congregation's answering *Amen*. Were I not weakened by long hunger, perhaps I would shout and stamp my feet like Buchan and some of the fellows about me. But in the main I feel tired, and not so greatly surprised at the Company's incredulity – for how could anyone at home understand what Darien is, least of all those who sent us off in a fleet laden with clean wigs and grand notions?

———

At last we make our sorry way back to Scotland, reaching the Clyde in November 1699. Here we hear that relief ships were sent to the colony, and a second expedition too – four more ships, put to sea before ever word reached them of the disaster that was Darien, and of its abandonment. They shall be met there only by the many graves, and the ruins of our badly built settlement. Over the next months, news trickles back to us: those on the relief ships tried to rebuild the settlement, but the Spanish, being out of all patience, finally attacked. Those Scots that survived were suffered to leave – I am told that they were few.

And what about us, those who had carried the hopes of our nation to Darien, and had buried them there in the swamp, and lived to tell of what we saw? None wants to hear it. The scheme has near bank-rupted the nation, so that far from sympathy for our sufferings in the Scots cause, we are greeted with contempt, for the stench of failure comes off us very strong. I learn quick that it is better to say nothing, than to say that I had any part in Darien.

———

'How do you like that, for an apprenticeship at sea?' I say to the goat.

'Yet you survived,' he says, 'where many did not.'

'Should I be rejoicing, then?' I spit on the ground. 'And thank-ing the directors of the Company, who sent me off with such promises of glory and riches? And the English, who ensured that we failed?'

The cat sniffs at the gobbet of my spit, where it lies in the dust. She says, 'You stink of anger.'

'May a man not have his anger, when he has nothing else?'

'You nurse it like a kitten,' she says, and walks away.

I throw out my arms. 'She is impossible.'

'Oh, surely,' says the goat. 'What else should a cat be, but impossible?'

'And what do you think? Am I not entitled to a little anger at what befell me in Darien?'

'Certainly, Mister Selkirk. You may have all the anger that you like. As to how it serves you, the rest of your story shall answer that.'

For several minutes there is silence, except for the sound of his chewing.

'You seem not to be inclined to anger,' I say.

He sticks out his bottom lip as he thinks, exposing his single row of teeth. 'A goat is a pragmatic creature, and not much concerned with his past. My worms trouble me far more,' he says. 'When a fellow's arse itches as mine does, all other concerns become secondary.' He backs against a tree, which he uses as a kind of scratching post for his behind.

'And what then?' he asks. 'What came after your return from Darien?'

And here I fall back to silence, for this part of my past I am not ready to tell him, nor even to recall.

water ▮ every where

Lift up
now thine eyes ▮ northward, ▮ southward,
eastward, and westward:

▮ Arise, ▮ I will
give ▮ unto thee ▮

an altar ▮

of ▮

salt ▮

I am a man of normal appetites, much besieged by desire, and plagued by thoughts of women. I cannot stop remembering Effie Breck in the fisherman's hut that first winter, and the way that when she rose to dress herself, the nets had embossed a mark on her thighs, as though she were a creature caught up from the sea.

On the first merchant ship I served on, the purser kept a young black dog. On long voyages, having no others of its kind, the dog took to forlornly fucking coils of rope, and looking mightily ashamed of itself as it did so. When my thoughts turn to women now, and when I pleasure myself, I think that I am become no better than that wretched creature.

'I'm no stranger to long voyages,' I tell the goat and the cat. 'But this – nigh on two years – it is too much even for the most seasoned sailor.' I sigh and set down the length of rope I am twisting. 'I do not ask for much. Even the ugliest of Leith's whores would suffice.'

'Is not your constant frigging enough?' Sleek is ever thus: very blunt.

'Hardly constant.' Indeed, I pride myself on my restraint. 'Many men would do worse. If you'd heard the stories of what my fellow sailors would be willing to fuck, given the chance—'

'Be silent,' says the cat. 'I tire of your noise.'

'I did not imagine a cat could be so readily offended.' For here on the island, the night's silence is regularly torn up by the amorous screeching of the cats. Even Pickle has by now whelped three litters, and in a range of colours that reflects poorly on her virtue. I look at Sleek. 'You lick your own arsehole. Can you really be offended by sailors' loose talk?'

'It does not offend me,' the cat says. 'It bores me.'

'What notion have you of boredom? I have seen you lie five hours at a time, barely moving, and then with a good deal of fuss and spectacle you stretch, only to roll over and rest another five hours, and more besides.'

'Do you imagine I am bored during such times? My fur is warm; my belly is full of meat. I want for nothing.'

'But what occupies your thoughts?'

She yawns. 'I have already told you: my warm fur. My full belly.' She gives a mighty stretch. 'It must be exhausting to be a man, and forever needing to exercise your thoughts, as you might exercise a hunting hound.'

It is a hard thing, to be held to the standards of a cat, which are sometimes mysterious to me, and sometimes monstrous simple.

'You are better in silence,' she continues.

'Then why did you and the goat bestir yourself to speak to me?'

'Because silence is a language you have not yet learned.'

'Do not take umbrage,' says the goat quickly. 'For myself, I find your company endlessly diverting. I would not want to be without it.'

'Nor I,' says the cat.

'Truly?' I ask her – for it is rare that she shows me affection. Even when she allows me to stroke her, she looks at me all the while as though she is doing me a great kindness.

'Truly,' she says. 'For I am grown very fond of goat livers.'

———

At the shore, the birds shriek at the sea.

Sometimes when I listen to the water, I fancy I am listening for the voices of the drowned. And my own ship, the *Cinque Ports* – is she down there, in the deep dark, where the restless water stirs the hair of my shipmates? I am sure of it – sure that she is long since sunk. What song can the dead sing, from fifteen fathoms down, drowned and gone?

Did I escape, or did I abandon them? And are they damned, or am I?

———

The goat sees me bent over my Bible with my charcoal.

'You labour mighty seriously over it,' he says, 'as though it were a form of divination.'

'Perhaps.' Back in Nether Largo there is an old woman who styles herself a mystic, and charges people to read the future from a sheep's entrails, or from the shoulder blade of a ram. 'Some people claim they can tell the future from bones, or from guts.'

'Good,' says the cat. 'Words may lie, but bones do not.'

I shrug. She may be right – certainly old Mrs Farrie made a decent living from her bones, despite the many imprecations of the Reverend William Moncrieff.

When I am done with this latest attempt, from Ecclesiastes, I read it aloud to them.

The sun ariseth, and the sun

returneth

into the sea; yet the sea is not

satisfied

it is

already

old

I gave my heart to

madness and I perceived

that this also is

wisdom

'You would do better with bones,' says Sleek.

The goat is less scathing. He says softly, 'And what is it that you are trying to do, my friend, with these scribblings?'

I am relieved that he does not chastise me, at least. But I cannot explain what I am doing. I think I am trying to make a kind of spell or invocation. By my reckoning, it is now two years since I was left on the island. I am so very tired. With my strange poems, I am trying to put an end to time.

22

I wake to the cat's claws on my neck.

'You are summoned,' she says. She is standing on my chest, her front paws on my throat, and when I don't respond at once she does not scruple to dig her claws in, slow and deliberate.

'Summoned?' I sit up and prise her from me, holding her at arm's length before dropping her to the ground. 'Have you run mad? On what authority?'

She merely looks at me – I should have learned by now that cats need no authority beyond their own. Then she says again, 'You are summoned.'

When she strolls from the tent I follow her. You will think it is I who have run mad – for what manner of man obeys a cat? But you must understand also that novelty is a powerful thing. My days on this island are so much the same – the interminable repetition of the same dull tasks, and all the while checking the horizon for a sail that does not come. Curiosity alone would have been enough to set me following the cat, even if there were not something fearsome in her tone, and in the very set of her slinking back.

We have scarce left my clearing when I see that the goat has joined us, slipping between the cat and me. His face is grave, and as he follows the cat they are silent, moving fast and in concert, sure of their destination.

We go up – a fierce up, not through the well-trod paths that I myself follow to my lookout. These are strange ways and new, where the goat and cat may pass with ease, but I am much whipped and scratched by boughs and thorns, for the paths of beasts make no accommodations for men. The animals do not slow for me, nor wait, and so at times I must scramble to keep up. At first I call after them, 'Wait,' and 'Would you at least tell me where we are heading, and why?' When they do not answer I continue in silence, except for occasional curses when thorns slice my arms and face.

By my figuring we are bearing south. When we emerge finally from the forest, I find we can go no further: the island itself ends here, dropping away in one of the tall cliffs that make this side of the island so inhospitable to sailors looking to come ashore. I pull up sharp, and the small stones dislodged by my feet skitter over the cliff's edge, falling so far that I cannot hear them land. This clearing is but a few yards wide, a rocky outcrop trapped between forest and cliff.

I retreat a step or two until my back is against a tree. The goat, however, is not in the least troubled by the sheer drop behind him. Many a time I have seen his brethren chewing cheerfully halfway up a cliff, so that you would swear goats have the gift of flight. The cat, too, is quite at her ease, and is already seated and licking her front paw.

'Why have you brought me here?' I demand.

'You chose to follow,' says the goat. 'You must know that we have business with you, and you with us.'

'Don't speak in riddles. Why are we here?'

'Why, for your trial,' he says.

What answer can I give to such a nonsense? I could almost laugh – yet how can I say that this is absurd, impossible, when many months ago I sailed over the horizon of what is possible? Can a man spend his days conversing with a goat and a cat, and then all of a sudden say, *Stop – what you say makes no sense?*

'The island demands a reckoning,' says the cat.

'If there is to be a reckoning,' I say, 'then I do not account the island a fair or a merciful judge.'

'The island is concerned with neither fairness nor mercy,' says the goat. 'It is concerned with what is true.'

He steps, with some dignity, onto a square rock by the cliff's edge. I wince to see him balancing there, his back to the cliff, which drops away barely a foot behind him. He stands as if on a pedestal, or atop an altar, and says in a sonorous voice: 'Let us now commence the trial of Alexander Selkirk, variously known as Selcraig, Selcraigh, Selcrigge, and divers other names.' I suspect he finds some pleasure in ceremony – he is a fellow much taken with pomp.

He goes on. 'We charge you with intemperate behaviour, viz. violent affray, drunkenness and fornication.'

'What punishment could this court impose?' I ask. 'Am I not the one with the blade and the gun? Do I not come here with goat meat still between my teeth from my last meal? Do I not have dominion over you beasts?'

'Sir,' says the goat. 'You are quite mistaken. In this court, as in your nights and days, the island has dominion. And you will find,' he says, looking about him, 'that the island is a most unforgiving place.'

This I know already.

I finger the knife at my belt. 'I could slit your throat right now.'

'I do not doubt it – I have seen you slay many of my brethren the same way. But you cannot slay us all.'

'You speak for all the goats?'

'No indeed. I speak for the island. Its judgment is both older and more terrible than the judgment of any single creature. We are very fleeting things, compared to stone, and sea, and even forest.'

'I will submit to no judgments of this court, nor tolerate this nonsense.' I did not flee the judgments of Largo's kirk session and travel to the far extremities of the earth only to find myself now called, in my privation, to answer before some court of beasts.

Yet there is nonetheless an authority in this stern place, and in the goat's words, that chills me as even the kirk session did not.

That cat speaks. 'It matters not at all whether you submit. Your trial shall take place regardless.'

The goat, not unkindly, adds, 'It only remains for you to decide whether or not you wish to speak in your own defence.'

You might think me a fool, or a madman – perhaps both – to fear the judgment of a goat, a cat and an island. You might say that I could simply walk away, return to my camp, and ignore the beasts and their demands. You might even say that I could put an end to this at once with my knife, and feast on goat flesh for my troubles.

To you I say that a man may believe a great many things under the grave gaze of a goat, on a sheer clifftop. I think of the cat's face as she drinks her bowl of blood – how the blood beads red on her whiskers, and how she licks her white chin clean. I think of the goat's eyes, strangely slit. And if you have been raised, as I was, on your knees in the kirk, with talk of devils and sin, then this horned beast, his eyes slit contrary-wise, is a god or a devil, and nothing in between.

I could run from them – kill them, even – but I can neither flee nor kill this island. I am subject to this place, whether I wish it or not.

'We begin,' says the cat.

The goat clears his throat. 'The court is concerned with the period following your return from Darien. A part of your story that you have been most reluctant to discuss.'

'You can have no concern with that part of my past, nor any need to hear it.'

'You mistake us,' says the cat, looking bored.

'Indeed,' the goat says. 'It is not we that need to hear the story. You are the teller of your own story, and you also must hear it.'

'A story is a tidy thing – it has a happy ending. My story is no such thing – and that part of it, most particularly.'

'It is yours nonetheless,' the cat says. 'You cannot be rid of it.'

'So let us hear it,' says the goat briskly. 'What have you to say? Are you guilty of the said violent affray, drunkenness and fornication?'

'Not guilty,' I say at once.

'And would you describe yourself as a virtuous man?' he asks. I gather that the goat is to be my main interrogator; the cat, I fancy, sees herself more in the role of judge.

'I no longer drink.'

'Did you not try making liquor, even here?'

'You know very well that I did that only once, and did not succeed.'

The Reverend Vicarious Cronch cocks his head. 'Can abstaining from liquor then be considered virtue, when you have no choice?'

'It hardly seems fair to dismiss it,' I say. 'Whatever the circumstances, it is true that I have quit it – and since I'll allow that drinking was previously a vice of mine, then quitting it must be seen as an improvement.'

'And if the temptation of drink were once again present?'

I kick at the ground. 'That is hardly likely to arise.'

'What other evidence have you, of your virtue?'

'I have never taken my pleasure with a goat.'

'And can that really be accounted restraint, or virtue?'

'These have been long years. I'll warrant many a man would have resorted to unnatural pursuits.'

The goat looks displeased at this, but keeps his counsel. As for the cat, I search her face, but she is as inscrutable as ever.

'And yet for all your claims of virtue,' the goat says, 'your behaviour after Darien cannot be described as virtuous.'

'How could you know what happened after Darien?'

Now the cat speaks. 'We know much that would surprise you.'

'You are so certain that you wish to hear this story? It does me no credit.'

'And yet you have pleaded not guilty?' says the goat.

'Because there are others in the story, with sins far greater than my own.'

'Enough,' the cat says. 'Speak.'

23

I come back to Nether Largo, much wearied and angered by what befell us in Darien, but with a notion of showing the town, and my family most particularly, the man I have now become. I am the little brother no longer, for I have seen and done things that my brothers could scarce have imagined. Many of those things were bad – but they made a man of me nevertheless. I left as a lad of fifteen and now, four years later, surely all must see that I am different altogether. And despite the failure of Darien, I am justly proud to have risen to master's second mate at such a young age.

Upon my return, my father embraces me heartily, but it is clear that he is delighted not by what I have achieved, but by my coming home again, which he takes as a surrender, for he seems certain that my years at sea should have reconciled me to a quiet life in Largo. He asks nothing of my time away, only says very gruff that he is glad I am returned, 'for it's past time that you settled down to a decent profession, such as many men would be grateful for, and not off chasing your fortune at sea – and what has that availed you, for you look half starved?'

Mam cannot refrain from kissing me, and exclaiming at how tall I am grown, and pressing her hands to my cheeks as though she would squash me back down to the lad she remembers. She sends Andrew running next door, to the house of my eldest brother, John, and his wife Margaret, and when they come Margaret takes great pleasure in bossing all of us about, and sighing very weary when she speaks of her clutch of small children. 'And if you had children, Alexander,' she says, 'you would understand, and would not have worried your parents so, by jaunting off about the world.'

Andrew fixes me with a grin and says at once, 'What makes you believe he has no children? Perhaps he had to flee back here to escape the mob of bastards and wronged women who are coming after him.'

Da slaps him with the back of his hand and says, 'We'll have none of that godless talk in my house.'

'You are wicked, Andrew,' Mam says, 'to say such things about Alexander.' She rubs my shoulder. She is almost the worst of it, my soft sweet mother, clutching me and fussing over me and acting in every way as though I am still her wee dote, and this shames and vexes me more than the casual mockery of my brothers.

And when at last we sit to eat I am given the same old stool that I ever had, its legs uneven and rickety so that there is no way to sit in comfort, nor with dignity, tall as I now am, with my knees up almost to my neck. You might think the stool an insignificant thing and yet I take to my bed that night in a fury. I want to shout at them: *Do you not see? Do you not see that I am a man now, and were I aboard a ship I would be treated with respect?*

Far from impressing my brothers with my learning, they are quick to call me a jackanapes and an upstart. When I try to tell them of my work as a navigator, or any particulars of what I have seen and done, Andrew says, 'If you are to prate on so very grand, take yourself up to the kirk, why don't you, and join Moncrieff − then the two of you can speak in sermons together, and spare the rest of us.' On my second day back, one of my treasured books, a mathematical treatise on navigation, goes missing, its scraps found in the ashes of the kitchen fire in the morning, and Andrew and David looking well satisfied with themselves. It takes all Mam's hushing, and stern words from Da what's more, to prevent us coming to blows. Andrew is made to apologise; in front of Mam and Da he does very prettily, looking solemn as he says, 'Truly, Pet, I am heartily sorry.' That old name is a knife in my ribs, and angers me even more than the loss of my book.

Yet although my brothers needle me, in truth they seem glad to have me back. Having failed to escape Nether Largo themselves, I think they are gratified to have me return, thin and weary, and to know that I, too, could not get clear of the place. John and his wife and their children are only next door; Peter, too, is wed, his second child due any day, but still in Nether Largo. William is lately wed and gone, but only as far as Largo town, and thus still sits in the family's pew at kirk. Only Simon has made it further, living now in Glasgow and working at a tannery there. As for Andrew and David, for all that they are working men now, they live still with our parents. It is a hard thing to feel a man when it is still your mother who puts your meal in front of you, and you sleep in the same bed that you grew up in, your feet hard against the board at the end unless you sleep sideways. Since I came back, David has a way of ruffling my hair, no matter how I swat his hand away, and Andrew begins to do it too, whenever he passes behind me. I do not mistake it for affection, knowing it instead for a way of showing that I am their wee brother still, and that although they live in our father's house, at least they are senior to me.

'And what of Effie?' asks the goat.

'You are a sentimental fellow,' I say.

'It is not I who is on trial.'

Indeed I have not forgot Effie Breck. The next day is Sunday and when my brothers dally on the way to kirk, I hasten them on.

'Why the hurry?' Andrew asks. 'Are you grown very pious at sea, to be so impatient to hear Moncrieff's sermonising?'

I shrug, for if I were to tell him the real reason behind my haste, he would mock me all the more.

Effie is there with her family. I watch her for the whole of the sermon. There it is – that dimple that appears when she smiles and then goes away again, quick as a wink.

'I had thought I should find you wed,' I say the next afternoon, when we are at last able to contrive to be alone together.

'Nether Largo is not such a grand, big town,' she says, laughing. 'Did you think there were so many eligible lads, vying for my hand?'

Aside from looking a little older in the face, she is just as I recall: the sweet turn of her waist, and her hips curved just so – and surely those hips were made for my hands to cup. 'And anyway,' she says, 'I had a notion that you would be back.'

This is both gratifying and burdensome, what with the great number of years that have passed, and the number of ladies who have given me their favour in that time. Being unable to say that I, too, have been waiting faithfully, I say nothing at all, but instead kiss her a good deal, which is a useful way of putting an end to all such talk. We keep ourselves mightily busy with kissing and, when we can steal away again, with more besides. I had forgot how her sweetness and her lewdness are perfectly matched, so that she will look shocked and scold me when I blaspheme, but then show me exactly how best to touch her to bring her to pleasure.

Yet having now sampled such a variety of women, I find that I cannot help but compare her to them, viz. that the hair on her arms is coarser than that of the redhead in Plymouth; that when she sits atop me, her breasts go each to their side, like the saddlebags of a donkey, unlike the whore in London with her small, high breasts; that at the conclusion of things Effie laughs very hearty, a thing I have never known another girl to do. None of this stops me from meeting with her – for which young man has ever refused the gift of a woman? – but I grow impatient with her throaty laugh, which I used to admire but which now reminds me of an Irish carpenter who was aboard the *Endeavour*. I grow sorely impatient, too, with her earnest desire to see me each day. And the truth is that the girl who years ago seemed a perfect marvel to me, mere lad of Nether Largo, may not seem such a treasure to a man who has seen so much of the world, and its women too, and who has risen to the great heights of master's second mate.

Even on Sundays, when we are in the kirk with our families, Effie turns and stares. She beams at me as though I am her happy ending, delivered to her by the sea. Indeed the only person in all of Largo who watches me more carefully than Effie is the Reverend William Moncreiff, who has not forgot my youthful indiscretions, and whose looks say perfectly loud that he distrusts me still. And this combination of staring is calculated to make a man uneasy, for there is in Effie's looks alone enough to make Moncrieff and his sister faint.

'You must be less obvious in your attentions,' I tell Effie. 'I cannot have your father come to make demands of me.' I confess I should not like to encounter Mister Breck in an ill humour, having seen the bruises on Effie, and on her mother, who often goes about veiled like a Spanish lady, in an attempt to conceal her black eyes. 'This place is too small, and full of gossips and scolds,' I say. It seems to me that Nether Largo is nothing but one giant mouth, set always to prattling – already my brothers have begun dragging rumours back to the house. And John's wife Margaret is a church bell, forever ringing out gossip.

'I hear that young Effie Breck is staying out all hours,' she says to Mam.

'Aye,' says Mam, not looking up from her needlework. 'Well, they were ever an unruly family – how could they be otherwise, with the father such a brute.' She straightens the cloth over her knee. 'She should be wed by now, a pretty face like hers.'

'D'you hear that, Alex?' This is David, smiling at me so innocent. 'Do you find her pretty?'

'I've never found her so,' says Andrew.

And the only reason I do not fight them there and then is that I can ill afford to be thrown from my parents' house. After the disaster of Darien I have but little money, and certainly not enough to set up a home of my own – and if I did that, Effie would surely start speaking of marriage, a conversation I ardently wish to avoid.

Thus the provoking behaviour of my brothers, combined with Effie's many intent glances, turns my thoughts seaward once again.

'Hurry up,' says the cat. 'Your mouth is full of excuses.'

Yet I find I cannot hurry.

Almost every morning, Sleek takes herself out of the tent and squats to cough up a slimy ball of fur. It is a fraught and ugly process, involving a great deal of coughing and retching. This story feels much the same – it does not come easily to my mouth. It resists, and chokes me.

'Sir,' says the goat, 'This court will not wait forever. And nor will your story go away for waiting. Your evidence has touched upon fornication – both with Effie Breck and with various other women in ports—'

'No more than is usual, amongst sailors, I assure you—'

'Other sailors are not on trial today.'

'Very well.'

Effie is importuning me more than ever. She comes to me with her arms stamped with bruises, one for each of her father's fingers, and she speaks of how it will be different when we have a house of our own. I am less interested in such talk than in the things that we do to one another in the long grass as spring turns to summer – but it seems I cannot have one without the other, for the more we lie together, the more she speaks of marriage.

That same night my father takes me aside.

'I thought the one good thing about you running off to sea would be an end to you wooing the Breck girl,' he says. 'They are not a good family – and she's ever been a flighty one. You'd be wise not to get entangled with her.'

Yes, I think. I am entangled, like a man underwater, snagged and ensnared in seaweed.

'D'you hear me?' Da says.

I nod. I have not often agreed with Da, but on the matter of Effie he is right. I resolve that it is time for me to go to sea once more.

But when I meet her by the seawall to tell her I shall soon be leaving, she becomes upset. This is when I know that we are in different stories – or perhaps in different parts of the same story. She thinks we are at the beginning, but I know it is an ending.

'I have my way to make in the world,' I say when she weeps and entreats me to stay. 'What choice do I have?'

'And what of my choices?' she spits.

It is better this way – easier to be hard with her now she is this envenomed thing, ugly with rage.

'I could just have left,' I say.

'Aye – as you did last time, without a thought for me.'

'But I chose to tell you instead.'

'Such thoughtfulness!' she says. 'Should I be thanking you for your kindness?'

'You do not need to harp at me, is all I mean. Just because I must go, does not mean I don't care for you at all.'

'*Must*,' she says. 'Oh, you are very faithful to your obligations, when they are to yourself.' She shakes her head. 'Was it not you who wooed me, and very determined too?'

'We did it together,' I say. 'All of it — it was not just me.'

'So you will abandon me now, and not even marry me first?'

'I have no wish to wed, and nor can I offer you a home.' She cannot understand the great expansive horizon of the sea. How could I explain to her how the ocean makes Nether Largo and everything within it seem petty and small, when so much more has been promised to me? If we wed, it will make her life bigger, but mine smaller — for she will tie me to this place, and the stain of the troublesome Brecks, and the scorn of the kirk, when my dearest wish is to leave it all behind.

'You have to understand,' I say to her, 'that I can offer you nothing.'

'You were not saying that when you were offering me your prick. That you were very happy to offer me.'

'And you were very happy to take it.'

'What has become of you?' she asks me. 'You're acting nothing like the man I know.'

I want to say: *The man you know is exactly what I am trying to cast off.*

'Perhaps you do not know me as well as you think,' I say.

She opens her mouth, then closes it again.

'Come.' I reach out to her, but she swipes my hand away, scratching me with her nails. She runs up the hill, her skirts caught up in her hands. Then she turns back and calls to me, the wind whipping her hair over her face. 'You have been the ruin of me, Alexander Selcraig.'

The Reverend William Moncrieff's sister finds her at dawn, face down in the water. Miss Moncrieff sets up such a great cry and hubbub that all of Nether Largo comes down to the shore. Thus I see Effie, laid on the shore where two fishermen have carried her. Somebody has spread an apron over her face, but I know her at once by her body — who knows it better than I?

I try to pick her up — she is much heavier than ever she was, her skirts soaked through, and probably a bellyful of salt water too, for the drowned drink the sea at the end. I cannot lift her clear of the ground – can only raise her halfway, and press her against my body as I kneel. Her head tips back and I lift off the apron that covers her face; she is perfectly white, her face washed clean of breath by the water.

My father grabs my shoulder. 'You don't want to be caught up in this, son.'

David takes my other shoulder and says, 'Come on, Alex – her father shall soon be here.'

I have no wish to face Mister Breck and his questions, let alone his fists – and so I let Effie slump back down to the sand. When I stand my shirt and trousers are both soaked – the print of her on me for all to see.

Moncrieff and his sister stand together by the water as Da ushers me away. They turn, the two of them, to stare at me, and then turn away, their heads drawn close together in whispered conversation.

Back at the house there is no respite from the water, for there is scarce a house in the village that does not overlook it. From the kitchen window I stare at the grey sea that Effie had ever loved, being a girl of Nether Largo born and bred, who grew up wading in the shallows by the harbour, and helping her father with his nets.

Even Andrew speaks kindly to me, and says, 'It is an ugly business,' and leaves me alone.

David says, low voiced, 'I have chopped the wood for today – you need not bother,' and this kindness is hardest to bear, knowing how little I deserve it.

'It's a sad, sad thing,' says my father at dinner. 'But we must not forget that it's also a sin, to kill yourself like that. It's for the best that you did not marry such a girl.'

'She could've fallen in,' says David. 'There's no proving it either way.'

I know the proof. I am the proof. *You have been the ruin of me, Alexander Selcraig.*

24

Only my mother, my soft sweet mother, brings her anger to me. My mother has always forgiven me everything and excused my many faults, but even she cannot find an excuse big enough to drag the whole of Effie's body through, wet and heavy as it was. In the kitchen she kneads the dough so violently that the legs of the table scrape against the floor each time she pounds.

'Did you trifle with that poor girl, Alex?' she says.

'Indeed not, Mam.' I dare not say otherwise. It is new, this anger of my mother's. Now her softness is all for Effie, and none remains for me.

They found no stones in Effie's pockets. It must have taken great determination on her part, for I have been a sailor long enough to know that the body does not wish to drown, and even a man who cannot swim will thrash and fight when pitched overboard. What dreadful resolve it must take to do otherwise − and how very like Effie, who was ever single-minded.

The whole village is sure it is self-murder, yet Moncrieff allows her to be buried in the kirkyard, although she is allotted a plot on the northern side − and if this is a slight then her parents dare not ask Moncrieff about it, grateful as they are to have her within the yard at all. The first clod of wet dirt landing on the coffin makes a terrible knocking sound, and for an instant I think it must be Effie banging on the lid, trying to get out.

'I am glad Moncrieff has shown mercy to that poor girl and her family,' Mam says, 'and let her be decently buried here.'

Mercy. I stare at her family, gathered by the grave in the mizzling rain. Effie's mother's face looks like a hill that has collapsed under too much rain: a landslide of features. Effie's father stands terribly stiff, as though it is he and not Effie who is dead.

I look and I look for mercy and I can find none.

———

Seeing no reason to stay and bear the censure or sympathy of the village, and many reasons to go, that same night I stuff my belongings into a bag and make once more for Leith. I pity those who have never been sailors, for they lack the great alibi of the sea, always ready to take them elsewhere.

In my haste, I am none too precious about my post, taking the first job I can secure, on a merchant ship bound for the low countries.

I had not thought that a dead woman would be so hard to outrun, but even at sea I am much beset by thoughts of Effie. A ship has neither time nor space for contemplation, and this ship less than most, being short-handed and with a veritable tartar of a captain. Yet still Effie comes to me. When I am taking a sounding of our depth, and reeling in the plumb line, I imagine that I shall haul up Effie's body at the end of it, like a fish on a hook. The cook boils a huge pot of cockles, and when I look at those small pink shells, all I can see is the neat, shiny nails on Effie's drowned hands.

My choice of ship could not be considered a success. The crew is put to much hard usage and works with an ill temper. When I leave the ship after just a few months, there is a dispute over my pay, so that I am obliged to return once more to Largo, where I can work for my father and hope to save a little before I take again to sea.

———

'You pass very smoothly over that dispute,' the goat says, interrupting. 'And over your sudden quitting of the ship, what's more.'

'There was a fight,' I say.

'You speak as though a fight were a thing that happens beyond the will of men – like a storm, or an earthquake.'

'Might it not be? Certainly it is not always within a man's control.'

'Some men seem to have more control than others.'

'Perhaps some men find themselves pushed beyond what is tolerable.'

'It would oblige the court if you would tell us how you were pushed.'

'In all the ways a man is ever pushed,' I say. 'The captain bad-tempered, and the ship's master having no idea of navigation, nor the humility to take counsel from those who know better.'

'Drunkenness,' the cat says. 'Speak of that.'

'You too would take to drink if you found yourselves on a ship so ill-managed, and with men inclined to sloth.'

'And did the drink not hamper your own work, or make you less diligent yourself?'

'Indeed not,' I snap.

My father is pleased to have me back, for I take to my tasks in his workshop with a new willingness – not only because this last hapless voyage has left me in dire need of money, but because I cannot abide to be still. If I have a moment of quiet or leisure, thoughts of Effie surface in my mind, like a bloated body in water.

So loath am I to be left with my thoughts, that in the evenings I have taken to preferring the company of my brothers to being alone.

'Good of you to deign to drink with us,' Andrew says, 'now you need not be sneaking off to chase that fat-arsed lass.'

I say nothing, and drink more. Our father being pleased with my work has put me out of favour with Andrew in particular, for Da is forever calling him lazy, and with good reason. I drink too much – too much by far. It is better this way, for when I am drunk I do not dream of Effie, nor dream at all, falling instead into a kind of bleary oblivion.

In the mornings, chopping wood is one of the tasks that falls to me – and it is my habit on coming back inside to take a drink of water, poured from the can on the sill. This morning, as always, I latch the door and take a hearty swig, for splitting wood is thirsty work, and all the more so when I drank too much last night. But as soon as I begin to gulp it down my whole body convulses and I retch and cough. It is salt water, horrid sharp on my tongue.

'You look sorely unwell,' says Andrew from his seat at the table, 'Will you not take another sip, Pet, to soothe you?'

I do not even need his smug grin to tell me it is he who has filled the can with salt water, the better to make a fool of me.

'Our father shall hear of this,' I say.

'And I am sure he will believe it, for you are quite the favourite, these days.' Andrew is still laughing, tremendous pleased with himself.

'You think to make me ridiculous,' I say. 'But you only show yourself for a fool.'

'Why must you always take everything to heart? It is only a little salt water – are you not the great sailor, after all?'

'At least I have ventured beyond Nether Largo,' I yell, 'and not stayed forever at home like a child, playing pranks.'

'Your sweet Effie did not scruple to drink salt water,' he says, his voice slow and deliberate. 'Oh, she drank her fill.'

And at that I seize a log from beside the kitchen fire and use it as a cudgel to beat him, and he squeals loud and puts his wretched thin arms over his head but cannot ward off my blows, and indeed I am striking fit to kill him, until the log itself snaps in half, and he looks up and, through a bloodied lip, says, 'You were never able to finish a damn thing – coward.'

'I will finish you,' I say. And I make for the door to the stairs to fetch Da's pistol, for he keeps it always in the trunk by his bed. But by now Da has heard the hubbub and come down, and he must see murder writ clear on my face for he stops me, slamming the door very firm and blocking it, so that I cannot get upstairs. Andrew has by this time fled to the yard, screaming all the while that I am out to kill him in his own home. I follow hard behind, but John's house is so close that he has already heard the great commotion and is at the door, Margaret right behind him and not even trying to hide the excitement on her face.

'Calm yourself,' she shrieks, in a voice not calculated to calm anyone.

'Let me deal with Andrew,' I say. 'He shall get what he deserves, and he well knows he deserves it.'

'The whole of Nether Largo will hear your yelling,' says John, who has ever been concerned with the good opinion of others.

'I don't care. Where is he?'

'Get inside,' John says, and my father now has come through to the kitchen and is yelling too, 'You damn fool, you will make of us a laughing stock.'

'It is Andrew who has done so, and he shall get his comeuppance,' I shout.

Andrew chooses this moment to come back inside, bolder now that he has John and our father to defend him. He saunters in mighty calm, as though he had not but minutes ago fled this same room in fear of me. I have only my fists, but these shall do. I dive at him again, but he, ever cowardly, jumps behind Margaret, who is still yelling. One of her and John's children has followed her into the house and is standing in the doorway watching with glee, as though the whole scene were a boxing match put on for his amusement.

Da tries to pull me away, and so I turn to wrestle instead with him, and Mam is there crying noisily, and Margaret is screaming at me, and I can taste not only the salt water in my mouth now but also hot blood, for I am hit. Then Margaret herself tries to grab at me, putting herself between me and Da. I shove her aside and being but a small woman she veritably flies against the door frame, her head striking it loud and brisk, with a sound like a log being tossed into the woodpile. That sound is enough to stop me, to stop all of us, and John runs to her, and my father says, 'Are you pleased, you brute, with what you've done?'

But I can only stare at Margaret on the ground, her hands pressed to the side of her head. And though eventually I hear myself say, 'I am sorry, and I did not mean to do it,' I know very well that I have never liked the woman and thus cannot acquit myself of wanting to hurt her.

With a tumult so loud and a village so small, it is not a surprise when the Reverend William Moncrieff himself knocks on the door a few hours later, stern and businesslike, his sister behind him, peering over his shoulder, her lips pinched very tight. They are cloistered some time alone with my father. Upon leaving, Moncrieff informs me that I am to appear at the kirk session the next day, at noon.

'For conduct out of keeping with the godly nature of this village, and of Largo as a whole,' he says.

I am about to give a retort, when over his shoulder I see Mam. The shame on her face silences me as Moncrieff's lectures never could.

The kirk is always a grave place, and never more so than now, when it is both kirk and courthouse. Even Andrew is solemn-faced – and although I have heard him say such lewd things about Moncrieff's sister as would condemn him straight to hell, he is now bowing low to Moncrieff and the other assembled elders, and when he takes his seat is careful to turn his head at just such an angle to best display his bruises.

'Young Alexander,' says Moncrieff. I bridle at once for he makes me sound like a mere lad and not a man, let alone a man who has seen far more of the world than he. 'You have been summoned today because of your disgraceful conduct in the scandal arising yesterday morning, which disturbed the peace of the entire village.'

'And shall my brother Andrew not be called to account also, for his part in starting all of this?'

Moncrieff shakes his head, as though greatly saddened. 'Your father has told me very clearly that you were the one who began the violence. Your brother John and his wife I have summoned as witnesses; as for Andrew, he has come and doubtless takes a most natural interest in these proceedings. And surely you will not dispute what your father has told me – for have you not sins enough laid at your door, without disputing the words of your own father, a godly man?'

'May a fellow not snap, after years of being plagued by his fool brother?'

'A godly man, and a temperate one, remains always in control of himself.'

Where was it decided that I am godly, or temperate? But in Largo it seems there is no choice. We are all deemed godly and in my case spend the rest of our lives falling short.

Moncrieff speaks again. 'Am I to take it from your answers that you are not ready to repent of your sins, and to make amends?'

There is no answer I can give that does not take me back to my own sin, my own guilt. I dare say nothing of Andrew's taunts about Effie — for that would only draw Moncrieff's notice to how I wronged her. Thus I stay silent.

Moncrieff consults the notes in front of him. 'In the early morning yesterday there was an infamous outcry at your father's house. Your mother was seen fleeing, in some distress. Your brother John's wife, Margaret Bell, was heard to cry out.' He refers again to his papers. 'She yelled, *Will you murder your father and my husband both?*'

'Well I did not murder either of them, though I was sorely provoked.'

'Then you struck this same Margaret Bell.'

And here I am silenced, for the charge is true.

'You have nothing to say?'

'No, sir. I did shove her.' For though I may be a bad man I am not a liar. If there is virtue in this it is a very small virtue, coming after a great sin — but a man such as I, having few virtues, must take comfort in those few. 'It was an accident and I never meant to do her harm.' Do I believe it? I turn to look; Margaret, in the front pew, has a bruise on her cheek. It puts me in mind of the bruises Effie's father used to leave on her, and I am doubly shamed.

While Moncrieff and the elders consult in low voices, I look down at my hands and I wonder how I have contrived to pull off this trick: surely a man must have a special talent for destruction, to be so sorely provoked and still make himself the villain?

'This unfortunate display having been a public one, and much disturbing the godly peace of the village, it is only fitting that your penance, too, should be public.' Moncrieff makes a note in his book. 'You are commanded to return at tomorrow's service, and to appear before the pulpit, and to make acknowledgement of your sin, before the congregation.'

All through the evening, you may well imagine my yearning to do as I have done before, and run away to sea this very night, to avoid the mortification of being hauled before the entire town and rebuked as a sinner and a ruffian. The sea is a sore temptation, being so big that a man may be forgotten, if not absolved. But Andrew's taunt of *coward* is still fresh in my mind, and I cannot bear to prove him right by fleeing.

Thus I appear at the kirk the next day, and keep my head down as I am rebuked in the face of the congregation. I speak clear and loud when Moncrieff demands that I promise amendment on the strength of the Lord, and when he asks me if I will resolve to be a more sober and upstanding man, even with Andrew smirking at me from our pew I am able to stay calm and answer, 'Yes, I am heartily sorry for my sins and will do better, and seek forgiveness from the almighty God.'

That night my mother puts her hand over mine and says, 'Alex, you know I have always held you very dear – but you must make penance and repent before God, or you shall come to a bad end.'

But who needs God when you have the sea, which lets you start over and demands no penance? I leave the next day, to find an ocean big enough to be lost in.

25

'That is all?' the goat asks.

'I have not returned to Nether Largo since.'

My story has been a long time in the telling. The sun is beginning to drop beneath the mountains to the west. I am tired – not wearied by labour, as I would be in the ordinary way of things. I am wearied now in a different way, from the work of trawling the past.

'Surely that is enough,' I say.

'It is not all,' says the cat.

I watch her warily. How much can she know? If anyone can spot an omission, I warrant it would be the cat, for she has a very unflinching way of seeing.

'You shall have no more from me today,' I say.

The goat shakes his head. 'Still you have not told us how you came to be on this island.'

I say nothing. They shall not have that story. Two years here has not been enough to grind my rage and fury down to the size of words.

'And what of your verdict?' I ask instead. 'What is it to be?'

The goat shakes his head. 'The island arrives at its judgment in its own time.'

'How shall I know, then?'

'You will know,' says the cat.

I look from her to the goat, and back again. 'So is it over, then, this – this trial?'

The goat cocks his head to one side. 'Let us rather say it is adjourned – for your story is not yet finished.'

'You are still not satisfied? Must you dig up every deed, and must I rehearse every transgression aloud, and—'

'It is you.' The cat stands. 'You carry the stink of your past with you, as if you have rolled in a dead thing.'

In the evening the goat leaves my camp, as he does each night – but tonight I am more aware of his going, and fearful of what it might mean. What kind of man am I, who fears the judgment of a goat?

Sleek sees me watching the track where the goat has gone. 'You are ill at ease,' she says.

'I confess I would be loath to lose his regard.'

'And mine?'

I give a small snort. 'I am not sure I have ever had it.'

When I was at sea and we spoke very free of women, it was just a notion of women, that great welcoming hole, and no one woman in particular. And when we came ashore it mattered little which women we fucked, for they were all the same to us, and served the same purpose. Yet since today's trial my thoughts are all of Effie, and of her alone: the roundness low at the front of her belly; the soft hair on her shins; the way she would smile as though she could not help it, a smile sweeping across her face like a wave breaking amidships. All things particular to her, and shared by no other person – and all of them lost to the sea.

The next day the Reverend Vicarious Cronch returns.

'I am heartily glad to see you, sir,' I tell him.

He raises one wiry eyebrow. 'Do I not come each day?'

'I confess I feared that today you would not.' I hasten to the Bible, for last night, by the grudging light of my seal-fat taper, I scoured the pages for a way to write about Effie.

'Here,' I say. 'I was last night reading the Book of Amos. Should you like to hear what I found there?'

The

dead
swallow
the   moon

we
refuse

the

drowned

and

they   wander from sea to sea, and   they

thirst.

'It is prettily done,' says the goat, 'if a little melancholy. But I wonder, still, at this scribbling of yours. I am not at all sure that it can be considered a Christian practice, or that I should countenance it.'

Can I still be counted a Christian, greatly changed as I am? Would God himself recognise me, in my goatskins? Am I better or worse in his eyes now, unlovely and wild as I have become?

The cat has walked across the pages of the open Bible. She sniffs the paper and sits.

'What does it do?' she asks. 'Nothing. You comfort yourself with your word games. It is for you, and not for her.'

'And what should I do?' I ask, my voice harsh and loud. 'Since you know everything, cat, tell me what we should do for the dead?'

'Leave them be,' says Sleek.

26

Because a man can only dig so many pits, and because the rats can always dig deeper, I have taken to carrying my tray of offal and scraps to one of the ravines that pierces the island. Here I tip them into the ravine and feed them to the sea below.

I take a fancy that this is a form of offering that I make to the ocean. But how many more offerings will it take to win the sea's mercy?

———

I wake, a bright and wind-scoured morning, and I understand with a calm but unflinching clarity that there is only one kind of mercy that I can be granted. Since the unsettling trial, I have moved sluggishly, as though wading through the deep waters of my shame. Now I understand what I must do: it is time to kill myself.

Have I not had more than enough reason, in the two years I have been here? A man may perhaps carry his shame, if he is tolerably comfortable in other respects. But my life being so exceedingly miserable, and without hope of improvement, my shame is too large to bear. No ship is coming for me, and I have failed even at escape. Why cling to life, and suffer it, when I am but a wretch, laden with every species of sin and disaster? And the goat and the cat, too, must bear their share of the blame – for what good has it done to dredge up all my shameful past? Why could they not let it lie?

Once, in the hills above Largo, I saw a cow whose calf had become stuck during calving. She staggered, unable to escape the caught calf, twisted and dead, halfway out of her and reeking. I think of her now, for I drag my bad fortune behind me in the same way. Even here, so far from everywhere and everyone, I cannot get free of it.

Better by far that I should be gone – better for me, certainly, for I shall be rid of the torments of life on the island.

So sure am I of this that it seems a wonder I have not arrived at this decision earlier. Unable to get off the island by my raft, I must escape it the only way I can.

I inspect my musket – its long barrel makes it ill-suited for suicide. If I turn it about to train it on myself, I cannot even reach the trigger. The island's cliffs would grant me certain death; the sea offers a man many ways to die. But I am a man who likes to trust to the work of his own hands – and so I make a noose.

If I were to leap to my death, or drown myself, the island would keep its secrets, and none would ever know what became of Alexander Selkirk, mariner. But if one day Captain Stradling and his crew return, I should like them to find me here, swinging. The rats will strip my flesh quick enough, but my bones will still tell the story. It gives me no little satisfaction to imagine Stradling coming face to face with my remains and knowing for certain what his cruelty drove me to do.

I tie the hangman's knot carefully, making eight turns, and testing that it draws up smooth and tight.

'You are making something?' asks the goat.

'Nothing,' say I. 'Only practising – it would not do for a sailor to forget his knots.'

'No indeed,' says the goat. 'Am I not always telling you that industry is the enemy of idleness, and thus of sin?'

Ordinarily I am short with him when he takes to preaching. Today I smile and make a show of tying a few more knots in the long tail of my noose.

As for the sin of self-slaughter, you may well reckon that it concerns me little. A man such as I, already so well practised in sin, can scarce go further astray. It is my litany of sins and failings that has driven me to this point – I am as lost to virtue as I am to everything else.

Yet I do not doubt that the Reverend Vicarious Cronch, ever devout, would take a graver view. I wait until the early evening, when he heads west. And if, before he goes, I am particularly assiduous in scratching him beneath his chin and behind his ears, he says nothing of it, and trots away before sundown to seek the island's high places.

I go about my preparations quickly. For a gallows, I choose a pimento tree that affords both a convenient bough and a view over the water. Climbing the tree to affix the rope is no difficulty for a sailor, though at one point I slip on the damp bark and as I catch myself, a cry of fear escapes me. I laugh at myself – how should I fear to fall and break my neck, when I have come up here to hang my noose for that very purpose? You might wonder that a man can laugh at such a time, but in truth I feel altogether lighter. The decision, having been reached, is a tremendous relief. For the first time in more than two years, I can see my way off this island.

When I clamber down, I see the cat watching me. She is chewing on the tail of a dead rat. Perhaps she has been there all the while, for when she sits thus, amongst the ferns, it is hard to make her out.

'You are come to be my audience?' I give the rope a good yank – it holds firm.

'Have you need of an audience?'

I shake my head. 'But as your court has heard the whole of my shameful conduct, you will understand why I do not deserve to live – nor wish to.'

'The court has not yet given you a verdict.'

'Then let this be my verdict.'

I drag my chair across the clearing and set it carefully beneath the rope. Atop the chair I place a squat, wide stump that used to serve as my stool.

The cat observes and says nothing.

'And shall you just sit there and watch?' I ask her.

'It is not my job to change your mind, though you might wish it.'

'Indeed I do not.' What man deserves death more heartily than I? My own stubbornness and folly have brought me close to death enough times. Finish it, Selkirk. Finish what you have begun.

I climb upon the stump. It wobbles a little as I place the noose about my neck. The rope is too long – I must take the noose off again and balance, haphazard, on the stump as I shift the knot up the rope. Yes, there. I place it once more over my head.

'I do this for Effie,' I say.

Sleek yawns. 'Do not imagine that this is for her.'

'Do I not owe her a penance?'

'Did I not tell you to leave the dead alone?'

'How better to do that than by ending it all? Then I can bother nobody – not even you.'

The rope is rough against my skin. How meagre a thing to figure in my thoughts, at such a time – and yet I cannot stop from scratching my neck, nevertheless.

It is time. An ending – yes, this is the ending.

I set one foot to the back of the chair, the better to tip it away. A deep breath. Another. I raise my hands to tighten the noose behind my neck.

My body knows my will. It does not lie. It answers me now, as it answered when I nearly slipped from the tree, and caught myself. It answered when the storm came and I was swept from my raft, and I did not surrender to the sea, nor let myself be drowned. I fought for breath and I fought my way to land; I fought as a wildcat fights, vicious and unquestioning. I chose the island, for all its miseries. My stubborn, faithful body. I chose to live.

Carefully, I lift the noose back up over my head. It snags a moment about my brow, stuck there like a dreadful crown. I jerk it free, and the stump and chair teeter as I climb down.

I sit on the ground, knees drawn up to my chest and arms wrapped tight about them. I am shaking very grievously. Effie – Effie who marched into the sea without even a stone in her pocket to weigh her down. Is it her courage that I lack, or her despair? As for her despair, I should know the exact shape of it, for it was my doing, after all.

But I am a stubborn man. The same stubbornness that has plagued me my entire life, and caused me no end of trouble, will not release me now. I will not take my own life. The sea has a death for me – oh, the sea, with its long patience, shall outlast me. But until then, I will not choose my death.

I look up at where the noose hangs, turning slowly in the night air. Through the noose, I can see the last quarter moon, as though it has been snared.

When I think to look behind me for the cat, she has already left, without so much as a word.

Does she scorn me for thinking of hanging myself, or for failing?

———

Sleek does not return. I call her, though she has never come when called. At dawn on the second day, when she is still not to be found, I call again, and take myself hunting though I have no need of meat. I kill a young goat so that I may lay out the liver and heart for Sleek, hoping that even though she has not answered me, she will answer the call of blood. Still she does not come. Pickle and the other cats tear at the heart, and the rats take the rest.

'I fear that she has left me,' I say to the goat. Her scorn for me – weak creature that I am – has become too much, and she has stalked into the forest and will not return.

'What passed between you?'

'Nothing,' I say. For how can I tell Vicarious Cronch, devout and godly, of what the cat witnessed?

'I would not be so quick to assume that a cat's actions have aught to do with you,' says the goat.

This is hardly comforting – for if she has not left me out of pique, then some harm has come to her.

'What if she fell?' God knows the cliffs of this island are merciless.

'A cat is no more like to fall than a goat,' Cronch says at once, and looks most put out at the suggestion.

'Then what?' She is not fool enough to tangle with a seal, nor a goat's horns – and the last of the sea lions have taken once more to the water, not to return until next winter.

'She is sick, perhaps,' he says. 'Or she has fallen foul of her own kind.'

It is true that the island's cats are avid fighters. If a man found himself here and did not know the island to be overrun with cats, he would surely believe in devils after his very first night ashore, for the cats make a violent tumult, setting up a tremendous long shrieking, rising and falling in pitch, and then flurries of hissing and screams.

'She is dead, then?'

'Don't be so sure,' says the goat. 'An injured cat is not like a man, to run home to be physicked. If she is hurt, or ill, she will have taken to ground.'

'How can that serve her?'

'If she is indeed dying, she will wish to die alone.'

I did not think I would miss Sleek as I do – for she is so scathing, after all, and has a most uncomfortable stare. Sometimes, and particularly since the trial, I have felt uneasily that she sees too much – that she knows the portions of my past that I have not yet been willing to speak. Yet I sleep poorly without her weight beside me on the hammock. And though she could not be described as affable company, she has been company nonetheless.

I walk the island's paths calling her name, and receive nothing but echoes. I climb into the densest forest, which closes its dark wet mouth around me. It closes around me like a pair of hands about the throat. Oh Sleek, see what a poet I am become. This island has made such a strange creature of me, full of goat meat and metaphors.

———

She has been missing four days when I make my way to the lookout, seeking her all the way.

You may wonder why I persist in going to my lookout, after more than two fruitless years. When I made my noose, I was despairing at how long had passed without a ship. Now, having decided to live, I must put a different complexion on it. The more time passes since a ship landed here, the more I consider it likely that one must soon come. My own final, disastrous expedition came here twice, not to mention the French warships that we encountered here. This island is damned by its remoteness, but also blessed by it, being the only place in such a very great distance where a ship may resupply and repair.

'A man is an optimistic creature,' the goat said last night, when I told him I would visit the lookout today.

'I've been prodigious unlucky thus far,' I said. 'But I think it more likely each day that a ship must come.'

'Men at cards will do the same, will they not?' said the goat. 'Bet with ever more fervour, despite loss after loss, because they feel their luck must change. And the longer they lose, the more certain they become that the change is imminent.'

'You may keep your little reflections to yourself,' I told him. And I set off today just the same, for I will not have it said that Alexander Selkirk can be discouraged by the garrulous philosophising of a goat.

I reach the lookout in early afternoon. There are no clouds; the horizon is a surgeon's neat incision on the sky.

There — I see it: a blemish on the ocean, to the nor'-east. I cup my hands to make a funnel before one eye, as if to fashion a looking-glass, though I know it cannot avail me. But the blemish grows, and I do not budge, and while I do not caper and holler as I did last time, I know very certain that it is a ship.

I light my signal fire at the lookout, and use my flint too, for all is urgent, all must happen now. I feed the fire to a frenzy, until it is loud.

The goat has smelled the flames and come to seek me out.

'There is a ship,' I call to him. It is still a great distance off, and the darkening sky makes it harder to see, but I feed my hope as fervently as I fuel the signal fire.

'It may arrive to find the place in ashes.' He gazes up at the blaze, and the flames rear and buck in his dark eyes. 'Do you mean to burn the whole island?'

'What care I for that?' I say. 'I am saved.'

The goat chews a while. 'Will you not at least take some sleep?' It is dark now, and I can see nothing beyond the circle cast by my fire. 'If it is indeed a ship, it will take a long while yet to draw near — and anyway, it will not risk an unfamiliar harbour in darkness.'

'No,' I say. 'No, I could not sleep regardless.' I pace the rocks and curse the waning crescent moon, as slender and useless as a trimming from a fingernail. I must not stop feeding the fire; when I have exhausted all of my gathered wood, I scurry downhill to gather more. It is good to be busy, for when I am stumbling amongst the black trees, arms full of fallen wood, time passes less slow. I am jubilant, giddy. I call to the cat as I walk, for my only sadness is that when I leave the island, I shall not be able to farewell her.

This dawn might have been calculated to show the ship at its best. It is a frigate, cast into relief against the rising sun. They must have sailed all night, for it is now close enough that I can make out each sail, taut with wind. She is coming.

If the night's wait was hard, this is harder. You would not believe that a man who has waited for two years and more would struggle to wait mere hours – but today each of these minutes is pulled from me like a tooth.

At last the frigate is close enough for me to make out the flag. For a moment I grasp at joy – the flag is red. More than anything I've longed to see England's red ensign. But no, it is the red saltire, that jagged cross on white – the Cross of Burgundy. A Spanish ship.

I kick dirt over the fire – I have built it so big, so big and so hot, and I burn my feet with trampling on it, but there is no time for pain, no time for anything. The fire is not out – I empty my water bladder on the flames, which sets up a great hiss and steam, and I curse very loud, for the white steam is more visible than the smoke, and still the fire burns.

'You are not tempted to take your chances with the Spaniards?' asks the goat.

I am still stamping, and hurling on the fire what dirt I can scrape up with my hands. 'The French, I would perhaps take my chances, things being as desperate as they are. But not the Spaniards.'

'You would not consider throwing yourself upon their mercy?'

'The Spanish have little concept of mercy, from all that I have heard.' There is a stinging stench – it is the hairs on my legs, all scorched away. 'It is one thing to be killed in an engagement – that at least is an honest death, and a quick one. But to be tortured or made a slave by the Spaniards?' I shake my head.

'And are you Scots and English so very well known for your mercy? And do you not keep slaves?'

'I have no time for your sophistry.' I stamp on the final embers. 'Not today, when I'm trying to keep myself from ending up in a Spanish mine.'

The fire is out at last. I squat, wincing, to examine the blisters that are already rising on my feet. When I turn back to the water, the ship is making good speed, her studding sails set.

'There was a fellow aboard the *Cinque Ports*,' I say. 'A former navy man, by the name of Alsop. A few years back, he'd been taken by the Spaniards, and spent a year or more in the silver mines. He never spoke of it if he could help it, but it was clear enough that it had been the ruin of him.' Alsop used to flinch whenever the bell sounded; once, a line snapped with a great whipping sound and he dropped to the ground and whimpered. He walked hunched over, moving like a dog that has been kicked so many times that, to him, all the world is a boot. When it was his mess's turn to eat, he could not share food, but would grab at it and turn his back to the table and swallow it down hastily.

We were playing at cards one night – a practice outlawed by most every captain, and therefore much beloved of the men. Having lost the wager, and a goodly quantity of his tobacco, Alsop sighed, as if expecting nothing less, and said, 'I was ever unlucky.'

'Would you say so?' I asked him. 'Some would say you have miraculous luck. You were spared from the mines, after all. You were freed – you got to leave.'

'You're mistaken.' He shook his head. 'There is no leaving such a place.'

The goat looks solemn as I recount this to him. 'But you're no navy man, captured in battle. Are you so sure the Spaniards would deal with you so harshly? And you're a Scot, not an Englishman.'

'I doubt the Spaniards would make such a distinction. And they guard the South Seas jealously – it's the key to their empire. Any foreigner they found here would find his life forfeit – let alone if they discover that I'm a navigator who knows these seas, and sailed them as a privateer, what's more.'

I am faced now with a dreadful choice: do I stay concealed in the high, rocky reaches and the forests, where no stranger to the island could hope to find me? Or do I head down to my camp, to try to bear away some of my few possessions, in case the Spaniards should locate my camp? If they saw my fire, and know the island to be occupied, it would take but little searching to find the place, close to the harbour as it is. I think of my possessions – so meagre, but so hard won, by painful labour.

But to retrieve them is to put myself in the Spaniards' way. It will take me over an hour to reach my camp, if I sprint, for it is largely downhill; some time more to gather or hide my belongings; considerably more time to regain this spot, especially if laden with any of my things. The ship is so close – close enough that I can count her gunports and make out all the little features of her construction that now mark her clearly as Spanish: the flat transom stern, and the great deal of giltwork. Any minute she could bear westward and enter the bay, or set down a boat.

I make a hasty survey of what I have with me: my knife, my empty water bladder and my flint. A little piece of smoked goat meat, stuffed into my flint pouch for safekeeping. Everything else I must consider forfeit, or risk my very life. But I do resolve, should I survive this, to find a place away from my camp where I may hide those other treasures that I do not need daily – my little store of powder; my flintlock musket; my mathematical instruments.

My eyes have not left the ship, but I lean closer to the goat. 'If she is to anchor in the bay, she must soon bear west.' I realise that I am whispering, which is absurd, for the ship is still well offshore, and could not hear me if I bellowed.

She does not turn, but holds her line south. Yet still I cannot be at all easy in my mind. A captain who does not know this island may think to find another anchorage; may not know how hostile are the cliffs on the island's southern side. The frigate may yet bear west, in search of another harbour; may come around again to my bay.

It is a strange feeling indeed, to wish this ship away from the island, when all my imaginings of these past years have been to summon a vessel. Crouched as I am amongst the rocks, I nevertheless feel mighty exposed to the gaze of every man aboard the frigate. A ship of that size could bear several hundred men – are they staring now, some of them through their spyglasses?

She is in good trim – that gives me hope that she has no need of this place. No ship comes here save in desperation.

She does not turn; the wind behind her is steadfast and she does not hesitate in her going, and I watch her all the way, hour after hour, until she is gone.

I slump to the ground, shaking. It is over. Over, and I do not know how to feel. I shall not be made a slave by the Spaniards; I shall remain here, to bear the terrible weight of my aloneness.

who shall   redeem

the ships

the sea

shall not

Remember

me

27

In the melancholy days that follow the ship's passing, my one comfort is the return of the cat, who limps into camp two nights after the ship sailed out of view. She is thin; her body is a tent of flesh, slung between her sharp hips and shoulders. Her fur has lost its lustre, and is patchy and dull. Behind one ear is a great scab, blackened and stiff.

When I squat and run my hand down her back, I can feel each lump of her spine, like a rope studded with knots.

'I thought you were dead,' I say. 'Or that you were angry with me.'

'This is not about you.'

'What happened?'

'Teeth and claw,' she says.

'You should have come to me. You should not have been alone.'

'All creatures die alone,' she says. 'Cats are wise enough to know it.'

'But you did not die.'

'Not this time. Bring me liver.'

In her honour, I slaughter one of my penned goats, for Sleek is so grievous thin that I do not trust that she will survive while I go hunting. I set the bowl of blood before her while it still steams. Her front legs give way as she bends to drink, so I steady her with my hand beneath her chest. When she has drunk her fill, I take the goat liver and dice it into tiny cubes which I feed her, one by one, from my finger. She eats with absolute determination, and instead of bathing herself as she usually does after a meal, makes at once for my hammock. I reach out to lift her, but she hisses; whether I have touched some injury, or whether it is a matter of a cat's dignity, I am not sure. She makes the leap herself, and curls at once into a tight ball, eyes firmly shut, one ear flicking like a restless moth.

'I am glad you came to me at last,' I confide to the dark. If she hears me, she makes no answer.

Over the next week she eats as though it is her profession. Not once does she thank me for the food I bring her; instead, her demands are as imperious as ever, and sometimes very specific. 'Goat milk,' she says one day, and the next, 'Fish. Not the spiny small ones. A fat soft fish, with big firm eyes.'

It pleases me to answer her whims, and it distracts me from my own sorrow after the passing of the Spanish boat. Sleek begins once more to wash herself. Her fur has been so wretched and dull that to call her *Sleek* would be a taunt; now she begins to shine again, and the scab on her ear has flaked away, revealing fresh swollen flesh, gaudily pink.

'Will you not tell me what happened?' I scratch her head, taking care not to touch the wound on her ear. 'It was another cat you fought, I take it?'

'He forgot himself.'

'And shall you fight him again?'

'I shall not have to. He will not make the same mistake.'

'I wish you had come to me,' I say.

'I was sick – it would not serve me to have the other cats see me like that.'

'She has a position to maintain,' says the Reverend Vicarious Cronch, somewhat officiously.

'Are there captains, then, and admirals, amongst cats? Rules of precedence, as amongst gentlemen?'

'Something like that,' says the goat, but the cat speaks over him.

'Teeth and claw,' she says. 'These are your precedence, your rules.'

Within two weeks, the cat is herself again: her bones no longer protrude, and her fur gleams. I am kept busy with my project of concealing some of my valuables, in case the Spanish come again and find my camp. Some things I cannot bear to stow away; apart from the daily necessities of life, I like to keep my Bible near me in the camp, and my musket too (though it has not been fired for well over a year). I gather only those treasures I don't need at hand day-to-day: my navigational tools; a fragment of my broken flint; my store of powder, leaving but a little remaining with my musket. These I bury carefully beneath a stone in a shallow cave, taking great care that the spot is dry, so that my powder shall not spoil.

I am also determined to conceal the approach to my camp from the shore, by readying a quantity of leafy boughs that I can cast over the main path should a Spanish ship arrive. However, the truth is that I am so often coming and going from the shore that the path is now very well trod, and even when I cover it thickly with the boughs, all but the most cursory glance would still reveal the path, which now ends abruptly where I have laid the branches. And even this poor conceit shall work only if I have time to drag the boughs over the path – I cannot by any means leave the path blocked all the time, coming and going as I am. Thus I must content myself with having hidden a few treasures, for to hide my camp more thoroughly would be to make my daily life sorely inconvenient, which I am reluctant to do, being already beset by every manner of difficulty.

In need of meat, I set out at dawn with my knife. This is the best time for hunting, while the goats make their way down from their rocky fastness on the island's west, by paths that I have long since learned. I am waiting, therefore, behind a boulder, where I have found that I may spy the procession of goats as they pass above, and take my pick, and then be ready to spring out and catch my chosen goat when the herd has turned on the crooked track to pass below me.

This morning there is particular piebald chap, unlike any others I have seen on the island, his hide a jaunty scattering of black spots on white. And even a man as abandoned as I may still have his little vanities – thus I take a notion that this piebald goat will make a fetching hide, for a jerkin or even a blanket, and I resolve to have him, though he is larger than what I want for meat. My knife in hand, I crouch and wait. The smell of goat is growing – I would never say as much to the Reverend Vicarious Cronch, but goats have a powerful odour, and bucks most especially.

The first of the goats are trotting below my rock now, orderly and quick. I note the grey buck who was ahead of my piebald in the procession. The hoof-falls behind him are crisp on the rocky path, so I jump – but what is this, squirming in my grasp and giving outraged squeals? Not my piebald but a white goat, and small too. I have mistimed my jump, or the piebald has stopped to forage. I release the white kid and turn, and there is the piebald, startled along with the rest of them into frantic motion. These goats take to speed the way a seal takes to water – they belong in it, so swift and sure on the stones. By the time I round the corner of the steep track the piebald is already ten yards ahead.

But I have not survived this long without some stubbornness of my own, and this island has made me nimble and fitter than I have ever been. I chase hard, and when we reach the ridge I gain on him, for he is slowed by coming upon a cluster of his fellows, all jammed in the same little pass, which he must surmount by hopping right atop their backs. By the time he has leapt from there to the rock beyond, my own path has taken me near to him, and with a great jump of my own I am able to grab him, at least by one of his hind legs, though I take a mighty kicking for my efforts, and am much scratched, for I have pursued him into a thicket. I have him now – but he gives one more spring. Staggering, I refuse to release his leg and am dragged forward, and suddenly we are both of us falling, falling, and this is to be the end of Alexander Selkirk, the end of all my stories, told and untold.

———

I am ushered back to the world by a rough scraping at the side of my face. It is so rough indeed that at first I have a fancy that I am being sanded, like a fresh-hewn plank – for I have been dreaming of ships, as I am wont to do, and of the ruined hull of the *Cinque Ports*. But this sanding is prodigious wet, and thus over time I realise that I am under the ministrations of Sleek, who is licking me very thorough and none too tender.

I am lying on my belly, my head turned to the side. Having washed my face, the cat now sets about my ears and there is no lying still for that, so I try to shift my head away, though the pain in my back and neck is fearsome.

'You are not dead,' she says.

'I would wish myself dead,' I say, 'if it would rid me of this pain.'

How I am not dead I do not know – surely I fell too far to have survived? Yet the answer is perhaps beneath me, for I am not on the ground. No – I am lying on the piebald goat, his body stiff and cold below mine.

The cat yawns. 'If you are to die, take off your jerkin first – goat hide is tough to chew through.'

'You would eat me?'

'How else should a cat honour its dead?'

I suppose all meat is the same to a cat, and what is a man but a particularly large sack of meat.

I shift upon the body of the goat. 'You would eat the goat first, surely.'

A languorous stretch. 'I tire of goat meat.'

Time is mighty uncertain – it has been knocked about, as has my body, and so I cannot say how long has passed, or whether I am awake or asleep, or both at once. My sight is blurred, and when I try to fix my gaze on any single thing, my head pains me so grievously that I must shut my eyes again and cease my trying. It is hot, and then it cools. The cat has not left my side. She has not yet begun to eat me, which I must take as a good sign.

It is just my luck that my vision at last begins to clear as it grows dark. I can see little but the face of the cat, who is perched close by, her muzzle stained with blood.

'What happened to you? Have you been fighting once again?'

'The blood is yours.' Her efficient tongue unfurls from her mouth and she licks at the blood on her cheek and chin.

I bestir myself and try to rise, but my limbs are grown disobedient, and my legs most particularly will not stir at all.

'If you stand, you will only fall,' says Sleek.

'It is the piebald goat's fault,' I say. 'He led me over the cliff – it was hidden by bushes.'

'You have that goat to thank,' says Sleek. 'He broke your fall.'

'Broke,' I echo. I have no energy to say more, for the longer I am awake, the more the pain is yanking at me with all its barbed hooks. *I am broken*, I want to say. My head, my back, my limbs. There is no part of me that is not in pain. I do not even know the site of the wound that marked Sleek with my blood. I am all wound.

———

A different pain – smaller. A nip at my ear, and then another. Then the swiping: she bats my face with her paw, extending just enough of her claws to let me know that they are there.

Is she eating me? Perhaps I am dead, after all, though I had not thought being dead would be so very painful.

'Enough,' Sleek says. 'Wake.'

Another swipe of my face, this time with more claw.

I open my eyes. It is dawn – I have lain here a full day and night, the dead goat beneath me. The flies have found its gaping eyes, and settled on them like black scabs. I close my eyes so that they will not start on mine.

Another swipe to my cheek. 'Enough,' the cat says again.

I am thirsty, I realise, and all of a sudden I can think of nothing else. My tongue is a sandbag in my mouth. The small water bladder I carry with me was burst in the fall – it hangs from my belt, flaccid and torn. The piebald goat beneath me has grown stiffer. He lies in a moat of his own blood. I reach out and touch the sharp tip of one of his horns – it is a wonder I was not impaled when we fell. I recall that my knife was in my hand as I pursued the goat - it is even more remarkable that I was not impaled on that. But where is it? My breath is fast and rasping – that knife, blunted as it is, is my greatest treasure.

Unable to stand, instead I heave myself onto all fours. In the dawn light I can now make out the precipice above me, and I cannot believe that I fell so far, nor that I lived. But it hurts my head to look upward, so I fix my gaze on the rocky ground, and begin to cast about for my knife. A blessing – it is there, a few feet from the dead goat. I crawl to it, heedless of my pain, and clutch it to me before examining it. If it has been damaged in the fall, it is already so sorely blunted and chipped that I cannot see the difference – at least, not with my blurred and yawing vision.

I scramble over the goat once more. I shall not have his hide after all, for I cannot by any means carry him, and even if I could, he has already the foetid stink of decay. When the cat leaves, the rats shall have him. Such a waste of a handsome hide. Before I leave I crouch and, with shaking hands, make my slit in his ear. 'There,' I say, 'you piebald bastard. I shall account you mine, though I got nothing from you.'

I was not more than a mile from my camp when I fell, and though I have never before been at the base of this precipice, to a sailor the dawn sun is as good as a signpost, and I know that I have only to make my way nor'-east. But I crawl like a wounded bear, noisy and slow, the pain much worsened by movement. My legs I had initially thought broken, but they bear my crawling well enough – it is my head that I fear for. My brain is a clapper in a noisy bell, crashing against the side of my skull with each tiny motion. And of course this island will not offer me anything as simple as a path, or even a straightforward route. No, instead I am foundering on rocks, and when I gain ground I am met by more small crevices, and it is several hours before I find myself again on a familiar path, though everything looks different from down here, crawling as I am. I have pissed myself, and my goatskin trousers chafe my legs something terrible. It is only a small pain but somehow as loud in my head as all the larger pains from the fall. Several times I stop to vomit; having not eaten for a long time, there is nothing to bring up but a sharp green bile.

The cat is gone – having wakened me, perhaps she considers her work done, and indeed I do not know what aid she could give me on this journey – yet I wish she were here, or the goat, to urge me on. Many times I long to lay on the dirt and be done with my dying. I do stop once, the pain being so very great and my progress so slow that there seems no point to it. I let myself slump forward to the ground and lie still. However, I find that the pain does not relent and so, with the stubbornness my father used to curse, I decide that if I am to hurt all the same, I may as well keep going and die in the comfort of my own camp. And if I do not die, then at least there I may drink, for my thirst is another pain in my grand collection.

When I crawl to the outskirts of my camp, the goat rushes to meet me.

'Friend,' he says, and looks mighty alarmed at the state of me. 'I have been worried about you.'

'I have had enough of goats,' I say. 'Leave me be.'

He does not. He draws near, lowers his head and sniffs me all over, raising his front lip to bare his gums, as he is wont to do. He sniffs the wound at my head, and my wet trousers, and though I must smell foul, he stays close by me.

I drink lukewarm water from my kettle, vomit, and drink more. I fall into my hammock and ignore the mewling of Pickle, begging for food. It may be sleep that takes me, or it may be unconsciousness – either way I welcome it.

Pain makes an old man of me. For days I am slow and hunched. My thinking is not clear, and nor is my sight. I take up my Bible but the letters will not be still, shifting and crawling as though the page is overrun with ants. I toss the book across the hut.

The goat and the cat keep me company. We speak; sometimes I am melancholy, and sometimes I find the slightest thing amusing and would laugh and laugh were not my ribs so sore. I eat little, though I am prodigious thirsty. I have neither the energy nor the appetite to slaughter one of my tamed goats, but I drink goat milk daily. The cut on my head continues to swell, straining at its scab.

'You look like a kid just beginning to sprout his horns,' says the goat.

Perhaps I have a fever, for that night I dream I grow a pair of splendid horns, curved and ridged. Even when I wake I can still feel their weight.

It is ten days before I am again able to go abroad, and even then only with a great deal of limping. Though I am much wasted, my body feels heavy.

'You do not easily die,' the cat says.

I nod. 'This island keeps trying to kill me nonetheless.'

'I have another riddle for you,' says the cat.

'You have not even answered me the first, to my satisfaction.'

She ignores me. 'Riddle me this, Mister Selkirk: what is cat and goat at once, and neither?'

This I cannot fathom. I can think of many things that are neither cat nor goat, but none that are both. Or is her riddle just some play on words, with no deeper significance?

'Is it *at*?' I ask. 'For it is in both *cat* and *goat*, but is neither?'

'Nothing so petty.'

'It is but a riddle – why should it be anything serious?'

'A riddle is always serious,' she says.

'Why do you torment me? Have I not enough to endure without you taunting me with riddles that have no answer?'

'Fool,' she says, almost fondly. 'I have given you the answer.'

28

I recover steadily and resume my ordinary routine. You might think a savage, castaway life such as mine would be rank disorder, but in fact I find my days on the island have formed an order of their own. I have no timepiece, nor a ship's bell announcing the changing of shifts – but the island has its own shifts, and after nigh on two and a half years here, I have learned them well.

I wake at dawn and lay abed a short while, the cats close about me. I scratch Pickle beneath her chin, though when she stretches her mouth in a great yawn, her breath does smell most sorely of offal.

I must rise soon enough – first to check the view across the bay, for each new day dangles the possibility of rescue before me, and replaces it with despair when the horizon remains empty. Next I must tend the fire, for its hunger never ceases. I bank up the coals overnight, but by dawn I must coax it back to a solid flame. And on damp days, of which I have a surfeit, the fire must be started afresh, and though I am much more skilful now than once I was, that is still half an hour of work with my rubbing stick, and careful tending to get the fire to a comfortable burn. All the while my she-goat is letting me know, with hawing and shrieking, that she is ready to be milked.

That job being done, I break my fast with a bowl of milk, and then must feed and water the goats with armfuls of leaves and grass, and check that they have not damaged their pen, for even goats as well fed as mine can be counted upon to gnaw at a fence.

If I'm in need of meat I head early to the winding paths, to catch a goat on its descent from the island's heights. This work accounts for much of the afternoon – not the catching nor the killing, which are swift, but the work that follows. I must butcher the carcass, and set out the scraps for the cats, not neglecting to pour Sleek her bowl of blood. I must begin the curing of the hide, and the smoking of the meat – all of it familiar work now, but dull.

If it is not a slaughtering day, and I have enough daylight hours, I go to my lookout. Whereas my camp gives me a good vantage point to the north, my lookout lets me survey the seas in all directions – little though it avails me. On the way back down I gather fallen wood, or anything else that may prove useful: palm fibres fit for ropemaking; a split rock sharp enough to be put to work as an axe; an armful of the pale grass that my tame goats like above all others. And as soon as I get back to camp, my first concern is to feed my fire anew.

If I have already been to the lookout within the last few days, I may go instead to the shore to seek some salt, or to slaughter a seal, if I need oil for tapers. Or there may be some particular task demanding my attention – indeed, there are usually several. A new pail to be carved; turnips to be dug and boiled; in summer, pimento berries to be gathered and dried.

In the late afternoon, I take my dinner. I have come to find that two meals a day suffices – and even with the aid of pimento or salt, the drudgery of my bland diet means I could stomach no more. Listlessly, I chew on my cabbage leaves and goat meat; often I close my eyes and try to remember the taste of cheese, or wine, or lamb.

On summer evenings, when the light allows, there are more tasks to be done: scraping a hide; rendering seal fat for tapers; the endless task of gathering wood.

The goat takes himself to the high places; the cats draw near. By firelight, or by the light of my tapers (though I try to ration these), I work at twisting rope, or mending my clothes, which now look exceedingly eccentric, being nearly all contrived of goat hide. I read my Bible, or take to it with my charcoal. The cats take to my bed before I do, for first I must set my fire for the night and ensure there is some wood put by for the morning. When at last I seek my hammock, the cats make way grudgingly, though oftentimes they slip from the bed at night, to hunt. Asleep, I dream of ships: ships sinking, or ships sailing to my rescue. Sometimes they are one and the same; I watch from my lookout as the ships approaching the island to free me are run aground on rocks. They sink fast, and I wake weeping.

This is the shape of my days: labour and drudgery. I have at once too much time – these fearsome uncharted years, stretching on forever – and too little – for every task here is made longer by my lack of proper tools or materials. And I can never entirely take my ease, for there is always more to be done, and between the rats and the insects and the rain, this island is parsimonious with comfort. You cannot imagine the tedium of it: the hide that I cured but a month ago now mildewing in the damp; the water bladder that I painstakingly stitched now chewed upon by rats; the woodpile that shrinks and shrinks and never grows, no matter how many logs I haul. I am trapped in a game with neither purpose nor end, and the familiarity of these days makes them no easier to endure.

I know that I have elected to live, and not to die. But on the worst of these days, when my labour seems as endless as the blank horizon, a man could not be blamed if his thoughts drift sometimes to the noose, or to a cliff.

But what would the Reverend Vicarious Cronch say, full of censure and godliness? And who would pour blood for Sleek, and suffer her scorn?

The *Cinque Ports* sails into my dreams. She wallows there, her worm-eaten hull and her clumsy keel, the wet rot stink of her. In my dreams she is foundering, and Captain Stradling himself is at the pump, pumping even as the waves top the gunwale, and she is a ship that welcomes the water, for she is already more worm than wood. She sinks with a sigh that sounds like relief, and Stradling takes his pumping to the bottom of the sea, and all our men with him.

'I dreamed of my old ship last night,' I tell the goat and the cat. 'Much as I hated her, it pains me to think that she is surely sunk.'

'Are you so very sure that she must be sunk?' asks the goat.

'A sailor knows when a ship is done for. It's not superstition – it's a matter of wood and water.'

'Then the sea gave you your death,' Sleek says, 'and you refused it.'

'And I for one am mightily glad,' says the goat quickly. 'Though still you have not told us about the voyage that brought you here, nor how you came to leave that ship.'

The cat ignores him and continues staring at me. 'Your death is not a gift you can refuse forever.'

She stretches, arching her spine and flaring her claws. The mast of her tail stands tall, so that every part of her is stretched at once.

'Do you really think you can refuse the sea's gifts?' She meanders away.

'Sleek,' I call after her. 'Sleek. Who would want such a gift?'

She turns. 'Still you think as men do. You think it matters what you want.'

———

I do not notice the stink of me unless I take myself into the bay to bathe. Afterwards, when I don my hides again, I realise how much I have taken on the odour of goat. In my long hair and beard, and my goatskin clothes, which these days I fashion not according to anything but my own comfort, I am goat-like indeed.

'You might easily be mistaken for one of us,' says the Reverend Vicarious Cronch.

Once, this would have offended me. Now I laugh. 'Though I might wish for a goat's nimbleness across the rocks – it might have saved me from the fall.'

He shakes his head. 'That we can never teach you. Nor would we, for you are become quite nimble enough, and we goats know it to our cost, for you have caught so many of us.'

'Yet you are still here,' I say. 'And we are friends, are we not?'

'We are good friends,' says the goat, very gravely. 'Though I should be most offended if you tried to eat me.'

'Sir,' I say. 'I would never dream of it.'

He turns his head, the better to fix me with one of his monstrous goat eyes. 'I know.'

I am not accustomed to making promises; I am even less accustomed to being believed.

———

behold,

a

plague

of

water

All men, I imagine, have some need of company; a sailor more than most, for his is a crowded life, crammed as he is below decks with so many others. Even as a child, my house had such a surfeit of brothers that I could not so much as roll over without Andrew elbowing me in the ribs. Altogether, I have never learned how to be alone. On the island, my aloneness has been so savage that I even find myself missing Andrew.

But sometimes, on these winter evenings, the goat draws close to the fire and lowers himself in his ungainly way, his legs folded beneath him. Sitting in front of him, I lean back against his warmth. A goat does not make a very soft pillow, particularly an old goat such as the Reverend Vicarious Cronch, being largely a collection of bones. Nevertheless when we sit like this, and when Sleek is by my side, the whole of her thrumming with purrs, and Pickle at my feet, I find that I forget to be lonely.

The goat summons me at dawn. It has been more than six months since my fall. I am healed – or as healed as I shall ever be, for still my bones ache, and my left hip clicks when I walk.

Cronch is polite but sombre. 'You are called upon once more to answer certain charges.'

'Now,' the cat says.

There is no arguing with a cat, and thus I follow her, the goat behind me, and we make our way to the appointed spot. If I was wary of that cliffside when first I was summoned there, you may imagine how wary I am since my fall, the scar on my head still tender to the touch. I stand as far from the edge as the clearing will allow, and watch the goat mount his stone pedestal.

He wastes no time. 'Let us commence the second trial of Alexander Selkirk.'

'On what charge?' I am weary – healed but not yet fit, so that this march has left me more tired than I would admit, and in an ill humour.

'Charged with the sin of murder—'

'That's a calumny,' I yell. 'I never killed a man outside of my duty. Would you try every privateer? And every sailor in the Navy, and all the admiralty too, for the deaths under their command?'

'Be patient, sir,' says the goat. 'For I have not finished the charge.' He clears his throat. 'Charged with the sin of murder against himself – self-murder.'

I spin to face the cat. 'You told him?' I had believed that my stringing up the noose was something we held in confidence – a sharing somehow more intimate even than her warm body asleep in the lee of my chest at night.

'Quiet,' she says. 'Listen.'

'I didn't do it,' I shout at her. 'I stopped.'

'Fool,' she says. 'This is not about the noose. You have harmed yourself in other ways – much worse.'

'A nonsense.' I turn away and make for the path, but Sleek blocks my way. Her back is arched in an angry contraction, and all her fur standing on end so that she is twice her usual size.

'You chose to come here,' she says.

'Begone.' I swipe at her with my foot, and she unspools a hiss louder than any I have heard.

The goat calls from behind me. 'So you claim you did not seek to make away with yourself, in the series of events that led to you being left on this island?'

'This is nonsense.' I turn back to him. 'I live, though this island oftentimes makes me wish I were dead. How can I be charged with self-murder when I'm still alive? And what business is it of either of you, whether a man wishes to live or to die? I had not thought wild beasts to have such a fine Christian morality.'

'Am I not a minister?' He speaks as though it is a thing that could never be doubted – as a man might hold out a rock and say, *Is this not a rock?*

'My own morality is of course Christian,' he goes on. 'And on the topic of self-slaughter, the church's teachings are quite clear. As to the rest of this island's creatures: while I regret I could not call them Christian, their morality is very much concerned with survival. You might say survival is a sort of commandment amongst animals. Thus this court considers self-slaughter a grave thing.'

'You would condemn even Effie?' How could she be blamed for what she did, when I left her with nowhere to turn but the sea?

'Selkirk,' says Sleek. 'This is your trial, and not hers.'

The goat resumes his recitation. 'This court charges that the said Alexander Selkirk, lately of Nether Largo, Fifeshire, did, on the fifth day of October 1704, conspire to commit self-murder, by causing himself to be marooned on the island of Más a Tierra, of the Juan Fernández islands.'

'You know nothing of how I came to be here.'

'Indeed. You have kept it close – which is itself a matter of some suspicion.'

'Is a man permitted to keep nothing to himself?'

The goat raises his chin. 'Mister Selkirk, you are on this island on sufferance. It is time to account for how you came to be here.'

The cat gives one more hiss, her meaning unmistakable.

My history being what it is, and my conduct so very far from exemplary, I am no stranger to being called to account for myself in a manner of court. And while at the time the kirk session in Largo seemed fearsome weighty, no court has been more chilling nor more stern than this island court, overseen by the goat and the cat, and the unrelenting sky behind them.

'Now,' the goat says, 'to the evidence. On your first morning alone on the island, when you discovered the length of rope, did you not say that it would be useful, *if only to hang myself with?*'

'That was a jest.'

'And yet such a jest reveals something of your state of mind, would you not agree?'

'I would not.'

'And have you not yourself often complained that you have been *abandoned to die on this God-forsaken island*, and many similar laments?'

'I have – and who could blame me for that, seeing how I am reduced to living?'

'And can you name the man who caused you to be left here?'

'Indeed I can. It was Captain Thomas Stradling – though he scarce deserves the rank.'

'You lie.' How the cat contrives to hiss this, though her words contain no *s*, I cannot say.

'I do not. It was Stradling who left me here, despite my begging.'

'Only he?' asks the goat.

'Captain Dampier deserves some of the blame – for it was he who led the whole disastrous voyage, and appointed Stradling captain, after Pickering died.'

The cat's growl is like a can of gravel being shaken. 'Who else?'

I press my hands to my ears. 'Enough. I have told you: Stradling and Dampier.'

'No,' the goat says. 'Mister Selkirk, this court is not a place for dissembling, and this island neither. It is time to tell the truth. Thus I ask you one final time: who was it who first said that you would remain on this island?'

'It was I.'

29

How big must a man's folly be, that it can cost him the whole of his life? As big as a ship; as big as an island.

It starts with Dampier. Since my second and final escape from Nether Largo, I have worked my way around several oceans. Brined in my anger and my disgrace, I work the trade routes and do a good job with an ill humour. I make no friends. I study my trade, and ashore I drink much, and alone. When I take a woman to bed it makes me melancholy, and this then curdles into anger against the woman. These days I am a compass needle, turning always towards fury. I take whatever posts I may, and I keep moving − for since Effie's death and my public disgrace, there can be no returning to Nether Largo. My family wants no part of me; the sea does not want me either, but at least it refuses nothing.

In May of 1703, in Kinsale, I secure a post on a privateering expedition, led by one Captain William Dampier, late of the navy, and with a reputation for prodigious travels. He has sailed the entire world, and even published a book about his voyages. He is to captain the *St George*, in convoy with the *Cinque Ports*. It is this smaller of the two ships that I am to join, and I shall be its master, under Captain Charles Pickering.

And if this role is given me with little interrogation, I do not ask myself why they have no master already, and are willing to take me on at barely twenty-three years old. I for one will ask no questions, eager as I am to be gone, having been three weeks ashore and drunk nearly the whole of my savings, and being out of favour with various men of Kinsale, by means of fighting and whoring. I wish only to be gone – for if I am not kept busy, I am much plagued by images of Effie Breck, floating like driftwood, face down.

Dampier's expedition does not only promise me an escape, but a great deal more – truly there is no end to Dampier's promises. He has announced that he will seize one of the Spanish treasure ships that ply the South Seas. These Manila galleons are the ocean's grandest prize, voyaging but once a year between Acapulco and Manila. 'And laden with gold, silver and other treasures you could scarce believe,' Dampier tells us. Oh, it is a manifest of riches enough to set any man's prick stirring. Sailors still speak in awed tones of Cavendish's capture of one such galleon, well over a century ago.

And if around Kinsale docks there is other talk, too – rumours that Dampier has an unsavoury reputation, and few are willing to serve under him – then I pay no heed to those whispers, for what can they offer me, next to Dampier's enticements of riches and glory?

When the purser, Mister Morgan, enters my name into the ship's articles, he makes it *Selkirk*, and I do not correct him, though it is usually writ *Selcraig* or *Selchraig*. Indeed I enjoy this idea of cutting off my old name, like slicing a cable that tethers me to my old life. The man who wore that name is burdened with all manner of disasters – let me be rid of him altogether. As for the *kirk*, that pleases me a great deal. I am leaving behind me the kirk and its judgments – see me sail away, Alexander Selkirk, taking the *kirk* in my very name, so little do I fear it or its censures.

The *St George* and the *Cinque Ports* are goodly ships, and well provisioned for a long journey, both in victuals and in war-like stores. The *St George* has twenty-six guns and carries 120 men. My ship, the *Cinque Ports*, has sixteen guns, sixty-three men. There, I tell myself: there is no shortage of men willing to sail under Dampier after all – and if they are an ill-assorted collection, that is only to be expected of a privateering crew. For what are privateers, after all, but men with the stomach to fight the enemy, but without the stomach for the navy and its discipline? As we work to ready the ships, I watch the crew muster. Excluding Dampier's officers, the men are a rabble: merchant sailors; former navy-men; ruffians with no experience of sailing but much in fighting; and those desperate cases who take to the sea because courts or creditors or importunate wives have made it unwise for them to stay ashore. How should I judge them – am I not such a man?

My only concern, upon first inspecting the *Cinque Ports*, is that her hull is not sheathed – nor is that of the *St George*. A good layer of tarred hair or felt, applied to the hull and overlaid with a layer of pine, gives some protection against worms. And we shall be sorely in need of that layer of sacrificial planks – for Darien taught me well about the voracious worms of the South Sea, who eat ships extremely hard, more so than in any other part of the world.

Dampier has come aboard to consult with Captain Pickering, and I join them and the other officers on the deck.

'Shall the hull not be sheathed, sir, before we sail?' I ask him.

'Sheathing spoils the sailing of ships,' he says at once, and marches ahead, to confer with Pickering.

'Do you know what else spoils the sailing of a ship?' I say to Funnell, the mate of the *St George*, who has fallen in beside me. 'Sinking to the floor of the damned ocean.'

Dampier looks back at me, his chin raised a little so that he is staring down his long, straight nose. 'Mister Selkirk,' he says. 'Have you an opinion on the preparations I have seen fit to make?'

Dampier may have left the navy, but he has still that martial aspect to his bearing. I have never been a prudent man, but even I am prudent enough not to pick a fight with him before we have even set out, and on my first voyage as ship's master, what's more. And if I announce that I have sailed the South Seas and know how viciously the worms thereabouts work at a hull, that will only serve to remind them all – Englishmen, by and large – of my part in the Darien disaster.

'No, sir,' I say.

A week after we sail from Kinsale, the *Cinque Ports'* officers are invited aboard the *St George* to dine. For all its luxuries, I am ill at ease in the great cabin, where most of the officers are gentlemen. I say little, for I fancy they will know me for an interloper; I fancy that the stench of Nether Largo clings to me: the herring nets, and my father's hides, hanging half-cured in his workshop. At the head of the table, Dampier holds forth at length about his famous travels. He styles himself something of a botanist, and gives a long disquisition on the sago tree of the Philippine Islands and its many uses, and of the avocado pears of the isle of Chepelio.

'Who knows what marvels we shall carry home in our hold,' he says, raising his glass. 'Not just Spanish treasure, but wonders of the natural world also. What a name we shall make for the *St George* – and the *Cinque Ports* too.'

Where most of the men pronounce our ship the *Sink Ports*, Dampier always says it French-wise, *Sank*, for he is at pains to show himself a cultured fellow. I think of the *Cinque Ports'* unsheathed hull; *Sink* or *Sank* makes no difference, for neither name augurs well for a ship.

Afterwards, when we take a turn about the deck, the *St George's* garrulous mate, Funnell, hangs back from the others to walk with me.

'You were mighty quiet during the meal,' he says.

'What can a man such as I say among gentlemen, and scholars too?'

At this Funnell laughs. 'Ah – the avocado pears, and all that fiddle-faddle? Do you know how our fine captain earned his bread, when he was a younger man?'

I do not need to ask Funnell to tell me, for it is plain to see that he is fit to bursting with his knowledge, and well pleased with it. On a ship, gossip is currency, just as much as tobacco or coin.

'A buccaneer,' he says. 'Pirating his way around the Caribbean.'

I shrug. 'How many privateers might be called pirates, except for a letter of marque?' It's the same job, after all – the only difference is that we privateers have the Queen's blessing for our raids, and are sworn to attack only enemy ships. That Dampier went pirating in his youth does not shock me, except inasmuch as it contrasts with his rather proper and haughty demeanour. He has let it be known that he shook the hand of the Queen herself, introduced by the Lord High Admiral, when he received his letter of marque for this voyage.

'And if he was indeed a buccaneer,' I say to Funnell, 'then he will know what he's about, when it comes to hunting Spaniards.' Buccaneers, unlike ordinary pirates, prey upon Spaniards most particularly.

'I'll allow that the buccaneering isn't the worst of it,' says Funnell. 'He even confesses to it in his book. But there's something that he'll never put in one of his books.' Here he lowers his voice and leans closer. 'Ask Dampier why he's taken once more to privateering, instead of another commission with the navy – I dare you.'

We both know full well that this is a wager I will not be taking up – for who would be brazen enough to ask Dampier this? A captain is king of his ship, and Dampier is more imperious than most.

Funnell's voice is still the merest whisper. 'He was court-martialled, after his voyage on the *Roebuck*. Found guilty, too – of *very hard and cruel usage* of his first lieutenant.'

'What did he do?'

'Abused him roundly, and in the end had him beaten and put in irons like a common sailor, and no officer at all.'

'Perhaps the man deserved it,' I say.

'The court martial didn't find so – declared Dampier unfit to command any navy vessel. Docked his pay too.' Funnell grins – for nothing pleases such a man so well as his superiors being brought low. 'Do you not wish you had enquired further, before signing up to a voyage under such a man?'

'And which of us is the greater fool?' I ask. 'The man who signed up in ignorance, or the man who signed up fully knowing what our captain is?'

And this at least shuts him up, which I account a mercy, because if Funnell fell overboard in fifty-fathom water, I firmly believe that he'd be talking all the way down to the ocean's floor.

As for Dampier, if he has gone from buccaneer to respectable man, I do not hold it against him. It suits me all the better, I think, as we are rowed back across the dark water to the *Cinque Ports*. I close my eyes and I see Effie Breck, floating, her hair spread out about her face. But tonight, when Dampier spoke of the Manila galleon and how we shall seize her, I could believe anything is possible. I could even believe that a man such as I – unsavoury in both habits and reputation – can be transformed.

If we are to hunt the Manila galleon, we must first travel to where it approaches Acapulco, half the world from Kinsale. You might think that after Darien, I would have no appetite to return to the South

Seas. But since Effie's death, and my disgrace, there is no place I will not go, as long as it is away.

From Kinsale, we must head south, to Madeira and then the Cape Verde islands, off Africa's west coast. Thence west, across the cruel Atlantic, to make our way down the coast of Brazil, and to round Cape Horn. From there, if we survive the Cape, we shall trace the coast of Chile northwards, until we reach the Spanish trade routes, and can seek our prey. But the Manila galleon is not all we shall take, for we have been promised other prizes along the way: Dampier speaks warmly of how we shall not only seize Spanish ships, but also raid their towns and grow rich on plunder. And despite Funnell's mutterings, it's a comfort to know that Dampier is one of the few men to have sailed the world entire.

Yet this is not a happy voyage. By the time we reach St Jago, of the Cape Verde islands, Dampier and his first lieutenant, Samuel Huxford, have argued so violently that Dampier has Huxford and his two servants put ashore and left there. St Jago being a very forsaken place, Huxford begs most piteously, saying, 'You would not be so barbarous as to turn me ashore amongst a parcel of heathens.' Dampier does not relent, and without Huxford we sail west for the New World.

I have little time for musing on the designs of Dampier, or on Huxford's fate, for I am kept busy at my work. A master's role is a grave one, for if I neglect my task, we shall be altogether lost. I take soundings with the plumb line, to test the water's depth; between the stars and my cross-staff I figure our latitude. Latitude is a puzzle that men have solved: a good navigator with clear skies can ascertain perfectly well where he lies, north to south. But longitude remains the bane of sailors, and of navigators most particularly. In figuring a ship's location east to west, there is a tremendous slipperiness. I take my readings diligently – measuring the heading, and our speed, all plotted on the traverse board – and against this I must set the currents and our leeward drift, all while consulting the sandglass, which does not run steady when waves toss us about, and which seizes with the damp, furthermore. I track our course using dead reckoning, but the longer a voyage continues from a known point, the more errors accumulate, like weeds on a hull. Our location is a certainty on the day we set sail from St Jago; after four weeks of sailing across the bleak Atlantic, it has become no more than a reasonable guess.

I am wearied, and talk little. My work demands vigilance – sometimes I think that growing up plagued by the pranks and japes of my brothers has made me well-fitted to such a task, for I know what it is to be ever watchful. At least this ceaseless labour gives me little leisure to think of Effie. But even now, bent over my logbook, her drowned body drifts into my mind like flotsam. Her eyes are open underwater, as naked and tender as the milky blind insides of an oyster, pried open.

In the long crossing the men grow restive. Rations are much reduced, and supplemented when we can by fishing. A shark is hauled aboard, which cheers the men a little, by way of its size. But we came to slay Spaniards and not sharks, and still have seen no action. The beer has soured and when we empty a butt, we find at the bottom a thick, stringy mass, congealed and foul. By mid-November a fever comes, and the surgeon bleeds the men conscientiously, but to little avail. Too weak to walk to the heads, the sick men shit in pails. Below decks is never a pretty-smelling place, but the stench of the *Cinque Ports* is fit to singe the very hairs off your nose. Worse, our captain, Pickering, is among the sick, so command falls to Stradling, first lieutenant – a young gentleman sailor, burdened with more wealth than wit.

'Now we shall see some prizes,' says Stradling, ever cheerful. 'You may count on it.'

He is always thus: tremendous certain, having not the habit of doubt. And doubt is a great gift to a sailor, who must be suspicious of the sea and its many tricks.

There is one man aboard the *Cinque Ports* whom I account a friend: David Loggia, the chief mate. He is a former navy-man, lately of Leicester, though his grandfather came from Sardinia, which explains his hair, absolutely black. He is about my own age, and tremendous broad and strong. I was drawn to him at first because I thought him a useful fellow – a man of his size is better as a friend than an enemy. Yet despite his strength, in all his dealings Loggia is slow and thoughtful. When he swears, he does so in a gentle voice – when one of the ship's boys is caught swiping Loggia's grog ration, he calls the lad a 'damned devilish shit' in a voice so soft that you might mistake it for an endearment. I begin to suspect that Loggia may not, after all, prove useful in battle, though Dampier has given us no opportunity to test this notion.

'And how do you find our esteemed leader?' I ask Loggia one night, when the two of us are alone at the taffrail.

'He is not quite as I thought him to be,' says Loggia.

'Better, or worse?' I ask.

'Only that he is not as I thought to find him,' he says, never one to be rushed. He is cleaning beneath his fingernails with the tip of his marlinspike, for Loggia is fastidious about cleanliness.

'How did you think to find him?' I ask. 'For Dampier's reputation would have him either as a peerless navigator, or as a mere brute pirate.'

'Indeed,' says Loggia. 'So if he is not as we have been told, I cannot yet say whether it shall be for good or for ill.'

We reach Ilha Grande, an island off the Brazilian coast, where at last we may take on fresh water. We have good fishing but the fresh food comes too late for many of the sick, and Captain Pickering is amongst the dead. He is buried ashore, with more ceremony than the others, and his death is a grave loss to the expedition altogether. It is a double blow, for the loss of Pickering himself, a steady man and well-liked by the crew – and for his replacement in Stradling. Stradling is not even twenty-five when he is made our captain, and this advancement up the ranks has been so rapid that he mistakes it for a tribute to his talents, and swaggers about the deck more cocksure than ever. And where a more experienced captain would let his men get on with their work, Stradling never misses a chance to give an order, high-handed and loud, as though it is his voice alone that keeps the ship afloat.

Furthermore, back in St Jago he bought a monkey, a small, belligerent creature with the face of an angry old man. Stradling has made of it a pet, letting it sleep in his cabin, and perch on his shoulder. Next to the wizened face of this beast, his own soft face looks younger than ever. He finds the creature amusing, and announces he will not be without it, and scratches behind its ears as it leers. 'I am become prodigious fond of the little fellow,' he says. The men are not, for the creature is given to shrieking at odd moments, and leaves stinking little shits on the deck which the men must clean.

Stradling does not seem to notice. 'Oh, he is a great favourite of all the crew,' he says of his monkey, chucking it under the chin, and he has no notion that this very morning the cook had offered a shilling to any man who would sling the creature overboard, for shitting in his pans.

At Ilha Grande we are busy refitting – already the hulls are showing signs of wear from these hungry seas. We have been four months at sea, and have not a single prize to show for it – only our dead, our weakening hulls, and the company souring and mutinous. Huxford being left at St Jago, Dampier's new first lieutenant is one James Barnaby, but the two are often at variance, and after a night of bitter quarrelling, Barnaby takes eight men and the *St George*'s boat what's more, and does not return.

'If Dampier keeps going through first lieutenants at this rate,' I say to Funnell, 'the boy who swabs the decks will soon find himself in that role.'

Funnell laughs. 'Rather that poor lad than me.'

'Some navigator I was,' I say to the goat. 'For I failed to see what was coming, writ perfectly clear. Ours was from the very start an expedition much beset by maroonings and abandonments. I should have seen it as an omen.'

'Men cling to omens,' says the cat.

'I didn't see,' I say, 'or not soon enough. I thought Dampier difficult; I thought our voyage had an inauspicious start. I did not yet see how my doom was written into all that had happened, as though it were marked on a chart.'

'That does not necessarily follow,' the goat says.

'Dampier was a devil for putting men ashore, or suffering them to leave – and Stradling was party to it. You must see how this habit made possible what was later to befall me,' I say. The past is always happening all over again – following itself like the inevitable curve of a goat's horn.

'And if a thing is fated,' the goat says, 'it follows that you need bear no responsibility for how you chose to conduct yourself?'

'Spare me your condescension,' I say. 'And what of Dampier, or Stradling? What of their conduct? What judgment do they face, for all their rough usage of their men?'

'The sea's judgment,' says the cat at once. 'Salt and dark water.'

Whether the judgment of this island will be more or less merciful than the sea's, I do not yet know.

30

After Ilha Grande, Dampier announces that we shall not touch land again until we have rounded the Horn and come to the islands of Juan Fernández, off the coast of Chile.

'He does not dare to land,' Funnell says, 'for each time we are in a port he loses men, one way or another.'

'He shall lose them overboard, if he continues in this manner,' I say – for the men are driven half mad with frustration. Instead of the promised riches, we have dried meat full of ants, and every other pea in the barrel is a rat's dropping. Fever and scurvy have each recruited a company of the dead. The dead men's belongings are sold on deck by auction; we argue over the price of our former quartermaster's shoes, and I buy a quantity of good thread. And where there should have been councils held to determine our plans, instead Dampier and Stradling and the purser, Morgan, decide all things in hugger-mugger among themselves, without consulting even the officers.

The sea is a bad place to flee the drowned. In these waters, with their grey slabs of waves, Effie comes to me more than ever. In my dreams she walks towards me slowly, heavy with water, and when I wake I expect to see her bare wet footprints on the deck. Even when I am at my work, I must fend off the image of her laid out on the shore, the apron draped over her discoloured face. I try to focus on my compass, but my hand has begun to shake, setting the needle juddering. I am a haunted man, a stranger to mercy.

Dampier is often aboard the *Cinque Ports* or inviting its officers to dine with him on the *St George*. The more I see of him, the less I can ignore his flaws. He speaks very bold of all that we shall win by this voyage – oh, he can paint a comely picture of that galleon – yet he is forever putting off the moment, and insisting that this target or the other will not serve, for why should we risk our ship or our lives for some small prize when the Manila galleon awaits us, fat with treasure? So much does he prevaricate that the men begin to doubt his courage. He counsels patience from the men but is hasty in his grand promises. And being careless with his words, he makes such a great many promises that even the most faithful sailor cannot but note the difference between these lofty expectations and the sad truth of our voyage, which has taken no prizes of any note. The crew grows restive and uneasy.

But it is the hull that worries me most of all, for the Horn and its storms are unforgiving, and in both ships the worms have been at work. The *Cinque Ports* is sailing sluggish and reluctant. I suggest to Stradling that before we brave the Horn, we should make once more for land, to scorch and tar the hull properly.

'If you want to be a shipwright and not a sailor, you would've done better to stay at home,' Stradling says impatiently. 'The men will stand for no more delays. Nor would you, had you more courage.'

It is easy to be brave when you have seen nothing. He has not sailed to Darien, nor seen the worms eat the ships and the hunger eat the men. He does not know the price the sea demands.

But I am Alexander Selkirk, notorious for my temper. I will not be shamed nor mocked by this mewling man who calls himself captain. And I am about to retort, when Loggia places his broad hand on my forearm. His grip, heavy as a shackle, is warning enough. Stradling raises his eyebrows and waits; when I do not speak, he strides away.

We make for the Drake Passage, that stretch of water beneath Cape Horn, where ships can pass from the Atlantic to the Pacific, if they survive. At first we meet with clear skies.

'Perhaps we shall have an easy passage,' says young Neil, a lad who has taken a liking to me for no other reason than that we are both Scots.

I say nothing, for the sea in these parts is not to be trusted.

In the first days of January a storm drops on us like cannon fire. It is blowing hard sou'-west, the ocean all torn up, and we lose sight of the *St George*. The sea swallows the sky and all is dark, the day turned to night and the air turned to furious water. A man falls from the tops; the surgeon physics him but he is not like to live. We are taking on water through our riddled hull; then through the gunports; then in great washes over the deck, my fingers and palms scorched by the lines that I must cling to. I am cold – who would have thought that such a little thing as cold could signify, when all the world is water and we cannot keep the *Cinque Ports* head-on but are tossed about carelessly? And yet the cold is so fierce that it loosens my grip and sets me to shaking until I think my teeth must come loose like a man struck with scurvy. We are going down; I think of the starving man at Darien who swallowed the stones, and I wish I had stones of my own to swallow, that I might have a quicker death when we go under, which we surely must. I think of Effie, who found her way to her own drowning without even the aid of stones. What a mess of dying is life – and how heavy it all seems now, amid the water that hurls us into each wave's pit, and heaves us out of it again, which would be a relief were there not always another pit coming, and all of it in the dark. This death is taking a prodigious long time, and I have never been a patient man – if I am to die then let me not be taunted like this and tossed about the deck in the meantime. If I could open my mouth without drowning, I would shout at the face-slapping wet sky: *Be done with it, be done.*

But we do not die. The sky lightens; the storm forgets us and moves on; we are riding heavy, and every man must take his turn at the pumps, and still there is no sign of the *St George* – but we are not dead, and now I welcome the bone-shuddering cold for it is proof I am yet alive.

Stradling's monkey has stopped its chittering; it is silent, shrunken with fear, and clings, shivering, to his shoulder. But Stradling himself is jubilant.

'How do you like that, Mister Selkirk?' He gives a grand sweep of his arm, taking in the sodden deck and the battered sails. 'Not too bad for a ship you would have seen condemned, eh?'

'He is the kind of man who will always mistake good luck for good decisions,' Loggia says, when Stradling and his monkey have gone below.

'And take credit for both.' I spit over the rail.

We limp our way northwards up the coast of Chile. We sailed from Kinsale with sixty-three men; now we are forty-two, half of us sick, and all of us angry. Where are the prizes we were promised?

Before we make landfall the anger is contained, for we have the business of sailing and survival to attend to, and heaven knows the *Cinque Ports* needs our efforts, for the storm has left her in a sorry state, much tattered, and leaking sorely.

But when we make anchor on the island, the anger bursts like a pustule. Stradling begins to give orders: these men to stay aboard, and these to go ashore. The crew ignores him entirely, rushing for the boats. The island, we have been promised, is not only good for watering, but is also well stocked with goats. At this point I could take a bite from a goat without stopping to kill it first, so great is my hunger.

'If you disregard me, this is mutiny,' Stradling calls – and judging by the straining of the sinews in his neck, it is costing him some effort to speak calmly.

'And if we regard you, it is death by starvation or drowning,' say I.

'Have I not brought you safely round the Horn?'

'Safely?' I say. 'More than half our company is dead – and to what end? For what?'

Stradling has his pistol at his belt, his hand only inches from it, and I stand still a moment, among the hubbub of the men lowering the boats. If Stradling chooses to reach for his weapon it may go ill. But he does not, just stands there, his chin raised a little, which might make him look defiant or even dignified, were it not for the monkey gibbering on his shoulder.

Thus we load the boats without trouble, though there are so many of us that we near overset them. We are giddy with hunger and relief and greed, and for all our weakness the rowers make good speed for shore. All the while Stradling stands at the gunwale and watches, the only man remaining on the *Cinque Ports*. The monkey grins fiercely on his shoulder, its antic and ancient face next to Stradling's making the captain seem more alone, rather than less.

We have not left Stradling a single boat or tender, so he is marooned aboard the ship, though he has food and water enough that we can be sure that he will not starve.

'Nor shall he be forced to eat his monkey,' I say to Loggia, 'however much we might wish it.'

On the island, the mood is triumphant. We gorge on the crawfish, so plentiful that they almost offer themselves up for the taking. Of powder we have plenty, and so we kill more goats than we can eat.

'Though I had rather we had less powder,' Loggia says, 'for if our captains were not so inept we should have seen some combat.' I have not before heard him speak so bold, and it bodes ill for Stradling that even gentle Loggia will speak thus.

The seals do not make for good eating, but the men club them nonetheless. A young seal clubbed from behind is a very meagre sort of victory, but for want of Spaniards and prizes the men take what they can. We hunt, we eat and we rest. As for Dampier, we cannot but assume that he is dead, the *St George* sunk. Were we less hungry, we might mourn – if not for Dampier, then for his crew.

But on the third day the *St George* sails into the bay. Had we arrived at the island at the same time, I cannot but guess that Dampier would have been met with the same anger as Stradling, still marooned alone on his ship. But now we are three days fed and rested, and in all that time believed the *St George* sunk. Thus the ship's sudden arrival is something akin to a resurrection – and while we have cursed Dampier, he has many good men aboard whom we cannot wish dead. For myself, I am mightily glad that Funnell is not drowned, despite his tiresome prattling.

Amongst this general rejoicing, even Dampier is greeted warmly enough when he comes ashore. And for all his flaws I will allow he has a commanding manner that Stradling sorely lacks. We bring to him our grievances, viz. the hugger-mugger manner of decisions being taken, without any consulting of the men or even officers; the failure of our captains to adhere to the design of our journey and its promised prizes; the sorry state of the ships, so ill-prepared.

Dampier listens gravely and says that he shall make amendment, and shall speak to Stradling of the same. He goes awhile aboard the *Cinque Ports*, and upon his return brings Stradling with him. For once Stradling does not have his monkey on his shoulder, which I take to be Dampier's counsel, and good counsel too, for the men despise the creature. And perhaps three days alone have given Stradling cause to reflect on his failings – or perhaps Dampier has rebuked him for letting things come to such a pass – for Stradling appears chastened. He speaks of his resolve to see the ships refitted well, and to seek our promised prizes, and Dampier joins in, and talks of all the riches that await us.

'All of this hubbub and disputing amongst the company benefits only the Spanish,' he says, 'for it delays our coming victories, which you have heartily earned.'

And a man with a belly full of goat meat and salted crawfish can easily believe that all our ordeals are left behind us like the Horn itself, and that now nothing awaits us but wealth and glory.

Stradling and Dampier seem true to their word. They order the ships careened so that we may clean and repair them properly. It is arduous work to haul the ships over to their sides, and arduous work to repair the hulls too, for the worms have made of them a mere tangle of holes, much waterlogged. Yet the crew is refreshed and hearty now, and works willingly. At night we take our ease; the sick grow well again and the weak grow strong, though all of us tire of goat meat and cabbage, and the oily taste of seal flesh. Funnell sidles up to me and insists that the reason for the *St George* being late to join us here was not merely the storm, but Dampier sailing straight past the island a week hence and insisting it was not Juan Fernández after all, and only relenting days later, and being forced to turn about. But here, with my belly full and the hull on its way to being repaired, it is easy to shrug, for Funnell is forever gossiping – and has Dampier not circumnavigated the globe? It is easy to turn away from him and to listen instead to Dampier and his generous promises, the Manila galleon that he offers to us as though he holds it in his very palm.

We have been on the island almost a month when, in late February, a ship hoves into sight. Our careening and repairs being just concluded, it seems fated that the prize now presents itself to us, tremendous neat. The *St George* gets up her yards and topmasts and gives chase at once; we in the *Cinque Ports* are not quite so ready to sail, and in our haste to follow we are obliged to leave behind a quantity of anchors, cables, sails and other supplies, not to mention several of our men who are inland, hunting goats. But so sure are we of our victory that we determine to return for them shortly, after we have seized our prize.

By eleven that night we draw close to our quarry – close enough to see that she sails under the French flag. She is well-manned, and has the advantage of us in both size and firepower; I put her at 400 tonnes and thirty guns. Stradling and Dampier exchange signals and elect not to engage until the next day.

The order is given at dawn. The *Cinque Ports* is first to come alongside the French ship, but we have not fired more than ten or twelve guns when we fall astern and are not thereafter able to keep pace with her without interfering with the *St George*, which is anyway better armed. She keeps alongside the French ship for seven long hours, exchanging broadsides, and several times Dampier's men might have boarded her, and I am baffled that they do not.

Then a small gale comes upon us and the French ship shears off; by the time we have come alongside the *St George,* the French vessel is outstripping us both. We officers go aboard the *St George* to consult – the men are heartily determined to give chase – not just from wishing to take the prize, but also to hinder her from telling the Spaniards that we are in these seas, which could spell disaster to our designs. But Dampier is most insistent that we should not pursue her. 'I did not come hither to fight Frenchmen,' he says. 'And anyway, I know of places where more gold may be had, and for less effort.' And I begin to understand why his men were never ordered to board the French ship.

Already it is as though the French ship were never here – for Dampier is speaking lustily of how we may raid the Spanish town of Santa Maria, and of how the Manila galleon is still to be had – and Stradling never countermands him, and indeed echoes him eagerly.

Thus ends our first engagement, with the men frustrated and the French ship, I must suppose, very well satisfied to have had the better of us. Nine men on Dampier's ship are dead, and several injured. So many lives to be fed into the great machine of Dampier's plans, the true purpose of which I cannot tell.

Before returning to the *Cinque Ports*, I find Funnell by the main-mast with his friend Welbe, a midshipman of choleric disposition.

'Why did you not board her when you had the chance?' I ask.

Welbe snorts. 'You would do better to ask our fearless captain that,' says he, 'for the only order he gave during the whole engagement was to make sail at the end.'

'And that we could scarce hear,' says Funnell, 'for on the quarterdeck he'd made for himself a barricade of bedding and rugs and pillows, the better to protect him.'

Stradling calls my name – the boat for the *Cinque Ports* is ready. I leave Funnell and Welbe with their anger. How much to believe of Dampier's cowardice, I do not know, but I do know for certain that his men hate him, and that bodes ill for any captain.

We stand away towards the island to retrieve our men and our stores, and two longboats what's more, that we were obliged to cut loose during the chase. We battle a heady southerly all the way, but on coming at last to the island, ahead of the *St George* and under oar, we see two sails in the bay. They are French warships, and fire upon us at once. We make for the *St George* and though the French ships do not give chase, our captains quickly determine that we must flee and leave the stores, and the wretched men, for we are sorely outgunned. It is a grave loss, for we can ill spare the supplies or boats. As to the men we have left behind, we can only say that it is very likely that they are already prisoners of the French, or shot.

The next months follow the same pattern: the men's angry appetite for prizes is foiled at every turn by Dampier, and Stradling goes along with him each time. We make it as far north as Callao, where we come upon the French ship once more, in company with a smaller vessel, and Dampier refuses to close on her, bringing the men to near mutiny. Before he can be persuaded, the French ships escape into Lima and beyond our reach.

'It is better this way,' says Dampier. 'For why waste our shot on such petty prizes, with the Manila galleon still to be had?'

He is saving himself for her like a bride. But we shall go to our graves starving and unconsummated.

Under such leadership, the men are forever fighting and vexing one another. And Dampier at every engagement proves himself a coward and an indecisive captain.

'He has a great aversion to gunfire, that one,' says Loggia.

'And Stradling is no better,' I say. 'For where Dampier is afraid of battle, Stradling is afraid of Dampier, and will never countermand him.'

We are briefly cheered when, the very next day, we seize a Spanish merchant ship, meeting with no resistance, for the ship was just leaving the harbour and ill-prepared for a skirmish. It carries a fair cargo – but Dampier allows us to offload but a small part of it, insisting that to load the whole of it shall be a hindrance to his greater design. Nor will he let us take the ship itself, for he says that he has no officer fit to command it – a comment calculated to further enrage his officers.

The next day we take another Spanish ship, and the same story unfolds: our men forbidden to rummage the ship nor to take all of its cargo, despite there being a good quantity of indigo, cochineal and more. As privateers, on our return we will have to satisfy the court that we did not steal cargo belonging to traders rather than to the Spanish crown, and sometimes this involves a careful assessment of the manifest. But Dampier does not even mention these ordinary dictates – he says only that we cannot burden our fleet with such petty cargo, for when we raid the town of Santa Maria we will fill our holds with gold. He orders the ship released, taking only its launches, which we have need of. There are mutterings aboard that Dampier has taken a bribe from the Spanish officers to release the ship, and that this private consideration he shall keep for himself, at the cost to all of us of our share of the plunder. A few days later we capture a bark, which Dampier consents to keep, whether to placate us or whether, as he says, because the small ship shall be useful for his planned raid on Santa Maria.

On the few occasions that a prize is won, Dampier neglects to keep any record of the goods seized, and these are not accounted for and divided between the ships and their companies in the manner agreed in the articles we signed back in Kinsale. Whether this is merely poor management, or a plot to defraud the men, it is not clear – but all the company is uneasy about whether we shall get our share, and the men take to watching one another vigilantly, and watching Dampier most of all. Another little bark, taken near Gallo, is not enough to placate us, even though Dampier maroons its crew on Gallo and permits us to take the ship.

Dampier's distaste for combat damns him twice in the crew's eyes: once for thwarting our ambitions for riches; and once for cowardice, which is the more dangerous for him. If we were in other regards well satisfied – by steady rations and the taking of rich prizes – we might tolerate such a captain; but these things being absent, there is much gathering in corners and against bulkheads, and even the incessant leaking of the *Cinque Ports'* hull is not enough to drown the sound of angry whispering.

I do my work, and I do it faithfully – following the orders of Dampier and Stradling and guiding us northwards. But I have come to realise that however diligently I may navigate, we are chasing a horizon that shall always retreat, for Dampier does not know his own mind.

31

Dampier announces that we are to raid the Spanish town of Santa Maria. 'It is a veritable treasury,' he says, 'for all the mines thereabouts send their gold there, whence it can be taken back to Panama.' You would think every building of the town itself is built of gold, to hear him tell it.

'And what of the Manila galleon?' I say. 'Was that not supposed to be our quarry?'

'Mister Selkirk,' he says, 'you lack ambition. Can we not take both?'

'Indeed,' Stradling says at once. 'Let us have both – and why not?'

It is not only Stradling who is persuaded by Dampier's promises. Many of the men are still credulous; young Neil cheerily tells me that after we have seized Santa Maria, he shall buy a plot of land in Fife with his share of the riches – and a carriage too.

'And you, Mister Selkirk?'

'Get back to your work,' I tell him.

We anchor off the Point of Garachina. Santa Maria is upriver, and we ready ourselves for the raid. One party heads upstream under oar; I am with Dampier's party, set to follow when the tide will permit us to bring our bark upriver. When at last the tide relents, we are away. But the reeds on each side of our ship draw closer, until we can go no further, and we founder some time amongst the reed banks before being forced to turn and make our way back. Awaiting us at the bay is the realisation that Dampier mistook the mouth of the river, taking us instead a up a blind inlet. Now the tide is shifting against us once more and we are forced to lay at anchor.

'How did this happen?' Dampier says, looking from me to Funnell and back again – and I realise that he is as confounded as the rest of us. It is one thing for us to have been seduced by his reputation, and to have staked our lives on the legend of William Dampier, indefatigable explorer, renowned navigator. But I realise now that he too has been seduced by that legend, which is a more dangerous thing altogether.

The men are silent with fury as we await the next tide; Dampier tries to stay jovial, but is drinking freely from the little cask of brandy that he brought aboard, and talking with a forced cheer. 'All shall be well,' he says, and takes another swig. 'Do not doubt it.'

When at last we are able to join our men upstream, they have ill news: the first village they passed was abandoned, and further upstream they were met with gunfire. The Spaniards must have been alerted to our presence, and have made ready.

'Sir,' says Funnell. 'It is madness to proceed – they'll be waiting for us.'

'What does that signify?' says Dampier. 'Are we afraid of a fight?' And I see that he has for too long placated the men with the promise of this raid to allow it be snatched away now, even if prudence would dictate that we should retreat.

We approach Santa Maria under cover of night. Neil, the young Scot, is beside me in the first launch, both of us hunching low. He turns to me, his eyes bright, and says, 'At last we shall see some action, Mister Selkirk.'

I do not have the heart to tell him that the action we are bound to see shall not be to his liking.

We take turns at our oar; the rowing is hard, but it is harder still when Neil takes the oar, for then I have nothing to occupy me but my fear, and I begin to imagine an ambush around each bend of the river.

A jungle is never silent but frightful full of noise – the buzz of insects, like some dread machine, and the great coarse shrieks of birds; the rustling of the very trees, not to mention the occasional alarming crack that might be a fallen branch or some beast of the night, or a Spaniard waiting with a musket trained on us in the dark.

Even my breath is loud, far too loud, and time passes with a terrible slowness — time is a river and we are hauling ourselves upstream, against its current. I put us at about a quarter-mile from Santa Maria; the darkness is more than dark — it is thick, a stubborn black so heavy that peering at the riverbank reveals nothing.

Shots from the northern bank. A musket ball hitting water makes a fearsome hard sound — there is no softness in it. We near overset the boat with our scrambling and are shooting back before Dampier can even order us. I get off a shot quickly. A cry from the riverbank — one of them is hit, at least — then scurrying and yells, and one last shot from a distance.

The rowers are pulling hard, and Stradling in a high, taut voice is screaming at them to row faster still. But the river's next bend unleashes another ambuscade, this one larger, and amongst the firing I feel Neil's body go slack — he makes no noise, but simply stops like a clock, so that merely by the press of my body against his I know for certain that he is dead, and that he can never again be set going. I shove him aside so that I can take the oar, which is dragging in the dark water.

We rush upriver, and there is more shooting, but this time we are ready and shoot back at once, and manage to scramble ashore. On the muddy bank I reload and shoot my musket, under fire from the Spaniards who are suddenly upon us. My wet hands fumble when I try to reload again, just as a Spaniard grabs me from behind, his arm tight around my neck, his breath hot on my ear and his free hand raising a dagger to my throat. But not for nothing have I grown up forever fighting with my brothers. I swing my elbow back and jab him hard in his guts. His dagger falters, and the grip about my neck slackens enough for me to twist around, wrenching my own knife from my belt. I plunge the blade into his soft belly. He slumps sideways, jerking my knife with him. When I pull it out there is a terrible sound of something unspooling wetly to the ground.

The men are raging — we have overcome the ambuscades and can take the town, but Dampier is insisting that no, it is too late, and Santa Maria will have sent away its riches.

'We shall be outnumbered,' he yells, 'and for what?'

'For all that gold,' shouts Stradling. It is the first time I have heard him speak against Dampier.

'The gold is gone, you fool,' says Dampier. 'The minute they knew we were coming, they'll have carried it off.'

Dampier will not be moved, and the men are frighted enough to relent, so we board the boats once more and let the current take us downstream, where we rejoin the bark about midnight. The men waiting there had expected to see us loaded with gold; instead we have nothing but our shame, and six injured men, and the slim body of Neil, which is cold by the time we shift it into the bark. My right sleeve is blackened and stiff with the Spaniard's blood.

Back aboard the *Cinque Ports* and the *St George*, the days that follow are distempered with anger. With hunger too – for soon we are so scant of provisions that we are surviving each day on five boiled green plantains between six men. Dampier and Stradling have withdrawn to their cabins and scarce emerge; the men talk openly of mutiny, and even we officers have nothing to say in our captains' defence – nor would we dare, for the men are in a lynching frame of mind.

I eye the door of Stradling's cabin. 'If he does not come out soon,' I say, 'we have crowbars aboard that are as good as keys.'

'Patience,' says Loggia.

———

This very night the ocean serves us a piece of handsome luck: we espy a sail at midnight, coming up to anchor close by us and unawares. She is a fat Spanish merchant ship, and we take her without any resistance, both Dampier and Stradling emerging to give their orders, eager and loud in their commands, as though both know that this is the chance that may save their necks. We board the Spanish ship smoothly, and her crew is made prisoner.

Oh what a treasurehouse she is – what a gift from the seas: flour, brandy, wine. Tonnes of quince marmalade, which we eat with a spoon, the sour sweetness stinging our ulcered gums. Plump bales of wool and linen, bulging where they are bound. No woman has ever looked as appealing to me as those bales, soft and firm – for they speak of riches. 'With this, we shall supply ourselves for years,' announces Funnell. The small bark we had seized earlier, Dampier now orders sunk – such small prizes need not concern us now.

Best of all, Funnell and I are set aboard to command the new ship: Funnell to represent the interests of Dampier and his company, and me to speak for Stradling's. I could forgive Dampier and Stradling anything, I think, as I stride the decks of the *Asunción* – my own command. In high spirits, we stand across the Bay of Panama, anchoring in mid-May by the island of Tobago.

It is while we are here, and offloading provisions from the *Asunción*, that we hear rumours amongst the prisoners of a great sum of money hidden in her depths: 80,000 Spanish dollars, taken aboard at Lima and concealed against just this sort of misfortune.

Yet the captain, a sweaty fellow, awful thin, insists that the money was put ashore at Truxillo, as a result of him hearing that we were in the region. 'If you find any money aboard, except that I have already given account of, you may hang me from the yard-arm.' This Dampier takes as proof – but the Spanish crew will not recant, and I am inclined to trust them, for having seen the desperate and furious looks of our company, they are frighted enough to speak the truth.

Yet still Dampier refuses the men permission to rummage the ship, nor will he consent to let us ransom her, insisting that if we delay to await a ransom, we shall be embayed for months, the southerlies being what they are. He will not take counsel from me, nor Welbe, nor Funnell when we tell him we can easily reach Port Pinas and there have an excellent anchorage. To this he argues that our company is in no state to guard the prisoners, nor to defend should the Spaniards send help, our men being drunk. And it is true that the men have made rather free with the wine found upon the *Asunción*, but who could blame them after their recent long hardships? And the men's mood is not improved by seeing Dampier and Morgan, the purser, shifting into Dampier's own cabin heavy ingots of gold and silver, and other riches.

After four days at anchor here, Dampier summons all the officers to the *St George*. We think he at last shall take counsel, but instead of consulting with us as the articles that we signed dictate, he merely gathers us on deck, along with the company aboard. Here he announces that the *Asunción* is to be turned loose with her crew and what goods are left in her. 'For the loss of any further time shall spoil our greater designs,' he says.

'What designs?' someone calls from behind me. 'What fucking designs?'

'The Manila galleon,' he says, as though it is obvious. That mighty galleon, which Dampier has conjured for us so many times, so vivid that I could almost smell the tallow oil on her pulleys – she seems now impossibly far away. What designs indeed.

Dampier's nostrils narrow as though he has smelled something foul. He turns to Stradling, for it is one of the *Cinque Ports'* company who called out.

'Captain Stradling,' he says. 'Do you stand for this kind of insolence from your men?'

'I do not, sir.' Stradling shakes his head. On his shoulder, his monkey imitates him, shaking its little head briskly. 'But you must allow that the men's expectations have been frustrated.'

'Am I responsible for their expectations? Am I to cater to the imaginings of a bunch of sailors?'

'And my own expectations?' Stradling says. He has still a young man's voice, and it has crept even higher. 'I note you have filled your own cabin with valuables – what share of that is due to me?'

'I counsel you to watch your words, Stradling.'

'And what share is due to us?' shouts another man – it may be Funnell.

Here the men start a strident chorus of *Hear Hear* and divers other shouts, much less polite.

'In a ship of war this would be considered mutiny,' Dampier says, 'and punished with death.'

'And in a ship of war the captain would be unafraid of combat,' I say.

This is the beginning of a great unravelling. The crew is in uproar, a mixture of laughter and jeers; a number of officers gather around Dampier, whether to protect him or to fight him it is not clear, amongst the tumult. Dampier is swearing heartily, and threatening all manner of punishments, and I see very clear that a man who cannot master his own temper shall never master his men. There is much pushing and yelling, and I confess that I am at the centre of it, and put my fists to good use on those men between me and Dampier.

Not for some time are things calmed by Dampier firing his gun into the air, and by a placatory speech from the surgeon, Mister

Lyons, who says he has physicked enough men this voyage and has no wish to heal any injured at the hands of our own company. Lyons is not reckoned a good surgeon, but he is well liked, and thus his voice has a calming effect. Lyons may not have saved many lives in his career, but he perhaps saves several today, Dampier's among them.

After that there can be no question of the two ships continuing in consort. Dampier and Stradling agree that they shall each go their separate ways, and to the rest of us, Dampier says loudly: 'I know you now for mutineers and scoundrels. Do not think I will forget it.' His gaze rests a long time on my face.

On a long afternoon in Dampier's cabin, he and Stradling arrive at a division of the prizes – a division not to Stradling's satisfaction, based on his sour face when he comes back aboard the *Cinque Ports*. When pressed, Stradling confirms that we shall each have our share, but when I compel him for more details he reveals that my share of prizes, after eight months of this cursed expedition, is to be seventeen dollars. What can a man do but laugh, then? So much has been risked, and so much lost, for so little.

To his credit, Dampier forces no man to go with him who does not choose – or perhaps he recognises that such men will only foment unrest. Five of his men join Stradling's company, while the same number abandon Stradling for Dampier.

I ask Funnell how he can bear to remain with Dampier.

'What is Stradling but Dampier's pup – the same arrogance, but without the experience?'

I can summon little to say in Stradling's defence – only that whereas I can see no hope of ever persuading Dampier to accept counsel, Stradling may prove more pliant once away from Dampier's influence.

Funnell only shrugs. 'That's as may be – but I will stay with Dampier, if only to get away from Stradling's monkey and its evil little face.'

I smile. 'Perhaps the *Cinque Ports* would do better with the monkey as our captain, in Stradling's stead.'

And thus Funnell and I farewell one another – neither of us confident that we shall meet again.

32

Before all the company, Dampier makes a great show of shaking Stradling's hand. 'I wish you well,' Dampier says stiffly. 'But I had not thought, Stradling, that you would so easily forget who had deputed you and made you Captain.'

Stradling gives a brisk nod. 'And how could I, sir, when you have always been at such pains to remind me of it?'

Thus the *Cinque Ports* sails from the *St George*. I watch Stradling carefully – I wait for him to become a man, rather than a stripling lad. Instead he is strangely diminished. Without Dampier to echo, he seems to have no voice at all. I recall my joke to Funnell about the monkey, and it no longer seems funny, for at least the monkey has a spark of anger in its eyes, which I would be heartened to see in Stradling's, instead of this new blankness.

We are vulnerable without the protection of our larger consort, and now would have no chance of seizing a galleon such as Dampier promised to us. There are other enemy ships to be taken – but to privateer successfully in such a ship such as the *Cinque Ports* requires boldness, and in this Stradling is sadly wanting. In months of cruising we take only one prize, and it is a meagre one, which we burn when we cannot ransom it.

The stores that Dampier allowed us to take from the *Asunción* have dwindled, until our faces look not so very different from the wizened face of Stradling's monkey. The hull leaks, and there is no respite from the work of pumping, and even the officers take our turn. Sailors are no strangers to hard labour, but there is something particularly numbing about working the pumps, for it never ends, and achieves nothing – we churn the water out, and it rushes back in, and that is the task of our days and our nights. Sometimes Stradling's monkey sits nearby and watches us at our pumping, and I fancy I detect a kind of scorn in him, to see us labouring while he takes his ease. I throw my marlinspike at him, and he leaps away with a girlish shriek.

We sail now like a plague ship: desperate, aimless and wanted by none.

I dream that the barnacles and worms that plague our hull have come aboard my flesh. I feel the worms churning in my skin; when I try to scratch it, I cannot, for all my skin is crusted with barnacles, and when I claw at them they slice my hands to shreds.

I wake scratching at my arms, leaving great red welts.

'It is only the fleas,' says Loggia, when I show him my arms. And it is true that the *Cinque Ports* has its cargo of fleas – in these, at least, we are well supplied.

I scratch at my skin; I dream of Effie, and of worms. I dream of the Manila galleon, but she too is all beset by worms. She rides dangerously low, the water coming over her gunwales; at her front, like a figurehead, is Effie drowned and dead. Her hair is still wet, her mouth still open.

Stradling announces that we are to head back to the island. In the absence of prizes, our last hope for refitting the *Cinque Ports* must be the supply of stores that we left on the island, many months back, when we rushed off in pursuit of that initial French ship. As for the men we left there that same day, I hold little hope for them, on account of the French warships we found there when first we tried to return.

Yet when we limp into the bay, in September 1704, two of our abandoned men are there, waving and leaping, and guiding us through the rocks as we row the launch ashore. Even long after we have spotted them, they will not cease from waving – they flap their arms wildly, as though they would take flight and get off the island that way. Ashore, they embrace us fervently, rushing over one another to tell their story. All the other men, they tell us, were captured or killed by the French. The two of them, Kemp and Hastings, only survived by taking to the depths of the forest and hiding there for many days, chewing on roots and leaves for their hunger.

When the French sailed they took with them the stores that we had left. Kemp and Hastings had not even a scrap of sailcloth with which to make a tent; instead, they show us the cave they had shared for all these months, a short way above the cove. It is a meagre, damp hollow, and we do not tarry there, for the whole area around the cave reeks and is befouled, where the men filled pit after shallow pit as their latrine. They must have seen me grimace at the stench, for Kemp says, with sudden venom, 'You would not have such dainty notions, Selkirk—'

Hastings interrupts him: '—had you lived as we've lived.'

Their long seclusion has made them cantankerous and odd. They seem to dislike each other heartily, and yet never stray more than a few feet from one another, as if they cannot conceive of being apart. Some tasks they do as though they are one person, and not two. They show me how they cook a goat over a fire at the shore: they move in concert, one turning the spit, the other feeding the fire, and all the time glaring at one another and speaking in strange half-sentences, which one begins and the other finishes. Two ends of a shipworm, they pull endlessly at one another.

I say to the goat and cat: 'Part of me thought we should have done better to have found the stores, which we were sorely in need of, rather than the men.'

'That is hardly a charitable thought,' says the Reverend.

'I have never claimed to be a charitable man.'

'You did not interrogate them more, as to how they survived here?' he asks.

I shake my head. 'Why should I? I had no thought of staying. And they were not good company – I avoided them when I could, for they made me uneasy.' I did not want to be near them, with their strange mannerisms and their clipped and angry way of sharing words. Their time on the island had marked them with a great and heavy strangeness, and I kept clear of them.

'Yet having seen the harm done to those two men by their long stay here, still you contrived to condemn yourself to the same fate?'

The goat has his horns lowered as he speaks to me. I have often admired their curves; now I am made aware how very sharp they are.

'I contrived nothing,' I say. 'Listen.'

We have careened the *Cinque Ports*, but without sailcloth or other supplies, she is still in a sorry state. Worst of all, Stradling will not attend properly to the repairs needed for the hull – for he is all impatience, and wishes only to be away.

'Sir,' I tell him, 'she should have been sheathed before ever we set out.'

'Sheathing spoils the sailing of ships,' he says. Even after splitting from Dampier, he is still obediently echoing Dampier's exact words. I picture Stradling perched on Dampier's shoulder, nodding and tame, as Stradling's own monkey perches on his.

'Even if she cannot now be sheathed, the worst of the rotted timbers must be replaced. And the whole of the hull must be breamed – breamed thoroughly, until we've scorched every worm.'

'Nonsense,' he says. 'Our refitting is almost done. I have the coopers at work on the barrels; we are well on our way to having the main mast spliced. The sails shall be patched as well as we can manage without more sailcloth.'

'And none of it will signify without a hull that can float,' I say.

'Watch your mouth, Selkirk,' he says.

I should feel more assured if there were any rage in his voice – but he speaks only as though exhausted. There is no captain there at all, I think – he is just an empty hull, in which the echoes of Dampier's voice can sometimes be heard, bouncing, bouncing.

The cat interrupts. 'Did you not owe Stradling your duty?'

'What does a cat know of duty?'

'I have two duties,' she says. 'Survival, and pleasure. Both of these I serve gladly. They serve me very well, likewise.'

'Do I not also have a duty to survival? You have charged me with self-slaughter, after all. And I was right about the hull.'

The goat's ears prick up. 'Did you not elect a different duty, when you joined the expedition?'

'It is a privateering ship – I didn't enlist in the navy.'

'Are privateers not also in service of the Crown?' he asks. 'And did you not therefore owe loyalty to your captain?'

'Loyalty must be earned through merit.'

Here the goat chortles heartily. 'Oh we have a fine man of ideals here.' He turns to the cat, and then back to me. 'What world have you sailed from, sir, in which each captain is chosen for their worth alone? And are kings, and all nobles, to be chosen thus also?'

'Do you want to hear my story, or do you want to discourse on theology, and politics, and all such things?'

The cat's tail switches impatiently. 'Speak,' she says.

———

We are on the island for a month. The *Cinque Ports* is loaded with stores – wild goats penned in the hold; casks of salted fish and crawfish stowed; the decks stacked with barrels of good water.

'We shall soon take a merchant ship,' Stradling says, as he makes his final inspection of the gun deck. He slaps the breech of a cannon the way a man might slap the rump of a horse. 'Then the East Indies, and then for home. Or we sail for Peru once more, and find Captain Dampier, and together we shall take the Manila galleon.'

Has he forgot his own anger at Dampier, and Dampier's many failings? Can the men likewise be so quick to forget? They are restless, bored with waiting here, and with this long catastrophe of an expedition. They are so hungry for battle, in a ship ill-fitted to withstand it.

Back on shore to oversee the striking of the tents, Stradling holds forth once more about the prizes we shall seize.

'We shall seize nothing,' I say to him, 'for she is not seaworthy.'

'Careful,' Loggia says quietly from behind me.

Stradling raises his voice. 'Our company is fit once more, and we are well supplied.'

The men nearby have drawn closer, and are not even bothering to disguise their listening.

'Captain,' I say. 'Without attending to the hull, all these supplies are only so much ballast, to hasten our sinking.'

'Mister Selkirk,' says Stradling. 'You overstep your authority.' He lowers his voice a little, so that only I may hear him. 'Look at the men — can you not see that what they need is a prize? If we linger any longer here, I shall lose them.'

'You shall lose them regardless, for the ship is not seaworthy, let alone fit for battle.'

'A man with courage would not be so shy of battle,' he says.

'I do not want for courage,' I say, 'but for a hull worth the name. Dampier's cheapness in not having the hulls sheathed shall cost us our lives, if you do not have the sense to fix it.'

Stradling turns now to the men, gathered all around.

'And what thinks the company? Do you wish to stay here, with Mister Selkirk, fiddling at our hull? Or do you wish to seek your fortunes, and to show the Spaniards our mettle?'

A muted cheer at this last — for a young man will hate the Spaniards even more than he values his own life.

'Come,' I call to the crew. 'If you won't stand with me, at least stand behind your own words. How many times have I heard each of you complain of the captain, and how he dooms us with his stupidity?'

But there is silence.

'Oh you are all fine, brave men,' I sneer. 'Speaking so bold behind Stradling's back, and mute now.'

None will respond. Even Loggia — steady, faithful Loggia — does not join me.

'I trust you will find your bravery soon,' I shout at them, 'for you'll be sorely in need of it when the ship goes down.'

I turn to Stradling. 'And it shall be your fault — for a good captain could salvage a voyage on a bad ship — but a bad captain and bad ship together cannot be saved, and you are as bad as they come — a weakling and a spoiled pup.'

'Sir,' says Stradling, very stiff and proper. 'You cannot expect me to stand for this. Make your apologies, or I shall account your conduct mutinous.'

'Then you may leave me here,' I say, 'for I should rather take my chances on this God-forsaken island than to trust my life to a ship full of holes and captained by a fool.'

The men around us fall silent, and Stradling himself looks pinched about the face.

'Would you care to say that once more, Mister Selkirk?'

Now my blood is hot in my ears and I let my rage become the whole of me.

'You heard me well enough, I fancy, but I will say it again: I had rather be left here than to sail under you.'

Few men get to choose the words of their own death warrant, but I realise that I may be one of them, for the words I spoke have surely condemned me. I see it now – too late, too late to realise that I have been speaking much too free, and that I shall pay for it. I know – for I am no stranger to setting my life ablaze. The dreadful circle of the past comes round again, the spiral of a goat's horn, the same story telling itself over and over.

Stradling swallows, his face entirely calm now.

'Very well. Let me consult a moment with some other of my officers,' he says, and he walks back to his tent, waving impatiently at Wilmot and Bell to join him. As for the rest of the crew, they watch me warily, keeping a wide berth, as they might from a man with the pox.

Yet I am not bowed. Stradling will surely now listen to sense and take my counsel. When he returns it will be with a plan to refit the hull, and a promise to moderate his own conduct.

And when he does emerge it is better than I had dared to hope, for he carries a cask, as a token of apology.

'This is for you, Mister Selkirk,' he says, and I have assembled my most gracious smile, for Stradling is only young, after all, and the *Cinque Ports* his first command. As his elder I should show him forbearance, now that he has come to make amends, and we shall share this drink together, and I can speak sense to him.

He hands me the cask. 'A good supply of flip, for you.' He gestures to Wilmot, behind him, who is carrying a sack. 'And here is tobacco, and powder, and a quantity of flour.' He turns and speaks now not for my benefit, but so that the crew may hear.

'For as Mister Selkirk has of late had plenty to say, I will not give him cause to say I treated him unjustly in leaving him here.'

The beach beneath me seems to yaw and tilt, as though I am standing on the deck of a vessel that has taken a huge wave amidships. I have to steady myself before I can speak.

'If you leave me here, I will die alone. We both know it.'

'Ah, but you, Mister Selkirk, navigator – with your great astronomical calculations and your tremendous wisdom on shipbuilding and all things – surely you ought to have made that calculation already, before declaring that you would not come aboard under my command?'

'It was but bold talk,' I say. 'You would not be brute enough to maroon me here.'

'Marooned?' says Stradling. 'That is hardly the word, when you elected of your own free will to stay here. I am merely obliging your wishes.'

'I was not serious.'

He raises an eyebrow. 'What could be more serious than my fitness to command, and the future of my ship?'

'I sought only to provoke you,' I say. 'To make you see the gravity of the situation.'

'What could be graver than mutiny?' he asks. 'Should you prefer to be taken back in irons, and whipped?'

'Yes,' I say at once, for at least aboard a man may plead his case – but there is no pleading against this island.

'You have forfeited your place on my crew,' says Stradling.

'Loggia,' I say, for he is standing but a few feet behind Stradling. 'Say something. Tell the captain – for God's sake – tell him he cannot do this.'

'You fool,' says Loggia, keeping his voice low. 'Is this not what you asked for? Can't you see you gave him no choice?'

I wait and I wait for Stradling to relent. The final boats are loaded, the final tents are struck. His is the last boat to leave. I note that there is room in the prow, enough for both me and my sea chest. Surely this hoax has carried on long enough, and I have been sufficiently humbled? Any moment now he shall turn and say, very stern, *Well, Mister Selkirk, you have learned a lesson from your impudence, have you not?*

Stradling steps into the pinnace and takes his seat astern without looking back. 'Row hard,' he says, 'or we shall miss the tide.'

'And the rest you know,' I say. 'For they left me.'

'They gave you what you asked for,' the cat says.

'No man would ask for this.'

'And yet you did,' she says.

'No.' I shake my head. 'I never thought he would go through with it. I did not think he would be so cruel – nor that he could afford to do without me, his ship's master.'

'Your pride cost you dearly,' says the goat.

'No,' I say. 'It was his pride that I did not account for.' Had I spoken thus to Stradling in confidence, away from the men, he might have listened – or at least taken less drastic action. 'That was my folly – being rash enough to say it aloud, before all the gathered men.' I backed the captain against the wall of his own pride, and what choice did he have but to strike back?

'Yet for all that, you were not wrong about the state of the hull.'

At this I give a laugh that sounds very much like a sob. For I know it now better than any: how a man may be right and yet still be a fool; may be correct and still damn himself.

'Go on, then,' I say. The spring sun is glaring, and this cliffside offers no shade. 'Let me have your verdict.'

'Are you in such a hurry to be condemned?' asks the cat.

'You two summoned me. Why, if you will not even deign to make a judgment?'

'You are hasty,' says the goat. 'Do you imagine your story is finished?'

'What do you want from me? Do you wish me to make confession, as the Papists do? Do you want me on my knees?'

'We want your story,' the goat says.

'The whole of it,' adds the cat.

'Jesus Christ,' I say. The goat looks at me sternly – he has ever disapproved of taking the Lord's name in vain. 'I thought when I condemned myself to this place, that at least I would be rid of difficult company.'

'You wished to get away from Stradling,' the goat says, 'and men such as he and Dampier – intemperate men, hasty to anger, and bad at taking counsel.'

'Men who could not get along with their fellows,' says Sleek.

'Yet you could not escape such men after all,' the goat says. 'For here you are.'

I am used to such barbs from the cat. I had not thought, however, to hear the Reverend Vicarious Cronch say such a thing.

'Are you not my friend?' I ask.

'Indeed,' he says. 'But a friend may still observe. And we goats are great ones for noticing.'

I wish I could be free of the goat and the immense slit lens of his eyes. When a man's life is built largely of shame, he does not want a witness.

'What a blessing,' I spit, 'that I should befriend the only goat in all the world who can list my failings.'

'Blessing?' hisses the cat. Never has the word sounded more like a curse. She leans forward from the rock on which she perches, so that her whiskers almost touch my face, and the meaty stink of her breath is warm on my skin. 'You escaped a doomed ship – blessing. You found yourself on a remote island, and yet you have not starved, nor been devoured by beasts nor savages. Blessing.' She bares her teeth, a rictus grin. 'Tell me, Mister Selkirk: what further blessing would you wish?'

33

The goat and the cat speak no more of it, but for several weeks after this latest trial, I am sore uneasy. It is not the trial alone that has set my teeth grinding and my jaw tight. I have reached a most unwelcome milestone, for by my reckoning it is now early October 1707, and three years since I was left here.

According to Dampier, when he rescued the Mesquite Indian slave who was abandoned here by buccaneers, the man had passed three years here alone. I admit that I had clung to that period as a kind of measure – and now that my third year has passed, I enter a fresh realm of despair. Even the Mesquite Indian had his rescue; none has come for me.

'This is a record I never sought to better,' I say to Sleek and the goat. 'I cannot stop thinking of how the Indian must have felt when the ship came to the bay.' Dampier told the story many times – and why not, for he figured well in it: a saviour, rescuing the helpless, wretched figure.

'Dampier had in his company another slave,' I say. 'A fellow of the same Mesquite tribe. When they came ashore, the two Indians rushed to one another on the beach. Dampier said their reunion was as joyful a thing as he had ever seen.'

'And what does Dampier know,' says the cat, 'of the joy of slaves?'

Sleek does not speak to me the rest of the day – she is very expert in ignoring me.

I ask her, 'Why do you come here, if you hold me in such contempt?'

'We are friends,' Sleek says, and rolls over.

'No. The goat is my friend.'

'We are friends,' she repeats.

'How so? You are forever harping at me.'

'Friend of blood bowl, of liver. Of the scratching behind my ears.'

'That is not what friendship is.'

'You are wrong.'

'When I fell from the cliff, you said you would eat me if I died. Is that a thing a friend would do?'

'May I not love you as well with my teeth as with anything else? With my belly?'

And I think of the goat, and how he once ate a Bible. Was that a goat's manner of devotion? Was it his prayer?

the

water   shall

not

be

forgiven

Late afternoon. I am stretching a hide on my makeshift frame; the goat has been holding forth on Corinthians, and what it means to *put away childish things*.

'And it would mean something very different to a man, I expect,' he says. 'For whereas your kind can scarcely walk at a year old, at the same age a goat is considered grown, and indeed may already have bred.' He scratches his chin against the rough trunk of a tree.

'You never lose an opportunity to harp on the superiority of goats.'

'As a minister,' he says, 'it is my duty to acknowledge the excellence of the Lord's design, for—'

He is interrupted by a great tumult of petrels, crying out and shrieking. I stand, pressing my hands into my back where it aches from hunching over the hide. The petrels are wheeling towards the bay, and do not cease from their furious cries.

Within a few steps I am at the side of my camp that affords me the clearest view over the water – and there I see it: a ship. Two, in fact: a ship of the line, in the Spanish style, and a frigate of at least twenty-four guns, already in the bay – they must have sailed through the night and made harbour this morning. And in my recent listlessness and despair, I have been lax in climbing to my lookout, or even checking the horizon from my camp.

Even at the same instant that I register the jagged red cross of the Spanish flag, I cannot help but marvel at the splendour of these vessels. I could not have been more astonished had some vast sea monster arisen from the water. The galleon most particularly is a thing of wonder – I have seen nothing of its scale these many years. A man who tumbled over the rail would not survive the fall, so tall is she, the great wall of her hull studded with gunports. For so long I have dreamed of ships as my rescuers; seeing the galleon now, I am reminded how mighty a machine of war such a vessel is. She must carry hundreds of men, the frigate half as many again, and each of them is my enemy, and would gladly see me dead or make a slave of me.

I curse my campfire, its plume of smoke the only blemish in today's clear spring sky, and I kick dirt over the flames. I stamp and stamp but it is too late – the smoke has done its work, for they cannot have missed it. And there – boats are already being lowered and loaded; this is the ruckus that has sent the birds wheeling. The first of the boats sets off, the oars leaving a neat row of stitches on the water. They are coming.

In my head I have rehearsed so many times how I shall make myself safe. I sprint to the path that comes up from the shore and grab the boughs I have laid by. Even as I haul them across the track, I am aware how slight a disguise they offer – my path is too well trod, and the obstruction too meagre to be effective. Dashing back to my camp, I waste precious minutes gathering those treasures that are not already hidden away, for I need them daily: my Bible, my kettle, my musket and small store of powder. My knife and my flint I keep always on my belt, but suddenly my camp, which I have often bemoaned as sparse and spartan, seems full of things I cannot bear to lose. The wooden bowls and pails, which cost me hours of carving, and many blisters and splinters besides. The hides on my hammock, each of which took weeks of curing. My few lengths of rope, much repaired – the longest of which is currently fastening the fresh hide to the frame. Such things would appear to the Spaniards as nothing but rubbish or scraps, but to me they have become infinitely precious. My fingers fumble as I undo the knots on the stretching frame that I was tightening this very morning. When at last I have recovered the rope, I race about my camp and gather what I can, swearing and dropping things in a great clatter that scares away Pickle and some of her young. I am glad, for I would not have the Spaniards come upon them – and I am glad, most particularly, that I have not seen Sleek since dawn. The goat, though, is watching me, his ears cast back, his hoofs dancing on the spot. Time – for three years I have bemoaned how one man should be burdened with so much of it, the creaking passage of the hours and days. And suddenly I have not enough time, and each second brings the Spaniards and their muskets closer.

At last I have tossed my scant treasures into the bushes a little way to the west of my camp, where a passing man at least cannot see them. Only my musket and powder do I keep with me. It has been years since I have fired it – I can but hope that this island's damp has not rusted it to ruin.

I throw open the gate to my goat pen, for I do not wish the Spaniards to have the benefit of my little flock. But the goats are too tame now and will not leave, only looking blankly as I wave my arms and hiss and try to scare them from the enclosure. With much effort, I manage to chase out three of them, but lamed as they are, they move slowly, and even when I have got them out the gate they do not flee, but merely stand about the camp, one of them testing the walls of my hut with his teeth.

All this has cost me too much time. I hear voices and human footsteps – how long I have dreamed of these! The steps are hasty, and fast drawing near. If they were watching my smoke, they will also have seen it stop – perhaps smothering my fire did nothing but advertise to them that I am an enemy. Certainly they are coming fast and determined, their voices louder by the instant.

By my side, Cronch is staring towards the oncoming rush of noise. He turns to me, his ears stiff and sideways, his nostrils flared. He does not speak – instead he gives a raw, goat-like cry, and it is this that startles me into speed.

I flee, the goat beside me – inland, by the paths I have walked these many years, heading always away from the water. Behind me the cries go up – they have found my camp, and again I curse my fire, for its ashes will still be warm, and that will spur the Spaniards on. And now I curse my well-trodden paths, for if they are swift for me, they shall be swift for my enemies too. I should have slipped into the lowland forests; here I am too high and too exposed, the trees thinning over bald rock. We startle a cluster of wild goats – they snort and bleat and scatter. It is no comfort that from a distance I could almost be mistaken for a goat – that will not spare me, for the Spaniards will be hungry for fresh meat.

A shot from below, then another. The sound alone does me violence, my ears ringing. For years I have heard nothing louder than a sea lion's bellow. A musket ball ricochets off the rock a yard to my right; stone shatters and sprays me with sharp chips.

'Cronch,' I shout, for the goat is still close by. 'Cronch – run!'

He is away, abandoning the path for the rocks. I cannot follow him, but I hear the consonant clatter of his hoofs on stone, and I am glad of his jerky goat gait, leaping side to side as he moves, for he shall make an erratic target. He is both cunning and fast – faster than his old-man visage and bony aspect would suggest – and quickly he slips out of sight.

I bless this island's fleet-footed goats as I run – I bless them for making me fast, for teaching me the hoof-wise wisdom of leaping and balance. I jump from the path and cut straight across the rocky spur where other men would founder and slip; here the Spaniards may shoot at me, but they will not catch me. I am jubilant with speed – surely no man can keep up with me, goat-chaser and mountain-scrambler that I have become.

They shoot again. My breath comes in hard, hot rasps. Each shot as loud as cannon fire, the whole island a clanging bowl of echoes. And if sometimes I have entertained the notion that the Spanish might not after all be so very dangerous, that they might show me mercy, I now know how wrong I was.

I have been fleeing westward – here the forest thickens below me and with one final exposed dash across bare rock I can drop down into its cover, then weave uphill through the grasping trees. It is slower-going now, and the musket slung over my shoulder makes me slower still, but I think I have shaken them off – I can no longer hear their voices, so I push onwards, quieting my own gasping breath the better to listen. No, they are still after me – they have paused their shooting, but voices still reach me through the forest. A man calls; several other voices answer. Are they spreading out to search for me? And is the goat safe, or have they shot him, my venerable friend?

I scramble always westward. I cannot tell how long this pursuit has lasted – only that when the voices reach me now, they have lost their urgency – they are less certain, more bored. There is a fallen tree across my way, long dead, its thick trunk softened with moss and even small ferns. I clamber over it; on the far side, beneath the trunk, is a dank hollow. It is not deep, but it is dark, the ferns hanging over it. I slide inside, lying on my back, musket pressed between my chest and the log.

In here, there is time for my fears to take shape. Stories of the Spanish silver mines are legion, and of the slave galleys too. I have so often complained of the privations of my life on the island, yet I have the freedom of my hours. I am not beaten, nor chained, nor forced to labour in stifling mines, nor chained to an oar to keep time to the beat of a whip.

Footsteps – closer than I had thought. I hold my breath and press myself against the earth as though it could close over me, a tender grave. More footsteps: a lone man, I think, walking, pausing, walking. My eyes have grown accustomed to the dark; above me on the log's underside, grubs squirm wetly, and a trail of ants follows itself across the moss. Such a busy world is hidden here, and has been around me, unseen, all this time.

The unmistakable sound of breath. A scraping on the fallen tree above me – then his boots drop into sight, barely a yard from my head. He stops – I am done for. I have my musket, but cramped as I am I shall never be able to raise it in time.

Then the boots take a step away and I can see his face. He is looking down – he has got out his prick, and then comes a steaming stream of piss, loud where it hits the fallen leaves and ploughs a shallow trench in the ground. But I cannot tear my eyes from his face – his face! His pupils round, not goat-wise and oblong, nor the crescent pupil of a cat's unforgiving eyes. I concentrate on keeping my breathing shallow and hushed – and yet part of me would burst from my hiding place as though born from the earth. I would run to him, embrace him, would press a hand to each side of his face and stare and stare, and embrace him for the gift of his face, a human face, which I have missed more than salt.

I shift the tiniest amount, the better to see him. That is a mistake, for while the ground outside my hollow is wet, within it are dry leaves and twigs that rustle beneath me when I move. At once the man stops his pissing and looks up, eyes darting around. Shall this be what kills me: my terrible hunger for a face? He grabs at his musket, turning side to side, his trousers still hanging open. He takes one step towards me. In this cramped hollow I am trapped, helpless, a crawfish entombed in its own tight shell.

A scattering of stones behind him – a sudden burst of sound and movement. It is a goat – it is the Reverend Vicarious Cronch, his white beard and his splendid horns, bursting from a thicket of ferns and darting northward. The man turns at once, a roar of alarm becoming a roar of laughter – he lets off a shot – calls something in Spanish that might be aimed at his comrades or at the goat. Then he laughs again, finishes his piss, reloads his musket and strides away.

I dare not move. Now is the time for the island's lessons of patience – but I am mad with haste. Was Cronch shot? Has he taken to the high places further west, where the goats take their wisdom each night? That he saved me deliberately I have no doubt – the whole island was his refuge, against men unfamiliar with its terrain, and a goat can go where men cannot. All those Bible stories about goats slaughtered as sacrifices. Has he sacrificed himself – and for such a wretched, sinful man as I?

I force myself to stay here in the hollow for many hours. I stare at the moss on the underside of the tree. Once I hear the hallooing of voices, but nobody passes near. Another time, around noon, there is a volley of shots; again I think of the goat, and while I am not a praying man, I make such prayers as I am capable of.

I creep out only when it is dark – only now can I account myself safe, knowing as I do the island and its many paths. I search for the goat, calling his name in a whisper as I scour the forest where last I saw him. There is nothing to be found, which gives me heart that at least he was not hit by that first shot. But there were so many Spaniards, and so many shots.

I make my way to a promontory at the bay's northern edge. There are lights on the ships, and a lantern sways on the water – another boat making its way to the shore. A camp has been set up a little way from the beach; voices reach me, calm and low.

Above the bay, from my own campsite, a light glows. At first I think it just a campfire – but it is too big. A bonfire, I tell myself – that is all. They will be in a festive mood, for it may have been weeks or months since they were last ashore. But already I know the truth, that this tall and flaring light must be the blazing of my huts. I weep, and I wish I had with me Sleek and the goat, not only for the comfort of their presence, but because I would then be assured they have not fallen into the hands of the Spaniards. I cannot countenance the thought that the Reverend Vicarious Cronch could even at this instant be turning on a spit in the same camp where we shared so many hours of conversation.

For two days I lurk in the island's deep places, creeping out only to spy upon the Spaniards' movements. It is November, and the nights are still long and cool. I sleep on the ground with only my goatskin clothes for warmth, and I think of how many times I have complained of the discomforts of my camp. What I would give for it now: for my dry huts; my hammock, covered with hides; Pickle and Sleek to keep me warm.

From a safe distance, I peer down to the bay. Many times, during these frigid and uncertain days, I entertain heroic schemes, in which I make my way in secret to the beach, and steal away in one of the Spanish boats, single-handedly seize the frigate, and sail to my freedom. With such foolish notions I pass my time, knowing them to be mere fantasies, for the shore swarms with Spaniards, and even if a man could somehow surprise or defeat the well-armed crew on the frigate, no man could sail such a ship alone.

At dawn on the third day they strike their camp, and the boats are made busy, ferrying men and water barrels to the ships. A good northerly has set in, and by the haste of their preparations I know them to be heading south, for they are rushing to catch the wind. *Blow, goodly wind*, I think. *Blow.*

The anchors are weighed; they are away, first the frigate and then its mighty consort. When they get clear of the bay, their sails fatten with wind. It is a sight I have so often imagined, the fleet of my most ardent longings – and it is leaving without me. My heart a ragged pennant, torn to pieces by that same wind.

For hours after the ships have slipped from sight, I mistrust the empty bay. Could they have left some men awaiting me, in ambuscade, and planned for the ships to return once I am caught? But it is too elaborate a charade for one man – all those boats loaded; the anchors weighed. They have seen my humble camp, and they must know there is no horde of slaves to be seized here. They have caught the strong north wind and will not return.

By evening I dare to go to my clearing. The huts are burned almost to the ground, and anything that the flames spared lies buried by ashes and dirt. The Spaniards killed several goats, the butchery done hastily right here, and the offal left where it fell. Whether these were wild goats, or my own tame flock, I cannot tell.

Night. The cats have all made themselves scarce. They have slipped into the forests and become darkness. I wrap myself tightly in my goatskin jacket, and from my half-sleep I watch the rats feast on the offal. I dare not light a fire, for fear of the Spaniards' return. There is a waning gibbous moon, pale and useless. It is a single lantern casting about to find a man overboard, in all the boundless sea.

The next morning four of my little flock of goats return, skittish and white-eyed. Pickle, too, appears at the clearing's edge. It takes much coaxing to persuade her to come any closer; only with a great many pieces of offal, tossed one by one in her direction, can she be lured towards me. Once here, it is most affecting to see how she nestles in my lap, and her diligent licking of my knuckles.

At noon, the Reverend Vicarious Cronch comes, moving stately and unhurried. I set Pickle down, though she clings with her claws to my trousers – for I have business with the goat.

'Sir,' I say to him. 'I owe you my life.'

'Whatever do you mean?'

'You know very well. You startled the Spaniard. You led him away.'

'That sounds most unlikely.'

'And has not my life on this island been one unlikely thing after another?'

'There are many goats on this island,' says he. 'To a man, one goat looks much the same as any other.'

It is not like him to be modest – rather, he usually tends towards smugness. But grateful as I am, I will not press him on it – and never a wordsmith, I have no way of putting into speech my gratitude. Instead I take his long goat face between my hands, and bend my forehead to his. I take a great deep breath of his scent – the grassy, animal stench of him.

When I step back, Sleek strolls into the clearing and sets about licking herself, as though nothing unusual has happened since last we saw her.

I look once more about the remains of my camp.

'Perhaps I should have thrown myself upon their human mercy. But I would make a poor slave, half mad as I am.'

'Mad with wisdom,' says the goat.

'Mad indeed,' says the cat.

34

I survey the scorched remnants of my huts; my empty goat pen, its fence trampled where it was not burned.

'I am ruined,' I say.

'You are alive,' the cat says.

'Spare me your homily on how very blessed I am,' I say. 'Today of all days, I do not have time.'

She yawns. 'I see that nothing has changed. You are still at war with time.'

———

time   is

                          the

                                              good

                                         disease

The sole advantage of having such meagre belongings is that those few things that survived the fire, the Spaniards did not bother to steal. The broken barrel hoops poke out of the ashes like the ribs of a carcass; two of my roughly carved wooden bowls are charred but still fit for use. I have many times cursed the damp of this island, but in the matter of this burning it has served me well, for when I set about digging in the ashes I find a number of hides, only part burnt.

The Spaniards did not find my hastily hidden Bible and rope, nor my more carefully concealed store of treasures: my remaining powder; my navigational tools; my broken piece of flint. Best of all are the items that the Spaniards themselves left, seeing them only as rubbish: some scraps of sailcloth and cordage; an empty cask that smells so richly of wine that I press my nose to it and take deep greedy breaths.

As I suspected, most of the goats the Spaniards killed were from my own tame flock. Those remaining, however, are not hard to recapture. Lamed, they could not flee far, and tame as they are, they do not know how to be free. They circle the clearing, bleating pathetically.

'Shameful,' says the cat.

I pretend not to see them, but keep up my work on the pen, and once it is done they re-enter of their own will. They should have learned by now to fear men. Yet still they come, their great goaty eyes and their soft bellies, their little udders swinging like so many soft bells, and all I need to do is make fast the gate behind them.

Near everything that I owned, I had made myself – and thus can make again. As Sleek has not scrupled to tell me, I am rich in time, if nothing else. The days pass quick, suddenly so full of tasks, and there are little improvements I can make here and there, so that as the camp begins to take shape, it is a finer camp than before.

These are strangely calm and spacious days, as summer settles on the island and I rebuild my camp. I work; I scratch the goat below his chin, and on the spot between his shoulders where he cannot reach. Pickle has another litter of kittens, and all but one survive. If the kittens dare to approach Sleek, she bats them away.

Before the island, I have always been a great one for leaving. I fled Nether Largo more than once, leaving my shame and disgrace like so much cargo; I fled Effie when she wanted to be wed, and when she died I fled Nether Largo once more, and the shame and sadness of her dying. Time and again I have taken to the sea – and when things aboard have turned ugly, I have taken again to land, even demanding to be put ashore, as I did on the island.

But this island permits no fleeing of any kind. The ocean is denied me. On land, if I were to run, I would eventually end up where I began, for the island is a noose. The ruin of my camp – the ruin of my past – none of this can I escape.

———

We speak little, these days, the goat and the cat and I. What need have I for words, when the things themselves are all about? I can touch them: stone, blade, wood. The generous arc of the goat's horns. I love to trace that curve, how it follows itself. How it does not break the promise of the coil but continues, right in on itself, its spiral perfectly inevitable. I think of my three landings on this island, twice upon the *Cinque Ports* and the third time on the wreckage of my raft. All follows time's curve; all is as it must be.

A man who stared long enough at such a curve could trace the arc of time itself, until the past bent right around into what is yet to come, and what is yet to come would already be behind us, in the neat curve of history in which all is connected. I would follow that arc all the way around – and the disaster of Darien would be undone, and the crumbling hull of the *Cinque Ports* would be made stout and strong. Effie would rise from the water like an anchor being weighed, and the water would stream from her, and she would turn her face to the unstinting sky, and all the world would be made whole.

———

the

water

is

not

alone

Autumn brings sea-mists that swallow sound, and soften the island's sharp edges. Then a long, slow winter — but in my new-found patience, I am learning to grant each day its time. The goat's stately beard is beaded with frost; Sleek sidles beneath my goat hide blankets and nestles against my legs for warmth. In the deep earth, spring is waiting. I will be here when it comes.

When I speak, I speak cat-wise. More abrupt — more like the declarations of Sleek, when she calls for 'hot blood', or hisses 'rats'. I say less now, and more to the point. I gesture at the thick grey clouds churning on the horizon; 'Storm,' I say to the goat, and no more. More often I say nothing: a storm announces itself, after all.

I throw down the diced liver of a goat to my cats – I have no need to say 'Eat.' And if Sleek wishes to wake me, it is not with words, for no word can wake me as sudden as her claws on my chest, or her hiss.

I let my body speak, for words get in the way. What could I say of my affection for Sleek that would express it better than a steaming bowl of blood set at her feet? How better to express my fondness for the goat, than with my nails on the underside of his chin, in that particular spot behind his beard where he best likes to be scratched? There is nothing that the goat can say to me of friendship or of loyalty that is not better said by the way that he wraps his lips very tender over his teeth to be sure that they do not nip at me when he takes a slice of turnip from my hand.

A word is both insufficient and too much. If I say *sea*, the name carries so much cargo – *ocean, distance, navy, buccaneers, fathoms, fear, hope* – that there is no room left for the real thing of it: this great pulsing salt mass that stings my feet with cold as I walk the shore. And words smuggle in other words, like contraband – *sea* is so close to *see*, and all that *see* brings with it (*look search horizon longing sail watch*). No – the words must stop their noise and allow the sea to be itself: its briny horizon and its white-tipped waves, all real, all now.

Once there were things, and the words for things. Now the words begin to fall away. What need have I to say *cat* when she is right here? The best word for *cat* is a cat.

My Bible poems grow sparser. Fewer and fewer words survive the ministrations of my charcoal. I blacken the paper until my charcoal wears down and my nails scratch against the page. I spend a whole evening labouring over the Book of Kings, until this is all that remains:

for ever

is

heavy

'Do you care less for the Bible, that you find fewer words to choose?' the goat asks, when I show him this latest fragment. He remains suspicious of my efforts with the charcoal, for they smack of sacrilege.

I do not know how to explain to him that though the Bible speaks to me in fewer words, it speaks more true than ever. Can I love a book by reducing it to silence? Once I would have said no. Now I know more about the expansiveness of silence – its spaciousness, its generosity.

I find my Bible all about the island, these days. I find it in the infinite, intricate branchings of a patch of moss; the perfect curlicues of a shell, which are found once again in the curved horns of a goat, and it is all the same, the same tune played on different instruments.

Now that I begin to slip out of words, I think of the cat, and how she said I should rely on bones and not my Bible games. I understand her better now, and after all these years I have more understanding of the faithful bones, which do not lie.

35

I wake the cat at dawn. 'Come,' I say. 'You are summoned.'

She yawns so wide that I can see the roof of her mouth, ridged and pale like a shell. 'You have no power to summon me,' she says, and closes her eyes again.

'Fine,' I say. My voice, rough from lack of usage. 'Then let this be enough: I am summoned. I summon myself, for a third trial. And if you and the goat care to be my witnesses, I shall be glad of it.'

She arches her back and pulls herself in two directions at once. She stretches as dough used to stretch between my mother's hands.

'Call the goat,' she says.

Thus once more we make our small procession, but this time I lead, followed by the goat, who came very prompt when I called his name. Last of all comes the cat, falling at times so far behind that I keep turning to reassure myself that she is still here.

When we reach the cliffside ledge, it is I who mount the stone block, though I do it more haltingly than the goat, and I must steel myself not to glance behind me to the long and certain drop to the rocks below.

Cronch and Sleek are before me now. For a long time I do not speak. It is not just that my voice is out of use. Now that I am here, I do not know how to say what I must.

'Sir,' says the goat, 'I believe you have something to say.'

'So say it,' adds the cat.

I take a deep breath, and then another. 'Let us commence the third trial of Alexander Selkirk.'

They betray no surprise.

'On what charge?' asks the goat.

I clear my throat. 'It concerns Effie.'

Sleek stands and paces across the clearing and back. A cat makes a natural prosecutor. 'Effie. You have told us nothing of her.'

'I told you her story,' I say. 'How we courted, how I abandoned her, and how she took her life.'

'That is a neat story,' the goat says. 'But it is not hers. It is your story – only of yourself.'

'Always Selkirk,' says Sleek.

'Do not badger him,' says Cronch. 'Sir, what is the charge?'

I hesitate. The cat waits. The patience of a cat is an implacable thing. Delay as I will, she will still be here.

'The charge of the wilful murder of Effie Breck, late of Nether Largo, Fifeshire, and her unborn child too, through my wanton and callous conduct.'

I was not lying at the last trial, when I told them that Effie wished to be wed, when I had decided to go once more to sea. But I did not tell them why she was so very eager to marry.

And so I tell the story again, but this time I tell the whole of it.

When I meet her by the seawall to tell her I am leaving, Effie tells me she is with child. She carries the news to me as though it is a gift or a benison. 'A baby,' she says, and she presses her hands to her belly, though there is as yet nothing to be seen.

'Can you be so certain?'

'Do you doubt me?' she flashes back. 'I may not be a scholar such as you fancy yourself to be, but I'm no fool.'

'No indeed,' I say quickly. And because she embraces me, I embrace her too.

Only last night, Da warned me not to become entangled with Effie. *Entangled* – yes, that is exactly what this child does: it is a knot, Effie and I snarled up together in something that cannot be undone.

'I ought to be afraid,' she says, 'but I cannot help being happy.'

This is when I know that we are in different stories – or different parts of the same story. Because she thinks we are at the beginning, but I know it is an ending. Some part of me almost feels relief – the news of the babe confirms that I have made the right choice. It is beyond time for me to be away.

'Effie,' I say. 'I am glad you are happy – and you know I wish you no ill. But neither can I help you with this.' I point to her belly.

'This?' she says, very loud. 'This? Do your mean your own baby?'

I do not answer.

'You cannot leave now,' she says. 'For I cannot walk away from this as you seem to wish to.'

'I have my way to make in the world.' I tell her. 'What choice do I have?'

'What of my choices?' she spits. 'What of your child?'

'How can I be so sure that it is mine?'

'Do you think me some kind of wanton slut?'

It is almost a relief that she is angry – for it is better this way, easier for me to be hard with her now she is this envenomed thing, ugly with rage.

'I could just have left,' I say.

'Aye – as you did last time, without a thought for me.'

'I chose to come here today, and to tell you instead.'

'Such thoughtfulness!' she says. 'Should I be thanking you for your kindness?'

'You do not need to harp at me, is all I mean. Just because I must go, does not mean I care nothing for you.'

'*Must*,' she says. 'Oh, you are very faithful to your obligations, when they are to yourself.' She shakes her head. 'Was it not you who wooed me, and very determined too?'

'We did it together,' I say. 'All of it – it was not just me.'

'But this,' she gestures at her belly, 'this I must do alone?'

'I am soon to sea again. How could I possibly help you?'

'So you will abandon me now, pregnant with your child, and not even marry me first? If you don't wed me then I am lost, as you well know. My father will throw me out, if he does not kill me first.'

'I have no wish to wed, and nor can I offer you a home.' She cannot understand the great expansive horizon of the sea. How could I explain to her how the ocean makes Nether Largo and everything within it seem petty and small, when so much more has been promised to me? If we wed, it will make her life bigger, but mine smaller – for she will tie me to this place, and the stain of the troublesome Brecks, and the scorn of the kirk, when my dearest wish is to leave it all behind.

'You have to understand,' I say to her, 'that I can offer you nothing.'

'You were not saying that when you were offering me your prick. That you were very happy to offer me.'

'And you were very happy to take it.'

'What has become of you?' she asks me. 'You're acting nothing like the man I know.'

I want to say: *The man you know is exactly what I am trying to cast off.*

'Perhaps you do not know me as well as you think,' I say.

She opens her mouth, then closes it again.

'Come.' I reach out to her, but she swipes my hand away, scratching me with her nails. She runs up the hill, her skirts caught up in her hands. Then she turns back and calls to me, the wind whipping her hair over her face. 'You have been the ruin of me, Alexander Selcraig.'

'You know the rest,' I say. 'She drowned herself that same night.'

'Still you have told us nothing of Effie,' says the cat.

My shame is that I have nothing more of her to tell – for I did not see her at all. I was so full of my own story, the various indignities and disasters of my life, that I gave no thought to Effie. What did I know of her home and her life there with her father, whom the whole village knew for a drunkard and a ruffian? Of the bruises on her body, a story I never cared to hear?

I had the whole of the sea, and a future to make in it – what did she have but Nether Largo, and her father's house, and his fists? If she took her disgrace home, her father would have beaten her, or killed her, or her mother sent her away to starve. Is it any wonder that she clung to me as though I could grant her a different life? I thought her regard for me made me special – was that not proved when she waited for me those long years when I was first at sea? But if you have been praying a long time for change, it is easy to mistake somebody for the answer to your prayers. Effie believed very fervently in me – yet I was just a man, and a worse man than most.

Sometimes, I confess, I have almost believed that Effie's death was a kind of benison – that she took a drowning for me. I wore her death like the caul I was born in, as another proof that I could never be drowned. I despised my mother for her doting on me, and yet all the same I believed her that I was born to be spared. Alexander Selkirk, seventh son, blessed indeed.

And when my fool brother Andrew taunted me about Effie's death, I was so busy attending to my anger at him that I did not pay heed to the true cause of my anger: myself, for I caused her death, as surely as the salt water groping its fingers down her throat. I claimed her for my own and then I cut her loose, and the child within her too. It is a sin the weight of which should crush a man, and so I turned my back to it, steadfast in denial. Only now, on this island, when all else is gone, and I have nothing else to place between myself and the truth, must I face the awful knowing. I killed Effie. It was I, and no other. I refused her until the only answer that remained was water, and the only mercy left for her was the sea's mercy. I took the babe in her belly and turned it into an anchor.

'My father called her suicide a sin,' I say. 'There was great sin in it, I see now – but the sin is mine, for what I did to her, in my cowardice and in my pride.' It is a sin the precise weight of a drowned body – it is fierce heavy, and I shall carry it all my days.

'Mister Cronch,' I say. 'Many years ago you and I spoke about the scapegoat in the Bible. I argued, then, that I was the scapegoat, sent to the wilderness for the sins of others.'

'I remember,' he says.

'I was wrong. If I am a scapegoat, sent into the wilderness, then I bear nobody's sins but my own.'

I am weeping. The goat draws closer; he sniffs my face as goats do, with a hoisting of his top lip. He is gentle, but I do not want his comfort, nor deserve it.

———

'Go on,' I say. 'Let me have your verdict.'

'No.' The cat stretches her mouth wide in what might be a yawn, or just a baring of teeth.

'Come,' I say, my voice louder. 'Give me your judgment.'

'You shall not have it,' says the goat.

'Why? Isn't judgment the whole purpose of a trial – to which you yourself twice summoned me?'

That cat stands. 'You have no authority to demand judgment from this court.'

I turn to the goat. 'I have told you the whole of it. I have told you what I did to her.'

He nods. 'You told us of your sin, your grief, your regret. And now you come to this court to seek your absolution.'

'Selkirk, Selkirk,' says the cat, speaking over him.

'Indeed,' the goat says. 'You have told us your story once more, Mister Selkirk. It is not Effie's story, and you shall not have a judgment from us.'

'I do not want your mercy – for I showed Effie none.'

'We are not giving you mercy,' says the cat.

'Then condemn me,' I shout, and my words echo off the rocks and the cliffs below.

'You have come here for absolution,' the goat says, 'but this island can offer you none.'

'Give me the judgment I deserve. Let me suffer as I should – let me make amends.'

'Your suffering is not a currency with which you can purchase absolution,' he says, not unkindly. 'What amends can you make, when the girl is long dead, and the child too?'

'Do I not know that, and better than you ever could? It was I who held her after she was drowned.' I am reaching out, palms up, as though I'm holding her still.

'Yet even at her death, you speak of yourself,' says the goat. 'That picturesque scene: her body in your arms; your tears, doubtless. You would put yourself at the heart of her death, as you did with her life.' He steps back from me. 'A story can be a very ravenous thing, Mister Selkirk. Your story will take the whole of her, if you allow it.'

I drop my head. 'What, then? What do I do?'

'Say her name.'

'Do not call it,' says the cat at once. 'She is not for you.'

He nods. 'But name her, for our dead should be named.'

'Effie Breck,' I say. 'Euphenia Breck.'

'It is not her job to provide you with succour, and to secure the salvation of your immortal soul.'

'I ask nothing of her,' I say. 'I only seek the court's judgment.'

'To comfort yourself,' says the cat.

The goat interrupts her. 'You wronged Euphenia Breck. Yes – I would be no kind of minister if I did not acknowledge that. But you cannot summon this court, looking to make her the vehicle of your absolution.'

No more words from the cat – only a long, slow hiss, the sound of a blade being drawn.

'Here is what you must do for Effie,' says the goat. 'Ask nothing more of her.'

'What I did to her was unforgivable. There must be an accounting. Will you not convict me?'

'You say *unforgivable*,' says the cat. 'So go. Stop asking for forgiveness.'

36

Spring. Each season knows the time of its coming and its going.

There is a place downstream from my camp where the trees hang low over the brook, and in the right light the reflection of the water is cast on the underside of the leaves, dappling them. Such a small thing, and yet it is as welcome to me as once a cask of brandy might have been. How strange for Alexander Selkirk, disgrace of Nether Largo, to find his delights in the underside of a leaf, and not in taverns nor brothels.

I have often wondered whether, if I were to be rescued tomorrow, anyone who knew me would recognise me. Now I begin to wonder whether I can recognise myself.

I have lately discovered in myself a new capacity for wonder. You might think there is nothing new to be found on this island after so many years, yet I am finding novelties. Often they are but small: the plump bell of each flower on the myrtle; how the smoke of my fire writes its calligraphy on the sky; sunset, when the sun is an egg cracked against the horizon. These things signify nothing, yet I notice them. I am of late a very avid noticer.

The island has taught me much about different kinds of hunger.

At first, it was belly hunger. I was still learning to catch the goats, and how to forage for shellfish. The unsalted meat of the seals and fish made me sick, and day and night my hunger was a fist clenched tight in my belly.

After I learned to feed myself, I discovered other types of hunger. My hunger for company. My hunger for touch. Not just the touch of women, but even the jostling, careless touch of shipboard life. Robbed of all that, on the island I hungered for skin. The cats were a comfort: the simple, warm weight of them beside me in my hammock. Even the old goat was a comfort when I scratched him under his jaw, though his beard is very coarse and his head bony.

But something has changed. I have arrived at a place I never thought to be. Now, in these patient and expansive days, I have no hunger.

———

strange

grave

of

the

ghost

282

Stone and flesh and salt water. Words are unmoored, set loose. Stripped of the burden of language and meaning, each thing becomes itself. The dark rock, a comb of tiny holes, raspy to the touch, that leaves my feet flecked with black grit. The grey stone, steel-sharp, that slices the soil in straight lines. The basalt that warms under the sun so that when I sit upon it at midday it scorches the back of my legs. Each rock full of its own particularity. Each one an ordinary marvel.

I am learning, very slowly, to let the stone be stone.

Silent, for the most part, I have the goat and the cat by my side. Barefoot and clad in goatskin, I trust my days and allow them their allotted hours. I am living in my full strangeness now, shoulders back and chest wide, mouth closed and eyes open. I am exposed to the world, and of it.

Some days I go to my lookout. More often I do not. The sea will not be hurried. It will bring me what it will.

I step over the bleached bones of a long-dead goat. Between the rats and the wind, the bones have been polished a startling white.

How we living gnaw at the dead, as animals do. We cannot let them lie, but instead mouth at them, and taste them, and drag at them with our teeth.

Effie is dead – and I, who gave her no peace when she lived, must let her lie.

It is a hard thing, to know myself for what I am, and for what I have done.

Effie Breck. I will no longer worry at her corpse as though it is carrion. I will leave her in her winding sheet, her last silence, which is not for me.

I wake one morning and say *ballast, ballast.* I have altogether forgot what it means – it has become merely sound. It occupies itself: the luscious rolling of the *l*, the longing of the *last.* It has slipped anchor from its meaning and become sound alone. *Ballast.*

My clothes rot away. My blade is blunted and rusty, its tip snapped.
Why not words
Why should they not also fade and tatter and snap
Ballast
Reverend
Ocean
Oh
O

O there are such holes in words

I am out of voice, outside of time.

I did not know what lessons I needed to learn from this island. The most difficult and the simplest of things.

More than ever I am my body. I am bone and flesh and good, good muscle. I am what I do: the quick steps up the mountainside; my feet, bare and hoof-hard; my trusty hands which know their work.

And I have never prayed as well as I pray now with my legs when I run swift-footed up the rocks, nor with my hands when I carve anew my chair. Is this not devotion? Is this not worship?

Having shed words I am closer to the world. I am in it, and of it. Ankle-deep in the cool water, wind on my face, my whole body an engine for wonder.

Unchurched, I have no need of a minister, nor even of a Bible and its wordy mutterings. Unchurched, I am all worship, I am all things.

I am Selkirk
the kirk is in me

the kirk is me

I have not become good. I have come true.

Enough. The path to silence is not made with words. Let be, good stone, true sea.

Let be.

Many years ago, the cat told me that silence was a language I had not yet learned. She was right.

She snorts. 'A cat is always right.'

Did I speak aloud? I had not realised.

I take up my Bible for the final time. The stick of charcoal, its good weight in my hand. I open the page and write this island's final poem.

PART THREE

37

Summer has almost finished its work, and bends towards autumn. In the early afternoon I am scraping a hide; beside me, the goat chews turnip flowers.

The cat walks into the clearing, her tail straight up, a mast.

'Listen,' she says, standing squarely before me. 'This is the last riddle I will give you.'

I still my scraping and wait.

'Mister Selkirk. What comes and goes?'

I think for a moment. 'The tide? The sea? The sun?'

'Selkirk.'

'What do you mean?'

'Selkirk.'

I do not understand.

'Look,' she says. 'Look.' And she turns away from me, to face the distant sea.

There, on the furthest strip of the horizon: a ship.

———

I peer – two ships, in fact, one a little larger. From here I can see no flag, for they are standing off at a great distance.

Down I run, over rock, fleet of foot and careless of flesh, hot breath and swift. There is a better vantage point but a little way down the path – yes, two ships, and frigates, I would wager. Surely they have not the Spanish line, full-bellied? Surely they are good stout British ships, sparse of ornament? Solid, and not built for speed as

French ships are? At this tremendous distance I cannot be sure – yet I could swear it.

With each step down towards the water I lose a slice of the horizon. At the shore I can see but a few miles – so it is an act of faith to trust that the ships are still there, that they were not a mere dream. I drag from its shelter my store of wood, to light my signal fire. If they are Spaniards, I evaded them before and must trust that I can evade them again, especially as I've spotted the ships in good time. Or perhaps I will not evade them after all. Perhaps I will not be able to resist the allure of a human face, a voice, whatever the cost.

Squatting at the huge pyre of wood, I allow myself to use my flint, husbanded away so carefully for so many years that I am clumsy and slow with it – but there is the spark, there, and my fire is good – a good strong fire, bigger than any I have made, and it roars and bellows and spits until the Reverend Vicarious Cronch, who has followed me down, must draw back so that his long beard is not singed. Nevertheless, it is still bright daylight, and there are enough clouds about that I cannot be sure the ships shall make out my spire of smoke. It is a big fire, but a bigger sky.

I cannot bear to wait here any longer, unable to see the ships. I climb once more to the higher vantage point, near to my camp. I cannot see them – has this whole thing been merely some hoax played upon me by Sleek, taunting my credulous heart, as a cat toys with its prey? No – the clouds shift, and the ships are there once more. Yet they have drawn no closer. Likely they await a southerly wind, so that they may more easily sail into the bay. But a boat has been lowered; it sets off from such a great distance, a heroic distance to cover by oar. I must content myself with that little boat – but its progress is slow, so slow.

'I thought you had of late learned patience,' says the goat, watching me pace.

'I am only human,' say I.

Do I imagine it, or is there pity in his look?

While I wait, I resolve to prepare a feast for the sailors – a celebration fit for the occasion. These men will have been a long time asea, and hungry for fresh meat. I shall kill three goats and roast them. Dampier told me that Will, the Mesquite Indian who was abandoned here, did the same when he saw his rescuers on the horizon. See, see: everything happens again, the curve of the goat's horn meeting itself.

There is no time to hunt goats in my usual manner. Instead, rushing back to my camp in haste, I slaughter three of my penned flock, for what need of them shall I have now that I am saved? They are very tame now and do not shy from me, but rather come willingly to the knife so that I may slit their throats. The blade does its red work.

I butcher the goats hastily – still it takes time, but I am grateful for it fills the hours that otherwise I would spend watching the boat's sluggish progress. I set the meat to roasting for I am determined to give a feast to these men – these hearty rowers – to put me in their favour. A blood price, to earn my place on their ark.

Back to the vantage point – and the boat is surely closer now. The dark is coming – they have set a lamp in the boat, its light swinging as they row. They are perhaps a league from shore – still an immense distance – and despite rowing for hours already, they are indefatigable. Back at my camp I turn the spits. The cats cruise the fire's edge, licking the drips of fat that spit from the carcasses.

When I descend, the boat is close enough that I can see it from the shore. I set a second fire, a little way from the first. Oh faithful flint, faithful flame. I feed the whole of my store of wood into it, until it flares higher than a man. The day is fading quick but now the beach is bright, my blaze lights all, my face scorching. They shall not miss me; I am here, I am here.

In the glare of my own fires, it is harder to make out the boat's bobbing light. I must squint and shield my eyes from the hot and racing light of the fire. There it is, the light. Yet it draws no closer – it is stilled.

I run back up to the vantage point – the dark is darker than ever after the blaze at the beach. Yes – there is the boat. But it is moving away, and moving faster than before. It is fleeing.

I let out an animal howl. If they can hear me they will believe this island beset by fearsome beasts, and will row all the faster. But I cannot stop myself from shrieking – for in my eagerness to guide them ashore I have affrighted them with my fires. Instead of a lone man they may think this is a big settlement, a veritable garrison of Spaniards, and now needs must be cautious. And I curse myself for having set the fires on the beach, rather than higher – for from a distance, they may appear to be ships' lights, and they may imagine a fleet in the bay. The boat is fleeing – they are almost out of sight. Oh Christ – in my hunger to be found I have driven them away. And if they are in poor shape – and for what other reason would a ship consider coming ashore in such a God-forsaken and remote place? – then they will not return, for a broken-down ship or an ailing crew will not risk an engagement with the enemy.

It was my own folly that left me here – and my own folly that has driven away my one hope of rescue. I drop to my knees then collapse forwards, palms to the ground, rocking and rocking so that my head strikes stone. I let it strike – I strike it all the harder. I wish more than anything to be released from this cursed spiral of time.

I am not alone tonight. The goat does not make his nightly retreat to the high places, but stays nearby. Sleek, too, stays close, though she is restless, waking me from my fitful sleep as she kneads, turns, and turns again.

It is light. The first thing I do is test the wind – yes, it has turned southerly. I look to where I last saw the ships – nothing. I stumble to the vantage point. The ships have not left – indeed they are closer by far, they have sailed past the bay and rounded back again, tacking in to lay close aboard the land. Close enough for me to be almost certain they are British ships, with none of the papish extravagance of the Spanish fleet's decoration. I whoop and cheer – they are coming. Then my hollering takes on a new fervour, for the gusty southerly stretches out the flag of the larger frigate and reveals the red ensign of England. No Scotsman has ever been more delighted to see an English flag.

I run to the shore. The frigates are entering the bay, but squalls and gusts are coming offshore mighty strong now and they are forced to reef their topsails. Still they come, and finding no enemy fleet at harbour here, they drop anchor. By noon they lower their yawl, and she makes for the shore. I rekindle a small fire in the ashes of last night's tremendous blaze – for now that I have sight of their flag, surely a fire can only signal that I am no enemy.

I count eight men in the yawl – and even from here I can make out their weapons. I take off my ragged shirt and wave it above my head like a flag, though it has been a long time since it was white. I leap and wave and caper, and if it does little for my dignity, at least it shall show them I am not hostile. And as they draw nearer I splash right into the shallows and gesture to the channel between the rocks, where they may safest moor – for I must show myself helpful in all things, show them how good I am, how good and how willing.

And they are here – all of a sudden it is so quick. This waiting that has taken years and years and the slow agonies of yesterday and last night, but now they step from the yawl and wade to shore, real human men with faces and voices, and though they carry weapons they come towards me without muskets lowered. They are cautious but they are coming. I fall to my knees in the shallow water and raise my hands in supplication or in prayer.

Such a clamour of faces, of stories, of limbs and hands that are not mine, and their voices so very loud and fast, the words that I cannot untangle –
you'dhardlyknowhimforaman
willyoulookatthestateofhim
canhetalkatall, d'youthink
oraspaniardmaybe
hehasmorethelookofasavagethanaspaniard

I want to say
save me
I want to say
I am already saved
I have saved myself and I did not think it could be done

All that comes out is one gasp: 'Saved.'
And the men set about a great clanging of words and cheers, and clap me on the back and say, 'Yes, yes my good sir you are saved – an Englishman after all!'

I open my mouth to say *No, Scots*, but words evade me – and they are making a tumult, turning to each other and drawing ever tighter around me.

'You are saved and need fear no more—'

'We will take you from this cursed place—'

'Someone give the man a pipe—'

'I'll warrant you'll welcome a drink and some good food, and some company what's more—'

I cannot answer. I have quite forgot the ways of words. I am looking about me for the goat and the cat – they were with me on the beach just before the yawl reached the shore. But there is no stopping the tide of the men's excitement, for where at first they feared me an enemy or a savage, with that single word – *saved* – I have made heroes of them. They are my very salvation, and that is a thrilling thing for any man.

'How long have you been here, sir?' asks one of them.

Four years, three months, two weeks. Four winters, four summers. I open my mouth to say it – but what sort of measure is a year? Better to say: four times the heavy tide of seals has come in, the whole shore a packed mass of good fat flesh. How many years? Better to ask: How many great roarings of the sea lions? How many evenings of peaceful debate with the Reverend Vicarious Cronch? How many hummingbirds flickering at the edge of my fire?

'Four years,' I say. I speak as though my teeth have been wrenched out and put in anew, all wrong and ungainly under my tongue.

'Four years – good God, man – if you're serious then you're a wonder indeed—'

'If this is not a miracle, I do not know what is.'

I do not want to be a miracle, nor a wonder. I am Selkirk. Where is the goat? Where is my haughty Sleek, to witness all of this? I try to turn around, but still the men are clapping me on the back and one of them lights his pipe and presses it on to me, talking all the while of how they must let Captain Rogers know of their discovery.

I lead the men to my clearing – it seems easier to guide them there than to talk, and I confess the pipe has made me dizzy. But I am dizzy anyway with noise and faces, such a babel of newness.

The sailors are greatly taken by my camp and my huts, and go about picking up my things and loudly marvelling at them. 'You are a most resourceful fellow,' says one, turning over in his hands one of my wooden pails. But they are more taken by the goats I set to roast last night. Being sadly neglected, the meat is burned on one side and raw on the other, and when the coals cooled the rats came and took their share – Pickle and her offspring too. Nevertheless the men fall very quickly upon the meat, which at least puts a stop to the barrage of questions, to which I have only been able to make clumsy and inadequate answers. I have given them the shortest possible version of my story: that I was left here after a disagreement with my captain.

The oldest of the men is Dover, second captain of the larger frigate. The other men likewise give their names, but in the blur of words and faces I cannot catch hold of them. The frigates are privateers, and sailed out of Bristol August last year.

The men admire Pickle and her family. Pickle purrs upon my hammock and takes their caresses as her due, exceeding smug. Of Sleek and the Reverend Vicarious Cronch, there is yet no sign. And I have no chance to search for them, for the men are still hungry for meat, and for sport also, determining to hunt some more goats for the crews remaining aboard the frigates. They take up their guns, and I offer to guide them along my own paths to the island's western cliffs, where the goats are to be found at this time of day.

'I'll warrant you know every stone on this island,' says Captain Dover.

Before I can answer there is a movement a little way behind me, between me and the cliff's edge. Dover swings around at the same instant that I turn.

It is the goat. He has nosed his way between two pimento trees, barely ten yards from me, his ears flaring sideways with curiosity, his upper lip raised to sniff.

A crack – Dover has raised his gun and got off a shot. 'There,' he says, well satisfied with himself – for Cronch is hit. I give a kind of yell and rush towards him, but he lurches away, and with a great clattering of hoofs and stones he falls backwards, right over the sheer edge.

I stagger at the brink of the cliff. 'Can we reach him?' I shout to Dover. The rocks at my feet are spattered with blood, bright and dark. In the crevasse far below I can make out the goat's white body, motionless. I lean forward, the better to see him; rocks skitter beneath my feet, some scattering over the edge. The crevasse is both narrow and steep – a split in the island, fifty feet deep, leading straight to the sea, which thrashes in a trap of sharp rocks.

Dover joins me and looks carelessly down. 'I will not hazard my neck for a parcel of goat meat,' he says. 'Least of all for one so old and grizzled.'

'We must,' I say breathlessly. 'A boat – lend me a boat and I shall reach him.' If I could but persuade them to lend me one of their boats, I will make the attempt by sea – though the rocks thereabouts are very fierce. 'We must get down at once.'

Dover has mistaken the cause of my alarm. He claps me on the shoulder. 'Friend, you are a castaway no longer, and need not worry so over a waste of powder, nor a shortage of meat. No boat can land there – and we will shoot a dozen goats more before this day is out, and you shall eat your fill.'

'No,' I say.

He is taken aback at the shrillness of my voice.

If I tell him the truth, I will be taken for a madman. How could I begin to say to them: *There lies my greatest friend, wiser than any of you, and my dearest succour during these many long years?* What sort of a man would confess that a goat has been the most patient and curious interlocutor of his life?

'No,' I say again, more quietly. 'In truth, sir, I am tired of goat meat.'

At this he laughs heartily and squeezes my shoulder. 'I don't doubt it. Then you shall have all the salt beef and ship's biscuit that you like, and leave the goats for us.'

I turn away from the ravine's edge – I can stare no longer at the wreckage of my friend. For the next hour, as I lead them west, I say nothing. I eat my sobs, and keep my head down. They are used to my silence, so they shall have more of it.

I am saved, and I am damned, both at once, for they have killed the best part of me.

38

I cannot shake off the men for several hours, until they are occupied with butchering the goats they have shot, and others with catching crawfish. I slip away from them and back to the shore. I scramble to the ravine's edge, where Cronch's blood has now dried black. Below, there is nothing to be seen. The rocks where he lay have been buried by the rising tide; the narrow inlet fills and empties, fills and empties. I lie there, peering down, until it grows too dark to see at all.

From the shore, the men are hallooing and hollering, calling my name. I rejoin them – they are in a hurry to return to the frigates, which have been signalling, alarmed that Dover's party has met with some misadventure here. 'And they will be happy indeed,' says Dover, 'to hear that we not only found no Spaniards here, but found one of our own instead.' And if I needed more proof that my words are ill-formed and clumsy, it is that these men still do not know me for a Scotsman.

I have one foot in the yawl when I hesitate. 'Stradling,' I say. 'Captain Thomas Stradling is not of your company?'

'There is no Stradling in our company – no man by that name. Our captains are Woodes Rogers, of the *Duke*, and Stephen Courtney, for the *Duchess* – with Dampier as pilot.'

Dampier. The word lands like a cannonball – so heavy that I expect the yawl to flounder under its weight. I can barely follow what the men are saying, as they continue to speak.

Dampier – Dampier who made Stradling captain and was the architect of the entire disaster of that voyage.

Dover is still speaking. 'Dampier has a particular charge to navigate the South Seas, for few men know these parts so well.'

I open my mouth to tell them everything: how Dampier could not even find his way to the island, sailing past it and only returning days later; how he mistook the entrance to the river and thus delayed the raid on Santa Maria; how obdurate he was, refusing to take counsel.

But words come slow to me these days, and 'Dampier' is all I say. They wait, a little impatient, for they are in haste to return to the ship. 'Dampier,' I say again. Once, I would have said, *I will not sail on any ship with Dampier, and if you are wise, you will put off here too, to spare yourself the same.* I would have let my anger rise in me the way a flock of birds rises – in a great noisy clattering and shrieking.

But the world will call you out – over and over, it will say: *Try me.* I need no grand gestures of rage. I will not be a martyr to my anger, which could cost me my rescue, but which would not trouble Dampier nor change him neither. It is time for me to make my own way.

I shake my head, step into the yawl, and say nothing. We make good time out to the *Duke.* We are taken up, and the frigate's crew crowds tight around me, full of questions and many of them desirous to touch my goatskin clothes or my long hair and beard. But they do not linger – disappointed, perhaps, by my slowness in answering the questions that they fire at me – and they are soon drawn off by the crawfish and goat meat their comrades brought from the island. They have been some months at sea, and having had a nasty time of it when rounding Cape Horn, the men are ravenous.

The captain of the entire expedition marches up to me. He shakes my hand very firm, both his hands pressing around my own.

'They told me you were clad all in goatskins, sir,' he says, jovial. 'Yet I did not think to find you looking even more wild than the skins' first owners.'

This is Captain Woodes Rogers, and he takes me to his great cabin, where he is full of questions about all manner of things, from my precise manner of catching the goats to how I use pimento to season my food, for want of a regular supply of salt. I say nothing of my attempt to flee on the raft, which seems a mad and shameful escapade. But I gladly share the many small details of my survival on the island, and all of these particulars he records diligently, and he is vastly pleased and takes to calling me *Governor Selkirk*, in a jesting way. 'For all this island was your domain, was it not, and you its sole ruler?'

I do not try to explain to him what the island itself took several years to teach me: that I was never ruler here, and that this island was not my dominion. That I was a mere subject of this place.

But Rogers is a fair man and above all in need of good sailors, so is inclined to like me and to treat me well. My rescue depends upon him, and I counsel myself not to jeopardise it by any flarings of my old self, that argumentative fellow, very fierce in objecting to every thing. Rogers calls me *Governor* and I nod and smile.

<hr />

'Now,' says Rogers, 'come above deck — for there is a man aboard you must be eager to see once more.'

Dampier is waiting on the forecastle. He looks older — he must now be sixty or thereabouts, a grand age for any man, and for a sailor most of all.

'Mister Dampier,' says Rogers. 'I bring you your old comrade, Mister Selkirk — though I'll allow you might not at first recognise him.' He steps back, and I can see from his manner that he is expecting a touching reunion of old comrades.

Dampier steps forward first. He shakes my hand and does not let it go. 'Mister Selkirk. You will have quite a tale to tell.'

'Indeed,' I say, and I look him direct in the eye.

Still he holds my hand, his grip tremendous firm. 'A story so marvellous that few will credit it.'

Is he warning me off?

If I tell of his cowardice and indecision, he will answer with stories of my mutinous conduct. Each of us with the other's ruin held on our tongues. If one of us speaks, we are both brought down.

'I am happy to find you well, sir,' I say. And with a final squeeze I pull my hand away.

That is all I can give him, but it pleases him well enough, and he turns to Rogers.

'I can tell you, sir, that when Mister Selkirk was ship's master, he was the best man aboard.'

This lie I acknowledge with a small nod, too small for Rogers to see. So that is his price – he will keep his silence, and I will keep mine.

Rogers beams. 'I had thought as much,' he says to Dampier, 'for no ordinary man could have withstood what he has.' He turns to me. 'I have in mind, sir, to offer you the post of second mate aboard the *Duke*. It wanted only Mister Dampier's endorsement – which now I have. Will you take the role, sir – though it may be a step down from absolute monarch of an island entire?'

'Gladly, sir,' I say, and he shakes my hand.

I would have been well satisfied with a hammock before the mast with the men, but Rogers insists on a bed in a cabin with Samuel Hopkins, a lieutenant who doubles as the ship's apothecary. I sleep in a kind of daze – untroubled by rats, but without the warm presence of Pickle or Sleek. All my dreams are of the Reverend Vicarious Cronch, and his long final fall. I dream that his horns were broken upon the rocks – the shattering of that splendid curve.

I wake to Hopkins' light snoring, and a fear that whatever salvation I have managed to find may not be taken with me from the island.

We are to stay here some little time, for the ships took damage in rounding the Horn, and a number of the men are suffering from illness of the scorbutic type.

For myself, my haste today is all to get off the ship and go once more to the island. I do not fool myself that I shall find Cronch alive – but regardless I must seek Sleek and check on Pickle. I go ashore with the first boat of the morning, promising to show the men the best place to gather cabbage leaves. Rogers does not seem a capricious man, but I am anxious to stay in his favour, and to prove myself both useful and willing.

When the men are busy harvesting the greens, I tell them I must retrieve some things from my camp. I go at once to the crevasse that swallowed the goat. There is nothing to be seen down there but water, and at the cliff's edge a diligent procession of ants where his blood was splashed on the rocks.

It means nothing that his body is gone – I tell myself this. The tide does not wait, not even for such an august character as the Reverend Vicarious Cronch. He has been taken by the sea, and is gone. Yet I cannot help but think of a goat's tremendous facility for climbing. Oftentimes in these years, a movement has startled me on a cliff face and I have marvelled to see it is a goat, so high and on rock so sheer that I could scarce credit it. As to whether a goat could climb the crevasse after being shot and falling such a great height – did not I survive a fall myself? And of all goats, I tell myself, the Reverend Vicarious Cronch is the most remarkable.

Perhaps it is typical of this island that it will not grant me the satisfaction of knowing. In the days to come I seek Cronch everywhere. Whenever I can contrive to be alone I call his name, all about my old camp, and various of the other places favoured by him: the turnip patch, now run to seed in autumn; a dead tree beside the path to my lookout, with a broken bough against which he loved to scratch his back. I call and I call, but my old friend does not appear.

Even Sleek is become most wary. She will not come out when Rogers' men are near, and the crew is often at my camp. Pickle is very taken with the sailors, who ply her with treats and marvel at how I have tamed a feral cat. When I point out all her offspring, Dover says, 'Your cat is a veritable factory of kittens.' But only once in these first days do I see Sleek, when I venture to my old camp alone, before dawn, to find her. She is skittish and silent, and will approach me only after I sit a long while without moving.

'You know what became of Cronch?'

She gives one of her menacing yawns.

'Sleek – Sleek.' I rub her soft ear between my finger and thumb. 'I can take you aboard. Ships welcome cats – you would find no shortage of rats.'

'I have all the rats I could want. The sea is no place for a cat.'

'Nonsense,' say I. 'Come with me. I have lost Vicarious Cronch – how could I manage without you?'

She does not answer. Instead she says, 'I have a riddle for you.'

'You said you'd given me the final riddle.'

'I did not say that.'

'You did. When the ships arrived – when you alerted me to them, for which I shall always be grateful.'

'Listen. This is the riddle itself: I did not say that. Who did, Mister Selkirk?'

'Stop,' I say at once. 'Say no more.'

'I never started.' She leaves, weaving her way between the trees, moving as smoothly as a fish.

'You are a very devil for staring,' says Hopkins, the lieutenant who shares my cabin.

'I am sorry, sir,' I say. 'I confess I am out of the habit of seeing faces.'

I put the men ill at ease with my scrutiny, for it is true that I am gravely besotted by faces. Hopkins has a narrow face, with the thoughtful and slightly puzzled expression of a sheep.

Captain Rogers himself is a commanding fellow, though I would not put his age at more than thirty years. His face is strong about the jaw, and between his eyes are two deep creased lines, as if his brow is forever furrowed – for he is an earnest man, always intent on some thing or other.

As for Dampier, he and I perform a strange duet: we avoid each other as much as is possible, and when it is not possible, we are exceedingly civil to one another. I will allow that he appears some-what humbled; there are rumours that he found himself in sorely straitened circumstances, after the disaster of his last expedition. Aboard he is treated with some esteem; they speak of him as an acknowledged authority. 'He knows the South Seas better than any Englishman,' Rogers tells me. If it is true, it is only true because so few Englishmen have thus far dared these parts, and not because of any particular skill or wisdom belonging to Dampier. Once I would have said as much – now I keep my counsel.

Rogers comes to my camp himself, for he is mightily taken with the story of my survival.

Like the other men, he marvels at my little huts and the neat pen for my goats, though all have now been eaten by the men except my stout milking goat, who has been taken aboard the *Duke*. Of Sleek, there is no sign.

'You found many ingenious ways to make yourself comfortable,' Rogers says, lifting and letting fall the goat hides that hang like curtains.

'I would not say *comfortable*.' I am packing up my things into my chest: my knife, much blunted; my Bible.

'Perhaps not,' he says. 'But ingenious nonetheless. A wonder simply to have survived so many years, entirely alone.'

'I was not entirely alone.' As soon as it is said I regret it, for Rogers looks at me sharply.

'Savages? Or was there perhaps another castaway, who did not survive?'

'Oh no,' I say. 'Nothing at all of that sort.'

And now his look is of confusion, or perhaps pity – for what am I but a madman, a rambling loon, amusing himself with shadows?

Then he sees that I still hold my Bible, and relief rises on his face like a dawn, and he says, 'Of course – for no Christian man is alone when he has his faith.'

Do I take it, this line that he is offering me, which shall very neatly relieve him of his awkwardness, and me of my madness? Rogers is known for a pious man – already Dover has complained to me that, at sea, Rogers insists on prayers being read twice a day.

'Indeed,' I say. For I cannot say: *A cat and a goat have been my great counsel and consolation.* 'Indeed. My Bible was a great comfort to me.'

He smiles. And if he should take up my Bible and find it much riddled with blackness, then he will assume it has been damaged or mildewed, like most things that I own.

And just as my Bible poems taught me, I see now that my time on the island is a story with many different tellings. To Rogers it is a story of piety and dominion; to others amongst the crew it is a story of virtue and endurance. The true story – the unfathomable story of a man, a goat and a cat – can never be told.

39

In these days that we spend in the bay, I am at pains to make myself useful, showing them the best ambuscades for hunting goats, and helping them to harvest cabbage leaves. Most of the men with scurvy recover well, being physicked with good fresh food, and only four are lost. This is accounted a great success, and the surgeon, Mister Wrasse, shakes my hand and credits me with this result, 'For you have been a physician here, or an apothecary at least, with all your foraging and good counsel.' I confess I am rather shocked than otherwise, to see these four dead, and given their burial from the ship – for although the crew fancies that my ordeal has made me a hardened man, the truth is that I have not seen a man die these four years past.

The shore is transformed. Tents have been pitched; the coopers are at work on the barrels, and a forge is set up too. All day huge vats of seal oil are being rendered, coating everything downwind with a greasy stink. Men take the boats out to fish, and salt their catch ashore. It is an industrious and noisy place now, my island, and much changed.

The *Duke* is a handsome ship, newly built, burthen about 350 tonnes, and with thirty guns. The *Duchess*, too, is new, and a little smaller with twenty-six guns. She has lately taken some damage, for they met a gale when rounding the Horn. Despite this, both vessels are in fair trim and handsomely fitted out. The men are a motley assortment, above one third being foreigners from divers nations, and few of the men being sailors before this voyage. Yet this collection of haymakers, tinkers, pedlars and the like have been fashioned into a passable crew, and I credit Rogers with this. Hopkins confides that there was an early attempt at a mutiny, but that Rogers quickly quashed it, 'and had one of the ringleaders served a public flogging by one of his own comrades.' I readily credit it – for while Rogers has been joviality itself to me, I would not wish to cross him.

My strangeness surprises me as much as the men. One day we are ashore, waiting for the pinnace to reach us. The men are rowing against the tide and their progress is slow; while we wait, I drop to my haunches to squat. The men are greatly diverted, and say, 'See how he crouches, like a Mahometan, or an Indian.'

'Or a man taking a shit,' says Blair, who fancies himself a fine wag.

I straighten at once and try to laugh along with the company. I had not realised until now how much I am in the habit of squatting like that, from my many hours each day digging turnips, or watching from my lookout, or waiting, hidden, to pounce at goats. The men make a show of trying for themselves this same pose, groaning when their muscles don't allow it. This mockery is, in the main, done in a spirit of fondness or curiosity – yet it is odd to feel oneself a spectacle. Being thrust back into the world of men, I am forced to see how very far I had strayed from it.

I seek Sleek once more – for we are to sail in two days. Vast stores of goat meat have been salted and packed aboard; the barrels have been mended and filled with water or seal oil.

Sleek is waiting for me when I reach the camp.

'Where is your answer to my riddle?' she says.

I meet her with a question of my own. 'Where is your verdict from my trials?' I cannot bear to leave this place without having it.

'You shall not have it – and you know why.'

'I do not.'

She sits calm in her silence.

'What of coming with me? You should do well as a ship's cat – think of the rats.'

'I am neither pet nor servant. You know I will not come.'

'Come with me – please.'

'Fool,' she says. 'Fool. I love you too well to come with you.'

Nothing in Sleek's strange and portentous manner frightens me so much as this fondness – for she has ever been scathing to me.

'What do you mean?'

'I cannot go with you,' she says, 'for if you speak to me aboard you shall be called mad, and the men will make sport of you.'

'How can you deny our friendship?' My voice is high and shrill. 'So many years, so many conversations? Did you not sleep at my side these many years?'

'Aye,' she says, 'I slept there, and I liked it very well. But as for the rest of it – it is a story you have made for yourself, like your poems from the Bible.'

'How could I invent you? You and the goat both – I know you. I have conversed with you for years.'

'Then how have you lost the use of your words? For were you not clumsy in speech, when your rescuers arrived?'

I have no answer for this. Instead I demand, 'What manner of man would conjure years' worth of conversations with a goat and a cat?'

'A man alone, beyond endurance. A broken man—'

I interrupt her. 'What about the goat, with his great knowledge of the Bible? How could I imagine that?'

'Have not you yourself spent these years reading that same book?'

'Even so – why would I invent conversations that have so often being provoking or infuriating? The Reverend and his perpetual discoursing on theology; you and your indifference. Would I not have conjured some companions more amenable – a helpmeet, or a lover, all breasts and arse?'

'And yet you conjured us.' A cat cannot shrug, but there is something very shrug-like about her gaze. 'You were surrounded by goats and cats. You made us what you needed us to be.'

'No.'

'It was all in your head,' she says, and rolls over into a languorous stretch. 'You summoned it all for yourself, to provide a diversion.'

'You were never a mere diversion.'

'We are, as we ever were, a cat and a goat. You made us otherwise.'

'And what of my trials? How could I conjure such an ordeal for myself, and why? Were they not solemn and grave? How could they be mere confections of a disordered mind?'

'Oh, not disordered,' she says. 'Most likely you may credit these imaginings with keeping you sane. But the trials were imaginings nonetheless. Your knowledge of the kirk sessions gave your imaginings that shape – nothing else.'

'And am I never to hear your verdict?'

'You have had it,' she says. 'You had it all along, in our silence.'

This is the most terrible verdict of all.

'Do not abandon me like this.'

'It is over,' she says. 'I was only in your head. The goat too.'

'He was not just any goat.' I am sobbing now. 'And how could I even have conjured such a name, when I know not even the meaning of *vicarious*?'

'*Vicarious* was a word you once heard. That goat was fond of you, no doubt, but he was not your loquacious friend.'

'That is not true. I know it.'

'Why, then, have you told these sailors nothing of our long years of conversation?'

'For fear of what they would think.'

'You know very well what they would think. You know it to be true.'

'Please,' I say. 'Please. Don't leave me.' It is the same thing I shouted at my shipmates when they left me here, so many years ago. Now I say it to Sleek, and I mean it no less sincerely now than I did when I screamed it across the waves to the departing boat. Don't leave me. Don't leave me here with the awful weight of this truth: that the very things that kept me sane have damned me for mad.

The cat looks at me for one long instant, my hand hovering before her face. Then she gives an animal hiss and is gone.

———

My chest is brought aboard the *Duke*, with the few possessions that were worth bringing. The Bible, my mug, my musket. My knife, which, although a blunted ruin, has been a trusted companion too long for me to forsake, even now that Rogers' men have furnished me with a new knife of my own. They delight in giving me such things, rightly knowing that even the merest trinket is a tremendous novelty to me. My goat hide clothes have been replaced entirely with such gifts. They are generous, these men, and my gratitude is unfeigned – but as the days pass, I feel more and more that my gladness does not belong to me at all, but is my part in an exchange. The quartermaster gives me a pair of stockings, and I put them on at once, and he beams; a midshipman brings me a fine pipe, and I am grateful indeed, for my own was long since chewed by rats. But I am aware that I must perform this gratitude, must give him a pipe's worth of story for it, so that he may say, later, 'How that poor fellow capered and grinned at such a trifle!'

In our cabin that night, I ask Lieutenant Hopkins, 'What does *vicarious* mean?' Hopkins is a bookish fellow, gently spoken, and I trust that if he does not know the answer, at least he will not mock me for my ignorance.

'Vicarious?' He thinks a moment. 'It means: *through another*. As in: *I've never travelled to New Holland, but have experienced it vicariously through reading Mister Dampier's books.*'

I thank him handsomely.

I will not bring Pickle aboard, though the men have entreated me to, for even a fine ship such as the *Duke* has its share of rats, and but one ship's cat, who is accounted lazy. No – if I cannot have Sleek, nor the Reverend Vicarious Cronch, I cannot bear to have Pickle, her muteness a sharp reminder.

On our final afternoon I spend an hour or more with her, holding her to my chest and stroking her in the spot beneath her chin that she likes best. I press my face to the top of her head and smell the reliable warmth of her – then I set her down. She shall do better here – she shall stay on the island and remember how to be wild.

It is almost sunset of the last day. Sleek is not at my camp. I head uphill, for I know where I shall find her.

There, at the cliffside where I faced my trials, she is waiting.

'Sleek,' I say, 'oh Sleek.'

'That has never been my name. You yourself gave it to me.'

'And you answered to it.'

'No,' she says. 'Not once did I claim it. You claimed me.'

I reach out my hand, cupping her face. She leans into my palm.

'You will never convince me that none of it was real,' I say.

'I told you from the start. It was in the very first riddle I gave you, and every riddle since. *What is a church for one man alone?*'

'Selkirk,' I say. 'But after that first one, I could never solve your riddles, except when you told me the answer.'

'*And who speaks, but is never heard? What is man, and cat, and goat, all at once, but neither?*'

I have my hands over my ears, rocking forwards and back, and to drown out her words I am saying the first and only word that comes to my mind, loud and over and over: *Selkirk Selkirk Selkirk.*

'I told you I had already given you the answer.' Her voice is strict.

'You did not.'

'Each riddle began with *Mister Selkirk*. The answer was right there.'

'Then you had not a very high estimation of my understanding.'

'No worse than you merited, for still you could not solve them.' She moves backwards, just beyond the reach of my hand.

'*Who comes and goes?*'

'This one I knew, for you told me already.'

'And my final riddle: *I did not say that. Who did, Mister Selkirk?*'

Despite my sobs, and my hands pressed to my ears, I hear her still. *Selkirk.* As she turns and dashes away, she puts a great quantity of hiss into that word – *Selkirk* lends itself to hissing.

40

If I had any notion of a grand farewell to the island, the work of putting out to sea precludes it, for all is haste and hurry. I do not mind – since the death of Cronch, I am not inclined to nostalgia, for thoughts of my time on the island are all bound up in memories of my conversations with that garrulous and surprising goat. And since the cat's merciless revelations, I do not even know how to understand my memories, which are not memories at all. Thus in my silence I wait out the final hours ashore before our departure, and contrive to busy myself as well as possible, rather than to muse on my leaving, or on the long years of my remaining.

In those final hours, I do not seek the cat – for there is no finding a cat that does not wish to be found.

———

On the fourteenth of February we weigh anchor. The wind is fair, south-southeast, and we are making north by north-east, for the mainland.

What can I say of these days aboard the *Duke*? I am well treated, and an object of fond interest for all the company. I find satisfaction in my work, and I do not suffer, beyond the sufferings that any sailor is subject to.

Why, then, am I lost and ill at ease, wading through my hours? Language has come down between me and the world like a veil, and nothing is as vivid, nor as real, as each day on the island. I miss the counsel of the Reverend Vicarious Cronch. I even miss the taunts of

Sleek. This grief is all the heavier for it can never be spoken. I carry it with me like the coin the ancients placed on the tongues of the dead.

Perhaps I am indeed mad. I think sometimes of that fellow, Alsop, and how he was freed from the Spanish mines but never escaped them. *There is no leaving such a place.*

I shall make my way back to the world – perhaps even to Nether Largo. I shall be once more a man among men. I shall make my choices, and doubtless my mistakes also, for a man's sins are barnacles, not lightly to be shaken off. Yet some part of me will always be on the island. Some part of me knows the truth of water, and of the great unfurling of a cat's belly as it stretches, and of how noise travels differently in the dark. I am still there – there, on the sharp striated rocks; there, in the place where words are no longer necessary. I longed for rescue – oh how bitterly I longed for it. But when you have pierced the veil of language and stepped out of time, there is no going back. I am there, stone underfoot and sun on my flesh. For good or for ill, I have not left. If anyone seeks the truth of Alexander Selkirk, let him seek there.

———

The *Duke*'s cook keeps a cat, a big ginger fellow who has grown fat on scraps.

I come across him a little after dawn, five days from the island. He has found the warm spot on the forecastle where the galley chimneys let out.

I greet him solemnly, as Sleek preferred.

'Good morning, sir,' I say, and give a small bow.

The cat looks at me with absolute indifference, and rolls over. Two lads, passing, who have witnessed the interaction, begin to snigger. I place my hands on the small of my back as though I were not bowing at all, merely stretching, and then make a show of stretching further.

———

Lieutenant Hopkins, whose cabin I share, I begin to account a friend. As well as being lieutenant and apothecary, it is his role to read prayers on deck each morning, a tradition kept much more strictly under the pious Rogers than on many ships. It's a mark of Hopkins' popularity that the men do not hold the prayers against him – he is well liked, for his patience, and for his gentle manner with the sick.

In our cabin one evening, I ask him, 'What if I were to tell you that, on the island, I was plagued by strange imaginings?'

'A man may imagine a great deal, in such circumstances.'

'But would he know them for imaginings? What if they seemed absolutely real? How could you be sure of the difference?'

'I am an apothecary, Mister Selkirk – good at the setting of bones and the binding of wounds. What you speak of concerns the mind, and not the body.'

'Is the mind not a part of the body? May it not be set?'

'Ah,' he says, and I fancy he is making an effort to keep his voice cheery. 'There you stray into philosophy, and there you lose me.'

I try to explain to him about a goat's horn – its polished ridges, and how its curve makes sense of time. 'It repeats, you see,' I say, and I trace the curve with my hands in the air, sweeping so wide that my knuckle grazes the bulkhead.

Hopkins reaches across the narrow cabin and places his hand on my shoulder.

'My friend,' he says. 'Do not exercise yourself over such things.' And I see from the alarm in his face that I have become too voluble, and am speaking too loud.

Thus I learn to keep to myself my stories of the island and its wonders, its horrors. The men are always hungry for stories of the island, but mine are not the stories that they want.

———

We have several days of heavy weather. Dover says to me, 'I warrant you'll not want to set foot aboard a ship again, once we have got you safe back to civilisation.'

Then, since they have gathered by now that I am a Scot, there are the usual jibes about whether Scotland may be considered civilised after all, and whether I might have done better to stay upon the island than to suffer the privations of Scots life. 'And the poor chap will know nothing of the Act of Union,' says Dover, and then they are at pains to explain it to me. I let them run on – I pay little heed to such things now. Though once I would have seized on any pretext to be outraged on behalf of my nation, I find that the concerns of parliaments and kings no longer interest me. The men speak, very animated, and I gaze at the timber of the deck, polished to a handsome shine. I admire the grain of the wood: its precision; the intricate repetition of its shapes.

Hopkins is asking something.

'Sir,' he repeats. 'Shall you go to sea again, then, after you have returned home?'

'Certainly,' I say.

Dover scoffs. 'Surely, sir, you have escaped death too many times to risk it once more?'

How can I tell this jovial man that there is no escaping death? If there is a death awaiting me at sea, then it shall have me, for the sea is patient and shall outlast even my luck. I have learned to let the rock be rock; I have learned to meet my death where I shall find it – for the cat told me that my death is not a gift I can refuse. Nevertheless I suspect that the death the sea has in store for me shall not be drowning – perhaps my mother was right, for I am a seventh son, after all, born in my caul already afloat, and I shall not drown. But I have tested providence far enough already: I have survived Darien, and escaped the doomed *Cinque Ports*. My own death shall come for me at the end, and this time I will not outrun it, for I am tired of running. And I am old enough to know that going to sea does not have to be the same thing as running away.

I boarded the *Duke* willingly. Whatever the sea has in store for me, I sail towards it.

———

A month after we left the island, the *Duchess* captures a small bark. While the *Duke* is not involved in the engagement, Captain Rogers has the vessel's unfortunate captain brought aboard, and some time thereafter I am summoned to the great cabin.

The prize's captain is one Antonio Heliagos, a Spaniard but of Indian blood too, and a very hearty, business-like fellow, resigned to his capture and sanguine of being ransomed. 'It is all business, is it not?' he says, quite cheerful.

'Selkirk,' Captain Rogers says. 'Our prisoner has news concerning your former captain, Stradling.'

And then the Spanish captain relates his tale: that the *Cinque Ports* foundered off Barbacour. 'All the men were lost but for a mere handful, Stradling among them – though they might well have wished themselves drowned for they passed years in a Spanish prison in Lima.'

Rogers grins. 'Where they would have found the living much worse than our Governor Selkirk on his island, I don't doubt.' And he thumps me across the back and says, jolly, 'There, Governor – how do you like that? You are proved right, after all – and had you stayed under Stradling you would be long drowned, or starved in some Spanish jail.'

And I thank him for bringing me to hear the news, and shake hands with the Spanish captain, but I cannot find it in myself to rejoice at being right. Once this was precisely the kind of vindication that would have given me great satisfaction, and about which I would have harped at length to all who would listen. Now I think of my shipmates, Loggia and all the others. I was only briefly right, but they shall be dead forever.

Rogers, ever civil, invites the captain to dine with us that evening. I hear the way that Rogers regales him with my story. 'And thus,' says Rogers, 'by his own industry, the Governor made of that barren island his own little kingdom.'

It is a flattering portrait – so flattering that it cannot be said to be a portrait at all. I am nowhere to be found in it.

That man whom he describes – this virtuous Governor, lord of beasts and ingenious survivor – did all the things that I did, though rarely for the same reasons. He did not speak to goats, nor cats, nor deface the Bible. Certainly he never indulged in self-abuse, nor despair, and nor was he the instrument of his own downfall. This man, a stranger to me, will go on, no doubt, to great things. Virtuous things.

But I have only myself to live within. Whatever I go on to do, I shall still be Alexander Selkirk, intemperate and of choleric humour. The island did not allow me change – indeed I begin to suspect few men ever change. It allowed me only to know myself a little better, perhaps, and to own the truth of myself, my sins as well as my virtues.

I hear Rogers tell my story. It is a good story – and we both come out of it well. It makes of me a pious man, redeemed; it makes of him the rescuer. Who will recognise Alexander Selkirk in that story? Give that man another name – he is not I.

All the world is water. I see in the horizon's curve the same line that I used to trace in the goat's horn. How time bends always towards itself.

I know how a man may become lost. I was lost many years before ever I came to the island.

But this I also know. I learned it under the ministry of goats, and the scorn of cats, and the kirk of salt, and the thick Bible of silence. Sun-blind, goat-mad, a tongue made dumb, walking the shores of loneliness. I learned it long before the sails of the *Duke* punctured the horizon. Listen. This I know: I know how a man may be saved.

Afterword

Selkirk profited from Woodes Rogers' voyage, which succeeded in seizing one of the Spanish Manila galleons. However, records suggest Selkirk's subsequent life was isolated and undistinguished. He spent some time back in Scotland, and some at sea. He appears to have committed bigamy – after his death, two women claimed to be his wives, and produced contradictory wills (although only one was able to produce evidence of a legal marriage). It seems that whatever lessons the island taught him, they were left there. In Richard Steele's 1713 account, based on his meetings with Selkirk, he claims that Selkirk told him: 'I am now worth 800 Pounds, but shall never be so happy, as when I was not worth a Farthing.'

In 1720, eleven years after his rescue from the island, Selkirk joined the *Weymouth*, a naval warship. On December 13, 1721, amid an outbreak of illness, the ship's log records 'Alexr. Selkirk, DD', which is clarified in a subsequent entry: 'P.M. Alexr. Selkirk Deceased.'

Daniel Defoe based his *Robinson Crusoe* on the various accounts of Selkirk's time on the island (although he made significant changes to both story and setting). There is no confirmed record of Selkirk meeting Defoe, nor is it known whether Selkirk ever read *Robinson Crusoe*, which was published in 1719, two years before Selkirk's death.

Robinson Crusoe is a household name; few have heard of Alexander Selkirk.

Historical note

This novel sticks closely to the facts of Selkirk's life, inasmuch as these have been recorded (with varying degrees of reliability). The outlines of Selkirk's family and youth, and his appearances at the Largo kirk session, are factual, including the salt water prank – however Effie Breck is my own invention. Selkirk's voyage with Dampier, his abandonment and survival on the island, and his rescue, are all drawn closely from contemporaneous sources.

In many places the language in these sources was irresistible, and I have either stolen or paraphrased particular turns of phrase (such as Woodes Rogers' description of Selkirk as 'a Man cloth'd in Goat-Skins, who look'd wilder than the first Owners of them').

The island on which Selkirk spent four years and four months was then known as Más a Tierra, of the Juan Fernández Islands, more than 650 km off the coast of Chile. In 1966 the Chilean government renamed the island Robinson Crusoe Island, to capitalise on the fame of Defoe's creation. Confusingly, the other main island in the Juan Fernández archipelago, formerly Más Afuera, was renamed Alejandro Selkirk Island. There is no record of Selkirk ever having set foot on this island, which lies 180km west of Selkirk's island.

My most indispensable source has been Woodes Rogers' account of his discovery of Selkirk, included in Rogers' book, *A Cruising Voyage Round the World* (Cassell & Company, London, 1712). This record of Selkirk's time on the island, and his rescue, gives details of Selkirk's survival, including his camp; his sources of food; his method of hunting goats, and of catching them for sport and slitting their ears before releasing them; his evasion of the Spaniards; and much more. Also useful is Richard Steele's account of meeting Selkirk after his rescue ('Selkirk, Alexander, an Account of his living alone above four Years in a desolate Island', *The Englishman*, No. 26, 3 December 1713, 168-173). There is no record of Selkirk attempting to escape the island on a raft – this is speculation on my part.

Regarding the cruise under Dampier that saw Selkirk abandoned on the island, accounts vary significantly between those (William Funnell; John Welbe) who blame Dampier and Stradling for failures of leadership, and Dampier himself. Funnell was the first to publish his account, *A Voyage Round the World. Containing an Account of Captain Dampier's Expedition Into the South-Seas in the Ship St George, in the Years 1703 and 1704* (James Knapton, London, 1707). Dampier responded with *Capt. Dampier's vindication of his voyage to the South-Seas in the ship St. George: With some small observations ... on Mr. Funnel's* [sic] *chimerical relation of the voyage round the world* (J. Bradford, London, 1707). In turn, Welbe published *An Answer to Captain Dampier's Vindication of his Voyage to the South-Seas* (B. Bragge, London, 1707). Their contrasting versions of events, and responses to each other's accusations, make for delightful and often bitchy reading. After the investors in the voyage made a case against Dampier, on 18 July 1712 Selkirk himself gave a deposition which is critical of Dampier for his mismanagement of the voyage. This novel has synthesised these different accounts to construct the version of events that seems most compelling.

For further reading on the fascinating life of William Dampier, I recommend Anton Gill's *The Devil's Mariner: A Life of William Dampier, Pirate and Explorer, 1651–1715* (Michael Joseph, London, 1997), and Diana and Michael Preston's *A Pirate of Exquisite Mind* (Doubleday, London, 2004).

Andrew Lambert's book, *Crusoe's Island* (Faber, London, 2017), was particularly useful in discussing the likely location of Selkirk's camp.

Diana Souhami's *Selkirk's Island* (Quercus, London, 2013), a biography as much of the island as of Selkirk himself, is vivid and thorough. I don't agree with her on every detail, but for her wise and thoughtful inspiration, I am grateful.

It is Souhami who claims that Selkirk joined the disastrous Scots expedition to Darien (now Panama). There is no record of Selkirk's involvement, but it seems plausible, given the numbers of sailors involved, the prominence of the expedition at the time, and the national excitement it provoked – and the Darien scheme provides material too good for any novelist to ignore.

For information on the Darien scheme, John Prebble's *The Darien Disaster* (Penguin, Middlesex, 1970) was extremely useful. Also essential was *The Darien Papers: being a Selection of original Letters and official Documents relating to the Establishment of a Colony at Darien by the Company of Scotland trading to Africa and the Indies. 1695–1700*, ed. John. H. Burton (The Bannantyne Club, Edinburgh, 1849). Some of the descriptions of Darien are taken from Francis Borland's *Memoirs of Darien* (Hugh Brown, Glasgow, 1717). Some of the phrasing describing the Darien scheme, particularly the gold worn by the local people and the details of the return journey, are drawn from primary texts found in *The Darien Shipping Papers, 1696–1707*, ed. George Pratt Insh (Scottish History Society, Edinburgh, 1924). The letter received in this novel by the captain of the *Caledonia* in New York is based on a letter that was in fact sent to the captains of the second expedition to Darien – but it was much too good to exclude, so I adapted it in a version sent to Captain Drummond.

There remains some uncertainty over Selkirk's date of birth. In this period there was more latitude regarding the recording of dates (as with the spelling of names: Selkirk's name was variously written as Selcraig, Selcraighe, Silcrigge, etc). The commonly accepted date of Selkirk's birth is 1676; however, Souhami notes that in his own 1712 deposition Selkirk gives his date of birth as 1680, making him twenty-four or twenty-five at the time of his abandonment on the island. Rogers wrote after the rescue that Selkirk was 'now but about 30 years old' – however in the context it isn't entirely clear whether he refers to Selkirk's age at rescue or at an earlier point during his time on the island. Like Souhami, I have chosen to trust Selkirk himself – but in this, as in so many other things, Selkirk may have been unreliable.

Selkirk's 'sea lions' were, in fact, southern elephant seals; I have called them 'sea lions' as this is what he (as well as many other explorers of the period) called them. Similarly, I have followed Funnell and Rogers in referring to the island's rock lobsters as 'crawfish'. The two species of hummingbirds that Selkirk describes in this book are actually male and female birds of the same species (the Juan Fernández firecrown), which displays such an unusually strong degree of sexual dimorphism that they were for a long time believed to be two different species.

It is recorded that Selkirk's few possessions on the island included his Bible – however, his use of it to create new 'poems' is my invention. While this form of writing has many precedents, I wish to acknowledge Austin Kleon's *Newspaper Blackout* (Harper Perennial, New York, 2010), and Jonathan Safran Foer's *Tree of Codes* (Visual Editions, London, 2010). These were beguiling introductions to the notions of texts carved out of existing texts. More recently, Nicole Sealey's *The Ferguson Report: An Erasure* (Knopf, New York, 2023) opened my eyes to the more radical potential of this form.

———

While it is true that the island was overrun by goats, cats and rats, it goes without saying that the Reverend Vicarious Cronch and Sleek are my own creations. It is documented that Selkirk cultivated the companionship of wild cats in order to keep the rats at bay. As Woodes Rogers notes:

The Rats gnaw'd his Feet and Clothes while asleep, which oblig'd him to cherish the Cats with his Goats-flesh; by which many of them became so tame, that they would lie about him in hundreds, and soon deliver'd him from the Rats.

In Howell's biography, *The Life and Adventures of Alexander Selkirk* (Oliver & Boyd, Edinburgh, 1829), he writes that when Selkirk returned to Nether Largo, 'Here he was accustomed to amuse himself with two cats that belonged to his brother, which he taught, in imitation of a part of his occupations on his solitary island, to dance and perform many little feats.'

I had finished the first draft of the novel when I came across the second edition of Edward Cooke's *A voyage to the South Sea, and round the world, perform'd in the years 1708, 1709, 1710, and 1711* (B. Lintot & R. Gosling, London, 1712). Cooke was a second captain under Rogers on the voyage that rescued Selkirk, and seemed irritated by the public appetite for details of Selkirk's time on the island, which Cooke had not mentioned in the first edition:

What then can it be that flatters our Curiosity? Is he a natural Philosopher, who, by such an indisturb'd Retirement, could make any surprizing Discoveries? Nothing less, we have a downright Sailor, whose only Study was how to support himself, during his Confinement, and all his Conversation with Goats. It would be no difficult Matter to embellish a Narrative with many Romantick Incidents, to please the unthinking Part of Mankind, who swallow every Thing an artful Writer thinks fit to impose upon their Credulity, without any Regard to Truth or Probability. The judicious are not taken with such Trifles; their End in Reading is Information; and they easily distinguish between Reality and Fiction.

Later, Cooke also notes of Selkirk: 'Some few Spanish ships happen'd to touch there, during his Stay; but he had resolv'd rather to converse with his Goats, than be beholding [sic] to that Nation for his Deliverance from that Prison.'

I suspect Cooke would thoroughly have disapproved of my conjectures – but his repeated references to Selkirk conversing with goats in fact served only to encourage me.

Acknowledgements

Juliet Mushens, my inimitable agent, is the champion every author should have — I am so lucky to have her as both agent and friend. I'm also indebted to her team at Mushens Entertainment, for their skill and care.

In 2024 I told my editor at Bloomsbury, Emma Herdman, that I wanted to write a weird book about a man alone on an island, talking to a goat and a cat. For her faith in me, and in this story, I will always be grateful. I've also been exceptionally fortunate to be supported by the rest of the outstanding team at Bloomsbury, who in their respective fields have all been superb advocates for this book. Particular thanks to assistant editor Gurdip Ahluwalia, managing editor Francisco Vilhena, and to my publicists, Grace Nzita-Kiki (UK) and Shaan Lloyd (Australia). The brilliant Carmen Balit designed the striking, witty cover. Sincere thanks to my copyeditor, Joely Day, and my proofreader, Erica Hesketh, for their diligent work. Any remaining errors are, of course, my own.

Alan Haig is a treasured and invaluable reader and editor, and this book has benefited from his wisdom. Andrew North, as always, gave thoughtful and sharp feedback. It's a matter of historical record that the brother with whom Selkirk fought is called Andrew — I hope that my own Andrew will forgive me for making his namesake so unpleasant.

Affectionate thanks to the booksellers and librarians who have supported my work, and who help to put books into the hands of readers — none of this would happen without you.

Selkirk's sailor friend is named after David Loggia, who won the right to have a character named after him in the charity auction at the 2024 F.I.T.E. Brain Cancer ball, and whose generous donation supported vital brain cancer research.

This book was written on the unceded land of the Wurundjeri Woi-wurrung and Boon Wurrung peoples of the Kulin nation. They were the first storytellers of the beautiful place in which I live, which remains Aboriginal land.

A Note on the Author

FRANCESCA DE TORES is a novelist and poet. She is the author of six novels, published in more than 20 languages. Her first historical novel, *Saltblood,* was awarded the 2024 Wilbur Smith Adventure Writing Prize. In addition to a collection of poems, her poetry is widely published in journals and anthologies. She grew up in Lutruwita/Tasmania and, after fifteen years in England, is now living in Naarm/Melbourne.

A Note on the Type

The text of this book is set in Bembo, which was first used in 1495 by the Venetian printer Aldus Manutius for Cardinal Bembo's *De Aetna.* The original types were cut for Manutius by Francesco Griffo. Bembo was one of the types used by Claude Garamond (1480–1561) as a model for his Romain de l'Université, and so it was a forerunner of what became the standard European type for the following two centuries. Its modern form follows the original types and was designed for Monotype in 1929.